BOOKS BY

Harry Brown

✿

THE STARS IN THEIR COURSES

(*1960*)

THE BEAST IN HIS HUNGER

(*1948*)

A SOUND OF HUNTING

(*1946*)

ARTIE GREENGROIN

(*1945*)

A WALK IN THE SUN

(*1944*)

THESE ARE BORZOI BOOKS

published in New York by Alfred·A·Knopf

THE
STARS
IN THEIR
Courses

THE
STARS
IN THEIR
Courses

by

Harry Brown

Alfred·A·Knopf   NEW YORK

1960

L. C. catalog card number: 60–7491

© HARRY BROWN, 1960

THIS IS A BORZOI BOOK,
PUBLISHED BY ALFRED A. KNOPF, INC.

FIRST EDITION

18

ZEBULUN *and* NAPHTALI *were a people that jeoparded their lives unto the death in the high places of the field.*

19

THE KINGS *came and fought, then fought the kings of Canaan in Taanach by the waters of Megiddo; they took no gain of money.*

20

THEY *fought from heaven; the stars in their courses fought against Sisera.*

21

THE RIVER *of Kishon swept them away, that ancient river, the river Kishon. O my soul, thou hast trodden down strength.*

22

THEN WERE *the horsehoofs broken by the means of the pransings, the pransings of their mighty ones.*

HAEC IMAGO, JUNIA, TIBI, CARA

CONTENTS

PART ONE

The High Places
of the Field

THE RANDAL meadows were high, but the mountains to the west were higher still.

Now, as they had since before men came, the Santa Marias nourished these ripened leas, smoothing them, covering their bones with a rich soil of mountain flesh, the Marias' body and substance. Once the peaks had been young and sudden, a jaw of jagged teeth, sawing horizons; but now their long parturition, sustained by the wailing midwife elements, had ground them down, dulled them, and scummed their sides, below timberline, with a green patina of spruce. Ancient and gentle, soothed and amused by the light winds stirring the freshened trees along their flanks, peaceful beneath a shock of sky, they slept a behemothic sleep, old children of the turning world, encompassed and lulled by the ending spring.

They were retired mountains, the Santa Marias, their work of generation nearly done, their heavy bodies settling ever closer to the warmth within the earth. They seemed themselves to have been put out to pasture like cattle; and yet these drowsy leviathans, ponderous under the bland sun, continued the rise and renewal of things, and their blood still fed the fields and wooded uplands of the rancher Percy Randal.

Deep somewhere in the Marias, near the sky, higher than any tree went, two streams, the North Tine and the South, were born of a coupling of zephyr and snow. As brooks, the Tines were conceived ten difficult miles apart and, although this happened another forty crow-flight miles from the Randal ranch house, they arose on Randal land. Old Percy owned the slopes of the Marias, all the way from the round old peaks to where, far east of his ranch house, the long plateau was broken abruptly into grotesque deep chasms. North and south, as well, the Randal ranch sprawled for more than thirty miles. And so, across an area greater than that of many kingdoms in the year of our Lord 1879, thousands on thousands of fat beef cattle wandered free and, browsing, bore on their hides the Broken S brand of Percy Randal.

Few of the men who worked the ranch knew where the Tines began. Percy himself had been there with his eldest son, when Hallock was quite a small boy. The foreman, Art Cospatrick, had also traveled to both, and the trail boss, Soap Damson, had once sought out the source of the North Tine—but it had been to win a bet, he was drunk when he did it, and two days after he came back from the place he had forgotten where it was. The rest of the ranch hands never gave the matter a thought.

Everyone, family and hands, however, was sure of where the Tines joined their currents. As they wound down from the heights of the Marias, now slowed by the bulk of great boulders, now speeded by sudden sheer descents, bucking and heaving in rapids above a slanted rocky bed, then curving in shadowed peace through a richness of virgin spruce, they gradually broadened, steadied, and came to a strong maturity. So, each nearly the other's equal in size, made dilatory by the level land, they flowed as two sides of a triangle of forest; and at last, in a gloomy, almost Gothic fastness known as Juncture Valley, the North and South Tines came quietly together. The result was the Forkhandle River.

It was neither a wide stream nor a deep one. Yet, as it curled its length along the upland meadows, on its way down the spine of a continent to sweeten with its clean bulk the muddy Rio Grande, it meant life, profit, and a high future to those ranchers through whose holdings it passed. And of all these men the most powerful, and therefore the one with the most to lose should any disaster strike, was Percy Randal.

He was not rich, except in land and children, but in the normal way of things his holdings and herds could at last become golden dollars; and if Percy did not live to enjoy them, he intended and was planning that his children should. He was a Scotsman, born in the Maritime Provinces of Canada, who had come down through Maine and Massachusetts in his young manhood and had then worked his way south and west. He was frugal and respected, hard-working and sharp. There had never been any question about his honesty; the size of his ranch was entirely due to his endless, aboveboard endeavors.

Randal had arrived in the Forkhandle country just before the Mexican war, bringing with him his wife, Harriet, and Hallock, his son, who was then five years old. The first shelter they had known on the uplands was a cramped square house of logs and sod, to which he had added rooms as the need arose. But as he prospered, and as the other children came—Cora, Pax, and, finally, Luke—he pleasured, after the last boy's birth, his wife's long wish for a substantial home, and so he built the place in which they all now lived, as soon after the Civil War as he could, with the best materials he could afford, from the mills of New England and the bazaars of New York.

The ranch house stood on a knoll roughly rectangular, two miles above where the Forkhandle River formed a stretch of the southern limit of Randal land. Shaded by aspen and spruce, which concealed in some measure its basic ugliness while stressing its air of comfort, the rambling wooden two-story dwelling was a focal point, around which were jumbled, seemingly to no purpose, a pair of corrals, a stable, a bunkhouse, a barn, and various smaller buildings.

The knoll itself rose gently more or less in the middle of a broad, open meadow which, too, was shaped like a rectangle, ringed by low, wooded hills. And it was here, on this wide trampled field, on a yellow Sunday in the last days of a good spring, while a concourse of people were enjoying the weather, their present relaxation, each other, and life in general, that certain pale threads, drawn out from dark hidden places, began to be wound inexorably together in an almost casual warping, until there had been wrought, out of such tenuous white and fleeting things, a taut trip-wire for the souls of men, destined, before its mindless work was done, to bring many tall sure riders down to earth, and below.

Maude Fletcher was the first to learn that Arch Eastmere was back again. Phil Hyssop was the second.

Arch appeared out of the dark, at two o'clock on that Sunday morning. When he came riding up to Maude's, he was returning from two years in Mexico, which was yet another of the places he had gone to seek his fortune, for the ninth time in an unfortunate life; and all he had to show for it was a marvelous silver-mounted saddle that gleamed like ice in the moonlight, and the clothes he wore on his back. He stood six feet, three inches tall, he was forty-two years old, a big old Colt hung low on his right hip, and, as he jogged his worn horse up to Maude Fletcher's house, he couldn't remember ever having been so tired before.

The place he stopped at was a two-room ruinous shack on the road to Divide, a half-hour south of the town that was also called Eastmere, after his grandfather; and the woman at whose place he stopped, Maude Fletcher, was a fading innocent of thirty-one who had been a respectable wife, then, briefly, a respectable widow, and who was now a respectable whore, as selective in her clientele as she was sparing of her passions. The passion she had always felt for Arch Eastmere remained, however, in full cry; he knew it quite as well as she did, and this was the reason he had made for her house.

Of course, life being a chancy affair, Arch wasn't sure, until he approached the place, that Maude still kept open bed there. But then the moonlight revealed certain objects lying somewhat away from the house in various states of disrepair, none of which had been moved during the two years of his travels, and he knew Maude continued to hold the fort. So, disregarding the fact that it was Saturday night, or Sunday morning, and that Mrs. Fletcher might be otherwise occupied, he rode his horse up to the bedroom window and called out softly: "Maudie?"

Silence held for a moment, and then he heard her say: "Who's that?"

"Maudie, the cat's come back," he told her.

Again the silence held: then there was a gasp, and he heard her cry: "Oh, *Jesus*, Archie Eastmere!" A scurrying came from inside the house; and even while he was getting wearily off his horse she was down below him, naked as a fading jaybird, and pulling him close to her. It was as though the two years had never gone by.

He took her in his arms and kissed her and lightly slapped her bare bottom. "No reason for you to doll up this way for me, Maudie," he said. "I like you just as well with no clothes on at all."

She was a custard excitement, shivering pale against him there in the moonlight. "Goddamn you, Archie, you didn't even write, I thought you was dead, why didn't you send me some word, goddamn you, oh, Archie, you *could*'ve wrote me now—"

He smiled at her. "Looks like you're alone tonight, Maudie, I swear."

"If I wasn't, I'd kick him clear out, goddamn you, why didn't you write me, Archie?"

"Never could learn Spanish," Arch Eastmere said. "You got to write Spanish down there."

"Big long catamountain, you can learn *anything.*"

"You wasn't there to teach me, Maudie."

"I'd've gone."

"Wish *I* hadn't."

"Didn't you do what you set out to do?"

"Not exactly."

"But you made yourself some money."

"Not even that, Maudie. No money at all."

"You Archie, tell me the truth, tell Maudie what happened down there, goddamn you, it's been so long—"

"I used up two years, that's about it, I reckon." He pulled their bodies together. "Ah, now, I'm plumb glad there wasn't nobody else around here tonight. I'm surely glad, little Maudie."

She thought she heard him sigh, and when she looked up into his face she saw that his eyes were closed. "Archie—" she said. She reached up and touched his cheeks; they felt hot beneath her fingers, and she frowned. "You feel sick, Archie honey?"

"Tired, honey. Just a little tired."

"Want something to eat?"

"Lie down for a bit, is all. And maybe a bite."

"You go in, Archie. I'll look after your horse." The untethered animal had wandered to a grassy spot.

"*Fun* you will." He slapped her bottom again. "Get in there yourself and warm us up something. And don't change your duds, hear?" He walked off toward his horse. Maude watched him for a few seconds, then scurried inside.

She fed soup to him, and he took it greedily; and then she made an effort to feed herself to him, and he tried to take her, too —but he couldn't quite make it. Then she knew for certain he didn't feel well, so she let him slip down into sleep on her wide, deep, gritty bed, stroking his hair and saying soft things to him, until his breathing was easy and very far distant; and then at last, after looking at his weathered face for a long long time in the moonlight, Maude Fletcher slept herself, without, of course, ever changing her clothes.

At ten in the morning Arch Eastmere woke up, with a fine high color on his cheeks; woke up sharp and alert. He surveyed the good-featured woman by him and read on her body many past and pleasant hours. He smiled and let twenty years drop from himself. Then, as quiet as his smiling, he rose from the bed and let the rest of his clothes fall as the twenty years had fallen, after which he came back down on the bed again and over the soft breast of Maude Fletcher, and started to take her sleeping.

She awoke by degrees, but deeply aware of him, and her waking was as profound as her sleep had been. She strained herself against him, and briefly then his body and his face were her whole world; until the body that was half her world bent bowlike in an agony, and the face that was the other half drained of all its color. Abruptly, the man who was all the world she then knew sought with bewildered eyes the breath he could not draw, before he rolled off her, frozen, down on the rumpled bedding. Maude sat up on the sudden, drawing her legs in, staring in horror at Arch, not knowing what to do and not even trying to stir, for any movement of hers, she felt, might somehow be the death of him. And he, on his part, stared at the ceiling as though at some descending god, nor seemed to breathe nor be alive in any remembered way. But he was alive, and Maude Fletcher knew it; and she also knew that he didn't dare move, for he saw in his head that if he moved he would break. All poor Maudie Fletcher could do was wail softly, low in her throat. She might have been humming to a child.

But at last, after a quarter of an hour, Arch Eastmere relaxed and took breath. And then he was able to turn to Maude weakly and smile and say: "What was *that*, now, Maudie honey?"

She could only shake her head at him. "*God*, Archie, you *must* be sick."

A few minutes later he was able to sit up. "It's not a sickness," he told her. "I don't know what it is."

"It's an *attack*, that's what, Archie. A *stroke*, like."

"Only old men get strokes, Maudie."

"You ever act like this before?"

His answer was a puzzled shake of the head. She caressed his hard back and leaned her cheek against his shoulder. "*Poor* Archie, god*damn* you, Archie, going off that way, down into that goddamned Mexico and getting sick, ah, long old Archie Eastmere—"

He drew away from her slightly. "I didn't get sick in Mexico," he said. "I never been sick in my life."

"You're sick now."

"I don't know *what* I am, I said."

"There's funny diseases down there in Mexico. I heard all about 'em, Archie."

"None of 'em come my way, Maudie."

"Where'd you go down there, Archie, what'd you go and *do?*"

"Oh, I worked for a feller down there. Big rancher."

"On his ranch?"

"Not exactly, you might say. I sort of looked out for him."

"Couldn't he look out for himself?"

"Guess not. Poor feller had more enemies than he had eyes."

"What happened to him?"

"Don Ignacio? Well, he was riding along one day, and this feller gunned him down."

"Oh. And you lost your job."

"That's what I lost, little Maudie."

"You know who shot the man there?"

"Yep. Same feller that took his fine silver-mounted saddle and rode back over the Border with it."

She sucked in air, and her eyes grew wide. "*You,* Archie? You shot him yourself?"

"Reckon I did, little Maudie." Arch Eastmere sighed. "There was all these wages he owed me. Made me mad."

"You don't do things for no reason, though, do you, Archie?"

Arch got to his feet slowly, as though he weren't sure his legs would bear him. "That's something I never found out yet," he said.

He began to dress, using great care. Maude Fletcher watched him in silence for a little while, then moved restlessly on the bed. "You ought to lay around here today, Archie," she said, pushing damp curls away from her eyes. "I don't like you feeling this way."

"I'm going in and see Phil Hyssop."

"He probably won't be home."

"He's always home."

"No, Pax Randal told me there's this big do out at their place today for his little brother's birthday—"

"Young Luke?"

"He's turned twenty-one. And the whole town'll probably be out there, Pax says."

"You been seeing lots of Pax, Maudie?"

"He comes around once in a while. A girl has to keep alive, don't she, when Archie Eastmere, goddamn him, is way down in Mexico someplace?"

He grinned down at her. "Listen, Maudie honey, don't you go getting yourself up on your high horse. I don't have nothing against Pax Randal, and you know it. Always got along fine with the whole Randal family, far's that goes. Matter of fact, Hallock and me, now, we seen the elephant together once or twice in our time. I was just surprised none of these girls around here hadn't roped Pax in by now. He must be slipperier than a greased pig."

"Mighty good-looking greased pig," Maude Fletcher said distantly.

Arch buckled on his gun belt, bent, and kissed her. "Yes, ma'am, Mrs. Fletcher, he's mighty good-looking," he told her. "And I sure do like that new dress you got on."

She pulled her naked body up against him, sliding her arms around his neck. "Do I still look as good to you, Archie honey? Tell me, do you think I changed a lot? Because I think I lost something when you went away like that."

"Honey, you didn't lose a blessed thing."

"Sure? Promise?"

"You're better right now this minute, Maudie Fletcher, than ever you were before. Best thing in the country, and that's the truth."

"Ah, damn you, Archie, damn you to hell, you're back with me, and you're all in one piece—"

"Let's us hope so," he said dryly.

"Take care of yourself, old sick cat, you. From now on, *I'll* keep you well, hear?"

"If I don't find Phil Hyssop to home, I'm going on out to the Randal place—"

"You'll be back here, won't you, Archie? You're not going off again, without a word, now, are you?"

"I'll be back here, honey, don't you fret. And I sure pray I don't have to go out to Perce Randal's, because I'd just as soon it didn't get around I was back in town."

"Be careful, Archie."

"Man can't be careful, little Maudie, till he knows what he's got to be careful about."

Doctor Phil Hyssop was home that day because his wife was ill; they were, in fact, almost the only two people who were left in the town of Eastmere on the Randals' bright festive Sunday. And if Hyssop was surprised to see Arch Eastmere, he refrained from letting his caller know it. The doctor had a splendid set of burnsides and a gravity to match; but this last was a professional pose, to a great extent, for Phil Hyssop could relax as well as the next man, if he had to, and better than most—away from the bedside, that is. Still, surprise was an attitude that came hard to anyone who had such constant dealings, and in such intimacy, with the naked essentials of life and death. So Hyssop greeted Arch Eastmere matter of factly, as though it had been a mere week since they met.

However, he could not keep himself from cocking an appreciative eyebrow at the fine silver-mounted saddle. "Looks like you did right well for yourself down there, Arch," he said.

"Won that saddle in a shooting-match, Phil. Other feller run plumb out of money. Man by the name of Dominguez."

"Looks pretty heavy."

"Got a rugged horse."

Later, when Arch Eastmere had described the attack he'd had at Maude Fletcher's, Hyssop's gravity was no longer a pose. Frowning, humming to himself, pursing his lips, stroking his thick burnsides, asking an occasional question, he prodded and tapped and listened to dim, important sounds inside Arch Eastmere's rib cage. Finally, after nearly an hour had gone by, the doctor sat down in the creaking chair by his desk and looked at his patient bleakly. "You figuring to work on one of the spreads around, Arch?" he asked.

"Hadn't thought much about it, Phil. Matter of fact, I'd be obliged if you didn't mention me dropping in this way. No point anybody knowing I'm back."

"Well, now, Arch—even young Pace Gray?"

Arch Eastmere's eyes brightened. "Why, Phil, how *is* that boy?

I declare, he's been on my mind a lot. He been behaving himself?"

"He thinks the world of you, Arch. Talks about you all the time."

Arch Eastmere stared at the floor. "Can't say as I set him many good examples."

"You couldn't prove it by Pace. Far as you're concerned, Arch, he can't see the wood for the trees."

Arch Eastmere smiled. It was a very warm, very happy, very pleasant smile, and it made him look almost boyish himself. "Well, Phil, when you see that old hoss Pace, tell him he can find me down to Maudie Fletcher's. But don't you tell nobody else, and don't let him, neither."

"I won't." The chair creaked as Hyssop shifted uncomfortably. "But now there's something I've got to tell *you*, Arch, and if I know you, you're not going to take to it kindly. That's what I'd begun to go into when I asked you if you planned to work on one of the spreads hereabouts—"

"I probably will," said Arch Eastmere.

"No, you won't, Arch," said Phil Hyssop. "Not if you want to stay alive."

Arch Eastmere stared at the doctor for a long time. "I never been sick a day in my life," he said.

"You're not *sick* now, either, damn it, Arch—not as the term is used around here. Now listen carefully. What you've got is, well, *heart* trouble. That thing this morning could've killed you—and the next one probably *will* kill you. So we've got to see you don't *have* that next one."

"My heart," Arch said flatly.

Hyssop nodded. "And as of today, you're living on, damn it all, borrowed time. Think you can get used to the idea?"

"Depends on how good my credit is, don't it?"

"Your credit's as good as the care you take of yourself."

"You can say right out, Phil. How long you figger I got?"

Phil Hyssop shrugged and sagged somewhat; at the moment Arch Eastmere had more gravity than ten Doctor Hyssops. "Hard to say. Maybe forty years. Maybe ten minutes."

"I don't want any forty years more," Arch Eastmere said

quietly. "Always figgered to die young, anyway. Runs in the family, to some extent."

"You *want* to die young?"

"Not right now, Phil. I'd like another week or so."

Hyssop was grave again. "I'm not joking, Arch, so don't you."

"Sorry, Phil, you're the doctor. Tell me what I better do."

"Take it easy, that's all, only thing you can do. Don't strain yourself, don't get all worked up, you know, *inside,* leave the booze alone, and the women too, like as not, with all due regards to Mrs. Fletcher. What it adds up to, damn it, Arch, I suppose, is: think before you move, and then move damned slow."

"Or I'll be dead?"

Phil Hyssop nodded curtly. "Or you'll be dead, Arch. Dead in your tracks."

Arch Eastmere rose and held out his hand. "I'm obliged to you, Phil," he said. "Will you be wanting to see me again?"

"Alive," Hyssop said, shaking hands. "Alive, that's how I'll want to see you."

"I'll have to owe you for helping me this way."

"Forget it. It's on the house."

"I want to pay my own way, Phil. Always have, always intend to."

"Some people think maybe you paid too much already. And, Arch—one thing above everything else: *watch your temper.* From now on, as far as you're concerned, getting mad's like committing suicide. Remember that, every day when you wake up. Don't you *ever* get mad."

On the way back to Maude Fletcher's, his horse walking, the sun barely past its zenith bouncing alarmed off the bright silver saddle, Arch Eastmere, his jaw sunk down on his chest, tried to review the life that had so nearly ended on this yellow Sunday morning. *Some people think maybe you paid too much already:* now what did Phil Hyssop mean by that? Too much, for *what?*

He couldn't have meant that first shooting-scrape, when fourteen-year-old Archie Eastmere put a ball from an old smoothbore pistol smack in his Grandfather Eastmere's thigh.

Old Black Jack Eastmere, who then owned most of the Fork-handle country, certainly deserved a certain amount of shooting, if any man ever did, but not at the hands of his own flesh-and-blood grandson. Arch, however, deserved all *he* got, he reckoned, for doing what he did, and he hadn't felt any rancor, either then or now. Arch didn't even feel it was wrong when Black Jack Eastmere, before he died, sold every square foot of the land he owned, wonderful grazing country to which Arch had been the sole heir. For, Arch had to admit to himself, anybody who'd shoot his kinfolks, no matter how much grievance he had, ought to be hung—and, for such a sinful man, anything less than a rope was just so much gravy.

It had grown very hot.

Was that why the joints of Arch's life refused to dovetail for him there, under the silver-reflecting sun?

Pieces of memory leaped to his vision, like trout breaking water for midges—and then were as quickly, as quicksilver, gone.

There was his mother, there she lay, she who had been Tessa Acton, a beautiful girl worn out by the Eastmeres, lying so pale and small on her deathbed, saying to Arch, who was small then too, a little boy barely eight years old, saying to her sober-faced, tearless son: "Little boy, little boy, they think they beat me, but they didn't, and they won't beat *you*, because I've washed your flesh in my own blood and strength, and none of the lot of them ever can hurt you." But then she had begun to cry herself, and she had tried to reach his hand and failed, until he found her frail fingers with his own. And then she had said: "Little boy, little Archie, poor little boy, I think *you'll* die young, too." And with a last, longer sigh than all the sighs before, the mother whose only delight he was went down into the darkness, with her cheeks still wet with tears. And Arch Eastmere, alone in the very be-ginning of all the aloneness to come, had awkwardly wiped her tears away before his own sorrow started to shake him.

It had been nearly thirty-five years ago; yet Arch Eastmere saw it as something just finished, something that had only now happened in the very next room away.

And there was something he and Hallock Randal had done together, a little before the War—but what *was* it? They'd laughed about it for weeks afterwards, the two of them, busting a gut every time they met, at the thought of whatever it was. Or had it been Hallock, after all? Perhaps it had been Ex Macleod.

It'd be good to lie down in Maudie's—

No, Ex Macleod was long dead at Shiloh. And there were other dead men, too. Some at the hands of Arch Eastmere? Who said *that?*

How many at Arch Eastmere's hands? And their names? And *where?* And *why?*

The heat made it hard to remember. The sun diffused things.

The dead faces all became one face, and—why, it looked like the face of Hallock Randal, one of the times they saw the elephant. But he couldn't be sure, because that Mexican silver was shining so on the saddle some Yankee *pistolero* had taken from somebody's horse. *Whose* faces? Who were all these *dead* men? *Why?*

He was at Maudie's and she was holding his horse and he was climbing out of the saddle. "You look hot, Archie honey, what'd he say, you going to be all right?"

"I'm hot, Maudie, little Maudie, he said it'll be fine, he wants me to lie down the rest of the day."

"I'll take care of your horse."

"You do that, Maudie honey."

He went into the house alone and threw himself down on his back on the same old bed and looked at the ceiling, and they were all still there, all the dead men. Who are you? *Who?* And *why?*

After all, Arch Eastmere had a right to know, if anybody did in the whole wide world. For wasn't it, after all, a dead man who was doing the asking, a dead man who had to die young? It *was*, indeed it was; and there he lay on his back, with not a penny to his name, on Maude Fletcher's dirty old bed—Arch Eastmere, with his big old Colt still strapped low on his hip, six feet, three inches tall, forty-two years old, a dead man by all accounts, and yet who once, nine lives ago, had been his lovely mother's only joy.

CHAPTER 3

Pax, handsomest of all the Randals, had started this particular Sunday with a drink, a good, stiff hair of the dog that bit him, while he was still in bed. He had ridden home late from Smiley's in Eastmere, and he awoke feeling heavy and lonely and chill. A pull from the bottle he had placed below the bedstead warmed his belly and lightened his thoughts.

Lying on his side, looking out the window, watching the sun come up, he reviewed the previous evening. He had sat in Smiley's with Drury Wynward from seven o'clock until well after two, drinking whisky with beer chasers. Toward the end they were the saloon's only customers, and, even when Pax was about to leave, Drury looked set to stay boozing all night, his mouth slack and his fine eyes glazed. "By God, now, Pax," he had said, "I never yet knew you to go running off home in the shank of the evening."

"I got this quarter-horse race with Mark Lacy tomorrow, Drury. You know that."

"Hell, you'll beat him."

"I better had. I've got a hundred-dollar bet on with Mark."

Drury had tried to whistle, but his lips were out of control. "You *seen* Mark's new quarter horse?"

"Nope. But I got a little tired of hearing him talk her up the way he's been doing."

"Hell, you'll beat him."

"Reckon it's in the cards I will, Drury, the way Mark's luck's been running this past year."

"Hell, you'll beat him, Pax. So just ease off, now. Tell you what, let's the two of us ride down to Maudie Fletcher's and toss for it."

"Then I'd never get home all night, Drury, and, goddamn it, the family's going to be at me every minute tomorrow to be doing something or other."

"Hell, you'll *beat* 'em, Pax. Have another drink, quiet you guts going home."

"One more, then, Drury. And that's all."

He could still taste that last drink, Pax thought, even over th hair of the dog that now soothed his stomach. He took three mo swallows from the bottle, corked it, and, getting to his feet, p it in the bottom drawer of his dresser. This second drink did t trick; he felt fresh and human again. Filling the basin on t commode with cold water, he splashed it on his face and g hair. The mirror above the commode told him that last nigh liquor and lack of sleep had left no mark on his even featur He shaved, still using cold water. Then he dressed quickly a went down through the silent house to the kitchen. He wan some coffee.

As he had been the last of the Randals to find his bed, he also the first one up. Dolores, Maria, and Concepcion, the ol eyed dewy daughters of the widowed cook, Luisa Costa, v already in the kitchen, however, decked out in gaudy dresses, full-skirted and heavily flounced. They seemed to l been expecting Pax, for when he appeared all three tittere one, giggled and shook, then turned their heads inward to each other and whispered in Spanish. Pax, after a first quick at the girls, ignored them while he sipped his blistering c

The half-heard sibilant talk continued in the bent-head of girls until Luisa pounded a knife handle down on the ta which she was rolling and cutting pie crusts. "Fools," sh quietly. "Stop it, fools." There was no anger in her voice

matter of fact, she was smiling. Yet the girls fell silent at once.

"Pretty fools," Pax said dispassionately, addressing the words to the lip of his cup.

"You know what they whisper, Pax?" Luisa asked. "They whisper to each other, who *you* think got the most pretty dress. *You,* Pax. These dresses, they make themselves. Especially."

Pax set his cup down. "They want to know, do they?"

Smiling softly, becoming on the instant modest, the girls huddled closer to each other like ewes in cold weather. "Well, let's see," Pax said. He stood up, improved by the coffee, and, in the spirit of the thing, solemnly walked over to them.

As he loomed above their braided hair, the three girls blushed, lowered their eyes, and peered wistfully up at him through jet lashes of a wondrous length. Pax studied each one in turn as they lined up before him; he frowned and pursed his lips, just as he would have done if he were inspecting some heifers with a view to buying them. He drew out one side of their skirts, as though to study the color and texture of the cloth, and he had them all turn around, in order, as he said, to study the workmanship that was in the back of each frock. "You *really* want to know?" he said at last.

The girls nodded eagerly, and their hands slipped unconsciously into each other's, as if they wanted to share a mutual courage in the endless seconds before a decision was given. Pax knew their delightful agony, and he could have prolonged it, in fact, he was tempted; but he was already bored, especially with Luisa watching. So he laid his left hand on a sixteen-year-old shoulder. The flesh, even beneath the gay cotton, was so hot that he was startled.

"Dolores," he said. "I reckon Dolores."

She was the youngest and loveliest of the three. Now, with a little squeal, she slipped forward under the weight of Pax's hand and, hugging him around the body, pressed her flushed cheek against his heart. Her eyes were moist, and she was very happy. "I hope *you* win, too, Pax," she whispered, just before he took a backward step and released himself from her arms.

Maria, who was seventeen, and Concepcion, all of two years

older—and therefore sadly wise in the disruptions of this world and widely versed in its confusions—smiled, but with their red mouths only; and while Pax had a second cup of coffee they wandered, disconsolate, back to their work.

But Dolores followed him everywhere, whenever she could, unnoticed and at a worshipping distance, all the marvelous day.

She did not, however, under Luisa Costa's watchful eye, follow him then, as he left first the kitchen and then the house.

Pax stood for a moment looking down the narrow road that led south to where a plank bridge across the Forkhandle River marked the lower boundary of Randal land. A half-mile along this road he could see a wagon coming toward him through patches of trees, bringing the first of the guests, in spite of the early hour. By ten o'clock, Pax guessed, there'd be at least a hundred and fifty people swarming around, while Luke Randal became a man in the meadow. Most of them would arrive, as had this first wagon, by way of the Forkhandle bridge. Others, however, riding from further west, would cross the river at Lacy's Ford, splashing through foot-deep water near the foothills where the Santa Marias began.

In reality, Luke's birthday had fallen on the previous Wednesday, and Percy Randal had purposely delayed the celebration. Although the spring roundup was finished, there remained, as always, the innumerable daily chores and duties to be carried out on the ranches through which the Forkhandle ran, and in the town of Eastmere, whose merchants, facilities, and minor pleasure palaces served this high segment of the earth. Only when Saturday's sun lowered behind the Marias did the clocks of work truly run down. And so Percy Randal had planned Luke's blowout for Sunday, when the biggest crowd could come.

"And he got himself mighty fine weather," Pax said aloud, looking up at the unmarred sky. He turned and began to walk aimlessly down the other side of the knoll.

His gaze, haphazard and semi-aware, roving with leisure over the various buildings, was brought up short when it fell on the near corral. A strange dappled mare, standing dead center in the enclosure, pawed the earth nervously, then reared up, whinnying. Over the top rail of the corral a saddle and a pair of saddlebags was hung, and inside the fence a man, whose face Pax couldn't see, was either taking something out of one of the saddlebags, or putting something in, and paying no attention to the horse, even when it reared and whinnied a second time. Pax thought, for a moment, that the man was either Jim Good or Sam Wadley, both of whom were supposed to be up in the Marias beyond Juncture Valley, making some repairs at a couple of the line camps. But any of the line camps was a hard six hours' ride, and this horse was too flighty to have come so far. Pax started toward the corral. He hadn't covered a dozen yards when the man peered around the saddlebags, grinned at him, waved, and headed for the corral's closed gate. It was Mark Lacy.

"Never you mind," Pax called to him. "I can still find my way up a fence."

Mark had lately fallen into the habit of carrying two bottles of whisky in his saddlebags wherever he went, and he had been guzzling from one of these when he saw Pax moving down the knoll in his general direction. He took another quick gulp, pounded the cork in with the heel of his hand, and replaced the bottle in the saddlebag. He had been fastening the strap when Pax saw him.

"Reckon you're just getting home," Mark said wryly as he and Pax climbed the fence from opposite sides.

"Just getting up," Pax told him, sitting on the top rail and hooking his insteps around the one below. "Hell, I was in bed by three o'clock. Haven't had that much sleep in a long time."

"I started *out* right about then," Mark said. He settled himself beside Pax and tilted his hat back. He was a man forty years old, with a thick black mustache and curly black hair which was beginning to recede above the temples, forming a widow's peak. His chin and cheeks were blue with a day-old beard. "Wanted this little beauty to have eight, nine hours' rest before we up and take your money." He nodded at the dappled mare. She had moved as far from them as she could and now stood against the rail, still pawing the earth, snorting, and tossing her mane.

Pax watched the mare in silence for nearly a minute. "So *that's* her," he said at last.

"That's her, all right," Mark said. "Best goddamned quarter horse this side the Mississippi."

"Looks to me," Pax said dryly, "like the most spooky goddamned quarter horse this side the Mississippi."

"She got a look at you, that's all. You know what that does to females."

Pax gave a short, barking laugh. "Well, by God, as far as females're concerned," he said, "there's mighty lean pickings in this neck of the woods, and that's the truth. Why, last night Drury Wynward wanted the two of us to go down to Maudie Fletcher's —*two* of us, mind you—and damned if I didn't near go."

"Drury go himself?" Mark asked with a grin. "I bet he did, the horny bastard."

"I don't know. Maybe. He was still at Smiley's when I quit there. Matter of fact, Mark, we figgered you might show up sometime, but then we figgered, hell, with the bedful he's married to, why should Mark Lacy go banging around barrooms at night with a lot of poor, lonely bachelors? That's what we said, by God, and I'll bet we were right, now, weren't we?"

The smile was swept from Mark's lips. "You do enough talking about my wife," he said, "so I reckon you're bound to be right some of the time."

"Where *is* Ellen, anyway?" Pax asked.

"Over there," Mark said. He pointed toward the mare, and some of the smile came back to his mouth.

"Your *wife*, I said, Mark. Ellen. Ellen *Lacy*."

"Oh, my *wife*. Reckon she's home. That's where I left her."

"*Ellen*," Pax said slowly. "I didn't figger I heard straight a minute ago. Ellen. You mean you went and gave this new mare the same name as your wife?"

"Why not?" Mark said brusquely. "They're both of 'em two fine females, only one's fast and the other's good-looking. And Ellen never minded at all about me naming the horse that way. You think I didn't tell her, for God's sake?"

"Well," Pax said, pouting as he brooded over the matter, "just so long as you can tell 'em apart."

"I can, don't you fret," Mark said.

"She coming on here with your brother? The *good*-looking Ellen, I mean?"

"Hell, it's all Alan can do to bring his *own* wife. Nope, I figger Ellen'll come by herself in the buggy."

"Tell you what, Mark, I'll ride over to your place and make sure she gets here safe and sound, what do you say?"

"The hell you will," Mark said.

Pax looked hurt. "Don't you trust me?" he asked.

"Far as women're concerned, I trust you the least of any bastard I know, by God, and don't you ever forget it."

"Well, now, Mark, I'm sorry, I swear," Pax said. "I didn't mean to rile you."

Mark drew in a deep breath, then expelled it with a grunt. "Ah, all right," he said. "It's no matter. It's just that I don't take to that kind of talk about my wife, and I get goddamn tired of hearing it."

"Yep," Pax said, nodding his head solemnly, "I reckon a feller that's married to a good-looking woman, like your Ellen, he has himself a lot of worries."

"By God, that's the true of it," said Mark.

"Well, I tell you what, then," Pax went on smoothly. "Instead of putting up that hundred dollars, why don't you put up your wife? Then, when I've gone and beat you, I'll take her off your hands and all your worries'll be gone."

"God *damn* you, Pax!" Mark exclaimed. He jumped down to the ground. "I'm not going to take any more of your guff."

"Mark, I'm sure sorry," Pax said, realizing that he had carried things too far. "I was only funning."

"I don't like that kind of funning," Mark said, still angry. "And, by God, if you keep it up, it'll lead to trouble."

"I'm quit of it, Mark. And I said I was sorry."

"Well, sure, then, Pax, never mind," Mark said. The tenseness went out of his face. "Reckon I got no call to be so damned jumpy, anyway." He looked up toward the ranch house. "Here comes your father."

Pax twisted his head around. "By God, that's who's coming,

all right," he said heavily, and he began to climb down on the outside of the fence, where he again joined Mark.

Percy Randal, with young Luke at his heels, came striding toward them. He was sixty-eight years old, but he looked ten years younger, his face unlined except at the corners of his eyes, his cheeks made ruddy by a circular network of tiny blood vessels, translucent under the clear skin. He wore no hat, and his unthinned hair was still a warm chestnut brown, save for those places above and around his ears where age had regretfully grayed it. His mustache was neatly trimmed. He had been a handsome, hard-working young man; he was now a handsome, dignified old one. "Howdy, Mark," he said with a warm smile.

Mark smiled back at him as they shook hands. "Well, Perce," he said, winking at Luke, "I reckon today takes care of the last of 'em."

"Thank the Lord," said Percy Randal. He turned to the gawky, long-haired boy at his side. "You know Mark Lacy, don't you, Luke?"

"Sure," Luke said. "Howdy." He shook hands with Mark.

"How does it feel to finally get your growth?" Mark asked.

"Same's it did last Wednesday," Luke said, grinning. "Only more so."

"By God," Randal exclaimed, "I'm already plumb sorry I'm giving this blowout." He glanced at Pax. "You know what your mother's told me I've got to do? I've got to crawl up on a wagon with this young feller here and introduce him to folks that've known him since he was a baby, and show him off like a god-damned side of beef. And do you know what Luke's going to do?" he went on, addressing Mark. "Why Luke's going to stand there kicking his toe against his heel and blushing till he's the color of Tennessee dirt and wishing, by God, he was still ten years old. Won't it be just that way, now, Luke?" He patted his youngest son's too-long hair, which fell nearly to his narrow shoulders.

"Reckon so, sir," Luke said with lowered eyes.

"I heard you come in, Pax," Percy Randal said. "Surprised you're looking so fresh."

"Figgered I had to, Father, on a big day like this."

"Well, while you're *still* fresh, and before the world and his wife gets here, I'd like for you to take a look at the course you'll be running. Luke's cleared it out pretty well, I reckon, but you're the feller that'll be riding on it."

"Yes, sir."

"I'll go with you, Pax," said Luke. The two of them walked away. Pax's arm was thrown across his younger brother's shoulders.

Left alone with Mark Lacy, Percy Randal turned his attention to the mare in the corral. The beast, much quieter now, was nuzzling the ground, blowing up small clouds of dust. "That's a mighty fine piece of horseflesh you got there," he said.

"Thought you'd like her, Perce."

"Want to sell her?"

"Hell, no. I've still got to get my investment in her back. And I will, too, by God. She's going to cost Pax a bit of money before the day's out. And maybe some of that cockiness, too."

"Could be, Mark, could be." A faint, wistful smile played over Percy Randal's face.

"I called her after my wife," Mark said suddenly, and with more than a trace of belligerence in his voice. "Ellen."

Percy Randal nodded slowly, his lips still fixed in the faraway smile. "Can't say as I blame you," he said. "They're both of 'em downright handsome. Why, now, if Pax could come up with a woman as handsome as Ellen Lacy, I'd be a happy man, by God." The smile broadened, and his eyes twinkled. "No chance of you selling *her* either, I suppose?"

A frown drew Mark's eyebrows together. "Not this year, Perce, I reckon," he said. "Haven't got *that* investment back, either."

"Well," Percy Randal said, "I hope they're all *boys* when you do." He leaned against a rail of the corral. "Things haven't been going too well with you lately, have they, Mark?"

Mark hesitated. "I've seen 'em worse," he said with deliberation.

Percy Randal was staring down at the earth. "We all have," he said.

"And they'll get better."

"They always do, yep."

"Funny thing about it, Perce, a couple of years ago, I couldn't do *anything* wrong. Then one day Arch Eastmere come to me and wanted to borrow five hundred dollars to go down to Mexico with, and like a goddamned fool I let him have it. And, do you know, by God, my luck's been bad ever since."

"Arch's a good enough man," Percy Randal said, "just as long as the things he's *doing're* bad. I liked Arch, but I'm damned if I'd ever've let him have five hundred dollars."

"Well, it's done now," Mark said wearily.

"What's done can always be undone," Percy Randal said. He studied the distant Marias for a moment. "Ever think of selling your spread?" he asked.

The remark was a casual one, but it took Mark Lacy by surprise. "Christ, no," he exclaimed, "any more than I've been thinking *you* want to buy it."

"I'll give you a good price, Mark."

"My God, Perce, you've got enough land for *ten* ranches as it is. What the hell do you want *more* land for?"

"Pax," Percy Randal said after a pause. "It's getting on to be time that boy settled down."

"You got a wife picked for him, Perce?"

"I reckon if I get him a spread, he'll get himself a woman."

"His own, Perce? Or somebody else's?"

"Hell, Mark, there's half-a-dozen unmarried girls around here that's got their caps set for Pax."

"Seems to me he's damned well had plenty of time to pick one or the other of 'em."

"He will."

"Maybe so, Perce, but when he does, it won't be to bring her to what used to be my spread, and that's a fact."

Percy Randal pushed himself away from the rail against which he had been leaning. "Fine, then, Mark," he said. "Fine and dandy. But if you change your mind, let me know, hey?"

"I won't be changing my mind, Perce. Not if I can help it."

"Sometimes folks can't help it," Percy Randal said. "And sometimes we change our minds in spite of ourselves. There's no telling *what* folks won't do. Anyway, I'm pleased I had the chance to ask you. Reckon I won't get to see much of you later, what with all that'll be going on." He clapped Mark on the shoulder in a friendly way. "Now I'd best get over and get 'em started on roasting that steer. A whole goddamned *steer*, Mark. That's a lot of meat to put away in just one day."

As he strode toward the pit that had been dug where the meadow met the knoll on the other side of the ranch house, Percy Randal was unaware that Mark Lacy's eyes, which had taken on an eagle's concentration, had settled their glare on his back. Nor was he aware that, as soon as he was out of Mark's sight, the strap of the saddlebag was unfastened and the bottle of whisky brought forth again. Nor could he hear Mark Lacy muttering: "God damn him, God *damn* him, God damn *them*," over and over again, bewildered and angry, as he drank.

Terry Sykes was tall and thin, with broad splayed feet, narrow shoulders, and a small bald head. His eyes were blue snowbanks reflecting the sky, and his skin was as white as a nun's. He never tanned, and he seldom talked. Usually when he was with other people, he stood brittle-backed, with a ramrod discomfort. He seemed no man, but a walking stalagmite; and he made some women shiver.

Now, however, in the cool Randal barn, leaning against one of the rough-hewn beams that supported the great loft above, listening to other men's inconsequential talk, Terry Sykes's attitude was, for him, very relaxed and easy. His arms were folded across his chest, and he was chewing ruminatively on a dead cigar.

Five other men, four of whom had ranches south of Percy Randal's, were lounging in the barn, passing around a bottle of whisky and dodging the noonday heat that yellowed the shimmering air outside the open doors. For the most part, they had ignored Sykes, although they had not begrudged him an occasional suck at the bottle.

Jock Menzies, who was bronzed and brawny and big as the side of a house, had wiped the neck of the bottle on his shirt-sleeve after taking a drink, and was handing it on to Oliver Swindon when he saw the cigar in Terry Sykes's mouth. There were several reasons why he might not have noticed it before.

Jock, good-hearted and gentle though he generally was, found Sykes distasteful to look at, and avoided the sight of him as much as he could. Too, Jock was neither very intelligent nor very perceptive; he might have seen the cigar ten times over before it occurred to him that it was in a man's mouth. "God *damn* you, Sykes!" he yelled. "You want to set everything afire, burning that rope? You're in a *barn*, goddamn it!"

Old Nelse Macleod chuckled in his whiskers. Nelse was over seventy, his tobacco-stained beard fell below the third button of his shirt, and his ranch was the second biggest in the whole Forkhandle country. "Thing's been out ever since he come in here, Jock," he said mildly.

Sykes's only reaction was to let his pale lids droop over his eyes, counteracting the movement at the same time by drawing up one corner of his mouth in what might have been either a semi-smile or a full sneer.

"Man never knows," said Jock Menzies. "Guns go off when they ain't loaded, neither."

"So do men, Jock, so do men," Oliver Swindon said, taking the bottle from the other's still-outstretched hand. Swindon, sturdy and sandy-haired, had legs that were somewhat too short for his body, a defect that went unnoticed on horseback; other than that he was a fine specimen. He tossed off a swallow from the bottle, wiped the neck on his sleeve, and gave it to young Pace Gray, who, curly-haired and boyish-faced, had barely turned nineteen, and was doing his damnedest to act like a man among men.

Nelse Macleod tugged at his beard and renewed his chuckling. The noise resembled an angry squirrel. "I always said Jock here could see less, in more time, than any feller I ever knew."

"By George, that's right," said Oliver Swindon. "Remember that girl he was courting down to Divide? Why, Jock courted that girl two years before he found out she was ugly."

"Bet it didn't take her that long to find out *he* was," Alan Lacy said. Alan was five years older than his brother, Mark, and heavier by fifteen pounds. He was clean-shaven, too, and his black hair was streaked with gray.

"Now, Alan," Jock said with a pleased grin, "if you'd been in these parts then, you'd have called it downright indecent, the way that poor girl took to me. Folks used to come up to her and say: 'Now, look here, uh—'" He broke off, frowning. "Uh—" He snapped his fingers in annoyance.

"By God, he can't even remember her name!" Old Nelse gave a hoarse, exultant laugh and slapped his thigh.

"Jennie Maggs, her name was," Pace Gray said.

Jock snapped his fingers again and nodded at Pace. "Sure. Jennie Maggs. She used to work for your aunts down there, didn't she, Pace? That's right—Jennie *Maggs*. Used to work for Pace Gray's aunts."

"And she *sure* was an ugly one, wasn't she, Pace?" Oliver Swindon asked.

"I was so young it didn't matter," Pace answered.

They all laughed. "By God, you still are, son," said Nelse. "And that's a fact."

"Oh, I don't know, now," Alan Lacy said. "Pace'd be a real heller, maybe, with a few more years on him, if it wasn't for some of these other stallions we got stomping around." He waved his hand in welcome to Hallock Randal, whose lean form was now silhouetted in the open barn doors.

"You talking about Sykes here?" Oliver Swindon wanted to know. "Or Jock Menzies?"

"Way I see it," Alan Lacy said, "George Throstle keeps the Eastmere fillies quiet, and Drury Wynward breaks in all the wild ones he finds on the range."

"Reckon my brother Pax does pretty well at loving, too," Hallock Randal said, coming up to the group. "Hope he don't get himself shot at one of these fine days. By an *accurate* man, I mean."

"Hell, he's the one that always keeps the most busy where females're concerned," Alan said.

"Goes without saying," sighed Jock.

Alan Lacy, who was sitting with his back against the side of the barn, cocked his head to look up at Hallock. "You seen Mark's new quarter horse?" he asked.

"Finally," Hallock told him. "Little while ago."

"What'd you think of her?"

"Hard to tell, Alan," Hallock said. "She looks fine on the outside, anyway. Good lines."

"If Arch Eastmere was back," Pace Gray said suddenly, his earnest gaze going from face to face, "they'd *all* eat crow, I swear. George Throstle and Drury and Pax, too, by God."

"And in just what way'll that be, son?" old Nelse demanded.

"Every damned which way," said Pace. "It wasn't only women and loving I meant."

Hallock and Oliver Swindon winked at each other, grinning. The cigar tilted upward, and Terry Sykes spoke bitterly through clenched teeth, his lips now curved in a definite sneer. "Arch Eastmere'll *never* come back here," he said. "He'll still be over the Border, waiting for the greasers to make him King of Mexico, on the day they shovel him under."

Pace Gray scrambled to his feet and took a step toward Sykes. "You're a goddamned liar!" he shouted, then looked desperately around for agreement. "Ain't he a liar, Hallock?"

"You sit down, Pace," Nelse said in a low voice. "World's *full* of liars. Taken me seventy-some years to find that fact out."

"That's right, Pace boy, sit down," Oliver Swindon said. "Arch'll be back one of these bright days, I reckon. And when he comes, we'll know it, sure enough, soon's he gets within a hundred miles of the place."

"Or if you don't, you'll sure as hell hear the noise when he stops to spit on his granddaddy's grave," Sykes said.

Pace Gray, who was resuming his seat on the floor, jumped up again. "By *Jesus*, you old bastard—!" he started to say.

Hallock spoke out sharply, and his eyes were suddenly hard. "*Pace!*" The boy, who seemed about to leap on Sykes, faltered, then sighed and sank down again, high color in his face. "He's got no call to talk like that," he said thickly. "Damned dirty old bastard."

Hallock's level gaze was now on Sykes. "And, *you*, by God— either stop drinking or stop talking. There's not going to be any trouble around here today."

"No trouble, Hallock." Alan Lacy nodded agreement. "No trouble at all."

"Hell with the lot of you," Sykes remarked. He swung his

back away from the beam and walked, stiff-legged, out of the barn. The others watched him until he blended with the yellow sunlight outside; then "Good," said young Pace Gray.

"Damned good," Jock Menzies said. "I feel a lot better now." He held his hand out to the boy. "Let's have a heave of that pain-killer, Pace."

Pace had set the bottle on the floor when he had risen to confront Terry Sykes. "God, I didn't have mine yet," he said. He raised the bottle to his lips, then passed it on.

Jock Menzies was midway through his pull at the bottle when he realized that Hallock was watching him with amusement. He swallowed what was in his mouth and grinned hazily at the other man. "By God, Hallock," he said, "what's a teetotaler like you *doing* in here amongst all us drinking men, anyways?"

"Matter of fact," Hallock told him, "I come in to tell you it's time to eat. Sort of wandered off the trail, didn't I?"

"Well, in that case—" said Jock. He drained the rest of the bottle. "In *that* case, let's all of us get back on it."

A few moments later Hallock Randal and Alan Lacy strolled together out of the barn. The others had hurried ahead. "What's troubling Mark?" Hallock wanted to know. "You got any idea at all?"

Alan considered the matter. "Nothing particular, as I know of," he said. "Why?"

"From what I hear," Hallock said, "he's been hanging around the corral all morning, all by himself."

"It must be that new mare of his," Alan said. "Mark's damn-fool crazy about that horse."

"You know what he asked me, when I stopped by there?" Hallock went on. "He wanted to know what happened to all our ranch hands. Said he hadn't seen but three Randal hands since six o'clock this morning."

"Why, hell, Hallock, I've seen eight or ten of 'em myself. Soap Damson, Art Cospatrick, *Drew* Cospatrick, Pete Adams— hell, yes, maybe a dozen."

Hallock blinked in the sunlight as they came out of the barn. "Sure," he said. "They're all here except Jim Good and Sam Wadley, and they're up in the Marias."

"What're they doing up there?"

"Repairs on the line camps. And they should've got back last night, come to think of it. It's probably that goddamned lazy Sam Wadley. Takes him three days to do what'd take any other man twenty minutes. Jim Good's probably having to do everything himself. Reckon Jim'll be boiling mad, once he gets back."

"Well, hell, Hallock, don't you pay no mind to Mark, hear? He's worked up over this horse race, that's all."

"I reckon I am, myself," said Hallock Randal pleasantly.

Far up in the Marias, however, and even while Hallock Randal was mentioning his name, Jim Good was concerned with a matter more grave than any laziness of Sam Wadley. For, as they were on the way from one line camp to another, cutting straight across the Santa Marias, he and Sam had reached the South Tine, which flowed across the trail there, and which had to be crossed by men moving between the two camps. But this time they never did get over the stream.

For they came upon a sight so startling—and, to their shaken minds, so terrifying—that, at Jim Good's command, and almost before he knew it, Sam Wadley was galloping hell-for-leather down the treacherous mountain slopes, on the first wild leg of the long ride home. And what he had seen had impressed itself on him to such an extent that Sam Wadley, who had always taken infinite care to exert neither his horse nor himself, was driving both man and beast as though the Devil were after them.

Which, in a way, He was.

CHAPTER 4

Harriet Hallock Randal sat, in the first relaxed time she had been given since the beginning of her day, under a shady tree on the top of the knoll by the ranch house. The steer had long since been served to the guests who, for the most part, having finished their meal, were now spread like patchwork around the meadow. Near Harriet, on her left, Luke sprawled; and on her right was Cora, her only daughter, stretched full length on the grass, her head resting on her hands. They, like their mother, were viewing the human landscape around them.

Gradually Harriet Randal let herself be enfolded by a gentle sadness. In recent years, most often when she was alone, she had found herself offering up a small quiet sigh on the altar of her life, for no apparent reason and much to her own surprise. Sometimes her eyes would look toward the far Marias and lock there for a little while, quite as though she awaited some messenger, loping across the old blue peaks, who would bring her an answer for a question never asked.

What had once been the broad high lake of her existence, swept by impassioned mountain gales that had raised a roil of whitecaps upon it, was now a placid and translucent pool, clear and cool and uncluttered down to its last green depths. Yet in the

first years of her marriage she had known strange upheavals in
the night, grim dreams and parlous nightmares that had sent her,
time and again, moaning and wildly distrait, into the strong com-
passion of Percy Randal's arms. These black and terrible midnight shocks were lessened much by the birth of Cora, and after
Pax came they ceased.

The clear blue eyes of Harriet fell on her only daughter. She
studied Cora's marble cheek and oddly coarse hair—dark hair
that never was able to stay in place, that Cora had never learned
to braid correctly. Pursing her lips a little, Harriet tried to understand what it was that the other lacked, both as a person and
as an object of male desire. She was thirty-two years old and
still unmarried. The reason for this long spinsterhood, in a place
so short of women, was beyond her mother's comprehension. For
several years, after Cora had turned eighteen, men had come to
the Randal ranch to court her, but none of them called again with
that purpose in mind after the first uncomfortable visit. She had
good features and a clean, incisive profile, along with a willowy,
well-shaped body; but there was something about her that made
all suitable men, after being in her presence for an hour, shrug
their shoulders, not necessarily with regret, and ride off to greener
pastures.

Perhaps Cora sensed her mother's eyes upon her, for she
looked around and wrinkled her nose at Harriet, in a way she
had done, in her better moments, ever since she had been two
years old. "I just can't get over it," she said. "Sallie and Dorrie
Pace haven't been this side of Eastmere since the American
Revolution, and there they are, big as life, sitting down there with
Pace Gray and looking modish as all get-out. If it was the mode
of eighteen fifty-seven, that is."

"Seventeen fifty-seven," Luke said without turning.

Harriet looked off to the right and down, where two gentle-
faced women in their late fifties, maiden ladies to even the most
unpracticed eye, were speaking to Pace Gray with some deliberation. Their words were of sufficient sharpness to make him
keep his gaze on the ground and his right hand busy with an
aimless plucking of grass. "Now, that's not kind of either of you,"
Harriet said mildly. "Why, I've known the Pace girls since before

even *you* were born, Cora, and if they're sort of queer and with-drawn, well, their lives haven't been exactly happy. You've heard that a hundred times."

"I didn't even know they'd been invited," Luke said.

"When I saw them drive up in that old surrey," Cora said, "I thought I'd sink right into the ground."

"How'd they know about the party?" Luke asked.

"Pace came by one day to watch Hallock with some mus-tangs," Harriet told him, "and I said I *especially* wanted his aunts to come. That's all there was to it."

"Poor Pace is getting Hail Columbia," Cora said. "And I know why."

"Sure, for drinking whisky in the barn," Luke said. "Little old Pace was in there getting likkered up with Alan Lacy and Jock and the rest of 'em." He giggled.

"You didn't follow him *in*, I suppose?" his mother asked.

"You know very well I've been out here every blessed minute of the day, getting my hand shook off and my back slapped till it's nigh broke."

As she looked at her youngest son, Harriet Randal felt her heart tremble and lurch. She had an almost overpowering urge to reach out and stroke his long hair where it broke jaggedly over his collar, below the nape of his neck—but she knew that he would be bound to resent such a public gesture on this official first day of his manhood. In spite of every effort, Harriet con-tinued to think of Luke as something or someone she could still carry in her arms. She persisted in seeing him as she had that first time, as the last living thing that would ever be taken from her body, small and helpless and soft, stretching a tiny unco-ordi-nated hand toward the glowing mother's face above him.

Harriet believed, too, that Luke would never make a really satisfactory adult. As she saw it, there would always be too much boy in him, too much delight in simple things, and too much belief in what he found in the landscape by which he was bounded. He had always been the best dispositioned of her three sons, and much the most gentle as well. Even tall Hallock, kind and patient and understanding as he was, especially with horses, lacked the pure gentleness of his youngest brother. Wide-eyed Luke had always embraced and loved the few small toys and pleasures that had come to him, and he enjoyed them for what they were, asking no more of them than that he might think them his own.

He could pass a whole innocent afternoon lying contentedly on his stomach, watching minute insects laboring at their instinctive tasks over a few square inches of earth that must have presented to them all the confusions men find in an African jungle or Amazon forest. Once, long ago, Pax had been this way, too, but his innocence and curiosity had somehow been more shrewd. Then a peculiar change had come over Pax, almost overnight, and though he still possessed the charm that had drawn people to him as a child, he now used the charm as a weapon; the pursuer, not the pursued.

Harriet Randal gave one of her small quiet sighs, then briefly looked surprised at herself. Luke heard her and instantly turned around, full of concern. "Something the matter, Mother?"

Smiling, she shook her head. "I'm happy, that's all."

Luke also was smiling. "Me, too," he said. Then he faced away from her again and returned to his own thoughts.

"There's your son *Pax*," Cora said sharply, pointing. The exclamation startled Harriet Randal. She followed the line of Cora's finger and saw Pax standing by the door of the barn. He must have come out of the cool gloom a bare moment before, and he was shading his eyes from the sudden bright afternoon. Then he strode confidently and steadily toward the second, more distant corral.

"He looks fine, just fine," Harriet said, more to herself than to Luke or Cora.

"He's stopped drinking, that's why," Cora said. "He hasn't had a drink since before his morning coffee." These statements of fact were uttered in an odd, echoing tone. Cora, too, seemed to be speaking to no one in particular.

"About time for the race, I reckon," Luke said, trying to be casual but betrayed by a sudden highness in his voice.

"Oh, yes," Harriet said. "I'd forgotten." She took a deep breath, then allowed herself a long exhalation.

Luke craned his head around, goggled at his mother, then sat up and stared at her with mock despair. "If you're not the most full-of-sighs woman I *ever* heard heaving," he said. "I sure hate the thought of you mooning around on *my* big day. Don't look right, somehow." He wagged his head at Harriet.

"Oh, I'm happy enough, never you fear," she said. "After all, it's *my* day, too, and don't you ever forget it, *Mister* Luke Randal."

"Sure it is." He put an arm around her and hugged her quickly. "*Everybody's* day."

"Sure it is," Harriet repeated after him. "And it's my day because it means the end of something for me. Because today the very last of all my children is grown up."

"If I was asked," Cora said in the same heavy voice, "I'd say it was the *beginning* of something."

"Beginning of what?" Luke wanted to know.

"This and that," Cora said. She averted her face even more from her mother and brother, looking off toward the far end of the meadow. "This and that."

"Big things, that's what," Luke said. "The beginning of big, *big* things." He kissed his mother sloppily on the cheek. "I'm going down and watch 'em saddle up." Jumping to his feet, he ran down the knoll in the direction Pax had gone.

For a moment Harriet Randal watched Luke's figure diminish in the hazy heat as he moved away from her, but Cora seemed completely unaware that her brother had left them. Then Harriet, after staring a while, her lips pursed in thought, at the back of her daughter's head, said: "Cora, what do you mean when you say—saying this is the beginning of something?"

Cora shook her head. "Oh, nothing," she said. Her tone was normal again.

"Darling, that doesn't make sense. You must've known what you meant when you said it. Now turn around, like the grown woman you are, for Heaven's sake, and tell me."

But Cora would not look at her mother. "I didn't mean anything, I told you," she said. "It was just something to say. Anyway—" Slowly she lowered her head until her face was brushing the grass it shaded. "Anyway, even when I *do* have something to say, nobody ever listens. I didn't mean anything, honest I didn't, and that's all I can tell you. It just slipped out, that's all.

It slipped—oh, what's the *use* of it?" Abruptly, Cora leaped to
her feet and ran past her mother toward the house.

Harriet Randal sighed, and this time she knew the reason for
her sighing. Never, while she lived, would she understand Cora,
no matter how much she tried. She had again made the mistake
of taking a molehill, not necessarily to make a mountain of it, only
to discover, too late, that the molehill had been, all the time, a
mountain in disguise.

There were half a dozen of Nelse Macleod's cowhands sitting in
the shade where the spruces began, considerably apart from
everyone else, midway down the meadow. They were full of
booze and happy as clams, and one of the lot, name of Randy
Worth, since his gut was gorged and he didn't give a damn, was
fooling around with an ill-tuned banjo, much to the pleasure of
his friend Will Clough, and the other four hands who were
boozed up too, plunking out a tune that was common and old
and making up the words as he went along:

> *"Come along, boys, and I'll tell you 'bout Soap—"*

And old Nelse's son, James O. Macleod, who was sheriff of
Eastmere and big as they come, riding toward the starting line
with Soap himself, grinned at the grizzled face and said: "By
God, they've got themselves around to a song on you."

> *"How his Maw was spooked by an antelope—"*

"She was, that's sure, and by every ought else," said Soap, and
spit terbaccer juice twenty feet away. He and J. O. were to start
the race, to be certain that the getaway was fair and square—

> *"So now every damn time Damson sees a gun—"*

They were the first to go down the course since the folks
around the ranch house had ate their grub. A man with his belly
full don't like to walk, a woman even empty don't like to feel the
sun, and the sun had been hotter than the hinges of hell, so

> *"He yells: 'Hell, Maw, now I'm spooked.' Look at Old
> Soap run—!"*

Soap and the sheriff had taken their time, especially since Hannah, who was J. O.'s wife, took a very dim view of her husband's going off when the business weren't official, and this business weren't—

Suddenly, with a sharp last twang, Randy Worth quit playing and he and Will Clough and the rest of them hollered over at Soap and J. O., who were passing slowly, walking their horses, taking their time in the afternoon heat. Soap waved at them unemotionally, took a plug of tobacco from his pocket, and bit off another chew. "You know what all that caterwauling was about, J. O.?" he asked. He returned the plug to his pocket without offering it to the other, for J. O. Macleod's wife saw to it that he had no bad habits, let alone filthy ones.

Macleod was an easy-going man, hearty and cheerful, as long as his wife, Hannah, was somewhere else. Now he threw back his head and laughed. "Damned right I do," he said. "*You*, by God, big as life and twice as pretty."

Soap shifted his cud and reconnoitered in the back of his mind. "Well," he began slowly, "that feller with the banjo was Randy Worth—"

"Yep," J. O. nodded solemnly. "Works for Paw."

"And that is the same Randy Worth," Soap went on, "that, let's see, it was the fall roundup three, no, *four* years ago—we was camped up to Big Wallow—*that* is the very same goddamned fool of a Randy Worth that let his short gun fall out in the fire pit, and he didn't even notice it was gone till it was too hot to take out, and even then he didn't have enough brains to lever it out with something. No, by Jesus, he comes to me and he says: 'Soap, for Christ's sweet sake, I went and dropped my damned Colt in the fire pit, what do you reckon I ought to do?' And I said: 'You stupid son of a bitch, you better start learning how to shoot a bownarrer right now.' But, hell, I walked over to the fire pit with him anyways and, Jesus sweet Christ, just as we was looking down at 'er, damned if one of them cartridges in the chamber didn't explode, and I swear the ball skinned my left tit closer than a snake's whisker. By God, I lit out of there like I had a prairie fire behind my britches, and I hunkered behind a tree till all those six cartridges'd gone off, and I was hollering for that

damned fool Randy Worth to high-tail it out of there, like I done,
and he was plumb idiot enough to stand right where he was
and look right down in the fire pit at his damned old pistol,
popping away, by God, like the goddamned Fourth of July. I
tell you, J. O., after I heard that last cartridge blow up I come
back there to the fire pit and I skinned the arse right off that
Randy Worth. And he ain't forgot it yet, goddamn his eyes."

"I never heard that story," J. O. said. "But I'd liked to've seen
you cutting for the timber, by God I would!" His big laugh
boomed out again.

"Never told the story before," Soap said, "and I guess Randy
never told it, neither, or you'd've run into it somewheres by now.
We was alone at the time, matter of fact." He glanced over his
shoulder once more, for old Nelse's cowhands were whooping it
up again, then he grinned crookedly at J. O. "Reckon when they
heard you beller like that they figgered I just told you the story.
Randy, goddamn him, must've went and spilled the beans." There
was a final yelp from the shade of the spruces. Soap waved his
free hand languidly in the air, although this time he didn't look
back. "Fellers must be feeling their oats," he said. "By God, now,
J. O., but I got half a mind to drag the six of 'em out here and
make 'em run the course themselves. Why, hell, they're half horse
already. You heard how the bastards whinnied."

Hallock Randal was in the near corral, holding the bridle of
Mark Lacy's mare. There was no call for him to be helping Mark
in this way, but something—having to do both with the new
quarter horse and with Mark Lacy himself—was causing Hallock to feel disturbed in spirit and unsettled in mind. And, because he hoped to find out what it was, he had left his dear wife,
Ann, and Simon, his son, who was not yet two years old, up by
the ranch house beneath a small shade tree, and had come down
here to the corral. He steadied the mare, stroking her quivering
nose, while he gave her half his attention.

The other half he gave to Mark Lacy. Mark, his eyes oddly
bright and darting, his lips pressed too tightly together, was un-
satisfied with his saddle girth, and was fussily adjusting the broad

band that encircled the mare's belly. A number of men and a few women were watching them through the rails. Pax Randal, too, already saddled, had ridden over from the far corral and, with one leg curled carelessly over his pommel, was lounging on his roan and observing Mark with amusement. "Man dear," he said sadly, "you've *sure* got your troubles with females."

The gleam deepened in Mark's eyes, and he compressed his lips even tighter. "Still at it?" he said, not bothering to look around.

"Got to keep myself amused," Pax said. "I'd hate to be hanging till *you* got everything set."

Now Mark turned his unsmiling face to Pax. "Twenty minutes from now," he said in a voice more strained than usual, "the troubles'll all be yours, by God, and I promise you they'll— *Easy*, girl!" The mare capriciously skipped her hindquarters away from him, dancing from hoof to hoof, snorting and tossing her head, as Hallock gave her rein, rather like a man playing a great fish. "*Easy*, Ellen! Easy. Easy! *There*, now, there—"

The mare steadied and again stood quietly. "Yes, sir, that's what I mean," Pax said. "She's skittish, Mark. I wouldn't trust that filly as far as I could throw a bull by the tail."

Mark continued to fiddle with the girth. "No reason for you *to* trust her, Pax. She's too much horse for you."

"You're right," Pax told him. "Knew it as soon as I said that about throwing bulls. Give old Mark a bull, and he'll throw it every time."

"Right you are," Mark said flatly.

"All over the man he's talking to," Pax went on.

"Right again," said Mark.

"Or the woman," Pax said.

"Yep," said Mark. With a grunt, he took a last sure tug at the girth, stepped back a pace, gave the mare a quick, professional conning and allowed himself a thin, almost bitter smile. "She'll do," he said.

"Sure you want to *ride* her out there?" Pax asked. "Maybe three or four of these gawkers here'd be glad to tote her along to the starting-line for you. God knows she's wore out already, what with all this tossing her backside around."

Mark took the reins from Hallock. "Obliged to you, Hallock," he said. He swung easily into the saddle, then held the mare in when she showed signs of wanting to prance some more.

"Luck," Hallock said absent-mindedly, giving all his attention to the horse. He had begun to realize what it was that had disturbed him about Mark, but he was still uncertain about Mark's mare. What he had learned about her in these few minutes, however, gave him a very uncomfortable feeling.

"With this little lady I don't need luck," Mark told him. "But thanks, anyway." He yanked on the reins, and the mare, rearing, pawed the air wildly, then dropped back again. "Now, just you tell me," he cried to Hallock. "Ain't she the prettiest piece of flesh you ever laid eyes on?"

"Your wife's supposed to be the pretty one," Pax said. "This here Ellen's only supposed to be fast."

"I'm talking to Hallock," Mark said. "You shut up."

"You figgering to start the race with a gunshot?" Hallock wanted to know.

"Yep," said Mark. "Why not?"

"I wouldn't," Hallock said. "Not if I was you."

"You're not me," said Mark. "So I will."

"Suit yourself," Hallock said. "It's always seemed to me," he went on, with almost more consideration than appeared necessary, "that a man ought to know what he rides himself better than anybody else can."

"There's plenty of men, though, that don't have the feel of what's under 'em," said Mark.

"But you're not one of *those* fellers, are you?" Pax said. He started to walk the roan toward the gate of the corral.

"No, by God," said Mark. "And I never will be, neither."

Just beyond the gate he brought his mare abreast of the roan. "I'm going to lick you good," he told Pax. "And don't you go trying any tricks, or I'll make you sweat for it, hear?"

"I don't have to try any tricks," Pax said, feeling mildly annoyed but shrugging it off. "Not with you."

"You're the kind that does, though," Mark said. "And the tricks always come back on your own goddamned heads. Just remember that."

"Ah, go to hell," said Pax.

Hallock Randal, lost in thought and with downcast eyes, the

last to leave the neighborhood of the corral, was starting back to Ann and his son, Simon, when, from somewhere off to one side, he was joined by olive heart-faced Dolores. Her eyes were opals in the sun, her moist mouth was open a little, and tiny beads of sweat stood out above the provocation of her lips. Hallock, smiling as she took his right arm in both her warm hands, noticed that, without a ribbon or a bow being obviously out of place, she had an odd disheveled look about her; and he wondered, with no special emotion, his mind being otherwise occupied, if some young visiting cowboy had been having some fun with her.

Hallock, of course, was not aware that within the past hour, when Pax had gone into the deserted barn to look for an old bridle he had some vague idea of using in the race, Dolores had slithered in after him and, with the heat of the day and one thing and another, she had found herself, much to her delight, being thoroughly kissed and, much to her regret, less thoroughly fondled by an otherwise willing but momentarily abstracted Pax, who, after just enough fooling around to make her haunches humid, had remembered first the race and then himself, and had gone off unbridled to the corral, leaving her, after a last probing kiss and a final promissory whisper, with a body that did not cease its shaking and allow her to seek the invigoration of the sun until Pax had been gone a good ten minutes from the barn. Hallock had been conscious, several times during the day, that wherever Pax might be, Dolores could be spotted not far distant; but he failed to connect her present appearance with this past approximation. Luisa's three daughters had always worshipped Pax, but Hallock was sure that, whatever his faults, his younger brother would never try any amorous tricks so close to home, certainly not with any one of the three virgin girls for whom, in the past ten years, he had developed an attitude more paternal than anything else.

"Pax will win, won't he, Hallock?" Dolores said, holding his arm with a grip of silk. "Oh, he *will*, *say* he will, *please* say it, Hallock."

Hallock had to laugh at such fervent pleading. "How much've you bet on him?" he asked.

"Nothing," she said. "No *money*, I mean. But he just *has* to win, he's *got* to. He said my dress was the most beautiful of all, and if *he* doesn't win I'll die."

Hallock laughed again. "Ah, that's it, then." He bent his head over hers. "Between you and me, *palomita*," he whispered, "just between you and me, I think he's going to win it."

"Are you honest to goodness sure?" A faint doubt still lingered on Dolores's face, anxious to be washed away.

"Yep," Hallock said. "And I'll let you in on a secret. The reason I know it is because I've got the evil eye." He waggled the index and little fingers of his free hand under her nose.

"Oh, you *Hal*lock!" She shivered happily and hung, a weightless trifle, on his arm. Together they continued on.

But now the brief joy went out of Hallock as he looked off to the distant starting-line. He didn't *need* any evil eye to help him, he thought; his own keen vision was enough. If any eye that day held evil, it was the unreasoning evil he had seen lurking deep in the flecked brown pupil of Mark Lacy's mare. He had watched her eyeballs rolling while he held her bridle and stroked her nose. She had a willful devil in her, that four-legged Ellen, if ever a horse did and if ever a smart man could spot it; and she was nearly primed to let that devil take over all her muscles and all her bones and move them as he pleased.

If Hallock had been given a chance to ride her, merely to get the feel and surge of her under his seat, he might have understood what was behind the hatred of men he had sensed in her heart. The skittishness itself was not necessarily abnormal, but the other thing imbedded in her he did not like at all. There hadn't been time, though; so now the whole matter was in Mark's hands and out of his own. As things were, unfortunately, if the mare took it into her head to spook at the starting-gun, or to make for the tall timber, bucking—well, she was capable of doing any number of things, depending on the patience of her devil or, and even more to the point, the acts of Mark Lacy himself.

That was, indeed, what everything hinged on: the way Mark behaved in the race. And Hallock, who knew the man much better than he would ever know that sinister dappled horse, found the idea full of dangerous possibilities. For Mark Lacy, although he was inexplicably capable of walking straight as the usual die and talking clear as the invariable bell, was, at that moment, as he must even have been when he asked where all the Randal ranch hands were, Hallock said to himself in angry sadness, blind drunk like the blasted fool Mark Lacy was.

George Throstle, pomaded, his hair carefully curled to cover a forehead he considered too high, his blue, Saxon eyes curtained against the sun like the half-drawn shades of his Dry Goods Emporium, his handsome behind-the-counter phiz bland as junket and the color of cream, stood with Alan Lacy and Lydia, his wife, entranced by the profile of Mark's wife, Ellen, poised but a step away.

Alone of the four, George Throstle was letting his gaze stray, and in a most subtle manner, from the tableau of the four riders, far down the length of the meadow. He enjoyed, as always, the sight of Lydia Lacy. She was a fine, strapping flame-haired woman who at one moment could be, he was sure, as quiet as the breathless space before a breaking dawn, and the next moment would, like as not, explode instantaneously like the red swelling sun itself, with a violence even more thermal and far more encompassing, especially for the lucky man who might then be sprawled beside her. At any other time his sidelong sly glances might well have glittered toward her, but this was a very rare day; it was seldom indeed that he found himself, and for so many hours, so opportunely close to the exquisite Ellen Lacy.

Whenever Ellen entered his store, she was either with Mark or, in Mark's absence, Alan and Lydia Lacy. Even today, when Mark had never come near her at all, she clung closely to Alan and Lydia, almost as though she were a child who had been frightened by the long, lonely ride to the Randals. George Throstle, however, darting quick looks at her, gulping down from a distance the essence and urgency of her honeyed body, saw a being far more desirable than any other female who had ever swept high-headed across his path. And there had been many of these.

Above all other interests, including his business if need be,

George Throstle was a connoisseur of women; although his presence—after some uncomfortable moments and a hasty flight from
New Orleans—in this scopeless western cow town should have
made it clear to someone in possession of other bits and pieces of
Throstle's history, that he was by no means a connoisseur of men.
He had managed, nevertheless, in his chosen avocation, and for
the most part undisturbed by emotional males, to collect a
number of specimens of females he had conquered. They were
of various shapes and sizes, but all, for George Throstle, were
beautiful in some particular way.

He had swept them up in the net of his charm, put them pain-
lessly to sleep with their faith in him as a chloroform, impaled
them on pins of desire with their varihued wings spread wide,
labeled them all in his neat clerk's hand, and placed them, to
be relished at his leisure, in the tidy museum of his mind. But,
cunning and secret curator though he might be, he knew with
a painful impatience that, should he ever achieve any mortal in-
volvement with Ellen Lacy, the glass cases of this museum would
crumble around his now-tawdry specimens, the old, long-admired
conquests would become immediate dust, and the whole array of
ladies suddenly passé, their colors still as bright as in that first
succumbent hour, gathered together with so much effort over so
many years, would be swept from his mind forever and into forgetful dark.

Yet she whose beauty was the lodestar for this small galaxy
called the Forkhandle country, the lodestone that even now drew
toward her George Throstle's strained metallic soul, stood ox-eyed
and unaware of the magnet her aureate flesh concealed, wrench-
ing the guts of the smooth man beside her.

From the golden hair with which she shamed the sun, to the
slim aristocracy of her ankles and feet, Ellen Lacy, she who had
been born Ellen Abigail Zane, was one of those gorgeous acci-
dents of nature, allotted with selfish infrequence to the sight and
amazement of humankind, a woman who, when she is seen to
pass, reaffirms men's faith in the works of their gods and the promises of their devils. Yet in her wildest fancies this mirror of perfection had never dreamed of nor desired more than a simple
life shared by some upstanding man who would keep her heart

unbeset by care, her glorious body warm and clothed, her eye-turning head roofed over, and her bed in continual double-backed motion.

Ever since they had arrived in the Forkhandle country Mark Lacy had complied, to a greater or lesser degree, to these reasonable expectations on the part of his wife. And in general Ellen had been well pleased with what fate had brought her. She was interested only in day-to-day living, wrapped up in her husband and his work, neither coveting the possessions of people better off than they were, nor having an eye for any man except the lawful sharer of her bed.

But over the past two years, and unknown to the Forkhandle people, Mark had gradually changed his attitude toward his marvelous wife. To begin with, the lawful sharer of her bed had made it move with decreasing frequency, though Ellen would never have thought to mention such a matter to him. Then Mark began to drink more heavily than usual, but due to his great capacity and greater control, this went unnoticed by everyone who knew him. Even with her limited perceptiveness, however, Ellen Lacy could tell, after seven years with her husband, just how much alcohol was sloshing around in him at any given time. Too, although Mark was pleasant enough with everyone else, he was growing short and quarrelsome with his wife. But as Ellen's ruminative disposition precluded any talent for domestic strife, she always kept her silence and her distance, and Mark was apt to end up alone, arguing with the side of the ranch house.

Everything that had been festering inside Mark came to a head eight days before this spruce-scented afternoon at the Randal ranch. They had returned from a shopping trip to Eastmere, where Ellen had learned, through a chance remark by George Throstle, that Mark's new mare was named Ellen, too. As they undressed for bed that night Ellen asked him the reason for christening the horse in this way. It was a casual, incurious remark, and Ellen might have been dimly fishing for a compliment; as a matter of fact, she felt pleased that he thought enough of her to give such a pretty, high-strung mare his wife's own name. But Mark, who, during the excursion to Eastmere, had

spent most of the time in Smiley's, drinking with Pax Randal
and Drury Wynward, the feet of the three of them up on one
table, talking about Lord knows what—well, Mark hit the ceiling
and started to yell about how there was now at least *one* blasted
female named Ellen around his ranch who could drop a foal if
she set her mind to it. Ellen, after a moment of silence, expressed
mild surprise at this outburst, for until he had so harshly vented
his feelings she hadn't known he was so distressed at their lack
of children. Of course, she seemed to remember he *had* mentioned it once in a while, but she thought he had only been joking.
Anyway, they certainly had tried hard enough, so maybe there
was something wrong with his manhood.

That was what Ellen had said, as she turned to hang up her
petticoat, and that had been when Mark Lacy, his face all at
once gone the color of brick, bringing his open palm across her
rose-velvet cheek, had knocked her clean across the bed, beyond
which she sprawled, stark naked, legs akimbo, on the rough boards
that met in the corner of the room. He had been instantly regret-
ful, but his unreasoned deed had hurt her, frightened her, and
made her cry, her pearl-breasted body heaving with sobs as she
huddled away from his ministrations. Even now, as she stood
near the finish line, her eyes grew damp at the remembered
shock and shame. And all because she had asked a harmless
question.

George Throstle, darting the last of two dozen hummingbird
glances at Ellen Lacy's man-melting face, abruptly turned to but-
ter as she whom he was so guiltily adoring laid her moist eyes
upon him and then, before he could recover his aplomb, lifted
them away once more, leaving his mouth as dry as a desert arroyo
and the muscles of his face like gelatin.

Had Throstle any idea, however, of what had turned the
golden head in his direction, its Lethe-deep eyes agleam, more
than his mouth would have shriveled away and more than his
face would have jellied. For, although no glare of angry accusa-
tion had marred Ellen Lacy's ivory brow when she swung to look
at George Throstle, the survey she had so briefly given him was,
for her, a condemnation, spread over a face unaccustomed, as
well as unable, to convey any emotional turmoil at all.

Oh, *you're* the one, she had thought, as she nailed him down on the cross of his embarrassment, *you're* the one who started this awful trouble.

She licked her lips with a darting tongue, and then the anger and shame which had clung, molasseslike, to her apology for a soul ever since Mark had walloped her, made her feel all hot and sticky. It was such a terrible thing to think about, the really worst thing in her whole life. She'd been a good wife to Mark Lacy, through thick and thin and ups and downs, and he hadn't any reason to slap her hard like that, just because she told the truth, crying all bare in the corner, with a great bruise that was black and blue and didn't go away for days, even with the raw meat held against it, with him off somewhere most of the time with Pax Randal and all those other wild men, probably, and probably telling them how his wife couldn't have any children. Well, that wouldn't get him anywhere with her, even if he thought it would, and hitting her that way didn't get him anywhere either. Yes, and if her poor dead brothers, big Duke and brave little Calvin, lying away off there in Gettysburg, Pennsylvania, hadn't been killed so young, she'd write and tell them, and they'd come out to the Forkhandle and fix Mark Lacy's wagon good. Well, maybe she hadn't said all she *should* have, after he hit her that way, but she certainly *had* told Mark Lacy that very same night, after she stopped crying, and right to his old red face, too, with that brush hanging down from his nose, all over his mouth, and tickling her sometimes, she just told him to his face that she had been a good wife to him, through thick and thin, no matter what he thought, and if he ever so much as lifted a finger against her again, let alone try to hit her the way he had already, well, it'd be *one* sorry day for him and everybody else who—

She gasped as, from the other end of the course, the crack of J. O. Macleod's pistol sounded loud in the anticipatory air. And then everyone around Ellen was cheering and carrying on, and she guessed the race had finally started, but she couldn't be too sure, because a couple of men had moved in front of her and were jumping up and down. But then George Throstle's "It's started, Ellen!" slithered along to her ear, and so she learned it *had* really started, and then she felt more relaxed, somehow.

WHEN Mark Lacy's mare came a cropper, Pax Randal alone, of all the people in the meadow, knew more or less what had happened, because Pax was only a couple of yards away at the time, to the right of Mark and a little behind him.

The mare had been skittish for several minutes after the two rode up to the starting-line, dancing around like a butterfly learning the polka, until Soap Damson, whose whisky-shellacked throat was drying and dehydrating out there under the sun, got off a few poignant words whose gist was that Pax and Mark had better dismount, take off their boots, and run the damned quarter mile barefoot. Immediately upon hearing this advice, and for reasons best known to herself, though certainly not through fear of Soap Damson, the dappled mare quieted down.

Thereupon Soap, cocking a bushy-browed, beady eye at the unpredictable horse, wondered aloud whether the signal to start should be a yell from him or a shot from J. O.'s pistol, making it clear that he himself leaned toward the former method. But Mark, with unnecessary vehemence, insisted that the gun be used.

Pax stayed aloof from this discussion. He was now too engrossed in the way he should run his own race to bother with the preliminaries. He knew his roan wasn't gun-shy, so it made no difference to him how they got things under way. The generalship involved in the four hundred and forty yards to be covered, however, could mean a Randal victory or defeat. The roan gelding, Pax believed, would be as good as any other quarter horse in the West over the first half of the course, but then, its early surge spent, already winded, it was apt to flag, and so it might droop sufficiently for Mark's jittery mare to forge to the front and stay there. It had happened in certain previous races; it could very well happen now.

So, when Mark made it clear that he wanted the pistol to be fired, Pax made no objection, for the odd urgency with which the request had been made gave him the strategic foundation he sought. For his intuition told Pax that the mare had never before heard a gun go off close to her ears, and whatever reason lay behind Mark's desire for the shot to be fired, there was every chance that the nervous horse might spook at the sound. And if the mare *did* spook, even for the fraction of a second, by the time Mark got her off and running Pax would be long gone, with a lead that she'd never overcome, not in a quarter mile. Hoping that he had judged the mare rightly, poised and tense in his saddle, Pax awaited the shot that would open the ball.

The two horses were maneuvered up to the starting-line. J. O. Macleod took out his big pistol, cocked the hammer, and pointed the muzzle at the meridian. His finger was squeezing the trigger when the mare took to dancing again. Soap addressed to her some words descriptive of her character that would have turned a mule-skinner green, J. O. brought his pistol down, and then, as abruptly as she had begun, the mare stopped her snorts and fidgets and moved back almost meekly to her place on the starting-line.

"*Shoot*, J. O., damn 'er eyes!" Soap roared. The pistol's louder thunder drowned his last three words.

As the shot's reverberation went over Pax's roan, it vaulted forward into a smooth, space-eating gallop; and Pax, who had given all his attention to the other end of the course during the lunge into pounding movement, and was on the point of glancing over his shoulder to see if the mare had spooked, was shocked to find Mark alongside him and actually pulling ahead. Mark's hat had blown off and he was bent over the mare's neck, his lips drawn back to expose the double row of his fine white teeth, clenched in a painful grin. Then Mark led by a clean length, and as yet they were barely seventy-five yards down the course.

The rowels of the spurs Pax wore were dull, but he beat them so hard against his roan's belly that the beast must have thought he used Bowie knives. So it stretched out its neck, flattened its ears, and really outdid itself. Before another twenty-five yards had been covered the roan's nose was in line with the girth that had so bothered Mark, and was inching ahead with every stride. At the same time the roan was edging in toward the mare, narrowing the lateral distance between them.

Mark Lacy looked at the encroaching roan, then turned in fury on Pax. Mark's brows were drawn down and inward until his eye sockets were nearly hidden, giving him the appearance of one of the more destructive Chinese gods. He opened his mouth as though to shout, but nothing at all came forth. Then, as Pax watched in amazement, he leaned in his saddle away from Pax, jerking his reins to the off side with great force.

Then Pax in disbelief saw Mark tumbling forward against the sky and the mare a grotesque tangle of brown dust and gray waving legs on the left, and a moment later he was passing Mark as the fallen man was rolled like a living tumbleweed over the hard ground; and then Pax was trying to rein up the roan, and he was saying to himself: "My God, he reckoned I was going to ride him down," and then he heard a terrible screaming. He could have sworn it was Mark, and the idea was like cactus spines in his bloodstream; but the roan was slowing, and at last Pax managed to look around, to see Mark on his back like a dead man, his arms and legs outflung, and the poor devil of a mare still screaming, trying blindly to fight her way up from the dust, with her eyes showing nothing but white, and one of her forelegs broken.

Soap Damson and J. O. Macleod, who had been cantering easily down the course after the two racing horses, kicked their own ponies into a gallop, reaching Mark Lacy's limp body even before Pax did. They leaped from their saddles there where Mark lay and were about to bend over him when the smashed mare screamed again.

"That'll do, now," Soap said evenly. He yanked the big pistol from J. O.'s holster, walked over to the crippled beast, and killed her with one well-placed shot.

When he came back Pax and J. O. were both kneeling by Mark and J. O. was saying: "Best not to try and lift him, hey? Something's apt to be busted on him, too."

Soap shoved the pistol back in the sheriff's holster. "What the hell happened, Pax?" he demanded. "You seen the damned thing, didn't you? Couldn't help but see it."

Pax stared at Mark's chest, rising and falling with the unconscious man's labored breathing. "Don't know, damned if I do," he said. "First I saw of it, he was going arse over teakettle. Soap, that damned mare must've tripped over her own feet."

The spectators were now running up, in a babble of idiot questions. Soap glared angrily at the increasing crowd as each member of it tried to get a better view of what might turn out to be tragic. "Get the hell back a ways," he said. "Let the feller breathe, if he figgers to keep at it." Shuffling, grumbling, the men fell back, their eyes never leaving Mark. But J. O. Macleod rose and gave place to Alan Lacy beside his brother's body; nor did Soap Damson object when Percy Randal, along with Luke, came up by the group and frowned down at the pallor he saw on Mark's still face. "Fetch some brandy from the house," he told Luke. "And move, son, damn it, *move!*"

Several minutes after Luke Randal had darted away, Mark painfully began to recover consciousness. First he grimaced as his lungs reached for new air, and his chest made great spasmodic movements. Then this gasping lessened, his breathing steadied and settled down to regularity; and finally, bit by bit, his flickering lids revealed his eyes, blank and unseeing. Twice he opened his mouth and closed it again. His face twitched as though a fly were on it. Then suddenly his lids snapped all the way open; the glaze left his eyes, and they cleared. A faint smile appeared on his dusty mouth. "Somebody shoot me?" he whispered. He was looking at Pax.

"Shot the horse," said Soap Damson.

The smile went away from Mark's lips, and he muttered a few words that made no sense. Then he wiggled the fingers of both hands and brought the smile back, even wider. "Reckon I'm all in one piece," he said in his usual voice.

Alan laid a tender hand on his brother's dusty hair. "You *sure*, Mark boy?" he said awkwardly.

Mark tensed the muscles of his right leg, then his left. "*Pretty* sure, Alan," he said. He raised his shoulders an inch from the ground, winced, relaxed again, and nodded. "Got a few sore sports on me, maybe," he told Alan, "but I reckon there's nothing broke." He raised both arms in the air. "Sit me up now, will you, fellers?"

Alan and Pax gently raised him to a sitting position. Mark touched a hand to his cheek and it came away bloody; for, along with a sizable stone bruise, his face had a slight cut where he had come up against something small but sharp. "Reckon I fell off Ellen," he said.

"How'd it all come about, Mark boy?" Alan asked.

Mark shook his head, after a glance at Pax. "Can't rightly say," he replied. "One minute I was there, next minute I was someplace else. Pax here knows, though. He was getting closer all the time. Pax knew what was going on, all right."

"Looked to me like everything was going fine," Pax said, "except I was getting beat."

"That so?" Mark said. "Didn't look like it to me."

"Well," J. O. said, "seeing as how we'll never know the way it might've come out, we might just as well figger it as a dead heat. Pax didn't win, Mark didn't lose."

"Mark lost a right smart quarter horse," said Alan.

"It can happen," Soap said. "It can happen."

"Yep," Mark said, surprisingly cheerful. "It can, and it does." His spirits grew even brighter as Luke Randal came running up with a nearly full bottle of brandy. "Now *look* at that!" Mark cried expansively. "Shouldn't take more than a lick and a promise of that stuff to have me rearing up on my hind legs, damned near good as new." He took the bottle after Luke had uncorked it, tilted his head back, and let two rich inches of the liquor run down his throat. "By God, Perce," he said, wiping his mouth on his dusty sleeve, "that's the best ever, for sure."

"It's all yours, Mark," said Percy Randal.

"No, by God," Mark said. "Not so long as there's somebody needs it more than I do, like old Soap Damson, say. Here, Soap, wrassle down some of this."

He held out the bottle to Soap, who hesitated a moment as though he were being offered the business end of a branding-iron; but then his valor got the better of his discretion, and he took the bottle from Mark. "Mighty hot out there in the sun," he said, making it sound more like a bald statement of fact than an apology. As he brought the bottle to his lips young Randy Worth, standing with Will Clough in the forefront of the crowd and still carrying his battered banjo, said "*Old* Soap!" and several men laughed, Soap included; and whatever feeling of tenseness that remained was broken.

Mark Lacy got to his feet unassisted, pressed his hands against the small of his back, rubbed the nape of his dust-powdered neck, and studied the faces around him. "Where's my wife?" he asked. "I don't see her anywhere. Where's Ellen?"

"Guess she was scared crazy," Alan said. "My Liddie stayed back, too."

Mark shrugged. "Just as well," he said. "Men can take care of their own troubles, by God, without a flock of women flitting around and getting 'em in *more* troubles, like as not." Then he saw his dead mare, but his face showed no change of expression. "You shoot 'er, J. O.?" he asked.

"Naw," Soap told him. "Me. Quicker the better."

"Obliged to you, Soap," Mark said quietly. "That was a mighty kind thing."

He walked across the few yards that separated him from the big dappled corpse and stood looking down at the twisted foreleg. "Sure messed things up, didn't she?" he said to no one in particular.

"I'll have a couple of the hands take care of her for you, Mark," Percy Randal said, "unless you'd rather—"

"Mighty kind of you, Perce," Mark broke in. "Just so long as it's no trouble."

"Least we can do," Randal told him. "And if you want anyone to drive you in and let Doc Hyssop take a look at you, just you say the word."

"There's nothing wrong I can't fix myself, Perce," Mark said. "But I'm obliged for the thought, all the same." Again he turned his attention to the dead mare, and as he studied her body he knew a queer resentment, along with a sense of futility that seemed to clog his throat. He coughed, and his eyes, as they took in the mare's wasted beauty, shone darkly in ponds of sorrow. "Don't you worry, old girl," he said in a low voice. "Nobody's blaming you. Nobody around these parts'd *dare* to go blaming you, not while Mark Lacy knows how the land lies. And I reckon he will know *just* that, and before very goddamned long."

No one, of course, heard him.

The wagons were moving down the road that led to the bridge across the Forkhandle. The residue of the sunset hung purple above the Marias, too faint even to make reflections, and things that an hour before had cast long shadows were now but shadows themselves. The big blowout for Luke had come to an end at last.

Percy and Hallock Randal stood outside the stable, talking with Art Cospatrick, the foreman, and Art's son, Drew. Art Cospatrick was a jumpy, bowlegged man, a few years younger than his boss. His brown face was eroded by weather, and his loose mouth was nearly encircled by a thick walrus mustache. Drew Cospatrick, without the mustache and the eroded face, was the image of his father a quarter of a century before. The four men were discussing a matter that had occupied odd corners of their minds for several hours—the horse-killing tumble Mark Lacy had taken, and why, in God's name, it should ever have happened. "What troubles me," Drew Cospatrick was saying, "is I always figgered Mark knew his way around horses, so when he—"

"*Used* to know his way around horses," his father broke in.

"Well, whatever," Drew went on. "But he sure must've knew that mare was gun-shy. My God, the way she lit out when she heard that shot—"

"No reason for him to," Art Cospatrick said. "Most of the critters are damnfool, anyways. And you can't tell but what Mark took 'er off on the quiet and broke 'er in to it."

"You have any idea she was gun-shy, Hallock?" Percy Randal asked.

"I figgered she was *something*, all right, Father," Hallock said, "but damned if I ever saw what. But I didn't like the look of her while Mark saddled up, and if I'd gathered he was in any shape to listen to reason, I could've maybe spoken up a mite stronger than I did."

"What's that about him not being in any shape to listen to reason?" Art wanted to know.

Hallock hesitated. "Mark was carrying a load," he said evenly. The three men looked blankly at him. "Drunk?" Art asked.

"Good and drunk," Hallock said, nodding.

Percy Randal rubbed his chin. "Can't say he appeared drunk when *I* saw him."

"Just how did *you* know he was drunk, Hallock?" Art demanded.

"Fact is, Art," Hallock told him, "I can't rightly say. I could tell, that's all. Why, hell, Art, I've been around Mark Lacy for—"

"Nobody's doubting you, son," Percy Randal interrupted.

"God, no, Hallock," Art said. "Don't ever get that idea in your head. But him being full of booze might clear up what's been troubling my mind, such as him making J. O. Macleod use his short gun that way."

"It don't clear anything up for me," Hallock said. "Because if Mark knew, and I'm taking it he did, if Mark *knew* how goddamned spooky his mare was, and he knew a gunshot was sure to spook her, then why, in God's name, did he lay the law down to J. O. about getting off that shot? What was he figgering to do, trying a crazy thing like that, let alone jerking the critter's mouth raw, like he did, just before she threw him, same as Pax said?"

"That's true," Art Cospatrick said. "A feller can get himself drunk and then fill some other feller full of lead, but it's no likker I ever heard tell on that'd set a feller to cutting his own throat. Mighty queer shenanigans, for my money, and goddamned if I like 'em much."

"Maybe he was mad at Pax," Drew suggested. "Maybe he had something planned on Pax."

Hallock shook his head. "Mark and Pax're good friends," he said. "Always got along fine, considering Mark's the older."

"Anybody heard anything about Mark acting funny otherwise?" Art asked.

"No word of it ever come to me," Percy Randal said. "And it wouldn't make much sense if it did. He's had his troubles lately, Mark has, but they're no worse than what the rest of us've went through, one time or another. And besides, any man that's got a wife as pretty as—" He looked off toward the clatter of a galloping horse, and anger entered his voice as he recognized the rider drawing near them through the gloom. "Now *what* the damned hell is Sam Wadley doing, thirty miles from where he ought to be?"

Sam Wadley, on his exhausted horse, saw the four men from the end of the near corral and bolted his way across to the stable. Then Sam reined up by the little group, slid to the ground and, his knees wobbling, gasping for breath, managed to hold himself erect by clutching the saddle horn. Horse and rider were blended together in a paste of sweat and dust. Unable to speak, Sam stared at one man after another, and none of them made a move to assist him in any way.

"If you figgered to make the party, Sam," Percy Randal said, "you're too damned late. Or did Jim Good get sick of watching you soldier?"

Wadley gulped down a lungful of air. "Not—Jim," he muttered. "—*Tine*."

"The stream up there?" Art Cospatrick asked, with a nudge in the ribs for Drew. "You trying to make us believe you and that pony swum all the way back?"

Blinking sweat from his eyes, too weary to wipe it away, Sam sucked in more air before he could speak again. "South—Tine," he said, "—all—gone."

The listening men began to drop their casual manner. "What the devil're you babbling about, man?" Percy Randal demanded, taking Wadley by the arm.

"Ah, let him get his breath, Father," Hallock said. Then, to Wadley: "Take your time now, Sam."

With an effort, Sam Wadley nodded. As they waited, his breathing became less labored; and at last, sufficiently steady to take his hand from the saddle horn, Wadley wiped away the eye-stinging sweat on a filthy sleeve. "Mister Randal," he said hoarsely to the tall old man, "I don't know—what's going on—up that place. Me and—we patched up Number—Two Camp and then we went—we figger to—ride right along—the Marias and come —down on Number Three—from above up there—and you know —cross both the Tines—when we come to 'em—but when we got to where—the South Tine—" His last words came out in a rush. "Honest to God, Mister Randal, that river was *gone*, the whole damned South Tine, with just the dry bed of 'er left!"

Amazement widened over every face. "Did you go upstream, Sam?" Percy Randal asked. "You find out what it was?"

"Mister Randal, Jim Good said to ride to hell-and-gone back here and tell you, and that's what I done, and that's all I know about it. Jim, he's still sitting up there."

"Well, I'll be switched!" exclaimed Art Cospatrick, shocked, if not scared, right out of profanity.

Drew Cospatrick's worried gaze was on Hallock, and Hallock was watching his own father as a majestic calm came over Percy Randal. The old man nodded to himself, as if this mysterious thing had been expected for a long time. "I reckon you'd best take a run up there, Hallock," he said. "And right away, tonight. Moon's nearly full."

"Yes, sir," Hallock said promptly.

"And I'll meanwhile go down to the bridge," Percy Randal continued. "See if maybe the Forkhandle looks any lower. Want to take somebody with you, son?"

Drew Cospatrick cleared his throat, on the point of volunteering to accompany Hallock.

But Hallock shook his head. "Reckon I've seen enough people for one day," he said. "There'll be time enough to take somebody with me when I find out just what I'm taking him for."

Of nearly a hundred people who crossed the bridge across the Forkhandle on that deepening evening, Mark Lacy was the only one to realize—and purely by chance—that something peculiar had happened to the river, and he knew it even before Sam Wadley slid from his horse. Mark had sat, glum and dour and with an aching head, holding the reins beside the equally silent Ellen, as the buggy which she had driven to the blowout moved down the two miles from the ranch house. Princess, the horse they always used with the buggy, aware that she was on the way home, clipped along smartly; and by the time she brought the Lacys to the bridge they were a half-mile ahead of the wagon behind them.

Then, just after she had clattered over the bridge, Princess threw a shoe. Mark, although he failed to see the shoe fly off, noted the instant change in her gait. Wordlessly, he drew her to a halt.

"What is it?" Ellen asked.

"She threw a shoe," he said. He got down from the seat and checked: the horse's right fore shoe was gone.

"Can we make it home?" Ellen called forward.

"Have to. I'm not going anyplace else." Mark was about to climb up on the buggy again when he noticed there was something odd about the sound of the river. He went back to the near end of the bridge, then walked down the bank to the water that hummed along under the rough planks.

What he saw left him completely perplexed. The level of the Forkhandle, at that narrow place, was barely half what it should have been.

For nearly two minutes Mark Lacy stood there. At moments he felt bewildered and angry, at moments he felt plain scared. The whole thing made no mortal sense. At one point he even considered returning to the ranch house and informing Percy Randal. But at last he heard Ellen calling his name, so he plodded up the bank and along the road to the buggy.

His head began to throb more cruelly as he mounted to the

seat, picked up the reins, and clucked his tongue at Princess. She moved on again, favoring her unshod hoof.

"Couldn't you find the shoe?" Ellen wanted to know.

"Didn't look," was all he answered.

They both lapsed into the sour silence with which they had started this homeward journey. Ellen's resentment was eight days old; Mark's, on the other hand, was much older in one sense, much newer in another, as far as the problem of his marriage was concerned. For, along with his deepening bitterness over their lack of children, and especially sons such as Percy Randal had, he was also angry with Ellen for not showing more interest, if not despair, when the other Ellen threw him. Even if a woman and her husband were on the outs temporarily, she should have made some kind of a show of grief or worry, instead of hanging back, like some guilty kid that'd wet its pants. Still, God knows, he didn't want to get into any arguments about it, not now, not tonight. He was pretty stiff from the fall, he felt tired as the devil, and here all the booze he'd put down was starting to kick its stale way out of him. He'd been a goddamned fool to drink all that whisky, soaking it up until he felt like the cock of the walk. Why, he was lucky he'd stayed in the saddle as long as he had—going out there on a new horse that he knew very well might spook at a gunshot, blowing his horn that way in front of Hallock and Pax. And then taking that header. God, it was a near thing he wasn't lying back there dead at this very minute. And in front of so many people, too. Now he was out a good quarter horse, and for all he knew there was worse to come. But tomorrow'd be time enough to worry about that. All he wanted now was to get home and get into bed, maybe have Ellen give him a liniment rub, and then sleep off his sore joints and the clanging bell in his head. That was all he intended tonight—

At least, that was all he'd intended before he saw the condition of the river. Now he'd changed his mind. Something was funny there, something that would take a lot of thought. Once he got home, by God, he'd wait until Ellen went to bed, then he'd crack open a bottle and sit around until he could figure out just what in blazes was going on. Some things that had been said to him today and some things he had noticed, too, made damned little sense by themselves, but perhaps over a bottle he could put them all together. For instance—

He glanced at the woman beside him.

For instance, Pax Randal had been mighty damned anxious to go and fetch Ellen out to the Randal place that morning, mighty damned anxious indeed, almost as though he knew she was waiting for him. In fact, Mark Lacy couldn't help but wonder just what the woman beside him *had* been doing when he wasn't around, these past eight days—or even, goddamn her, before that.

He wished he could talk to Alan.

CHAPTER 6

Hallock Randal was famed as a breaker of horses.

Bronc-snapping was second nature to him, and few were the mustangs, brought to him foam-nostriled and rearing, that could not be handled by the average ranch rider after five or six saddles with Hallock. He was much in demand for this ability all over the Forkhandle country, and he had even traveled down into Texas and the Indian Territory, on urgent invitation, to break certain difficult beasts. At roundup time he was always the rough-string rider for the Broken S, with a mount of ten or twelve of the saltiest horses to be had.

Hallock's understanding and handling of horseflesh was half instinct, half skill. The skill he had gained the hard way, by breaking horses ever since he had been so small that Percy Randal had to lift him into the saddle. The instinct, on the other hand, was something mysterious that he had been born with, something he could neither explain in himself nor pass on to anyone else. But he had it, and he would have it right up until the last few minutes of his life.

As he made his moonlight ride toward the Marias he did not try to force the horse under him, but it was a tiring journey for all that. Not long after midnight he reached Juncture Valley, and decided to make camp there. Two or three times, as he wound through the approaches to the valley, he had glimpses of Jim Good's fire, a flickering pinpoint much deeper and higher in the Marias. There was nothing to be gained, though, in extending either the horse or himself in order to reach Jim's camp before daylight. Jim would be waiting up there until somebody came, and by spending the night in Juncture Valley, Hallock would be fresh and in sunshine when he found him. So he tethered his pony, built a small fire, boiled some coffee, and settled down to sleep.

He had poor success at first. Lying awake in his blanket, as the weird shadows thrown by the westering moon grew longer, his thoughts lingered for a while on the odd disappearance of the South Tine. But not for long. He had brooded about this problem during much of the ride out, and he believed he already knew what had caused the stream to vanish. Too, he saw no reason to make any further plans until he knew at firsthand that what he believed had happened had actually taken place.

So it was that under the mottled moon he found his mind meandering back to the time of the Civil War, when he had lain so often like this, under other moon-bright skies; and his thoughts, which could often be elephantine, soon bounded along like an antelope herd on the rimless plain of the past.

He was aware—was this the first time he had been thus aware?—that most of the people who lived by the Forkhandle had favored, or fought for, the South. The Lacys, for instance. Alan had even ended up as a Major on Longstreet's staff, or maybe it was Bragg's; and Mark, captured in a skirmish in Tennessee, had spent twenty months in a Yankee prison. Lieutenant Exeter Macleod, Nelse's other son and J. O.'s older brother, had been killed leading his men as they overran the Union camp that first day of Shiloh. Ollie Swindon was invalided right out of his tattered butternut pants after Chickamauga, with shell fragments in both his short legs. Drury Wynward, a damnfool plume in his hat, had ridden with Stuart and later, both plume and hat gone, with Moseby until the end.

For a few moon-drenched moments he was of the belief that he, Hallock Randal, had been the only man in that neck of the woods who had fought on the side of the North. But then he remembered another: Arch Eastmere, too, had gone off early, and he had been with Sherman, from the first dragging days around the Mississippi until they all went waltzing through Georgia.

Even on the Randal spread, he remembered, at least Art Cospatrick had taken the Rebel side, and there had been a good many hot arguments between Art and Percy Randal, for Art, ten or fifteen years ago, had a lot more fire in him than he seemed to have now. But the arguments had always burned themselves out: Percy had never sent Art packing, and Art had never been mad enough to quit. And as for Soap Damson—well, that old devil didn't know who was President of the United States half the time, let alone allowing a Civil War to get in the way of his job of moving cattle from Randal land to a railroad track.

But the fact still remained, only two from the Forkhandle had worn Yankee blue, and the other man had been Arch Eastmere.

Then Hallock's imaginings leaped away to recall Percy Randal's advice to him when he headed east after Fort Sumter. "For God's sake, son," he had said, "stay out of the Cavalry, because they won't let you ride the way you want. And as a favor to me, you go join some Massachusetts regiment in Boston, because I had some mighty fine times in that city before I married your mother, and I reckon I owe the Commonwealth a little something on account."

And then he saw himself getting off the cars in Washington one fine October morning in 1862, on his way to New York City with his furlough papers and a wad of greenbacks on fire in his pocket, and there was a woman and her daughter getting out of another car as he passed, and they both had their arms full of packages. The girl was about fifteen and as pretty as they come, and when the raft of packages fell from her mother's arms Hallock ran over to pick them up. And it turned out that the woman's name was Mrs. Horace Dover, and her daughter's name was Ann, and Sergeant Hallock Randal knew right then that his whole life had been leading up to this bright October day when he stepped off the Washington cars, and he never got to New York City at all.

And then Ann's dear face, as it was on their wedding night

in 1868 came closer and closer to him, the way it had in that candlelit hotel room; and then he fell asleep.

The dream that was sent him toward dawn in the chill fastness called Juncture Valley was a dream he had known before. Over two dozen times it had been sent him, and it was always the same dream, never advancing beyond the place where it shocked him awake.

He stood with his company in line of battle at the edge of a clearing a half-mile square. Sergeant Randal was in command, he alone; there were no officers or other NCO's to be seen. The sky was sullen and black above them as he turned to dress up the company; and then he realized with surprise that many of those in the front rank were men he had thought were killed. But they dressed smartly, and Hallock, full of a calm resolve, surveyed the landscape they were in. Behind the company were pine woods, and directly to the rear began a winding road through these pines, along which they must have marched to their present station. The clearing, full of the stumps of pines lately cut, sloped down from where Hallock's company was aligned and then, reaching its nadir in a little, soggy marsh, swept up again to the standing pines that marked its opposite side. Then suddenly, even as Hallock was observing the silence of the spot, Rebs began to sift through the trunks of these ominous pines, hundreds of Rebs, a whole regiment of them, and they formed their own line of battle along the fringe of trees, and then started to move, in complete and terrifying silence, down the slope toward the marsh. Hallock looked along his line of battle, and now it seemed to him that the men who formed it were all asleep, and the sight of their motionless bodies angered him. He shouted at them, and they paid no attention. He singled out particular soldiers and called their names; still they paid no attention. And then he became aware, and horror filled him, that what he had thought was his company was nothing more than a hundred and twenty wax dummies, dolled up as soldiers of the 13th Massachusetts, with dead, painted faces and eyes of glass. Then in agony and fear Hallock gaped at the gray mass of men that had already passed the marsh and was moving up the near slope, with every enemy eye full of his death and on him. And he knew, as he quaked before their automaton approach, that if he wanted to save his skin he would have to run back, a coward and alone, along the dark twisting road through the man-dissolving pines—

The dream always ended there. And when Hallock started up from it this time he was, as always, drenched in sweat, and cold.

Recovering somewhat, he saw it was already first light. He built a new fire and made breakfast. He ate quickly and quietly, then broke camp, found a place where the lowered water made it possible to ford the Forkhandle, crossed over, and began a further ascent beside the drying bed of the South Tine.

Six miles on, at around eight o'clock, he came upon Jim Good waiting for him. Jim could add nothing to what Sam Wadley had already said, so the two men rode on deeper and higher into the Marias, following the tortuous track of the South Tine. The going was hard, with no available trails. Boulders, crags, and virgin thickets impeded their progress time and again. Often they had to dismount and help their hesitant horses along when they came to stretches that were particularly harsh.

After nearly two hours of this, they had pulled up for a few minutes' rest when Hallock heard a faint sound of falling water, coming from somewhere not too far above them. They went toward the noise on foot, scrambling over rocks and catching their clothing on thorns and bushes, while the splashing of the water grew ever more loud. Finally they came out below and to one side of a crag, perhaps twenty feet high, and both of them froze in astonishment.

Over this crag the South Tine was tumbling down in a waterfall, to vanish in a newly opened natural hole in the earth.

There had been, after uncountable centuries of careful balance, an inward collapse of rock, leaving a jagged, roughly circular gap, ten feet in diameter at its widest point, in what had been the bed of the stream. Hallock went as close to the yawning hole as he dared and gazed in wonder at this cancer of the Marias. But it was impossible to get close enough to it to peer down, and the falling spray would have only compounded the original danger, so, as the noise made any talk difficult, he and Jim Good slid and stumbled back to where they had left the horses.

Hallock had seen what he had expected to see, but he felt no relief at having his reasoning confirmed. Now he explained to Jim, as well as he was able, what he thought might result from the South Tine's having gone so irretrievably underground. There were, as he saw it, three possibilities.

One was that there was some kind of big but defined hole in the earth below the crag, and when the stream's rocks had fallen inward, it was like a cork being pushed down through the neck of a bottle. When the bottle, or in this case the hole, had been completely filled with water, the South Tine would disgorge itself and continue, as before, along its original course.

Another possibility was that the stream had fallen into what might turn out to be a huge, many-chambered network of caves, through which it might wander, ever downward, beneath the worn flanks of the Marias, until somewhere it would manage, by the sheer growing weight and pressure of itself, to force an outlet from one of these chambers and appear once more above ground.

The last possibility was that these subterranean caverns were of such an extent and dimension that the South Tine would be lost forever to the ranches in the Forkhandle country. And, in this eventuality, when the Forkhandle herds increased, as increase they would, water would become an ever-mounting, ever more serious problem and concern.

These, then, were the three things of which the future would make its choice. And of them, Hallock said, the last had best not be even considered, the first should be ardently desired, and the second must be actively explored, by men scouring the east slopes of the Marias to locate the stream when and where it should emerge; and, if necessary, redirecting any tangental course it might have assumed, making it once more blend with the Forkhandle.

This reconnoitering, Hallock went on, would have to get under way at once. He would leave Jim Good to fan out alone from his present camp, combing the hollows of the Marias immediately adjacent in the hope of stumbling on the re-emerging stream. Hallock, meanwhile, would return to the ranch house, report what he had found to his father, and then come back with all the men that could be spared from other jobs. They would divide this force into two parts, working out of the line camps, until they either found the South Tine again, or gave the thing up in despair.

Jim Good agreed that this was the only logical and sensible plan. So Hallock left him there and headed home down the Marias. He rode hard and he rode fast, and he punished his horse to his own sorrow. But by sundown he had reached the ranch house, a very weary man.

Mark Lacy, too, had spent a harsh night and day, but without having been in a saddle, or even out of doors.

There had been neither light nor movement around the Lacy place when he and Ellen got back from the Randal party. Mark let Ellen off at the porch and then took care of Princess and the buggy. He had no need for a lantern as he went about this work, so strongly did the moon reflect the unseen sun, even within the brown depths of the stable.

Walking back to the house, he again had a great longing to talk to someone about the ideas that were beginning to twist themselves inside him. He even considered waking Charley Samuels and persuading that grim-jawed man-of-all-work to sit with him for a spell, but then he remembered that Charley, along with being so damned religious that ten minutes of talk with him was as good as a year of Sunday School, was teetotal in the bargain, and Mark was in no mood to open his heart to a man who wouldn't drink with him. He would have to oil the hinges of his thoughts by himself.

When he entered the house he saw that Ellen had gone directly into the bedroom; she hadn't even bothered to turn up a lamp. Mark lit the big one on the center table, keeping the wick down low, and sank his sore body into the comfortable old rocker that Ellen liked to be in when she sewed. After a few minutes had passed the bedroom door opened and Ellen, as he had known she would, peered out. But he hadn't known she would be naked, as one bare shoulder proved her to be. He thought she'd have put on nightclothes, as she had more and more often these past few months, especially after they'd had a fuss—although, come to think of it, they had not really fussed today.

"Aren't you coming to bed, Mark?" she asked softly.

Her voice sounded naked too, Mark decided. "Not yet," he told her. "There's a few things I want to go over."

She paused. "I'm sorry about the mare. And you nearly getting killed that way. I should've told you before, I guess."

"Yep, it's too goddamned bad about the mare," he said harshly. "Now the only damned Ellen I've got is the critter that can't drop a foal."

The lamp made gentle shadows on her beautiful blank face as she studied him in ruminative silence, her eyes neither hurt nor angry, before she faded back into the bedroom darkness, closing the door behind her. Soon Mark heard the bed creak subtly under her far more subtle body.

The instant after he uttered his last sharp words against her, Mark was guilty and ashamed. He wished that he could withdraw what he had just now said, but he knew, and was sad, that he couldn't. Although he might have gone directly to the bed and taken her up in his arms, whispering to her the things she wanted to hear, until she forgave him and came warm and willing to his broad chest, he felt that such an act on his part, even though he did not trouble to ask for her forgiveness, would somehow be a defeat for him—and he had been defeated enough for one day.

But he was thinking like a fool, he told himself: there hadn't been any defeat. What had happened to him had been the mere repulse of a probing action. He had sent out skirmishers, and they had drawn the fire of a considerable force that had spread itself across Mark Lacy's advance. So now he at least knew the enemy's strength; and that, in itself, was a victory.

The victor, however, was low on ammunition. Mark rose, went to the kitchen, took an unopened bottle from the cache he kept on a cupboard shelf there, and brought it back to the rocking-chair, not bothering with a glass. Then, having pulled out the cork and tossed it into a corner, he lifted the bottle to his lips and let six substantial swallows go gurgling down his parched and welcoming throat. After a quiet belch of contentment, he waited for the anvil behind his brow to be lifted and tossed aside.

In a very short time the anvil was gone, but he gulped some more of the whisky to keep its ghost from returning. His world and everything in it began to stand out solid and clear.

Let's *see*, now—

To begin with, there was all that talk from Pax about Ellen. Wanting to come over here and get her, then being so goddamned boldfaced as to suggest that Mark bet *her* instead of the hundred dollars. What did he mean by talking like that? He'd never talked like that before. And there were other things he'd said. They'd slipped Mark's mind for the moment, but they'd come back, *they*'d come back, don't you fret about that, Pax Randal, God *damn* you.

What old Perce had said, though, hadn't slipped his mind, not so's you'd notice it. Wanting to buy Mark Lacy's ranch, saying he'd give a good price for it. And *why* did he want poor Mark's ranch? So Pax Randal, the son of a bitch, would have someplace to live once he took a wife. But *whose* wife? That was it, sure. Not that old Perce Randal or anybody else could make Pax marry somebody he didn't want to. Or did they have the woman picked out already?

And where had all the Randal ranch hands gone?

Why, hell, it was simple, once you started putting these little things together. They wanted Mark Lacy's ranch for Pax Randal, and they wanted Mark Lacy's wife for Pax Randal. And by God, they wouldn't stick at nothing to get 'em both. Jesus, they'd tried to murder him right there this afternoon, in front of all those people. They'd tried to kill him right out in the open, cool as you please, goddamn 'em.

But he'd known what they were up to, by God. He knew Pax figured to bump him in the race, trusting Mark'd be kind enough to get his neck broke. Well, Pax had failed, but the Lacy luck hadn't, because Mark had fixed it so he did his own falling, in exactly the way he wanted to, even though he knew it might ruin his nice new mare. Yep, he'd even made them think he was knocked kicking, lying there acting like he was dead, on the off-chance he'd hear old Perce or Hallock or that bastard Pax spit out something or other that'd give their whole game away. But they were smart, they played it close to the vest, yep, they allowed as how they were real upset. Sure.

And where were the Randal ranch hands all day? Mark Lacy
knew where they were, all right. Because Perce Randal had no
more idea of buying Mark Lacy's ranch than he had of growing
a tail. Not on your life. Which it almost *had* been.

The bottle was half gone now.

Damn it, though, you had to hand it to old Perce. He was a
cute one, by God. Any man with enough sense to pick a wife that
could foal him three sons, even though the one daughter she'd
foaled acted a little crazy—well, *that* was a man to watch out
for. But the woman Perce married could never have held a candle
to Ellen Lacy, as far as looks went, on the best day old Harriet
Randal had ever seen. But how about the woman Pax figured to
get? How about *her?* Was she lying in the next room now? Right
now?

Ah, Perce was a cute one, for sure. It wasn't enough for him
to put his goddamned woman-stealing son up to killing a man in
a horse race so Perce could buy the dead man's ranch for beans
and have his widow thrown in for bacon. Hell, Perce Randal
knew he didn't have to go to all that trouble. Because at the same
damned time he was throwing a big blowout and pretending it
was for his last boy's birthday, just so he'd have every rancher
around under his eyes in the one place, and on the one day. And
meanwhile most of his own hands were up in the Marias someplace, building a pair of dams that'd turn the Forkhandle River
into Percy Randal's own private lake. *That's* where they were,
up on the Tines. *That's* what they'd been doing. And, by God,
Mark Lacy had seen the result with his very own eyes, all the
long way down here. And he hadn't been drunk then, neither.

Perce Randal wanted more than Mark Lacy's ranch. He
wanted the whole Forkhandle country. And he didn't care how
he got it.

And once he had it, Pax would have a big ranch, and Luke
would have a big ranch, and even that goddamned looney Cora
would have a big ranch to be looney on. Because without water
everybody would have to let their land go.

And as soon as Perce'd made them sell out and he had every
square foot of land to the south of him, dead cattle and all, well,.
then the old Yankee bastard would blow up his dams and let his
one-man river run on as before. And meanwhile he'd send that

damned Pax nosing around, licking his chops over Ellen Lacy, stripping every stitch of clothes off her, probably, in his dirty damned mind, and counting the days until he dragged her into bed beside him, once Mark and the rest of them had been got out of the way, every man jack of them jerked from the picture. Except, by God, that *wasn't* how it was going to be. Not while Mark *Lacy* drew breath, it wasn't. And Mark had lots of breath left in him, which was maybe why Pax had tried what he did.

And plenty of *death,* too, if it came to that. God *damn* them! The bottle was empty.

Mark went and fetched another and, as the night died, this second bottle died with it. And as the morning sky yellowed Mark Lacy's brain spun in a wilder and wilder dance, until it wore through the thin, sodden floor of hate on which it had whirled for hours.

Mark had temporarily exhausted both himself and his wrath. He rose from the rocking-chair and walked, drag-footed and glassy-eyed, into the bedroom. And there, dead-drunk, as drunk as any three other men together, he fell face down on the bed, beside his beautiful, childless wife, who barely stirred at his collapse.

He slept dreams of rage and fire throughout the long following day. Ellen awoke and left him for her chores. The daily tasks of the household and ranch were carried on as usual. The noises of men and animals were bruited outside the windows. Some birds sang as the sun rose high, and others as it waned. But Mark Lacy remained oblivious to all but the seething pit into which he had cast himself until, at about the same time Hallock Randal came home from the mountains, he opened his redveined eyes, knew he was back in his own house at last, swung his sore body up from the bed, and strode to the other room. There he found his ox-eyed and patient Ellen placidly mending a shirt in a rocking-chair he seemed to remember having sat in for a little while before he went to bed.

"I reckon I could eat something now," he told her.

"You needed the sleep," she said.

CHAPTER 7

You need some sleep, son," Percy Randal had said, after Hallock, his voice frayed by fatigue, had told him the fate of the South Tine and what he believed should be done. "We'll talk about it in the morning."

But what began, the next morning, as a discussion between two men assumed, by degrees, the proportions of a town meeting. The first thing Hallock had undertaken, after he rose refreshed from the side of Ann, was to go to the stable to learn how his horse had weathered the strain; and it was as he was coming from there, satisfied that the beast had stood its ordeal well, that Percy Randal found him.

They resumed their talk at once, with Hallock scratching a rough map in the earth with an old branding-iron that leaned against the wall. Gradually father and son were joined by other people, until nearly a score of persons were gathered at that end of the stable, shielded by its bulk against the increase of the sun. All the Randals were present save Ann, who was occupied with Simon in the house. Even the three olive-fleshed daughters of Luisa Costa were there, although Dolores heard little that was said, so intent was she on the wonder of Pax Randal's will-melting face. Soap Damson was there, and the Cospatricks, father and son. The rest of the group was made up of various ranch hands, who had trailed along in the wake of Art and Soap.

It was a serious matter, all agreed, this business of the South Tine's vanishing, but in no sense disastrous yet; and general accord greeted Hallock's plan to search for its re-emergence. However, as might have been expected, some question arose as to the best way to go about the hunt for the missing stream.

The attitude taken by Percy Randal was, as much as anything else, paternalistic. By his nature, he felt a moral responsibility toward the other Forkhandle ranchers, especially since the unfortunate event had occurred on his own land. Nelse and J. O. Macleod, disturbed by the lowered waters, had ridden over the morning before in an effort to clear up the mystery, and later in the day Oliver Swindon had stopped by for the same reason. Percy could only tell them that Hallock was then up in the Marias, trying to find out what had happened. Everybody else, meanwhile, knew as much about the situation as Percy Randal himself did: as soon as Hallock reported to him, he said, he would pass the news on to those concerned. Then Pax, riding into Eastmere the same afternoon, had been driven half-crazy by all the questions that folks had thrown at him. The whole town seemed to look upon the Forkhandle as its personal property, and the sudden shrinkage of the river's body affected the citizens of Eastmere as would the mortal sickness of some dear friend.

So Percy Randal considered himself to be laboring under a far greater weight of accountability than any private inconvenience might cause. "How many hands you reckon we can spare?" he asked Art Cospatrick.

Art frowned, looked off at the distant Marias, then dropped his eyes to the ground. His lips moved silently as he spoke, to himself, the names of men. "Maybe eight or ten," he said.

"No more?" In turn, Percy Randal was frowning.

"We could call on some other outfits, Father," said Hallock.

But Percy Randal shook his head, adamant and proud. "I don't want to," he said sharply. "Not if I can help it. I want us to handle this ourselves."

"Aw, hell, Mister Randal," Soap said, after a sidewise glance at Art, "let's say fifteen, sixteen easy. And with your own boys, we'll have nigh on twenty."

"There's a lot to be done around here, Damson," Art said.

Soap rolled his chaw of tobacco around in his mouth, offered what might have been either a smile or a grimace to Harriet Randal, and said: " 'Scuse me, ma'am," before squirting what seemed to be half a pint of brown juice over his shoulder. Then he swiveled his gunmetal eyes against Art. "They was a lot to be done around here last week," he said, "and they'll be a lot to be done around here next week. And the week after that, mostlike. But that goddamned, 'scuse me, ma'am, consarned river better be looked to right now, with all the looking we can give it, or the whole goddamned, 'scuse me again, buggerly countryside'll find itself up the crick, and with nary a paddle this side the Mississippi."

"Sixteen, you say, Soap?" Hallock asked.

"I said fifteen, sixteen, but, hell, make it full sixteen."

"You counting yourself in?" Art wanted to know.

"Yep," Soap said blandly. "Otherwise they'd only be fourteen."

"Counting me in, too?" Art said.

"Naw," Soap told him. "That way they'd only be twelve."

"No need you talking like that, hear?" Drew Cospatrick exclaimed, stretching a gamecock neck toward Soap.

"Shut your face, boy," Soap said pleasantly.

"That'll do now, both of you," said Percy Randal.

"You know you're needed back here, Art," Hallock said, conciliating the old man. "And you know you'll get plenty done."

"Not as much as should," Art said stubbornly; then, in some surprise, he added: "You mean just *me*, all by myself?"

"You and Drew," Hallock said. "There'll be five or six of you altogether, probably. Don't you fret."

"I ain't," Art grumbled. "It's just that I got my job of work."

"Percy—there's no need of *all* our boys going, is there, Percy?" Harriet Randal asked.

"Them most of all, Hattie," her husband told her, "which *I* know, if *you* don't."

Harriet glanced pleadingly at her eldest son, and Hallock immediately made her cause his own. "I guess maybe one of us ought to hang around the place," he said casually. "You never can tell when he might come in handy."

Percy Randal shrugged. "If you feel that way, Hallock, well, all right," he said.

The stare his wife gave him was a cold one. "I feel that way, too," she said, putting her arm around the waist of Luke, who was standing beside her. "Luke'll be just as well off here."

But Luke, with the corners of his mouth pulled down, jerked free of her. "I'm a man, much as anybody else here is," he said. "And not just since Sunday, neither."

In spite of himself, Percy Randal had to chuckle at his youngest son. "By God, so you are, Luke," he said. "Might as well start earning your keep, too. All right, boy, consider yourself part and passel of what's going on, and see you pay attention and do what's told you."

"I will that, Father," said Luke, so happy that he failed to notice as his mother spun on her heel and hurried off.

"Pax can stay," said Hallock.

Pax, who was looking incuriously at Harriet Randal's receding back, now laid hot eyes on Hallock. "Doing *what*, for Christ's sake?" he demanded.

"Being around in case I need you, that's what," Percy told him. "You got something better in mind to do?"

"No, sir, I'll be around," Pax said promptly, with a last angry glare at Hallock. "When you need me, holler." He pushed past a couple of cowboys and went on into the stable.

Dolores, who had felt black-winged fear hovering over her head when she thought golden Pax might be riding to the mountains, could hardly repress the cry of delight that was swelling inside her. She wanted to follow him into the stable, but she knew that she couldn't. Not in front of all these people. Not now.

With Pax gone, although not because he had left the group, everything else went smoothly. When the men who would go into the Marias were ticked off by name, one by one, they came to a total of sixteen. Soap would take seven of these, including young Luke, and they would work out of Number Two Camp; Hallock, with Jim Good and six other hands, would base themselves above both Tines, at Number Three, further north. And they would be on the move by ten o'clock, in order to reach Jim Good before sundown. Along with a few spare ponies, they would pack in enough food for a week.

Piecemeal, the group dissolved, until only one person remained: Cora Randal. Her unbraided hair hung flowing around her shoulders. She had kept to one side throughout the discussion, noticed by no one save dark-eyed Dolores, who, lingering in the hope she might enter the stable unseen, realized at last that Cora intended to stay where she was.

So Dolores flounced off to the kitchen, and Cora, alone, leaned her weight on the stable's dry boards, immobile in the warm shadows. Hallock's horse shifted restlessly in the stall inside, but the motionless woman was not attuned to hear such mundane noises.

Cora was listening to something, however, her closed eyes lifted to the sky and a veil of thought drawn over her face. But the time came when her lids rose and she looked down glassily, as a woman drugged, at the earth on which was scrawled Hallock's crude map. Then, moving as one moves in a dream, she took the old branding-iron used by her brother and, smiling as one smiles in a dream, moving the rusty brand over the ground in measured concentration and with considerable grace, she returned the map once more to the dust from which it came.

At half past two that afternoon Mark Lacy rode up to the Randal ranch house.

After he had risen from his stupor the previous evening, Mark had eaten a huge meal, and for several hours he appeared to be a chastened, muted man. Yet, after he and Ellen, who persisted in her calm bearing toward him, had gone to bed, he had suddenly rolled upon her and taken her with a savagery that startled and dismayed her. She was tempted to offer some sort of resistance, but too late, for by the time she had marshaled her resentment things had gone too far, and his will had become her own.

Neither of them, that morning, had mentioned this bleak act

of darkness. Mark did a few chores around the ranch house and then, a little after nine o'clock, he saddled his horse and rode to Alan's place, only to learn that Alan had gone into town with Lydia. Resenting their absence, for he felt more unsettled than ever, and thus even more anxious to speak with his brother, Mark bitterly went back home where, even before he dismounted, Charley Samuels was telling him that Ellen, too, using the buggy, had gone into Eastmere, alone.

Outwardly calm but with a fury in him, Mark was on the point of riding to Eastmere after her, but for the time being he brought his wrath under control. Leaving the horse for Charley to unsaddle, he entered the house, strode directly to his kitchen cache, and bore back with him to the rocking-chair an unopened quart of understanding.

He drank steadily and undisturbed, without any food, until the sun reached its zenith and beyond. Then, without any visible change, either in his manner or his face, he left the house, saddled up again, and rode northwards.

Approaching the Randal ranch house, Mark was struck by the lack of activity around the place. Usually, at this time of day, a man could see ten or a dozen people busy with things in the corrals or the outbuildings, where now not a living soul moved. When Mark cantered his horse over to the near corral, he realized that, in place of a score of ponies which ordinarily would have turned lustrous eyes upon him, only four remained to watch him dismount, and all of these looked low grade.

Sure that he was on the right track in the way he had been thinking, Mark walked up the knoll to the ranch house, feeling a profound confidence in himself. Percy Randal himself opened the door. "My God, Perce," Mark said. "I wasn't sure if this was a working outfit or a burying-ground."

"Well, now," Percy said, smiling, "I guess we better call it a burying-ground. Everybody's gone up in the Marias to look for rocks to chisel into tombstones."

They're up there, all right, Mark thought, but that's not *why* they're up there. "Too hot a day for it," he told Percy, moving past him into the big main room of the ranch house. "And not enough dead folks around."

Percy shut the door behind them. "Can you force a little whisky, Mark?" he asked. "Or did that header you took put your mind off hard liquor?"

"I don't have to force it at all, Perce, thanks," Mark said.

While Percy Randal filled two tumblers his guest crossed to one of the windows, beyond which he could see most of the outbuildings. There was still no human movement anywhere. "Here you go, Mark," Percy said, coming up beside him.

Mark took his drink with a nod and a quick smile, gulped down half of it directly, then moved away from the window, prowling in an aimless fashion around the room. "I reckon you know the Forkhandle's low, Perce?" It was a flat statement as well as a question.

"Hell, yes. Knew it two nights ago."

"I wasn't sure."

"Hell, everybody in a hundred miles knows it by now."

"Perce, I haven't seen a soul." Mark was looking out another window, along the road that ran to the bridge. "Matter of fact, I felt right poorly once I got home Sunday night. Spent some time in my bed."

"Didn't Alan tell you?"

"Haven't even seen my brother." Mark turned from the window, finished his drink, and set the tumbler carefully on a side table.

"Another one, Mark?"

"Obliged to you, Perce, but no, thanks. Your whisky's too rich for my blood."

"You never yet saw the day," Percy Randal said cheerfully. He sank into his own big chair at one side of the fireplace and revolved his glass slowly between his gaunt hands. "I think the whole thing'll right itself before folks get too upset, though," he said. "Every man I can spare's up in those damned mountains now."

And maybe some you can't spare, thought Mark. "Yep," he said, "the place is a graveyard, and that's a fact."

Percy Randal sipped his whisky. "No cause to trouble anybody else, I figgered, long as we can handle it ourselves. But if it looked like we couldn't—"

"Hell, Perce, *you* can handle it. Yes, *sir*, you can handle it, and then some."

"Well, we do know where the trouble *starts*, anyway."

Mark's voice suddenly became very soft. "Just where *does* all the trouble start, Perce?"

"You mean you don't know?"

"I said I was feeling poorly, Perce. Lost a whole day. Didn't hear anything."

"By Jesus, yes, Mark. Hell, I'm sorry, I forgot. Well, the South Tine's dumped herself clean back into the Marias. Hallock seen a big hole opened up in the ground right across her bed, and that's what she's running into, up there between Number Two Camp and Number Three. You've done roundup work in that country. You know what it's like up there." Percy Randal took another, longer sip of his whisky.

"Oh, indeed I do, Perce," Mark said in the same soft voice. "I know what it's like up there, all right."

"Well," Percy Randal continued, "the way Hallock sees it, and I go along with him, that damned stream ought to come out someplace lower down the mountains pretty soon—if she don't fill up the hole she's going in now, that is—and there's a passel of 'em up there looking for 'er when she shows herself again. They'll be up there maybe a week, unless she sticks her nose out sooner."

"But just *your* people're up there? Nobody else?"

"If we need any more people, we'll come asking, Mark. Don't fret yourself."

"Can't help it, Perce," Mark said. "I'm fretting."

"What the hell about?"

"Mainly because I know you won't be needing any more people," Mark told him. His voice was like silk, his eyes like barbed wire.

"Hope not," said Percy Randal.

"And you know why?" Mark went on. "Because you don't *want* any more people up there, you old son of a bitch, except your very own."

Percy Randal, not sure that he had heard Mark clearly, looked up in some confusion. "I told you my outfit could handle it," he said.

"This is one leg you're not going to pull, Perce," Mark said. "I'm not buying any. And neither are you, by God, if I have anything to say about it."

Still not sure that he was understanding Mark's import, but angered by his tone, Percy Randal rose to his feet. "What the devil you talking about, anyway, Mark? You got *any* idea at all?"

"You're damned right I have, and I'm itching to pass it around. Because I know what your people're doing up in the Marias. And it ain't hunting any lost rivers."

Percy Randal walked slowly over to Mark, his jaw drawn down against his neck; he understood the man now, all right. "If you came here to get yourself some trouble, Lacy," he said steadily, "you'll get it, and then some. I promise you that."

"I got it without even coming here," said Mark. "And so's everybody else around the Forkhandle. I can see what you're doing, goddamn you, even if nobody else does."

"Then suppose you *tell* me what I'm doing," Percy told him. The old man's fists were clenching and unclenching as though of their own volition.

Mark jutted his head forward. "You're putting dams across those two streams up there, because you want to get us all off our land, that's what you're doing, you goddamned old thieving bastard."

"That's what *you* say, Lacy?"

"What do *you* say, Randal?" Mark was sneering now, and cocky; he'd broken the thing wide open.

Percy Randal, however, did not blanch; instead, a twisted smile distorted his face, and when he spoke his voice sounded like a file on iron. "I say you're right," he replied. "Right as rain. And I say I *am* damming up both those streams, because the one thing in this world I want to do before I leave it is to get rid of you, you two-cent piss-cutter, and everybody who tries to ride along with you is going to get the same medicine, hear? So you better run off crying to your big brother right now, while you still got eyes in your head to cry with, and tell him Perce Randal aims to drive you right into the ground, all the way through to China, by God, so he'd best get you out of my sight before some Chinaman finds you messing your britches." Percy pointed a shaking hand at a

Winchester carbine that hung on the wall above the fireplace. "You see that Worcestershire, by God, over there? Well, this is the first and last time, goddamn you, that anybody's going to beard me in my own house, and if you ain't away from here and riding by the time it takes me to tell you, well, by God, I'm going to fill your hide from stem to stern with every hunk of lead that gun's got in her. And in case you don't think I can cut you down slow and painful—" Percy Randal turned and went for the Winchester.

Before the old man had reached the weapon, Mark Lacy was out of the door; and by the time he had crossed to the door to shut it, Mark Lacy had reached his horse; and by the time the door was shut, Mark Lacy was larruping out of there, bent low along his horse's mane, with never a backward look.

As the clopping of hooves faded, Percy, breathing more deeply than he liked, had fought his way back from his rage. His first reaction to the unexpected and violent scene was to shake his trembling head from side to side. His second was to chuckle softly, but whether through pleasure or relief he could not say. And his third was, with shoulders sagging and oddly unsteady feet, to find his way back to his big chair and, sighing, drop down in it, heart-heavy and depressed.

Harriet Randal, her features composed, stepped into the room from the hallway outside. "Who was that just rode off?" she asked.

"Mark Lacy," he said, not looking at her.

"You were terrible loud," she said. "Were you having an argument?"

"You ever know me to argue with Mark?"

"No, but—well, Percy, he rode away fast enough."

"He had someplace to go," said Percy Randal.

After his wife, still dubious, had gone up the stairs to their bedroom, Percy Randal sat alone for over an hour, trying to escape from a web of thought. He realized, before Mark Lacy had been gone five minutes, that in saying such things to the younger man, whatever the provocation, he had been stupid and vindictive and childish. God knows, he was old enough to have kept his head and talked sense, instead of carrying on like a drunken riverboat man, especially when Mark himself must've been drunk, puking up all those crazy notions. Hadn't Hallock been able to tell that Mark had been drunk last Sunday, when nobody else had noticed? Yep, he had, and he'd been right as rain. Ah, Hallock was a sharp one, make no mistake. But here his old father had bulled ahead, making a damned fool of himself and, like as not, an enemy of Mark Lacy, when a little common sense might've cleared things up in jig time.

Percy had to admit that this South Tine business had pricked his skin deeper than he'd thought; but for the life of him he couldn't say why it had. He'd undergone many harsh trials in a full and, at least until he met young Harriet Hallock, reckless life; but whatever vultures of adversity had torn his vitals from time to time, he'd always managed to keep his head, nor ever howled with the pain of it. Maybe he was, God forbid! getting old: maybe the day had come for Hallock and the boys to take over the ranch and put the old man out to pasture. It would be real fine, come to think of it, to go east once more with Hattie, to see, maybe for the last time, the places they had known and loved in their high-horse youth, and to visit again with the few old friends they had there who were still above the ground—

"God *damn!*" Percy cried to the echoing room. "What the *hell* am I thinking about?"

Heaving himself up out of his chair, Percy began to pace back and forth across the rugs his wife had hooked or Ann had braided. Any old bull whose mind was beginning to wander along trails like that didn't deserve to be put out to pasture; the slaughter-house was the place for him, and the quicker the better, by God! Mark Lacy had been damned lucky. He didn't *know* just how lucky he'd been. Few men, in Percy Randal's prime, ever dared talk to him like that, and those who had, every last one of 'em, ended up dripping claret from someplace and, like as not, with something busted in the bargain. But now the tide had ebbed so low that Perce Randal could be cussed up, down, and sideways by a drunken crow-turd, and a guest in his own house to boot, yet never lift a finger in his own defense. He should have shot Mark Lacy, by God, where he stood; or at the very least dusted him off with a ball or two when he yellow-dogged down the road.

But then Percy Randal remembered that the Winchester carbine wasn't loaded, and hadn't been for a good six months.

He sighed and slowed his pacing. Once a man got in the habit of being a fool, it was pretty hard to stop, and it sure looked like he'd started to take up the habit this very day. Hattie, too, ought to have more sense, instead of trying to hang on to Luke like he was a lapdog or one of those long-haired sofa cats or worse. Why, when she'd come in the door a while back, it was the first exchange of words they'd had since she fussed about Luke at the stable. Maybe they both were getting too touchy about matters of no account. But, damn it all, this trouble with Mark Lacy *did* matter, and it could easily turn into something ugly, if not downright dangerous.

He was blowed if he could figure what had got into Mark, but, whatever it was, nobody with a grain of sense would help the man nurse his resentments along. If, for instance, Mark was taking it hard because he'd lost that new mare of his, well, Perce Randal could appreciate anybody's feeling low over a good quarter horse like that—but why in God's name didn't Mark come right out and say what was riding him, instead of laying a fuze of crazy talk the way he'd done? Hell, Perce Randal liked Mark, always had liked him; and it would have to be a mighty old man who couldn't enjoy the sight of that Ellen Lacy, seven days a week and twice on Sunday. No, sir, when the chips were down, there was no point in trying to scare the table with cards you didn't hold. So there was neither rhyme nor reason in letting the sore of this afternoon's cussing-contest fester any deeper than it had already. And he, Perce Randal, had better stop his tomfoolery and start applying some poultices to the wound before it got too late—

He opened the door and walked outside. He knew Pax wasn't in the house, and he hadn't gone to town, so he must be tucked away someplace nearby. "Pax!" he called.

No answer. "You *Pax!*" he bellowed.

Faintly, from some indeterminable spot among the outbuildings below the knoll, he heard Pax's muffled shout that he was coming. Percy Randal went back in the house to wait.

Pax was lying in the hay. He was stretched full length in the stifling loft of the barn, wearing nothing but his unbuttoned shirt. He was embracing the hand-burning body of Dolores, who was wearing nothing but a languorous smile and a little dust from the hay, and who, for the past fifty-three minutes, had been sundered from the virgin state she had lately found incompatible, having undergone her initiation into the sisterhood of seduced woman with little pain, less bleeding, and no regrets at all.

Her damp arms encircled the waist of Pax. She nuzzled his neck with her nose, and then began to lick his golden throat, for all the world like a lazy puppy. Ungirt Dolores, who had never dreamed that life could encompass such throbbing delights, wonderful beyond all sensation and yet so simple and ready to hand, was eager to make the double-backed beast again; and Pax, who hadn't had as much innocent fun in five years, was coming around to the same idea.

He flashed her an anticipatory smile and she stopped what she was doing, her pink velvet tongue peeping out from between moist lips. "Does it tickle?" she murmured drowsily.

"No, *palomita*. I like it."

"It makes you happy?"

"It does, by God. And so do you."

She slithered herself higher until she could lay her lips along his, which she did wetly and open-mouthed and for a long time. Her brown hands were pressed against the back of his head, while his own massaged the dimpled base of her spine and the softnesses swelling below. "That's all I *want* to do, ever," she whispered against his teeth. "Make you happy, Pax Randal. But I can't, I never can—"

"You're doing it right now, *palomita*."

"You know what I wish for you, Pax? I wish I was the most beautiful woman in the world—"

"You're the most beautiful *girl*, hear?"

"No." she buried her face in the curve of his shoulder. "But what I wish for you is, oh, I wish I was as beautiful as that Mrs.

Lacy, even, because you're *my* Pax Randal, and you're going to have the most beautiful woman in the world someday, for your very own."

Pax was already deciding that what he wanted for his very own, right here and right now, was the fledgling beauty whose breath was scorching his cheek. He lightly entangled one hand in her unbound hair and pulled her sloe-eyed face back to kiss her into another conquest.

And then, coming faintly to him across the still, humid air of the loft, he heard his name being shouted. "Damn all!" he said. "God *damn!*"

Dolores pressed hot against him. "Don't answer," she begged. "Oh, *please* don't, Pax, not *now*. He'll think you've gone off someplace."

"You *Pax!*" Percy Randal bellowed.

"*I'm coming, Father!*" Pax yelled. He freed his hand from Dolores's damp, dust-matted hair. Then he released the rest of himself from contact with the clinging girl and climbed to his feet in a rage, sweeping up his pants in the same movement. "He knows I'm around, all right," he told her. "Nobody fools old Perce."

She lay limp on her back in the depression in the hay that their joint efforts had flailed out. One knee was drawn up slightly, and sadly she watched him dress. "You'll come back here, won't you?" she asked, in a low, urgent whisper. "*Won't* you come back to me, Pax?"

"Don't see why not," he told her. He kneeled and kissed her quickly. "Don't move at all, you hear? Don't even put your clothes on."

"I won't," she whispered, "I promise. I only wish I never had to dress again."

When Pax came into the main room of the ranch house, he found his father sitting in his chair by the fireplace; and he caught himself thinking that Percy Randal had a tired, beaten look about him, utterly alien to the idea that all his sons had of their confident sire. Pax instantly threw the thought out of his head, however, when his father fixed him with his usual steady gaze. "Took you long enough, boy," Percy Randal said.

"I was fixing something in the barn, sir."

"Well, now you're going to do some fixing for me."

"Yes, sir," Pax said coldly.

Percy Randal rose from his chair and began to pace the room. "This is just between the two of us, Pax," he began. "And I'll want you to ride over to Mark Lacy's place, soon as I've had my say, and try to repair a little damage—"

CHAPTER 8

THERE WERE three saloons in Eastmere. The ranch people went to Smiley's.

Men who had businesses in town, or worked there, drank, for the most part, at Kopfner's; and Dundee's, which was really part of the Dundee Hotel, was patronized mainly by transient riders or travelers off the stages. But for anyone making the trip to town from a neighboring spread, Smiley's had a fine central location, between the Forkhandle Bank of Darius Oliphant and George Throstle's Dry Goods Emporium. A man driving in to Eastmere usually stopped at the bank, for better or worse; and if his wife came in with him, she never failed to prowl through Throstle's, giving her husband time to toss off two or three at Smiley's, meanwhile picking up some news and gossip. Then the wife, having finished her inventory at Throstle's, could stick her head inside Smiley's doors, demanding the husband's immediate presence.

Directly across the dusty street from Smiley's was Terry Sykes's Livery Stable, which drew most of its income from drummers who had to rent a rig with which to cover the Forkhandle territory, or young bucks who had an urge to do a little private, sit-down sparking. Sykes, George Throstle, and Oliphant were three townspeople who preferred Smiley's. Doctor Phil Hyssop came in occasionally, too. Most times, however, the doctor did his drinking at Dundee's, for reasons at bottom professional; people who'd stumbled into the hotel after eight or ten bouncing hours on a stagecoach were apt to want some medical attention, one way or another.

Smiley Brann, who ran the place that was called by his name, was a gimpy old gamecock who had been the best trail boss Nelse Macleod ever had; but Smiley had been badly smashed up, twenty years before, in a night stampede while moving stock north after the fall roundup. This had been the fault of J. O. Macleod, who was still a young sprout at the time, and who certainly would have been trampled to death if Smiley Brann hadn't bent the course of the rampaging herd, at a cost of five arm and leg fractures and seven broken ribs.

That night's activity had finished Smiley as a working cowhand, but he'd had some money saved up and Nelse Macleod had put some more with it, as well as paying all Smiley's bills until he was able to get around again; so now Smiley had his saloon. Both Kopfner's and Dundee's were bigger and more comfortable, but the men who came to Smiley's place made sure he got a living from it.

The saloon was nothing but a long narrow room, in a long narrow two-story building. Smiley and Pete Post, the man who helped him out, slept in tiny bedrooms on the second floor. There was also an upstairs room that held a big, round table, used only for serious poker games, whose players wanted a minimum of spectators and a maximum of peace. The downstairs bar ran almost the whole length of the narrow room, with barely space enough for two small tables in the rear, seating eight men all told, beyond which a door led to a privy behind the building. The decorations of the bar were utilitarian rather than fancy. On the dingy wall opposite the long, flaking mirror were two lithographs of sad-eyed dogs and one lithograph of General Washington, looking remarkably doglike himself.

There was one distinct touch about Smiley's, however, that belonged to no other building in town: in the ceiling above the bar were three hundred and seventeen bullet holes, their total checked and rechecked by various late-comers, the result of a great fly shoot on the afternoon of July 4, 1876. This had been started by Jock Menzies, three sheets to the wind and impelled by Pax Randal, who convinced him that the flies which infested the place were tiny disguised Redcoats, sneaking back on the Centennial of Liberty to give it another try. The toll of slain flies had never been ascertained, nor had the number of slugs later plucked out of Smiley's second-story walls; Pax Randal had been heard to say, though, that if ever there should be a call for a lead coffin, just give Smiley Brann the measurements, a hot fire, and a little time, and he'd lay you out in style.

The fly shoot had been a special thing. Usually Smiley's was a two-drinks-and-get-home, low-voiced place before the sun went down. On this particular afternoon, with the sun very close to setting, Terry Sykes was nursing a beer near the swinging doors. Drury Wynward, Nelse Macleod, and the Lacy brothers were drinking whisky at the one table which couldn't be seen by anyone entering from the street outside.

The four men in the rear had been indulging in futile argument for a long time, ever since Mark Lacy, finding his brother, Alan, at the bar with the other two, had pulled them off to this deepest table and begun to blurt out a lot of foolish talk about Perce Randal damming the mountain streams and trying to gun Mark down and planning to steal away Ellen Lacy as a bride, or worse, for Pax. Terry Sykes had wandered in later, heard what they were talking about, and decided to hang around to see which way the monkey jumped.

"Dear God in Heaven!" Mark exclaimed, for what seemed to him the fiftieth time. "Don't you all understand what it *means?*

"Mark boy," Alan Lacy said patiently, "you're not talking good sense. And you know damned well you haven't been, either, ever since you bust in here. I figger you ought to ride home, get yourself a good night's sleep. Maybe all day tomorrow, too, for aught I know."

Mark hit his forefinger again and again on the table. "I'm telling you I don't need any more sleep," he said. "I'm telling you what the old son of a bitch *said* to me. With his own Yankee *mouth,* goddamn it."

"Ah, you went and riled him, Mark," said Drury Wynward, taking the cigar from his fine-turned lips and blowing smoke toward the ceiling. "Made him mad enough to say anything come into his head."

"You ever know Perce Randal to say something he didn't mean?" Mark angrily drained his glass.

"Never was a man yet born," said Nelse Macleod, stroking his beard, "who didn't once in a while say something he didn't mean."

"Do it all the time, myself," Drury said. He grinned at the listening Smiley, who was polishing glasses near them.

Mark fixed furious eyes on Drury's dark, good-looking face. "Trouble with you, Drury, is you weren't out there on Sunday."

"Damn right I wasn't," Drury said. "I wasn't going to share that little filly I found with the likes of Pax Randal or Nelse Macleod."

"By God, boy," old Nelse cackled, "that's the talk I love to hear."

"They were saying some mighty queer things on Sunday," Mark went on, brushing a fly away from his face. "And doing some queer ones, too."

"Not when I was around, they wasn't," said Nelse Macleod in a firm voice. "And it was a fine Sunday, by God, and we all of us had a lot of sport, except maybe for a few of us that broke their quarter horses' legs and've been busier than all get-out ever since, trying to get some other fellers to carry their cross—"

"Damn you, Nelse Macleod," Mark cried, pounding his empty glass on the scarred table, "it's the cross of every single blessed soul around the Forkhandle. I *told* you what the old bastard told me this afternoon."

"Over and over again." Nelse glanced at Drury and studied the younger man's guileless face. "Drury, I want the truth. You didn't have an honest-to-God young filly out to your place Sunday, now did you?"

"Since you asked me man to man, Nelse, I'll tell you." Drury blew a smoke ring across the table. "What I had was a solid-gold attack of drunkenness that I carried over from Saturday night, like a blasted fool, and I couldn't have made that Randal hoe-down if I'd been dragged there by naked women. The only fillies I had were in my head and, I don't know, they all kept talking like greasers or something."

"Ah, Drury," Nelse said. "I *like* an honest man, even when he's only honest the second time 'round." Now Nelse looked along the bar at Terry Sykes. "You hear us all right from down there, Terry?"

Sykes kept his gaze fixed on the bar's polished surface, but he gave Nelse the courtesy of shaking his head. "Wasn't listening," he said.

"Hell you weren't," Nelse said blandly. "No feller nurses his beer the way you been nursing that one, unless he's got his ears cocked this way or the other."

"I been nursing this beer because it ain't fit to drink," said Sykes.

Smiley Brann winked at the men around the table. "That's particular beer, Terry me lad," he told Sykes. "Particular about whose gullet it goes down. It's fighting you every step of the way."

"It was good money paid for it, it ought to be good beer," Sykes said, finally turning his eyes toward the far end of the bar.

"You Terry," Mark said suddenly, swinging himself around in order to see the man he spoke to, "anything those Randals said strike you funny last Sunday?"

"Ah, now, Mark—" Nelse started to say.

"Yep," Sykes replied quickly. "Everything *they* jawed about then, and everything *you* fellers're jawing about now, it's all funny as hell."

"You're no help, by God," said Mark, turning away again.

"I might be," Sykes said, "if you all went up the Marias to roost them Randals off their dams."

This time Mark not only swung around but rose to his feet as well, his eyes gleaming, and knocking his chair over in his excitement. "*You* believe what I'm talking about?"

"Why not?" said Sykes with a shrug. "Time something took place around these parts. Perce Randal's as crooked as the next snake, and I've knowed that for a long time."

"Give him another beer, Smiley," said Mark.

"Never you mind, damn you," Sykes told Smiley, "or I'll bust a gut here on your floor." He gulped down his beer and moved toward the entrance doors, stopping there to look back at the other men, his stance stiff and awkward as always. "That damned Hallock Randal," he said, "is going to get his comeuppance one of these days, goddamn him. And I bet he's the feller that's behind everything's going on. You mark my words, all of you." Sykes strode out into the sagging day.

"What'd I *tell* you?" Mark exclaimed triumphantly, picking up his chair and resuming his seat. "There's one, anyway."

"One *what?*" Alan said with contempt.

"Sure, Mark," Drury Wynward said. "Terry Sykes even hated his maw, soon's he got a look at 'er."

"I would have, too, by God," snorted Nelse Macleod. "Old Man Sykes must've had 'er in a coal hole at midnight."

"God *damn* it, Nelse!" cried Mark. "Of all the people who ought not to go taking this careless-like, seems to me you're the main one. After all, you're the feller owns the most land around here, next to Perce Randal."

"I do indeed," Nelse nodded, "and my son J. O. Macleod'll own it after me, once he gets over being sheriff. And if you want to put your spread up for sale, Mark Lacy, well, I'm listening, and the bank opens early in the morning. You can get rid of it right easy."

"Get *rid* of it?" Mark shouted. "By God, that's what we'll all of us be doing, before we know what's hit us. As sure as I sit here in Smiley's, by the time Perce Randal's got through with the work he's doing right now, he'll be able to buy up the whole Forkhandle country for two cents and some spit. And he's got a houseful of both, the old bugger."

"Now, you look here, Mark Lacy," Nelse said. "Perce Randal's been a mighty close friend of mine, and a man can get terrible tired, hearing you slang him the way you been doing."

"A man can get terrible tired hearing an old Yankee bantard being stood up for, too," Mark said.

"Mark, *Mark*," Alan murmured.

"War's over, Mark," said Drury.

Mark raised his hand for silence, nodded, and stared straight at Nelse Macleod. "That's right," he said, "the War's over. And a lot of us paid a big price to end it, and maybe not in the way it ought to've ended, neither. I never knew your boy Exeter, Nelse, but I hear he was quite a lad. The War got over for him *terrible* early, didn't it, now?"

There was a silence. Nelse frowned and looked away from Mark; the memory of Exeter, so early dead, always brought him pain. "It was Ex's luck, that's all," he said gently.

"Yep, Ex's luck," Mark said, equally gentle. "Poor Ex Macleod's bad luck." He began to speak faster and louder. "But the Randals didn't have any bad luck, did they, with Hallock all dolled up in that blue Yankee sergeant's uniform, and everything going fine? The only dirty Yanks around the Forkhandle?"

"Arch Eastmere fought Yank," Nelse said.

"Sure, old Arch only wanted something to do," said Drury. "The different sides didn't make no difference to him. I reckon Arch fought Yank because the first *re*cruiter he run into was a damn Yankee."

"If Arch Eastmere was around *now* he'd see some difference in the sides, I swear," Mark said. "He'd see some difference, and he'd be on *my* side, by God."

"Why should he?" Drury asked.

"Because of a favor I did him," said Mark.

"Never heard tell of *that*," said Drury.

"I have," Nelse said. "You lent him five hundred dollars for when he went down to Mexico."

"That I did, by God," Mark said, "and I reckon I'll never get it back, neither. But Arch'd be with me, I swear, if only to clean up the debt."

Drury chuckled. "You don't know Arch Eastmere, by God."

"Neither do you, son, neither do you," said old Nelse Macleod.

"You'd see, by God, if he was here," said Mark.

The saloon doors swung open, and George Throstle entered, greased and pomaded and sharp as a fishhook. "The usual, Smiley," he said, and then came toward the group in the rear. "Now where's that lovely wife of yours, Alan?" he said. "Don't tell me you're letting her run around town by herself while you sit and booze?"

"She went on home, George," Alan told him. "I had more to do than I figgered."

And so had George Throstle much more to do that afternoon than he had thought, or Alan Lacy could have imagined—in the back room of the Dry Goods Emporium, where a few things were stored and where there was a full-length mirror. Lydia Lacy had gone in this back room to pose in front of this mirror with a bolt of new cloth draped over her excellent breasts, turning and twisting and watching it cling, and, the store being otherwise empty, George Throstle had followed her in, to offer what assistance he could. There had been some run-of-the-mill remarks on patterns and folds, followed by an adjustment of the new cotton print across the proud bosom of Lydia Lacy. And then, for no apparent reason, there was a tumbling down of the bolt of cloth, followed by a hungry embrace and much desperate kissing and whispers and promises and plans. All that awaited the ultimate embrace that would surely follow was the opportunity and the leisure; although George Throstle, as he calmed himself after the encounter, wasn't quite positive whether the conquest would be his, or Lydia Lacy's. Time, as they say, would tell. And meanwhile he allowed himself to beam down blandly on the lady's soon-to-be-cuckolded spouse. "Unusual thing, her leaving you here," was his offhand remark to Alan.

"Been a funny day," Alan replied.

"It has indeed," said Throstle. "Especially for the Lacys. "Why," he continued, turning to Mark, "today was the first time I can ever recall that your wife came to Eastmere alone."

"Anything wrong with it?" Mark asked.

"Lord love you, no," said George Throstle. "But I'm sure the whole town'd like it to happen more often."

"I don't reckon it will," said Mark Lacy.

There was an odd finality about his words that made Throstle change the subject. "Anything new about the Forkhandle?" he asked.

"There will be, don't you fret," Mark said.

"Like what?" Throstle asked.

"Like no goddamned river at all," said Mark.

Alan Lacy slammed his open palm down on the table, making the glasses jump. "Oh, *Jesus,* Mark, let it *alone,* will you?"

"That's what I say, too," said old Nelse Macleod, getting to his feet. "My God, all I've been hearing is that the Randals're damming up the Tines with one hand and feeling up Ellen Lacy with the other. They're both of 'em the silliest damned ideas I ever heard tell on, and I'm damned but if I ain't going over to my daughter-in-law Hannah's house, who don't do nothing but *shout*."

Old Nelse made for the swinging doors. He had nearly reached them when they were burst open and Charley Samuels entered the saloon, looking as though his mere presence in such a place meant everlasting damnation for his teetotal, hard-shell Baptist soul. Old Nelse, seeing him, stopped dead in his tracks. "Well, I never reckoned I'd see the day," he croaked. "Here's old First'n'second Samuels, taken to drink at last."

Charley Samuels's face was a mountain crag, with a horizontal fissure for a mouth. "I come looking for Mister Mark Lacy," he said in a monotone, "and not for any transgression."

The sight of Charley Samuels, whom they all called First'n'-second, actually in a saloon, had surprised the men around the table, too. "Here I am, Charley," Mark finally managed to say.

Samuels walked directly up to Mark. "I'm sorry, Mister Lacy," he said. "I wish I'd've found you in a more fitting place."

"Dundee's, by God," said Smiley. Drury and old Nelse laughed.

"What's so important, you had to find me in town?" Mark asked.

"Well, Mister Lacy," said Charley Samuels, "the evils men do run before them and find them out in evil places. But the sin of one need not answer for the sin of another, not until we are all called to a Higher Judgment. So I thought you'd better know right away, Mister Lacy." Charley's own brows met in merciless judgment on the sins of all the world. "About an hour or so ago, Mrs. Lacy run off with that Pax Randal. I rode in here right after he took 'er."

Nobody moved except Nelse Macleod, who slowly creaked back to the table.

"Now, then, Mark boy," said Alan grimly, in a voice like shattering glass, "*that's* a horse of another color."

The events which had taken place in the Lacy house much earlier that afternoon, when Mark had come back from his set-to with Percy Randal, progressed with a certain logic from a most illogical premise. "Where you been?" wild-eyed Mark had asked Ellen; and, "I had to—" she started to tell him. Then he had driven his fist into her stomach, and the blow contained all the shame he felt because of his flight from Percy. And when Mark himself rode for Eastmere and Smiley's, Ellen was still lying on the floor by the rocking-chair, among the scattered new spools she had purchased barely an hour before, holding her belly and gasping for breath.

For a while she thought she was going to die, that Mark had broken something inside her. Even the sunlight in the room was dark, and all the air in the world was reserved for the living, and her lovely mouth opened and closed, opened and closed. But when it seemed as though the end had come and the dark would be everlasting, a miracle of air approached her lungs. They accepted some of it, and then a little more, and the room and her coal of life grew brighter. But she lay on the floor a long time, until her breathing was as it had been before Mark struck her down; and when she finally rose to her feet, it was with difficulty and pain, for below her navel all was fire.

Slowly the fire died, however; and eventually she felt recovered enough to get out an old portmanteau and begin to pack it. Her movements were all deliberate; she wasted no time on tears. The portmanteau was half filled when she heard the beat of a galloping horse. Briefly she knew the returned chill wings of fear, for she thought Mark Lacy was back. Then she looked out the window and saw that the horseman was Pax Randal; and all at once he became to Ellen Lacy the distillation of everything good and beautiful in men. And even as he was dismounting by the corral, she had made up her mind what she must do.

She closed the half-filled portmanteau, and she shut the bedroom door on the sight of it, and she walked in her beauty out into the afternoon to greet the approaching Pax. He seemed, she thought, nervous and ill at ease, nor did he greet her with his usual warm smile. "Howdy, Ellen," was all he said. "Mark around?"

She shook her blond locks, and sunlight shimmered golden on them. "He's gone off, Pax. There's just me."

"Expect him back soon?"

"I hope not." These three cryptic words went over his head, and his face showed it; so she beckoned him toward the door of the ranch house. "Come in, Pax, please, for a minute. I've got to talk to you. I want you to do something for me."

"Sure, Ellen. If I can."

Once they were inside she stood close to him. "God must've sent you," she said. "I know it was God."

Pax felt like laughing for the first time since he had been summoned from the loft. "We don't call him 'God' around the house," he said. "Not yet."

"But just at the right time, Pax, just when I needed somebody so bad." She pressed both hands against her belly and winced at the pressure. "He hit me here," she said. "Mark, I mean. And with all his strength, too. I thought I was dead."

Pax let his jaw sag. "*Mark?*" he exclaimed. "My God, Ellen, what for? Why'd the damned fool hit you *there?*"

Her bovine eyes were wide with wonder. "It's not the first time, either," she said. "He knocked me all across the bedroom not two weeks ago. I was all bruised. And he tore all my clothes off, too, so I didn't have a rag to cover me. I think he's gone crazy or something."

"*Jesus*, Ellen. Why didn't you *tell* somebody?"

"I guess I didn't know how bad he was, even though I could tell he was drinking something terrible. And now I'm scared he'll kill me. Oh, Pax, listen, *would* you—I mean, do you think your *father*'d let me stay at your place for a few days, until I—?" Her face turned up to his, luminous.

Pax forced himself to look beyond her, at the green world glowing outside the windows. The combination of Mark's brutality and Ellen's desperation had thrown him into confusion. The life Pax led might perhaps be overexuberant, but it was stable, and seldom was its tenor disturbed; therefore, when confronted with a sudden decision, forced on him by circumstances equally sudden, he found it difficult to choose a course of action.

"Well, I—I don't rightly know," he said distantly. "Father sent me over here for this one particular thing, and he might—"

"But I've got to go *some*place, Pax. If I stay here, he'll—oh, God, I'm *scared*, Pax."

Running his tongue across his dry lips, Pax changed the direction of his thought. Suppose he *did* bring Ellen Lacy back home with him, what could they do to him? Or *her*, either? It was an act they ought to pound him on the back for, saving a woman maybe from being killed. And, by God, Ellen had a right to be protected from that wife-beating husband: Percy Randal'd be the first to admit it. And as for Pax Randal, from whom the original decision would have to come—well, Pax Randal right then and there could see himself as the Spirit of Good, driving the Forces of Evil back into the Bottomless Pit. But he made one last effort to hold his decision off. "Mark won't take it sitting down," he said slowly. "If I bring you over to our place, I mean."

"But it's a *Christian* thing to do," she told him. "And everybody'll *know* it for a Christian thing, once the word gets around."

Pax still was hesitant; but then he saw tears in those loveliest of eyes, and he dissolved like dew in the sun. "All right, Ellen," he said. "I'll bring you along with me. You get ready the things you want to take, and I'll go hitch up the buggy."

"No, Pax, I want to leave everything here," she said, and her voice broke. "There's nothing I want to remind me, not even the buggy. I'll ride Princess, she's my own horse, I bought her with my own money I saved."

Pax looked helplessly down at the hem of her dress. "Like *that?* You can't ride in a get-up like that."

"I can if I have to, Pax, don't you worry. *Please*, let's go before he comes back. He may even have somebody to help him. I don't want to put you in danger, Pax, you're being so good and kind to me."

"We'll both of us be all right," Pax said. He opened the door, then looked quickly around the room. "You *sure* there's nothing you want to bring along?"

"Just you." High-headed, she preceded him into the sunlight.

Ellen waited by the corral gate while Pax saddled Princess. Then the rock-bound fanatic face of Charley Samuels appeared around the corner of the stable. Charley watched them for a moment, then walked cautiously over to the corral gate. "Ain't you got enough horses to home, Pax Randal?" he demanded.

"It's me that's riding Princess," said Ellen.

"With a *man's* saddle and *female* clothes?" Charley stared at her as though she had confessed to a child murder. "That's work for hussies," he said in his hard-shell, fire-and-brimstone voice, "and you're a respectable woman, Mrs. Lacy."

"I'm going off to the Randals' with Pax," Ellen said dispassionately. At a sign from Pax she strolled over to Princess and let him boost her astride, swinging her right leg cleanly across the saddle. The resultant tightening of her dress, drawn up behind the pommel, showed six or seven inches of fine curved calf above a shapely booted foot.

Pax unhitched his roan and mounted.

"Mister Lacy know about this?" Charley asked him.

"Mister Lacy didn't say," Pax answered.

Charley Samuels was overcome, not only with the shock of Ellen's Babylonian behavior, but also because he couldn't fathom exactly what was going on. None of it added up, somehow. "When you coming back, Mrs. Lacy?" was all he could think of to say, carefully averting his gaze from that rounded calf.

"Not while *you're* alive, Charley Samuels," she shouted, for no discernible reason. Then she dug her heels into Princess's flanks and galloped away, with Pax behind her and closing up.

The truth hit Charley Samuels then, the way truth used to hit the prophets; he knew what was going on *now*, sure as what happened to Jezebel. His eyes began to smolder and gleam as he watched the riders dwindle in the distance.

"Ah," he said with great sonorousness, " 'thus will I make thy lewdness to cease from thee, and thy whoredom brought from the land of Egypt: so that thou shalt not lift up thine eyes unto them, nor remember Egypt any more—' "

Pax Randal and the fleeing Ellen saw no one as they crossed Mark Lacy's land, nor later as they cantered along the road that paralleled the Forkhandle below the Randal boundary.

Nearly a mile above the bridge the road to the ranch house wound through a grove of spruce. The riders had gone but a short distance into this when Ellen brought Princess to a halt. The beauty's breathing was deep and, to Pax, she seemed in some pain. "I've got to rest a bit," she told him.

He eased his horse against hers. "Does your—" He couldn't bring himself to say the word, but touched his belly with his free hand. "—hurt?"

"No, but—well, riding this way, it's hard. I'm not used to it. Let's please rest off the road a little."

"We're almost there, Ellen."

"I know. But just for a minute."

She rode off through the spruce, and he had to follow. Then, after the trees had completely cut off the sight of the road, Ellen drew rein. Pax slipped down to the yielding earth and adroitly tethered both mounts. "We could even walk it from here," he said, raising his arms to help Ellen descend. Casually she swung her right leg over the pommel in a breeze of flesh and linen, poised herself in disheveled loveliness briefly above him, then slid into the compass of his arms.

Nor did he let her go, but held her; nor did she try to break from him.

Instead they read the legends in each other's eyes, and believed them, and became as legends themselves, with two bodies entwined and lip against lip and soft, open mouths probing. And then they were part of each other on the earth and part of the sustaining earth herself, these lovers who had passed no words of love between them, ever, or even now.

And there was, on the sudden, such a perfection in their sunset grove that all was gold that had been dust before. The hair of their heads was mingling gold, and the tall, sad spruces were gold, and the softness of the earth flowed gold, and the sky their blanket was a golden sky, and "Gold!" exulted the passing birds, and "Gold?" the worm echoed beneath the bending root. And all the known oceans and new-found seas of Pax Randal and Ellen ran together and were running gold, and the desires of these aureate two were as liquid gold, running, running away—

Later, as they prepared to leave, she said: "Dear heart, take me up behind you."

"Can you manage now? We could walk it."

"No, dear heart, I can manage now. But, oh, Pax, I want to ride close to you, touching you. I don't care about my horse, somebody'll find my horse. Or she'll follow you. How could any creature help but follow *you?*"

So Pax Randal took his new, golden love up on the horse behind him, and *By God,* the warm thought came over him, *looks like I got what that little piece wanted for me, yep, little Dolores sure got her wish.* The arms of his new love encircled his waist, and so together they went along the darkening road that led to the house of his father.

Percy Randal, alone, had walked some distance toward the bridge, so eager was he for Pax's return and the report that he would bring.

The sun had swung down behind the Marias, and the richness of red that had held above the peaks for some time after its descent was fading to shades of mauve. Percy leaned against a great boulder by the side of the road, whittling restlessly at a piece of dry branch he had picked up. He had kept to himself since he'd sent Pax off to Mark Lacy's. This slanging-match had so upset him that he didn't trust himself not to go spilling the beans to somebody, just to take the pressure off his mind. Percy might even have liked, now that the horse had been stolen, to have Hattie help him lock the stable doors; but he knew this Lacy nonsense would upset her, and the Forkhandle trouble was disturbing her enough as it was. So, if everything could be settled between Mark and himself without anybody other than Pax, who could be close-mouthed enough, being involved—well, then, that was fine and dandy, and nobody'd be the wiser. And Percy

Randal was beginning to feel sure that it could all be smoothed over without too much grief. Why, for aught he knew, Pax might've settled it all by himself. He'd certainly been gone long enough to—

Percy Randal heaved up from the boulder, alert, at the noise of a horse coming up the road: only *one* horse, he judged, so Pax couldn't be bringing Mark back with him. Just as well, he guessed, in the long run.

Percy tossed his whittled stick away as, in the failing light, he saw the rider appear around a clump of aspen a hundred yards away. But then he saw that the horse held, not one rider, but two, and one of them was young Pax, and the other—the other—was, my God! *Ellen Lacy,* her arms around Pax's waist and her nose nuzzled up against his ear.

In one awesome moment Percy Randal's mind encompassed and knew everything that had happened on this fatal afternoon and everything that would come to pass in the deadlier days to follow; and in that single instant he lost forever the power of making decisions. "God help us," he whispered to himself, "that boy's gone and sunk his teeth in the Devil's tail."

And he could listen to black-winged fear as, with open talons and rending beak, it lowered its bulk down upon him, even while he opened his mouth to name his fairest son, God-forsaken.

PART TWO

The Stars
in Their Courses

CHAPTER 9

HE SAT in the old rocker on Maude Fletcher's porch, creaking it restlessly back and forth, back and forth, looking now at the woman who huddled beside him, now at the settling dusk beyond. At last he rose and reached out his hand to her. "Let's take us a stroll to the river, pretty Maudie."

"Oh, Archie honey, I'd love to walk over there with you, but you reckon you're well enough, Archie? goddamn you, it's nearly a mile to the river, and coming on dark, and all."

"I don't mind a mile, Maudie honey, and the dark never bothered me yet." He raised her to her feet.

"All right then, poor sick old catamountain, and if I have to, I'll carry you back."

They walked to the river as dusk turned to darkness, hand in hand, as two children might go. But the moon was up and the way was easy.

They stopped on a bluff that was twenty feet high and dropped straight down to the water. Arch Eastmere stretched out on his back and spread his arms, listening to the water and looking at the moon. Maude Fletcher, crouched by his lean flank, drew up her knees and tossed pebbles, one after another, into the river below. They remained like that for a long time.

"Archie?" she said at last. "What're we going to do, Archie?"

"Just this, little Maudie, lie here like this."

"I mean *after*, once you're well, Archie."

"I'm not sick, Maudie honey."

"Damn you, big old cat, you won't ever tell me what Phil Hyssop said."

"He said *hello* and *good-by. That's a right pretty saddle you got there*, he said. *Found it lying in the road down there in Morelos*, I told him."

"I'll find out what he said, don't you fret, the next time Phil Hyssop comes calling."

He turned and looked up at her. "Phil Hyssop comes calling on you?"

"He does and he will, old hair-face Phil Hyssop, and if anybody saw him slip in, goddamn him, he'd probably say I was sick. But next time he comes, you Archie, I won't let him even touch me until he says what you're sick of."

"Phil won't come calling while I'm hanging around, little Maudie, not while he knows I'm at your place."

"Then I'll go and see *him*, you hear? I'll walk into Eastmere and ask him right out."

"I'd say, take my horse, little Maudie, but you'd find him too much of a handful."

"I don't need your damned horse, old longshanks, I don't need a horse at all. *Everybody* comes to see Maudie."

He grinned at her, and gently touched the tip of her nose with his finger. "*I* did, and that's the truth," he told her. "And I'll save you a trip, Maudie honey. I ought to live forty more years, that's what Phil Hyssop told me."

"Oh, Archie, did he, honest? You're not just funning, now, are you, old long devil you, because if you are, I'll—"

"What, little Maudie?"

"Die, that's what I'll do, crawl into a hole, goddamn you, and pull the hole in after me."

Smiling, he pulled her down to him, and her head rested on his chest as he held her with an encircling arm. "Don't you ever," he murmured. "Because that's what Phil said, I swear. Forty more years, Mrs. Fletcher."

She moved her cheek against the rough wool of his shirt. "I love you, old catamountain," she whispered.

"Little Maudie honey." His hand caressed her tousled hair.

"Want me to show you the love I got?" She tried to raise her head, but he held her tightly, keeping her caught where she was.

"Not yet, little Maudie, not for a while, Phil said I'd best take it easy.

"For how long, goddamn that old fur-face doctor, for how long, Archie, a week?"

"Maybe a week, about that long, I reckon, can you wait a week out, little Maudie?"

"I can after two years, yes, I can, but after that, tell me, Archie, what do we do after that?"

"Anything you say, honey, anything you want."

"Will you be staying on here for good? That's what I mean, Archie, damn you."

He sat up and stared across the river. "Depends on just how bad I'm wanted," he said.

"I want you bad, Archie, my love and my heart, oh, *how* I want you—"

"I don't mean you, little Maudie, I mean other people, not you, honey."

"What other people?"

"Some there, some here, I can't tell just who, or how many."

"For work, Archie?"

"Work of a kind, it'd keep my feet busy."

"I hope it's here, oh, I hope they want you near where I am."

"I like it near where you are, Maudie, yep, Maudie honey, I like it fine, just you and me alone, and nobody knowing I'm with you."

"Ah, yes, Archie, that's it, not a living soul in miles, and nothing to do but live easy a week, until you're all rested and well. Look at the moon on the river, Archie, let's us take off our clothes and go in that nice cool water, just the two of us, all by ourselves."

"I'd like that Maudie, I swear I would, I'm starting to stink like a Guerrero goat."

He got to his feet and lifted her up and pulled her to him and

kissed her. Then they went along the bluff until they came to a
path and followed it down to the water. They stripped mother-
naked and waded in, still hand in hand, still like two children,
and they splashed each other and laughed. And they were so
happy that, although both of them noticed the Forkhandle
seemed very low, they gave it but little concern. For Arch Eastmere, who had spent the past spring and winter in hotter places,
believed that the level of the water was due to scant snowfall and
rain up in the high Marias, and little Maude Fletcher, for whom
life without her old longshanks had been one drab sunless season,
didn't give a good goddamn about the Forkhandle River, just so
long as the water was wet and the naked body beside her belonged to her old moonlit catamountain.

CHAPTER 10

It was an agonized evening for the Randals.

Old Percy called his family together after he had walked back to the ranch house beside Pax and Ellen Lacy. As they went, he had listened to their story, coming for the most part from the mouth of Pax; listened in sullen silence, for a tight-lipped anger was mingled with his fear then. But the fear and the anger had canceled each other out by the time Percy summoned his household to the big main room, leaving him mentally half submerged, and with no emotional straw at which he might grasp.

At the beginning things went smoothly enough. Ellen Lacy, with some help from Pax, told again of Mark's violence toward her, embellishing the tale a bit, and the Randal females were properly shocked and properly sympathetic. Pax certainly had done the only fit and gentlemanly thing, bringing her home with him; and poor, abused Ellen could indeed stay at the Randal ranch house, as long as ever she wanted. And she would have everything she needed, including clothes, because she and Ann were much of a size. Any woman could understand another woman's running away from such an awful place with nothing but what she wore on her back. And the Randal family would see to it that Mark Lacy kept his distance until he promised to stop drinking and mend his ways. "Why, Ellen dear," said Harriet Randal, "if you'd only told us last Sunday, it would have saved you a lot of grief."

"I guess Sunday I didn't know it would happen," said Ellen.

"What everybody ought to know right *now*," came the thick voice of Cora Randal, from the hidden corner in which she sat, "is, just what was Pax doing over at Mark Lacy's anyway?"

"I was *sent*, hear?" Pax told her sharply.

"Tell the folks why," said Cora.

"It's not my business to," Pax said. "Folks don't have to know everything."

"Folks will, though," Cora said calmly.

"How is it *you* know so much?" Pax demanded.

"How is it you *don't?*" his sister replied.

"You got any idea what you're blabbing about, Cora?" Percy Randal asked.

"I'm talking about why Pax was over at Mark Lacy's." Cora's face was so deep in shadow that they could not see her mouth form the words; her voice seemed to rise from emptiness.

"He was over to Mark Lacy's because I told him to go over," Randal said. "There was something I wanted to tell Mark. *That* answer your question, Miss Cora?"

From the shadows, silence.

Harriet Randal, however, was sending her mind back in time. "But Mark was here just this afternoon," she said.

"I know, I know," Randal said impatiently.

"Then you *did* have a fuss with him, Perce."

"Look, Hattie," Percy Randal began, "there's no sense in—" He broke off, frowned down at the floor for a moment, then nodded to himself. "All right," he said. "You might as well know what went on."

So he told them of his encounter with Mark earlier in the day, and how Mark had made him mad with some crazy notion that the Randals were damming up the North and South Tines in order to dry out the neighboring ranchers. Eliminating only the profanity, Percy Randal gave a precise and lucid account of what had occurred.

When he had finished there was a stunned silence, finally disturbed by the noise of Art Cospatrick sucking his teeth in thought. Then Harriet Randal gave one of her small, mild sighs. "I don't see why you couldn't have reasoned with him, Perce," she said, "instead of threatening him like that."

"I got mad, I told you, Hattie," Randal said. "And you would, too, if somebody talked to you that way, and in your own house, besides."

"Well, maybe," his wife conceded. "But when somebody's acting that way, I don't think you should treat them as, well, *you* know—" She gave a little bewildered shrug.

"It's been such a slow-rising thing," Ellen Lacy said. With lowered eyes she was studying her hands, which were folded demurely in her lap. "I guess maybe it's been coming on for a long while. But, well, living with somebody day to day, you just don't notice, I guess."

"Sunday, it busted *wide* open," Pax exclaimed.

"Why, he seemed nice enough the few minutes I saw him on Sunday," said Harriet Randal. "It was after he took that bad fall."

"That's when I saw him, too," Ann said. "Why, he even took Simon up and held him nice as you please and talked to him and was as gentle as anybody could be."

"That's because he wants children, I think," Ellen said, twisting her wedding band. "It makes him mad because we don't have any."

"Does he blame you for it, Ellen?" Ann asked.

Ellen blushed. "Who else can he blame?"

Art Cospatrick cleared his throat. "Well, you can talk about not having kids all you want," he said, "but the true of it is that Mark Lacy was likkered up good last Sunday, now ain't that so, Mister Randal?"

"That's what struck Hallock, yep," Percy Randal said.

"Mark was *drunk* on Sunday?" cried Harriet Randal. "Oh, Hallock *must*'ve been wrong, Perce."

Pax, who was standing behind Ellen's chair, now leaned over her. "Tell 'em," he said. "You ought to know what he was."

Ellen lifted her eyes to Harriet Randal. "I guess he was drunk, yes," she said, as though reciting a lesson. "And he drank all

Sunday night after we got home, and yesterday, when he told *you* he was sick, Mister Randal, well, he was just sleeping off all the drink he took. And today, when he hit me that way, he was drunk then, too, because when I came back from town there was this empty bottle lying on the floor that wasn't there before."

"I simply can't believe it," said Harriet Randal. "Mark *Lacy*."

"I'd rather believe Mark'd been drinking too much," Ann said, "than that he was out of his mind or anything like that."

"Well, Ann honey," Percy Randal said. "I've been around some mighty heavy-drinking men in my day, but none of 'em ever carried on the way Mark Lacy's doing."

"That's the truth, now, Father," Pax said. "Pulling his horse's head that way, even a drunk man wouldn't do *that*, not to a fine new mare like Mark had."

"You mean he *made* that mare fall?" Harriet asked. "Now, *Pax*." She knitted her brows in disbelief.

"Mother," Pax said, "I was right beside him. I saw it."

Harriet Randal sighed. "Oh, I just don't understand the whole thing. As if this river business wasn't bad enough."

"I thought about that a lot, ma'am," Art Cospatrick said. "And if Mark Lacy happens to bring some other folks around to his way of thinking, this river business'll be a whole lot worse. I'd sure hate to see something like that."

"You won't, Art," Randal said. "Nobody's going to listen to Mark while he's in such a state."

"Some folks might," Art said grimly. "I'm not so sure now."

"Why should they?"

"Because," Art said slowly, choosing his words, "*you* got what you got, Mister Randal, and *they* got what they got. Which is *more* for you, and *less* for them. Nobody trusts the feller with the biggest house."

"Damn you, Art," Percy Randal said without rancor, "you're starting to sound like Mark yourself."

"No, I ain't, Mister Randal. I'm just telling you that maybe other folks won't get mad at Mark and make out to take a gun to him."

A snorting laugh burst from Randal. "What do you reckon I

better do, Art? Run around to every rancher on the Forkhandle
and tell him to pay no mind to Mark Lacy?"

Cora's deep voice again rolled from the shadows. "The best
thing you can do, Father, is to send Ellen Lacy packing off
home."

Percy Randal whirled on his daughter. "Now, that's a plain
nasty thing to say," he told her. "And you better apologize *right*
now, hear?"

"And send Pax packing off with her," Cora went on, as though
she hadn't heard.

Percy Randal, frowning like doomsday, pointed a shaking
finger at the door that led to the dark hall. "By God, that'll do
now, girl!" he cried. "Get up and get out of here, go up to your
room and stay there!"

Cora did not move. In the gloom of the hall, however, doe-
eyed Dolores, who had heard everything, and who was glowering
with anger at Pax, took fright and, silent and unseen, darted away
through the house.

Percy Randal's jaw muscles were rippling under his cheeks.
"Did you *hear* me, girl, damn you?" he shouted at Cora.

"Now, Percy, *please*," said Harriet Randal, while the rest of
the group fidgeted uncomfortably. "You know Cora doesn't mean
what she says half the time."

"She doesn't even *know* what she says half the time," Percy
said. "But Ellen Lacy's here under our protection, for better or
worse, and—"

He was interrupted by an exclamation from Art Cospatrick,
who was standing at the window nearest the door. "Hey, Mister
Randal! They's a rider coming."

"Mark Lacy, by God!" Pax said. He crossed from behind Ellen's chair to the fireplace and reached up for the Winchester.

"*Pax!*" his father said sharply.

Pax's hand hovered by the breech of the weapon. "Just in
case, Father," he said; but there was no real confidence in his
voice. He let his arm drop to his side.

"Been enough of that this afternoon, and the gun's not loaded,
anyway," Percy Randal said. "And if it *is* Mark, he's got a pretty
good reason for showing up. His wife's here, if you'll recollect."

"But she's not going back to him, by God!" Pax said.

Percy Randal looked steadily at his son, and then at Ellen Lacy. "I didn't say she was," he said.

The hoofbeats came fast beyond the door, then stopped: the rider was leaving his horse at the near corral. Percy Randal straightened his shoulders as he moved across the room, threw the door open, and stepped out into the darkness.

A man was coming up the knoll from the corral. When he was about twenty feet away the light that came through the open door struck him and Randal saw who he was: Drury Wynward.

"Well, now, Drury, this is a pleasure," Percy Randal said, smiling and extending a hand in greeting. "Sorry you didn't get up here Sunday."

"Howdy, Perce," Drury said. "No sorrier than I was. Hear you had quite a do." The two men shook hands.

"Nobody went to sleep, I reckon, Drury. How is it you didn't show up?"

"Well, Perce," Drury said pleasantly, "it was just one of those days. A man don't rightly know what he's going to be like from one day to another, now does he? Or even what he'll *do?*"

There seemed to be something in Drury's tone, however innocent, that set Percy Randal's nerves on edge, but he shrugged the disquiet off. "Come on in, Drury," he said. "Better late than never. Wet your whistle and sit a spell." He put his arm around the young man's shoulders and steered him through the door.

When they saw Drury, the group in the big room relaxed. "By God, Drury," Pax said with naked relief, "don't tell me you went and got lost in the dark?"

"Happens to me all the time, Pax, you ought to know," Drury said with a grin. Then he turned his handsome face to Ellen Lacy and showed his white teeth in a warm smile. "Evening, Ellen," he said, as if it were the most natural thing in the world for her to be sitting there.

Drury exchanged greetings with the others, with the exception of shadow-hidden Cora. Then Percy Randal said: "A little whisky, Drury, to stave off the night air?"

Drury surprised the old man by refusing. "Not tonight, Perce, thanks all the same. Not with some business to do."

"A little whisky never hurt a little business," said Percy Randal.

"Usually not, no," Drury said. "But *this* business—well, Perce, I better get to the point right now. I come over to ask politely if I couldn't escort Mrs. Lacy back home."

"Oh." Percy Randal's gaze went first to Pax, who was staring openmouthed at Drury, then wandered to Ellen, whose own eyes were downcast again. "Why didn't Mark come himself?" he asked finally.

"Or Alan?" Pax managed to say.

"Surprised that *you*'d want to see either of 'em," Drury said coldly, then turned his attention to Percy Randal. "Matter of fact, Alan's standing by his brother, and he's the one that asked me to come here. Understand, Perce, I don't like this mess much, but I reckon since they're the wronged ones, I better be on their side."

"Now, wait, Drury, what the hell's this about 'wronged ones'?" Randal demanded. "If Mark Lacy's going around beating his wife, what else could decent folks do but take her in?"

"Wife-beating, Perce?" Faint surprise came and went on Drury's face.

"That's what I said. *Wife*-beating."

"Nobody mentioned wife-beating to me, Perce, and that's a fact," Drury said patiently.

"Reckon Ellen'd mention it, if you asked her," Pax said in some heat.

"Reckon Ellen'd say just about *any*thing you wanted her to, now wouldn't she, Pax?" said Drury.

"Watch your words there, Drury," Pax said, "or there'll be some trouble between you and me."

"I didn't come here to make any trouble," said Drury, and his voice held a measure of sadness. "I was hoping maybe to nip some in the bud."

"Well, by God, you won't nip any lighting into *me* that way," Pax told him.

Drury nodded, quite as though he agreed with the statement. "Probably won't do it *any*way, Pax. Judging from the looks of things, that is, and what I heard today."

"Just what did you hear today, Drury?" Harriet Randal wanted to know.

"A lot of things I didn't like much, Mrs. Randal," Drury said. "Things I didn't even believe, first off."

"Such as?" demanded Randal.

"I have to tell *you*, Perce?" Drury asked blandly.

"You *better* tell me, Drury."

"Well, Perce, before anything else, I'd kind of like an answer."

"Answer for what?"

"I come over, I said, to ask politely if I couldn't escort Ellen Lacy back home."

"And the answer to that is 'No,' " Pax said.

"Yep," said Drury. "That's what I figgered it would be."

"Now, hold your horses, Pax," Percy Randal said. He gave his attention to Drury: "Where's Mark now?"

"With some people, Perce."

"At *his* place?"

"Maybe. Maybe not."

"Look here, now, Drury," Randal said with considerable annoyance, "you and me, we've always got along fine together. There's no reason you can't lay your cards on the table."

"No point in even bothering," Drury said. "It's a stacked deck."

Randal was holding in his temper. "How do you want me to take that, Drury?"

"Anyway you like, Perce," said Drury Wynward. "That's about the size of it, I reckon."

"All right, then," said Percy Randal. "Mrs. Lacy will stay right here."

"Sure," said Drury, nodding.

"But tell Mark to come around tomorrow. There's half-a-dozen things we ought to talk over."

"Sorry, Perce, but I reckon the damage is done already." Drury started toward the door.

"For God's sake, *what* damage?" Percy Randal cried.

Drury paused at the door and turned around. "A man's wife has been took off by another man," he said. "And probably that ain't all he done, the way I see it, knowing Pax Randal as well as I do. Right, Pax?"

Pax's face went red. "You're a goddamned liar!" he shouted.
"Ah, go look in a mirror," Drury said. "The *both* of you." And
he jerked his head at Ellen Lacy, whose cheeks became on the
instant crimson.

Ann Randal flushed, too, and dropped her eyes; and Harriet
Randal said: "Oh, *Pax*, Pax dear—" in hurt confusion.

"You know, Perce," Drury continued, careless of the tension he
had caused, "we all thought Mark was talking through his hat,
going on the way he did about how you folks was damming up the
Tines and figgering ways to steal his wife—"

"Now, those're two goddamned lies!" roared Percy Randal.
"The one's bad enough, but—my God, steal his *wife*—!"

"Well, Perce," Drury said calmly, "when I first heard it, it
sounded like it was cut out of the whole cloth, and that's a fact.
But, well, here's Mrs. Mark Lacy, sitting in your parlor big as
life, so I reckon maybe Mark's right about what's going on up the
Tines. And I'm sure sorry about it, Perce, but I got a feeling you
bit off just a little more than you can chew. It's sad to think about,
too, you know, because things was running along just fine. I'll
tell the Lacy boys Mark can't have his wife back."

"What happens then, Drury?" Percy Randal asked, low-
voiced.

Drury considered the matter for a moment, then broke into
a grin. "Aw, hell, Perce, we'll come up with something," he said.
"Don't you fret."

He went out quickly, leaving the door agape. A little while
later his horse could be heard, galloping off in the direction it
had come. Everyone listened as though mesmerized to the sound
of these fading hooves. No one said a word. Then at last, as the
sharp clopping died, Percy Randal crossed to the door and shut
it; then he strode over to Pax. "What's been going on between you
two?" he demanded, and looked straight at Ellen Lacy.

"Nothing, Father," Pax said, facing the old man unflinchingly.
"There hasn't been and there won't be."

"You telling me the truth?"

"You ever know me not to?"

"Sometimes I don't know you at all, blast your eyes." Randal's
glance strayed to Art Cospatrick, who hadn't budged from the

window. "Art, you better have one of the boys ride up to Hallock and tell him to get himself back here."

"Good idea, Mister Randal. It come to my own mind."

"Send Sam Wadley. He damn well ought to know where to find 'em."

"First thing tomorrow morning."

"No, goddamn it, Art, *now*."

"All right, Mister Randal, I'll do that little thing." Art hurried out of the house. He was careful to shut the door behind him.

When Cospatrick had gone, Percy started to pace. "I can't get it through my head, Hattie," he said to his wife. "I swear I can't get it through my head at all."

Ellen Lacy, the lodestone, the lodestar, the paragon of women, who had been clasping her hands until the knuckles were ivory ever since Drury Wynward left, rose stoically to her feet, her breast heaving in a long sigh. "I guess I'd like to go to bed, if I might," she said. "I don't feel very well. I don't know what's the matter."

"Ann, dear," Harriet Randal said, "show Mrs. Lacy up to a spare room, please." She did not look at Ellen.

"Yes, Mother." Ann got up from her chair. "It's time to look in on Simon, too." She quietly led Ellen through the hallway door and up the staircase.

Percy Randal wandered over to the window Art Cospatrick had left and stared bleakly out at the night. Pax, meanwhile, found himself stuck, like some insect specimen, upon the steel pin of his mother's eyes. Harriet Randal's face was drained of emotion and her whole body was motionless as a statue; this vacant rigidity made Pax uncomfortable. "I don't care *what* you're thinking, Mother," he said. "I only did what anybody else would've done. You said so yourself. I heard you."

"Nobody's blaming anything on you, Pax Randal," she said, her body itself still frozen, and only her mouth moving. "*Nobody*. But whatever's been done can't be undone without a lot more grief."

"Well, by God, if they want grief, we'll give it to 'em," Pax said. "We *will* dam the Tines, by God!"

Percy Randal spun around from the window. "Shut your fool mouth, boy!" he said.

"Shut *my* fool mouth?" Pax cried. "You'd better shut Mark *Lacy's* fool mouth, going around saying we stole his goddamned wife."

"She's *here*, ain't she?" Randal demanded.

"Just because it happened to turn out that way," Pax said. "Why, if—if Drury *Wynward*, even, had come by the Lacy place when I did, why, by God, she'd probably be in his parlor right now."

"But she's not at Drury's, she's under *my* roof. And *we're* the ones Mark said was fixing to carry her off. And folks aren't going to believe it just *happened* that way."

"I don't give a damn *what* they believe, you hear? I don't give a single goddamn."

"There's been too much cussing here tonight," said Harriet Randal. "And I never yet have liked such talk. But *I* do, I *do* very much give, as you say, a goddamn, and *there*, it's out, and I'm glad. I don't know why, or how, all this trouble has come on us, but it surely does make us look to be in the wrong, and it puts us in *such* a bad, shameful light—"

"Hattie dear, don't you mind, dear heart," said Percy Randal gently. "Everything'll straighten itself out, the way it always has."

"Ah, I hope so, Perce," she said with a sigh, "I really do hope so. But so *much*, all at once. It's a far cry from Sunday."

"It *is* that," said Percy Randal. "A mighty far cry from Sunday. I wish to God Hallock was here."

"Ah, yes, yes, Hallock," said Harriet Randal. "Sometimes I wonder what the world's coming to."

Then she jumped, startled, as a coarse laugh leaped from the corner. Cora, whose presence they all had forgotten, came from the shadows and moved palely into the light. "The world's coming to a head, that's what it's coming to," she said in a fierce whisper. "I know it, and you know it, too, but you stand there and you don't dare move, because you can't run away from what's coming."

"Cora, goddamn you, be quiet!" Percy Randal cried.

His daughter shook her head so furiously that the rough black hair tumbled down around her shoulders. "It was there last Sunday for all of you to see," she hissed, "but not a one of you saw it, because none of you wanted to see it. And it was up in the mountains, too, and it was out there crawling around in the dirt by the stable, and the sound of it was over our heads, but none of you would listen, so none of you ever knew. And it's upstairs now, getting ready to go to bed, and readying *all* our beds for us, because you wouldn't drive it out into the night, and my dear brother Pax out with it, and in the morning it'll start to drive you, every last one out, all on fire, the lot of you, and you'll be driven, driven, *driven*—!"

"God *damn* you, Cora, you dirty bitch!" Pax shouted.

He moved close, then gave her a backhander against the face that sent her in staggering retreat against the hallway door jamb. She ignored the blood that began to run from her nose, and, stretching forth her neck, she fixed her brimming eyes on her brother. "Oh, I'm the *last*, Pax Randal," she spat at him. "I'm the last human being you'll use your hands on *that* way. And I'll see you drowned in your *blood*, Pax Randal, just the way I've always seen you, ever since you—"

"*Cora!*" Pax screamed like someone on the rack.

His sister broke off, breathing heavily. "Oh, *my*," she said. The words were pitched very low, and came out in her own voice. "Oh, my," she said again. Then she circled around the door jamb and disappeared into the darkness beyond, nor did her father nor her mother nor her brother hear her feet mount up the stairs.

Pax's face had gone corpse white, and his mother was gnawing her lower lip.

"My God," Percy Randal said brokenly, "what did we bring forth *that* day?" Sweat ran down his face and dripped on his shirt.

Percy Randal's night was a troubled one; it was near dawn before sleep took him.

He did not wake until the sun was well up, and even then he only managed to fight his way through into consciousness because he seemed to hear the sound of a wheeled vehicle somewhere near the ranch house. But when he rose and went to the near window, he saw nothing except the long shadows cast by the early sun.

Harriet Randal, pallid and spent, slept on and ignored the morning noises. Her husband dressed quickly and quietly, went downstairs uncombed and unwashed, let himself out of the house, and headed down the knoll toward the stable.

He had nearly reached its gaping doors when he saw Sam Wadley come out. Percy Randal stopped in his tracks. "What're *you* doing here, Sam?" he demanded.

Sam leered at him sleepily. "Aw, morning, Mister Randal," he said. "Doing as little as I can, I reckon."

Percy Randal frowned and set his jaw. "Look here, now, didn't Art Cospatrick set you off to the Marias last night, around nine, ten o'clock?"

Sam Wadley's bewilderment was sincere. "Art Cospatrick? Hell, *no*, Mister Randal, I ain't seen Art since, let's see, oh, yesterday afternoon sometime. And if he was fixing to send me back up there in the Marias, I'm plumb glad I missed him, and *that's* the truth."

"Sam, by God, if you're lying to me, I swear I'll—"

"So help me Aunt Susie, Mister Randal, I ain't seen Art since—"

But Sam Wadley was already talking to a retreating back.

His face a fixed mask of rage, Percy Randal hurried past the far corral to a neat shack near the bunkhouse, a place which, both by right of seniority and his position as foreman, was Art Cospatrick's, and which he shared with his son, Drew.

When Percy Randal reached the little house he threw the door open and stomped inside. "God *damn* you to hell, Cospatrick—!" he began.

But he could have saved his breath.

The single room that the shack contained was not only empty of Art and Drew Cospatrick, but empty of all their belongings as well. For, as Percy Randal seethed by their deserted beds, the Cospatricks, father and son, were already four long hours away from the trouble that Art had seen coming and feared, four hours north and riding hard.

CHAPTER 11

THE LACYS came up with *something*, sure enough, just as Drury had told Percy Randal they would.

In point of fact, they had drafted a plan even before they left Smiley's place. The four of them—Mark and Alan, Drury and Nelse—had remained at the same scarred table for nearly two hours after Charley Samuels had exploded his bombshell above their heads. But now Mark was no longer ranting, nor were the others chafing him in disbelief. What they at last decided to do, after threshing the matter out between them, was simple in the extreme.

Since Mark had been so stunningly right in assuming that the Randal clan was showing an undue interest in his wife, therefore his assumption of what was being done in secret, far up the slopes of the Marias, was equally correct. There remained, however, some confusion as to the way the Randals were going about things. According to Nelse Macleod, one stream, or even both, might be slowed temporarily high up in the mountains, but actually to dam them was a problem that could only be solved in a place where the blocked and backed-up waters would have an area wide and hollow and deep enough to let them form a lake of substantial size. This would have to be done where the land was fairly level, and it certainly could not be achieved above the foothills of the Marias. It seemed to Nelse Macleod as, with half-closed eyes, he unrolled in his mind the panorama of the Randal ranch, that if *he* were set on drying up the river, he couldn't think of a handier spot in which to bring off the job than Juncture Valley, where, less than a half-mile above the point where the Tines met and merged as the Forkhandle, the earth was so configured along each stream as to make the construction of two temporary dams a fairly easy thing.

They decided, though, that guessing got them nowhere. The damming of the Tines had to be stopped before it was too late; but the only sure way to find out where the damming was being done would be to get a slew of men together, ride across the Randal land, locate the dams, and, if Percy Randal still wouldn't listen to reason, destroy the obstructions out of hand.

The matter of Ellen Lacy's defection could, in the meantime, wait.

This dam-wrecking project, when struck, gave off a hard ring of illegality. Trespassing always had been a touchy, if not downright dangerous business; and, although none of them thought any real violence would result, they decided that when they crossed into Randal territory they ought to have at least as many men, armed and ready for trouble, should any trouble arise, as Percy Randal himself could muster, or, and better, many men more.

After an offhand enumeration, they agreed that Randal could oppose them with at least thirty men, including his own sons. As to their own forces, Nelse said he could supply a baker's dozen, Mark and Drury could each bring four, and Alan could call on seven. These, along with the ranch-owners themselves, made a total of thirty-two riders. As this seemed an insufficient number, it looked as though they had better ask Jock Menzies and Oliver Swindon to join them. That would certainly mean another eight or ten men, and the scales would be tipped the way they wanted.

Their design had been advanced to this point when Terry Sykes returned to Smiley's for his nightly tot of whisky. Silent, sour-faced and ignored, he sidled down the bar to the rear table, just in time to hear Mark once again bemoaning the absence of Arch Eastmere, in view of how valuable Arch could have been to their cause. Then Mark, becoming aware of the pallid, hateful

listener, and remembering Terry's bitterness when he spoke of
Hallock Randal, made a recruit of the wretch over the numb dis-
approval of his companions. After that Nelse and Drury and
Alan talked among themselves in desultory monosyllables, as
though Mark and Sykes were not there, until the latter, the chill
of their distaste finally seeping through his pale hide, sneered at
the ceiling, spat on the floor, gulped down his whisky, and left.
Mark Lacy, by now rather shamefaced at having drawn Sykes in
with them, came up with the idea that they all ride out to his
place where, undisturbed, they could work out more details of
their plan.

It was then that Nelse Macleod, perhaps upset by the inclu-
sion of Sykes, perhaps because some spark of conciliation still
lingered on in his heart, suggested that, while the other three
stopped at Mark's ranch, Drury should continue on to the Randals', on the slim chance that they might let him bring Ellen back
with him, or on the slimmer chance that she might be able to
leave of her own volition. To this idea, oddly, Mark made no
protest.

Drury, of course, had gone to the Randals'; and Drury, of
course, had returned empty-handed. So the four men agreed that
the fat was now in the fire and, after catching a few hours' sleep,
they began to translate talk into action. And thus it was that, even
before Percy Randal came out of his house to find his foreman
gone, Alan and Nelse and Mark and Drury were loping across
Mark Lacy's land, on their way to recruit Jock Menzies.

When they came upon Jock, he was shoeing a horse, for he enjoyed the noise and glow and sheer muscle of blacksmithing, keeping his own small forge off to one side of his stable. They waited
while the big, engrossed man, his naked torso reflecting with its
own sweat the long rays of the morning sun, happily clanged the
last nail home and dropped the new-shod hoof. When he saw his
four friends watching him Jock showed no surprise. He grinned
broadly at them, swept a forearm the size of most men's thighs
across his forehead, and tossed the hammer aside.

"You know," he said, moving out of the forge, "sometimes I

wonder if a pretty girl could stand the *noise* of being married to a feller like me."

"Well, now, Jock," said Drury Wynward, "*me,* I'm all the time wondering if she could stand the, well, *hard pounding* of being married to you. And you know, I don't reckon there's many fillies around, could stand all that hammering. Yep, Jock, if you ever marry, it best be to one great big *iron*-gutted girl, or at least two regular-size ones."

That was the last joke anyone made at Jock Menzies's expense that morning, for then Alan Lacy, acting as spokesman, told Jock what had happened, what they all thought was happening, what they intended to do about it, and how much they wanted him with them.

It took an hour of patient persuasion, intermingled with a certain amount of browbeating, before Jock, heavy-hearted over the whole affair, sadly and grudgingly said he would join them, bringing three of his own hands along.

"But you better know right here and right now," he told them with wistful belligerence, "that if it comes to shooting or anything like *that,* I'm pulling me and my boys out. Damn it all, Perce Randal and his whole family's always been nice as pie to me, and whether they're doing what you say they are or not, well, I like 'em just as good as I do you fellers, I guess, and I don't want any more harm to come to 'em than I want to come to myself."

Oliver Swindon, it turned out, was another kettle of fish.

It was nearly noon when the four men reached his place and left their horses at the corral. As they walked up to the ranch house Nell, Swindon's wife, came out on the porch to greet them. She was a rawboned woman, as tall as her husband, with a plain, patient face and straight black hair that had a touch of gray in it, parted in the center and drawn back over both temples into a tight bun. Beside her, possessed of that wide-eyed, pucker-lipped wonder that four-year old boys so well manage, came Thaddeus, her only child.

Her arms folded under her flat breasts, Nell Swindon contemplated the saddle-stained callers. "Stars," she said dryly, "if you all don't look like folks with a purpose." And that was the only greeting she gave them.

"Why, Nell," said Nelse Macleod, scratching himself beneath his beard, "we're the most purposeless fellers you ever did see."

"Then why so many noise tools?" she wanted to know—for both Mark and Drury were wearing their gunbelts.

"Oh, *them*," Drury said with a grin. "Well, I'll tell you, now, Nelly honey—"

"Don't you 'Nelly honey' me, Drury Wynward, you snake," she said in the same level tone.

"Then I'll tell *you*, Mrs. Swindon," Drury went on smoothly, slapping his holster. "We need these here noise tools to protect poor old Nelse from all these jealous women that's breathing down his neck."

"Well, if the old devil's paying you by the head," Nell Swindon said, "I guess you and Mark'll starve to death."

Nelse cackled with pleasure. "Eat themselves sick," he said, "that's what they'll do."

"Truth is, Nell," Alan told her, "we come to see Oliver."

"Truth is, Alan," said Nell, "poor Ollie's in bed."

"Not *sick?*" Mark asked.

"His legs're giving him trouble again. All that damn Yankee iron in 'em."

"He can ride, though, can't he?" Nelse said.

Nell Swindon shrugged. "Not in bed, he can't. No, Nelse, it looks like he can't ride or walk or anything else much, except maybe whine and grunt."

"Well," said Alan, "we can see him, though, I reckon?"

"Don't see why not. Say, now, Mark, Ellen didn't give you a recipe to give me, did she? She told me Sunday she'd see I got it some time this week."

"She didn't mention any recipe to me," Mark said steadily.

"Mark left before she was out of bed, anyways," Drury said cheerfully.

"Well," Nell Swindon said, "I been without that recipe for more than thirty years. A few extra days won't make much difference." She stepped aside to let them enter the house. "I got work in the kitchen, but you all know where the bedroom is. Mind your manners when you go through the parlor."

The four men went to the bedroom, little Thad Swindon trotting along at their heels. Oliver Swindon was sitting up in bed, wearing a cotton nightshirt, his face twisted in pain.

"Thought I heard someone out there," he said. "Howdy."

"By God, Ollie," said Nelse Macleod, with his eyes as sad as a decrepit bloodhound's, "by God, now, I do hate to see you like this, a man at the crown of his years."

"Hate it myself, Nelse," Swindon told him, pulling his mouth down. "Blasted thing hits me every once in a while. Not often like *this*, though. Like to drive me crazy, by George."

"Ever think of having the pieces taken out?" Alan asked.

"Yep," said Oliver Swindon, "just *long* enough to make me change my mind. Blasted doctors'd mess me up even worse, I reckon."

Drury had slumped casually down in the only chair in the room, and Thad Swindon was rubbing his little hands lovingly over the bone-handled butt of Drury's pistol. Drury winked at the child and ruffled his hair. "Mighty fine boy you got, Oliver," he said. "Grows a couple of inches every time I see him. Or maybe *I'm* shrinking, hey?"

"He's worse'n a monkey, way he noses around," Oliver said. He spoke sharply to his son: "Thad, stop messing with that short gun, hear?"

The child had pulled Drury's pistol from its holster and was holding it out in front of him, its muzzle pointed at the bedpost. His thin arms trembled with the weapon's weight. Drury ruffled his hair again, at the same time taking the pistol from his unwilling hands. "So you like guns, hey, old Thad?" he asked.

"Oh, *Thad* likes guns," the little boy said eagerly. "Boom!" He clapped his hands together and laughed.

"Well, judging from the size of you, I figger we're safe for a few years yet," said Drury.

"How long you reckon to stay in bed, Oliver?" Alan wanted to know.

Oliver grimaced with pain. "Hard to say, Alan, mighty hard

to say. This one feels like it'd take a week to work itself off. Yep, a week, easy."

"Ah, that's too bad," Alan Lacy said. "We were kind of hoping you'd give us a hand doing a little something."

"You can tell me what I'm missing, anyway," Oliver said. "A feller can get mighty bored, lying alone in his bed day and night, with nary a single soul to talk to."

"Well, Oliver," Alan began, "this is the way things stand—" And he told him a less simplified version of what he had told Jock Menzies.

When Alan had finished Oliver Swindon looked glumly thoughtful for a spell, then screwed up his face and grunted with pain. After the spasm had passed he relaxed again, brooded a bit more, and sighed heavily. "By George," he said, "I sure wish I was up and about, and that's the truth. You know, I was over to Randals' the other day, after I seen how the river was, and old Perce pulled the wool so far down over my eyes it made my nose itch. Yes, sir, if it wasn't for this Yankee iron acting up like it is, why, I'd take a few of the boys and go along with you all."

"*Would* you now, Oliver?" Nelse Macleod asked, almost petulantly.

"I would indeed, Nelse, I swear," said Oliver. "If I could just get up on my feet, now." He winced, leaned forward painfully, and stroked his right thigh beneath the bedclothes.

"Ah, I know what you're going through, Ollie," said Nelse with great gentleness. "Don't you ever think that I don't. And I sure wouldn't expect a crippled man to—" He broke off and extended his hand toward Drury Wynward. "Say, let's have a look at that gun of yours, Drury," he said.

"Treat 'er gentle, Nelse," said Drury, passing the pistol over. "She's hair-trigger, just like her Paw."

Nelse hefted the weapon, tossing it from hand to hand. "By God, she's a heavy cuss, ain't she?" he said. "Lord, I couldn't even *lift* one of these critters till I was nigh on fourteen years old. That *must* be quite a boy you got there, Oliver."

"Ah, they didn't even *have* guns like that when you were fourteen years old," said Drury.

"In *my* part of the country they did," Nelse said blandly. He smiled through his beard at Thad: "You ever *shoot* one of these great big guns, boy?"

"Oh, no," Thad said, and his eyes started to shine with hope. "But I can. Oh, Thad *can*."

"You can, hey?" Nelse said. "Well, then, Thad Swindon, you just come on outside with me, and we'll fix it so's you can shoot something or someb—"

"*No*, by God, Nelse Macleod!" Oliver roared. "Don't you dare leave that boy go shoot off that pistol. He'll break his damned arms!"

Nelse took Thad Swindon's sweaty little fist. "Now, Ollie," he said, "anybody that's big enough to hold a gun is big enough to shoot it. So you just lie back and rest yourself and be careful of those sore legs you got." He left the bedroom, pistol in one hand, boy in the other.

"*Thad!*" Oliver yelled, sitting bolt upright and trying to see out the bedroom door, "you come *back* here! God *damn* you, Nelse, you leave that boy *be!*"

"I'll get him, Oliver," Mark said. He took a couple of steps toward the door.

"Mark boy," Alan said mildly.

Mark stopped. "It's all right, Alan," he said. "Oliver just wants his—"

"I reckon Nelse knows what he's doing," Alan said. "So you let him be, now."

"Alan, are you *crazy?*" Oliver yelped. "The damned old fool's in his second *childhood*. Drury, please, for *God's* sake, get out there and—"

BOOM! came the thunder of the Navy Colt. And then came a long, tortured wail from Nelse Macleod.

"*Jee*-sus Christ, the kid's *killed* the old bat!" Oliver bellowed. He threw the bedclothes off and, his nightshirt flying up around his buttocks, went galloping high-kneed out of the room.

He hit the open air of the front porch as he might have hit a brick wall, for there was young Thad Swindon doubled over, giggling fit to die—and there was old Nelse Macleod, calmly waving away a pall of powder smoke that hung around his head.

Oliver Swindon opened his mouth to say something, found he had nothing sayable, and then forgot to shut his mouth again. Meanwhile the Lacy brothers and Drury came out on the porch and flanked him.

"Oh, you're a *cute* one, Oliver, sure enough," Nelse said, and he winked at Alan Lacy. "But I'm a cute one, too, and besides that I got nigh on thirty years on you. I take it you get my drift, Oliver."

Swindon shook his head dumbly.

"Well, then, when I come in here," said Nelse, gesturing at the corral, "I happened to take a look at that mare of yours out of the corner of my eye. Why, Oliver, she was plumb *dripping* with sweat. I bet, now, that you ain't been back from town, *and* in that sickbed, much more than half, three quarters of an hour."

"Ah, *you* old bastard," muttered Oliver Swindon. His eyes shone with admiration.

Nell Swindon came out on the porch. "What've you fools been doing out here?" she demanded. "Who's been making all this noise, and me with a cake in the oven?"

"I been curing your husband's sickness," said Nelse Macleod. "Got him right up out of bed, good as new."

Nell Swindon studied the gun in Nelse's hand and then surveyed her husband. "Stars, Ollie," she said, "you *must* be getting old, letting them catch you that way. I told you it wouldn't do any good, but you wouldn't listen. Oh, no." She grabbed her son by the upper arm. "Now, you come with me, Thad Swindon," she said, pulling him back into the house, "before you start picking up bad habits. All it takes is ten minutes of watching your father."

"Well, Oliver, since you're up on your feet," Alan said, "I reckon we can deal you in, hey?"

"I don't cotton to what you all're up to, Alan."

"Nobody does," said Alan. "But you swore."

"I know it," Oliver said. "And, goddamn it, I'm dealt in. But I don't have to like it, do I? Why do you all think I got in my bed?"

"Tell me, Oliver," Drury said. "I sure would like to know."

"Because I went into town first thing this morning," said Oliver. "To the bank. And you know who told me what was going on, what all you fellers was up to? Darius Oliphant, that's who told me. And he had it down pretty pat, too, by George."

Nelse Macleod tugged at his beard. "How'd old Darius get wind of it?

"From Smiley Brann, who else?" said Oliver. "He didn't say, but I could put two and two together."

"If Oliphant knows, then it's all over town," said Mark.

"Don't matter," Alan said.

"The hell it don't," exclaimed Oliver Swindon. "Next thing you know, J. O. Macleod'll be paying us *all* a visit. This ain't what you might call *legal*."

"Neither's what *they're* doing legal," Mark said gruffly.

"Just don't pay no mind to J. O. Macleod," said Nelse. "*I'll* take care of J. O. Macleod."

"But if you wanted somebody else," Oliver said, "why'd you have to come to me? Why the hell didn't you call on Arch Eastmere?"

"Because Arch Eastmere's in Mexico," Alan said, with a quick glance at his brother.

"*Arch Eastmere*," said Oliver, emphasizing every word, "*is right here in town*. Yep, that's right, so don't you all stare so. I saw him and Pace Gray going down the Divide road when I was on my way back here."

"You *sure*, Ollie?" Old Nelse was rubbing one side of his beard.

"Listen, Nelse, God couldn't make two people to look like that. It's been maybe three years since I seen Arch, but I couldn't make any mistake. A big, high-arsed, mean-eyed son of a bitch, sitting straddled across the fanciest silver greaser saddle I ever set eyes on. And riding down the road with the Gray kid. Arch *Eastmere*, by God!"

"Well, now, Mark boy," said Alan Lacy, smiling and slapping his brother on the shoulder, "*that's* what you've been begging for. That makes everything fine, just *fine*."

Mark Lacy felt his heart beating faster. But somehow, he knew, it wasn't from joy.

CHAPTER 12

WHEN Miss Dorrie Pace forgot her knitting, she killed a dozen men. Of such is the Kingdom of Indirect Causes.

The Misses Pace, along with their nephew Pace Gray, who had made the arrangements earlier, had spent Saturday and Sunday nights in two rooms at the Dundee Hotel, on their way to and from the blowout for Luke Randal. They did not do this because of the distance they lived from Eastmere, for a leisurely three-hour drive was all it took to reach their cool, shaded house, lying well off the road to Divide in a bend of the Forkhandle River. But the reclusive maiden ladies needed some kind of conditioning area in which to steady each other before the Randal party, and to which they might withdraw and unwind after the nervous excitements that were certain to be engendered by the sight of so many people.

A trip to Eastmere was, to the Misses Dorrie and Sallie Pace, what a voyage around the world would have been to an ordinary woman. Very seldom these days did they make excursions outside themselves and the remembered past that was slowly immuring them. Sunday, as a matter of fact, had been the first time they had seen Luke Randal since the week after he had been born.

Much to their surprise, they had enjoyed the outing immensely. Their pleasure had been so great, indeed, that, full of an unabated high animation, they had spent most of Sunday night without sleep, lying on the big bed in the Dundee and chattering to each other in the dark. And on Monday morning, when they left for home with Pace, they were still so flustered that Miss Dorrie failed to notice that her knitting had fallen from the commode on which she had, half thinking, placed it, and had rolled under the bed.

Pace, who lived most of the time in Eastmere, boarding with a family named Potter, on his aunts' sufferance and money, had been ordered to spend a week with the Misses Pace, which to him was the same as a prison sentence, because the two ladies had smelled liquor on his breath after he had helped to drain the bottle in the Randal barn. He sulked around the house on Monday after they all had returned, and he spent most of Tuesday lying on his belly on the bank of the Forkhandle, roasting his soul in the hell of being but nineteen years old. He had seen that the river was low, but he was much too busy brooding on his own bitter torments to pay any mind to a level of water.

Then, on Tuesday night, which was the first time since the party that she felt sufficiently calm to take up the blue shawl she was knitting where she had left off, Miss Dorrie discovered the shawl was gone. The last place she and Miss Sallie remembered seeing it was, they were sure, on the commode in their room at the Dundee. There was nothing they could do, then, but send Pace back to the hotel in the morning to pick it up.

At the same time, he could return the rented surrey to Terry Sykes's livery stable. The Misses Pace had long since sold their father's old surrey and buckboard, as well as the horses he'd had, and on the few occasions they left their house, they had always gone in rigs that were rented from Sykes, which Pace had driven down to them.

Young Pace Gray, of course, was pleased as Punch at this happy accident. On Wednesday morning he was off before sunup, driving the surrey, with his own horse tied on behind. He reached Eastmere before eight o'clock, going directly to the livery stable.

Sykes, pale and cadaverous, was there alone. For some reason,

he seemed to be happy, with his mouth twisted awry in the inhuman expression that meant all was well in the world of Terry
Sykes. He kept his own counsel, however, while he checked the
condition of the horse and surrey. Then, after Pace had paid
him and was on the point of mounting his own horse, Sykes said:
"I suppose *you're* in with 'em, too, a hard younker like you are."

As Sunday's encounter with Sykes was still an acrid memory,
Pace had not wanted any talk with him, except on what was owed
for the rig; but the enforced restlessness of the past two days was
a memory even more acrid, so he found himself curious enough
to ask: "In with who?"

"Why, the Lacy boys. Everybody else around is, I reckon.
Why, the way they're talking, damn 'em, they might even send
all the way down to Mexico and get Arch Eastmere back here, if
the greasers ain't killed him by now, that is. That's how bad they
want him."

"Ah, get off Arch, you old puke. The way they're talking
about *what?*"

"Fixing Hallock Randal's wagon, that's what. Taking care of
all them goddamned Randals, by God."

"Sykes, you're plumb out of your old dead head. The Randals're the biggest people around these parts. And the finest people, too." Pace swung into his saddle. "There's men around here
that'll bust your jaw, they hear you talking that way about the
Randals."

"Not since the river went down, by God, they won't."

"What about the river?"

"It's down, ain't it?"

Pace thought for a moment. "Yep," he nodded. "Reckon it is."

"And how do you reckon it *got* so down, hey?" Sykes crowed.

Pace threw one leg over the pommel and jumped from his
horse. "Suppose you just take a little minute," he said, "and *tell*
me how it got so damned down. I got plenty of time to listen."

His fine-boned face was perfectly composed when, twenty minutes later, Pace Gray entered the lobby of the Dundee Hotel,
even though what he had heard from Terry Sykes was making
his brain seethe and bubble.

Arthur Brill, at the desk, handed over Miss Dorrie's knitting; he had been holding it, sure that young Pace would be sent after it as soon as the loss was discovered. But when Pace asked him, mysteriously, "You know anything about it, Mister Brill, what's happened to the river?" Arthur Brill, secretive for once, would say only: "See Alan Lacy. He's the feller that's going to put things right."

Pace stood at the desk for a moment, thinking. The best thing for him to do, he decided, would be to ride to Alan Lacy's and get the whole story straight from the horse's mouth. He still wasn't sure of the whys and wherefores of the action that was being taken, but it sounded like a hell of a lot of fun, and he was nigh crazy for something to do. And, since he was going out to Alan Lacy's, he couldn't rightly say when he'd be seeing his aunts again, and so the Misses Pace, since they wouldn't be able to smell his breath, couldn't rightly say whether or not he'd had some drinking-liquor. Which was exactly what he intended to have. He made a beeline for the barroom, the half-finished shawl dangling out of Miss Dorrie Pace's knitting-bag.

Doctor Phil Hyssop was taking his time over a glass of beer while he waited for the arrival of the nine-o'clock stage. He waved Pace over beside him.

"Morning, Doc," Pace said. "How's Mrs. Hyssop? Better, I hope."

"She'll live," said Phil Hyssop. "They always do."

"Shot of rye, Lige," Pace said to the bartender.

"I've got a message for you, Pace," Doctor Hyssop said, lowering his voice as the bartender moved away. "If you want to see Arch Eastmere, you'll find him down to Maude Fletcher's."

Pace's eyes grew round with astonishment. "Arch *East*—?" he started to say.

Hyssop cut him off with an upraised hand. Then, satisfied that Lige hadn't heard, he went on, in an even lower tone. "Nobody's supposed to know it," he said. "He told me, just tell—"

But Pace was already running out of the bar. "Pour it back in the bottle, Lige," he called over his shoulder to the bartender as he burst out through the swinging doors.

"I be dogged," said the gaping Lige. "Damned young flea-britches."

Seconds later Doctor Phil Hyssop, staring down at his beer, heard Pace's horse galloping off. *Damned young flea-britches* is right, he thought; didn't even ask me how I happened to know Arch was back.

"Archie, damn you, big old catamountain, it's all wonderful, the best there is, even if you don't do nothing but hold me, but we got to live and you know it, know it as well as you know your damned name. I'll take care of you, Archie, till they start burning haloes in hell, but goddamn you, oh, Archie honey, with you here there's no money coming in, and nobody lived on love yet, without no money at all. But I couldn't and wouldn't work with you around, old Archie-cat, I love you so, not for all the goddamned rice in China, and a dozen rats thrown in."

"I'll get some money, Maudie honey, don't you go fretting about it."

"What'll you do, damn you, old tall wildcat, not sell your new silver saddle, you won't sell that, will you, Archie?"

"No, not that, Maudie, not my new silver-mounted saddle. But we'll make out, don't you worry. I always have and I always will. Something always happened just in time. One day the cards'll be dealt just right."

Arch Eastmere lay on the dirty, unmade bed with his hard eyes closed and his big feet bare. He wore nothing but his shirt and trousers, and his huge hands were locked behind his head. Maude Fletcher, curled up naked beside him, had her own head resting on his belly.

"Next feller that comes around, damn you, Archie, I just don't know what to tell him."

"Tell him to scoot, Maudie honey, and any other fellers the same, no matter how many come by. I reckon I'll never come down to that."

"Down to what, Archie, down to *what*, honey?"

"Living off *you*, little Maudie. I'll ride into town one of these fine days, see who's alive and who ain't. We don't figger to starve this week, now, do we?"

"Not from love, you old high-haunch, ah, I missed those big

long legs of yours, goddamn it, I *did* miss those long old legs, Archie honey."

"Maudie?"

"Ummm?"

Arch Eastmere sat up, displacing her. "Somebody's heading this way."

A hard-ridden horse was coming closer. Arch Eastmere swung off the bed in an easy motion and went to the open window, pressing himself along the wall next to it and peering cautiously out. Maude Fletcher scrambled to her feet and fluttered over beside him. "Nobody ever comes here in the mornings, Archie, never in all these years, goddamn it, can you see who it is, Archie honey?"

"Not yet, little Maudie." He chuckled, and the tenseness went out of him. "I can *now*, though," he said. "It's my hoss, Pace Gray."

"Oh, Lord, Archie, I better get myself dressed, with him so young and all."

"I reckon you better, Maudie honey."

But Arch Eastmere went out on the porch as he was, still in his bare feet. And if his eyes remained hard when he greeted Pace Gray, well, it wasn't Arch Eastmere's fault. They were, after all, the eyes he was born with, and the only eyes he had.

At half past ten that morning Arch Eastmere and eager young Pace sat on an old feed bin in the shed that had once served Maude Fletcher for a stable. The place was filled mainly with dust and clutter, and Arch's gleaming saddle stood out like a sore silver thumb in the littered shade; but Pace Gray had blurted out all he had learned from Terry Sykes about the trouble between Mark Lacy and the Randals, and now the two had more on their minds than Mexican silverwork.

"We'll go together, won't we, Arch? You and me."

"You mean, over to Alan Lacy's?"

"First there, then up in the Marias with the rest of 'em."

"No, old hoss, I reckon not."

"Ah, now, Arch, *why* not, for God's sake? Damn it, a man like you—"

"Seems to me, Pace, you talked a little more polite before I went down into Mexico."

"I reckon I do cuss a lot, Arch. Sorry."

"I never cottoned to cussing much, Pace. It's so easy, everybody does it. So the feller that don't use swearwords, well, he's got a leg on everybody else, way I look at it."

"I didn't use to, Arch, and you know it. I must've got careless, with you gone so long."

"If ever I had me a boy of my own, he'd no more go around cussing than I would."

"You got *me*, Arch."

"Well, now, looks like you're about as close to the real thing as I'll ever get." With a smile, Arch gently pushed his closed fist against Pace Gray's jaw. "So you do what the old man tells you, hear?"

"All right, Arch, I will—but why won't you do what *I* want, too?" Pace spoke plaintively. "We'll have a lot of fun up in the Marias, and nobody'll get hurt."

"Somebody always gets hurt," Arch said.

"Ah, there won't be any shooting."

"Feller can get hurt without being shot," said Arch Eastmere. "Or without a hand being laid on him, even."

"How?"

"You'll find out someday," Arch said. "And I hope I'm not there," he added coldly, "for both our sakes, yours and mine, too."

"But I won't *this* time, Arch. Aw, now, is *that* the only reason you don't want to go?"

"There's plenty of reasons I don't want to go. One is, I got nothing against the Randals and never did have. Another one is, I don't own a spread around here, so I don't give a hang what happens to the Forkhandle. And another one is, no wife of mine went and run off, and I don't see no cause why I got to wash Mark Lacy's dirty bedclothes for him."

"He helped *you*, Arch, and you can't deny it. He lent you that money, didn't he?"

"He did, hoss. And I'll pay him back."

"He'd like it if you did him this favor, Arch."

"Reckon he would. And I also reckon I won't be doing it for him."

"How about for *me*, then?"

"Not even for you, hoss."

Pace looked unhappily at Arch, hung his head for a moment, then pushed himself off the feed bin and started out of the shed.

"Pace, where you off to?"

The boy stopped, hesitated, then turned around slowly. "Don't rightly know, Arch."

"You come back here, hoss."

Taking his time, avoiding Arch's gaze, Pace shuffled back to the feed bin. "Never figgered you was a man to avoid trouble," he said sullenly.

"Thought you said there wouldn't be any trouble?"

"There wouldn't be, if you come along."

"Pace, my own trouble is, once I get into a thing, I'm like to get in it 'way over my head."

"But these fellers won't be looking for trouble, Arch. They just want to, well, set things right, you know."

"Listen, hoss, you know I've been in trouble once or twice, don't you?"

"I reckon so," Pace Gray said, "and more than just once or twice, too. And every time it was hard lines on the other feller."

"Not just *him*, hoss. But it weren't *my* fault, ever, you hear? I never went *looking* for trouble, any more than the Lacys and the rest of 'em'll be *looking* for trouble. And I don't want you to go thinking that's the way I am. Why, half the time trouble's blocking the street, when all a man wants is to walk along quiet." Then, as Pace, standing there with his jaw sunk down in his neck, seemed to be growing more and more glum, Arch Eastmere became conciliatory: "Aw, now, look, old hoss, another reason is, I don't want nobody to know I'm around these parts just yet."

"Doc Hyssop knows you're around, Arch."

"I just chanced to run into Hyssop along the road. And I said for him only to tell *you* I was back."

"He'll go and tell somebody else."

"I reckon he won't."

"You wait, Arch, you wait and see. He'll be in Smiley's drinking whisky and the Lacys'll come in, and they'll say: 'Ah, we sure wish Arch Eastmere was around,' and Doc Hyssop'll say: 'Why, he's down to Maudie Fletcher's, that's where you'll find Arch Eastmere,' and the next thing you know there'll be eight or ten of 'em down here, just begging you to come along and give 'em a hand."

"Now, why should Phil Hyssop do a thing like that, Pace?"

"I don't know," Pace said. "But anyway, for all you can tell, maybe somebody else seen you when you didn't see them, and they'll pass the word on to Mark and the rest."

"I don't reckon I was spotted coming in, old hoss."

"*I* might tell 'em, even." Pace raised defiant eyes to Arch, whose only reply was a gentle smile. Pace found himself smiling back. "Naw, Arch, you know I wouldn't do that," he said with a shake of his head. "Not something you didn't want me to."

"I don't know much, but that's one of the things," Arch told him. Then his smile faded. "The truth of it is, Pace," he went on, "and this is the *pure* truth—I'm feeling mighty done in these days. I had two hard years in Mexico, and a lot of things went on there, and now I'm plumb tuckered out. I need some quiet, and I got to get my bearings back, before I can do much of anything."

Pace was immediately sympathetic. "Ah, I never thought of that, Arch. Reckon I ought to've known."

"No reason for you to. You don't know what it's like down in Mexico."

"Maybe we can go there sometime, Arch. You and me, together."

"Not for a while yet," said Arch with unusual harshness. Then he lightened his voice: "Why, I plumb forgot to ask you, old hoss. How's Miss Dorrie and Miss Sallie?"

"Pretty fair, Arch. They went to that Randal party last Sunday."

"*Did* they, now? That's right nice to hear."

"Don't mean much at all, Arch. The two of 'em act the queerer every blessed time I see 'em."

"Living way back *there*, hey? In the old times?"

"That's about the size of it. With dead folks, mostly."

"They ever talk about me?"

"You know, now, they *do*. Talk a lot about you, come to think of it."

"*Do* they, now?" Arch Eastmere actually blushed. "Why, I don't think I've laid eyes on those two fine ladies in, oh, ten years, easy."

"Neither's anybody else, much, and that's a fact."

Arch Eastmere slapped his thigh. "Hoss, I got me an idea. I figger it'd be real nice to ride down and pay 'em a visit. You and me, that is."

"They'd sure like that, Arch. Sometime pretty soon."

"Naw, hoss, right now. Soon's we saddle up."

"Uh—what about Maudie?" Pace was taken aback, but he knew he was beaten.

"Little Maudie can always get along. So how about it, old hoss?" Arch rested his hand on Pace's shoulder.

"Sure, Arch," Pace said, and he brightened. "Long as it's you and me, together."

"Wouldn't have it any other way," Arch said. He got off the feed bin. "Tell you what," he went on, "you saddle my horse, and I'll go see Maudie."

"I'll do that little thing, Arch." Pace went over to the silver-mounted saddle and hefted it. "Sure weighs a ton. Can I use it sometime?"

"Sure. Some dark night instead of a lantern."

"You buy it, Arch, or win it?"

"I got it dirt cheap, old hoss," said Arch Eastmere, "from a feller that all of a sudden went bankrupt. Señor Ugalde, his name was. Lived in Chihuahua, the Señor did."

Like some great prowling cat, he padded out of the shed.

The Misses Pace liked to eat supper early and then sit in twin rocking-chairs out on the porch, watching the shadows of late afternoon double and triple their length. Nor, at the close of this fine day, did they make any change in their usual custom, even though Pace had returned with Arch Eastmere. As the four of them sat on the unpainted porch, watching the sun surrender to a curtain of aspen and spruce, Arch Eastmere found only contentment in the fact that a man who, in certain quarters, was considered too savage to live, should be sitting with two timid, aging spinsters and a boy not yet full grown.

Arch was relaxed and comfortable, and more completely himself than he had been in a long time. A mission Indian couple even older than the ladies worked for the Misses Pace; and, while Arch watched old John scything some high grass along the crown of the seldom-used road, he could hear a casual rattle of dishes inside the house as old Flora cleared the table.

The tall man closed his hard, cold eyes and sighed. He felt *safe* in this place, too—safe from a number of things. The Lacys might well have tracked him down, back there at Maudie Fletcher's, but they'd never find him in this backwater. And, while he was gone, little Maudie just might pick herself up a piece of change, if she had a mind to. It was none of Arch Eastmere's business what she did, as long as he wasn't hanging around her place, like one of those Mexican fancy men, whatever it was they called them down there, expecting to live off her money. Little Maudie Fletcher's life was her own, as everybody's life was his own—and as, up to a point, was Arch Eastmere's very own life. Now, he guessed, that point had been passed. He now had to live as a nurse to the sick thing that pumped and drove his blood.

But Arch knew he'd done what was right, if, as Phil Hyssop said, he had to take things easy from now on. Ever since he and Pace had arrived, Arch Eastmere found himself removed to a world he had nearly forgotten—the soothing, undisturbed past in which the Misses Pace preferred to live.

There, everything remained frozen and ordered in memory; all the bridges had been crossed, and all the decisions had been made. In that timeless world a man was neither dead nor alive, but whatever the person who called up the past chose to make him; and neither young nor old, but however the person remembering chose to see him. Arch Eastmere, to these soft-voiced, indwelling ladies, was sometimes a babe in arms, sometimes a boy of fourteen, sometimes a man nearly thirty. And the woman who had once been Tessa Acton, who had wept as she closed her eyes

forever on the face of her eight-year-old son, she, pretty Tessa
Acton, who hated to die so young, she was—

"Tessa, I remember, brought you here once to a party, Archie,"
Miss Dorrie Pace was saying. "We used to have, oh, a great many
parties in those days, when you were very young. At this one you
couldn't have been more than— No, I remember exactly, you
were almost eight years old. Do you recall that night your
mother brought you, Archie dear?"

"No, Miss Dorrie," Arch Eastmere said, "I don't. But I sure
wish I did."

"Tessa was so proud of you," said Miss Dorrie. "You could tell
by the way her face lit up. You stood there, cool as a cucumber,
singing a song for us, while we all—"

Pace giggled. Arch looked almost languidly at the boy. "Something funny, Pace?" he drawled.

"Picture of you singing," Pace said. But he stopped his giggling.

"Fact is, there's a pretty good voice in me," said Arch. He
turned to Miss Dorrie: "You recollect the name of the song,
ma'am?"

" 'Bendemeer's Stream,' " Miss Sallie exclaimed.

"That was it," said Miss Dorrie. " 'Bendemeer's Stream,' by
Thomas Moore, and you sang it right through, Archie dear, every
word."

"Reckon I still can," said Arch Eastmere.

"Archie, you *can?*" cried Miss Sallie. "Why, isn't that nice?"

"It was Tessa's favorite song, I know," said Miss Dorrie.

"My mother was the one taught it to me," Arch Eastmere said.
"Want me to sing it again?"

"Oh, yes!" exclaimed Miss Sallie.

"You're very kind, dear Archie," Miss Dorrie said.

Arch glanced over at Pace Gray. "All right with you, old
hoss?" he asked.

Pace nodded, and not a muscle in his face moved. He wasn't
going to giggle again, not if he knew what was good for him.

"I'd mostlike do better in a saddle," said Arch, as he swallowed
twice in quick succession, "but a feller might as well be hanged
for a sheep as a lamb. Here goes.

There's a bower of roses by Bendemeer's stream,
  And the nightingale sings round it all the day long;
  In the time of my childhood 'twas like a sweet dream
    To sit in the roses and hear the bird's song—"

He had a good baritone voice, had hard-eyed Arch Eastmere.
The others listened to him entranced, for he sang the old words as
though they meant much to him. And they did mean a great deal
to him, too, though he wasn't quite sure why they should. But they
flowed from his throat as water from a spring. Even phlegmatic,
half-deaf old John, twenty-five yards down the road, stopped
swinging his scythe and leaned on it to listen, while

"That bower and its music I never forget,
  But oft when alone in the bloom of the year,
  I think—is the nightingale singing there yet?
    Are the roses still bright by the calm Bende-
      meer?—"

poured from the mouth of tall Arch Eastmere.

The Misses Pace, behind their closed lids, retreated completely
to that long-gone, perfumed summer night. Old Flora in fascination came to the door of the house. And, although none of them
realized it then or, in fact, knew it later, they were listening to the
last song Arch Eastmere would ever sing in his life.

"No, the roses soon wither'd that hung o'er the wave,
  But some blossoms were gathered while freshly
    they shone,
  And a dew was distill'd from their flowers, that gave
    All the fragrance of summer, when summer was
      gone—"

And, even as it was, they didn't get to hear this last song
through to the end. For Arch, who had kept his eyes on old John
while he sang, had reached

"Thus memory draws from delight, ere it dies,
  An essence that breathes of it many a year—"

when he suddenly stopped. Pace Gray and his aunts looked at
Arch Eastmere, perplexed, and then, hearing the sound of hooves,

they turned to stare at the five riders whose appearance around a bend in the road had made the singer cease.

Miss Dorrie uttered a cry. "Oh, dear, *more* people," she mewed. "And so *many*, too! My goodness, Sallie, who on earth can they be?"

"And what can they *possibly* want?" said the frightened Miss Sallie.

"I know who they are, Miss Dorrie," said Arch Eastmere quietly.

He knew who they were, all right. Alan Lacy. Mark Lacy. Drury Wynward. Oliver Swindon. Old bearded Nelse Macleod.

And he knew what they wanted, too. Arch Eastmere.

They wanted Arch Eastmere, six feet, three inches tall, forty-two years old, with a sick, unhappy heart hung high in his left breast, and a big old Colt hung low on his right hip. *Especially* they wanted that big old Colt, in the worn holster tied to his thigh.

A man mostly had no say in things, Arch thought. If this was the way the cards had been dealt him, though, he guessed that whoever it was moved him hither and yon wanted him in the game. But, Arch Eastmere said to himself, if the five men hoped he'd sit down at their table, they'd have to make the ante a high one. Yes, sir, if they wanted old catamountain Arch Eastmere bad enough, it would cost them the money he still owed Mark, say, and $100 in gold to boot.

They wanted him bad enough, it turned out. As bad as Miss Dorrie Pace had wanted the knitting she left behind her.

C H A P T E R   1 3

HANNAH MACLEOD may have looked like an overstuffed pillow, but the stuffing consisted of broken crockery, rusty nails, iron filings, and thorns. She had the voice of a randy jack burro and the temper of a starving wolverine.

J. O. Macleod had married her, soul unseen, because she was the first female he'd ever run into who was anything near him in size. He'd also been sorry since the second day of their life together, when, in emphasizing a point she wanted to make, the rosy-fingered Hannah had put a seven-stitch gash in her husband's scalp with the aid of an oil lamp casually swung.

Ever since this bit of conjugal by-production, wedded bliss had become, for J. O. Macleod, an exercise in self-defense, and he had become so adroit a practitioner of the art that he seldom opened his mouth at home except to say: "Yes, Hannah. Yes, love." And, although Eastmere was a singularly law-abiding town, he also made sure that he spent as much time as possible at the jail, which was usually empty of prisoners, playing checkers with Ty Quarton, his deputy, or dozing with his feet up on his roll-top desk.

On Thursday morning Ty went to meet the nine-o'clock stage, returning with a package for Hannah and two letters for J. O.

Macleod. The package was the important thing: it contained a coffee-grinder to replace one that an inaccurate Hannah had heaved at her husband and smashed against the wall, well over three months before. Hardly a day had passed in which Hannah had not bewailed her loss or growled over the slowness of St. Louis merchants; and to see the grinder finally arrive took a big load off the mind of J. O. Macleod.

Stuffing the letters, which, it looked like, were from law officers in El Paso, Texas, and Grant's Pass, eighty miles below Eastmere, in his breast pocket, to be read at his later leisure, J. O. was about to start home with Hannah's package when Ty Quarton said: "Arch Eastmere's back in town."

"*Hell!*" said J. O. automatically. "You talk to him, Ty?"

The deputy shook his head. "Seen him riding by, is all. Him and a lot of other fellers all went in Smiley's."

"What fellers?"

"Well, they was Drury Wynward and Jock Menzies and Ollie Swindon and some of Jock's and Ollie's boys. Your old man, too, with half a dozen of his hands, looked like."

"Paw?"

"Yep. Beard and all."

"I guess it weren't just talk, Ty, all this stuff we been hearing."

"Looks that way, J. O."

"Paw ought to have more sense, the damned old fool. Reckon I'll take me a stroll over to Smiley's, once I get to drop this passel off home." And J. O. went out.

J. O. Macleod never did get to take that stroll over to Smiley's, however, not until nearly a week had passed, when it no longer mattered much, one way or another.

Hannah, to her husband's surprise, showed only annoyance when he brought her the new coffee-grinder. "I could've gotten this thing here from St. Louis sooner," she said, ripping open the package, "if I'd crawled on my hands and knees, pushing it with my nose."

"Yes, love," murmured J. O. Macleod.

"And you'd like to've seen me do *just* that, wouldn't you, you big tub of guts?" Hannah glared at him fiercely.

"No, now, Hannah, love, I sure wouldn't."

She pointed to the letters jutting from his pocket. "We got *more* mail?"

"Just official stuff, love." He pulled them out and glanced again at the envelopes. "Grant's Pass and El Paso."

"Official business?" she snarled. "And you don't even bother to *open* 'em to see what they say? *Some* sheriff, you are."

"They're probably just circulars, love. That's what I most always get."

"You won't know *what* they are till you *look*, will you? Here, give *me* one of those things—" She snatched away the letter from Grant's Pass and tore it open. "*This* don't happen to be any circular, Mister Gassy-Guts," she said, reading it through quickly. "It happens to tell you they think they got the man that robbed the Denver stage just west of town eighteen months ago, and they want you to come take a look at him."

"Billy Weltz?"

"This man calls himself Webber, but they reckon he's Billy Weltz. *That's* a circular for you, Mister John Law." She threw the letter down on the table by the new coffee-grinder. "Come on, what's the other one say?"

J. O. Macleod opened the El Paso envelope with great care, as though he feared it might crumble to dust in his huge clumsy hands. Then, unfolding the sheet of paper, he read what it contained very slowly and deliberately, moving his lips the while. As he scanned line after line a frown spread over his face and deepened, and at last his lips were pressed tightly together and did not form words at all.

"Well, what's it *say?*" Hannah demanded loudly.

He kept his eyes on the letter, in spite of the danger involved. "I'm not through it yet, love," he said.

This was all the fuze that was needed to blow buxom Hannah sky high. "But I'm your own *wife!*" she howled. "And you got no business keeping inform—" She checked herself and whirled suddenly on Nelse Macleod, who at that moment was coming through the kitchen door. "Now, what are *you* up to, Paw, pussy-footing around here and scaring folks out of their skins?"

"Glad somebody *can* scare you, by God," Nelse said mildly.

"Howdy, Paw," said J. O., glancing quickly up from the letter.

Old Nelse ignored his son and went over to the table. "Finally got a new grinder, hey?" he said to Hannah, who was mottled with rage and breathing heavily. "Well, let's see if you can keep *this* one on the table, where it belongs."

"Let's see if *you* can teach your big fat stupid son some manners!" his daughter-in-law spat at him.

"I don't feel like bandying words with you this morning, Hannah," Nelse said through bared yellow teeth. "But if I did, I'd say don't go blaming my boy, because it ain't his fault. You know what they say—if you lie down with dogs, you rise up with fleas. That's the thing J. O.'s faced—"

"Damn you, Paw, you calling me a *dog?*" Hannah screamed.

To the astonishment of J. O., Nelse Macleod strode over to Hannah and shoved his face against hers. "I'll call you worse'n that, you ten-cent slut," he roared, "if you don't keep quiet, by God! I come here to have words with J. O., and *nobody* else, and if I can't have 'em in peace, you mean pig-eyed bitch, I'll truss up your tongue with your own skirts, hear? Now *shut* your goddamned mouth, before you find out to your sorrow that Nelse Macleod ain't funning!"

The mouth of Hannah, which had been startled open by the unexpected assault, promptly closed with a snap. "Always thought a woman had a right to—" she began to mutter.

"*You* ain't got no rights at *all*, God blast you. Go on and get out of this kitchen. *Scat!*"

The resistible mass that was Hannah Macleod lumbered obediently into the living-room, slamming the door behind her in one final and futile gesture of defiance.

"Maybe you oughtn't've have done that, Paw," J. O. said dubiously.

"Hell, boy," said old Nelse, "you ought to lambaste that woman good, every morning, soon's she gets up."

"Ah, I don't want any more trouble than she gives me," J. O. said.

"Only way to make that kind listen to reason is bat 'em around. Same as mules."

"Well," J. O. said glumly, "with what I heard about this Fork-handle thing, looks like I *got* me more trouble, don't it? And not in my own house, neither."

"Yep, that's what I come over to talk about," Nelse said. "To tell you not to get all het-up. Won't be no trouble at all, boy."

"I been hearing some mighty funny talk, Paw."

"Wouldn't be at all surprised," said Nelse Macleod.

"About a lot of folks taking it on themselves to go riding over Perce Randal's land and maybe mess things up a little."

"Now, that's stretching the truth somewhat, J. O. We just want to see what kind of devilment's going on up the Marias."

"Perce say you could trespass on his land?"

"He ain't said we couldn't."

J. O. Macleod fell silent for a moment, the hand that held the El Paso letter hanging limp at his side. Finally he said, not without effort: "Paw, I reckon I better tell you fellers to leave off what you figger on doing."

Nelse Macleod picked up the letter that Hannah had dropped by the coffee-grinder and casually started to read it. "J. O.," he said, his eyes on the page, "I reckon we'll do what we set out to do."

"I'd hate to have to arrest my own father," J. O. said hesitantly.

"You won't, J. O., you won't," old Nelse said, still reading. He finished the letter and put it back on the table. "Well," he said, "so they finally caught up with that Weltz feller. Never thought they would. Reckon you'll be going down to Grant's Pass, hey?"

"Paw, goddamn it," J. O. exclaimed, "if you all go on Perce's land, like that, I'll have to do something about it."

"Such as, J. O.?"

"Such as—hell, Paw, I *mean* it, now. I'll have to do some arresting."

Nelse Macleod tugged at his beard. "Well, boy, just don't do any of your fancy arresting till we *do* go on Perce's land."

"Well, no, sir, I won't, but—"

"And don't do it *after* we go on Perce's land, neither, hear?"

J. O. rubbed the back of his bull-muscled neck and swallowed in discomfort. "I'm sheriff of Eastmere, Paw. So *please*, Paw, I'm asking you, don't go making things rough for me. Life's hard enough, without my very own father—"

Nelse Macleod cut him short with a wave of the hand. "Son," he said in a dangerously quiet voice, "you got no *idea* how hard your life's going to be if you don't keep out of our hair. By God, if your big brother, Ex, was alive he wouldn't be whining about things being made too rough for him. Not *Ex*, by God."

"If Ex was alive, he wouldn't be sheriff."

"Damned right he wouldn't. He'd own half the country by now. And he'd sure have more gumption than to want to squat down and sport a badge and brag about how he's the sheriff."

"I got gumption enough, Paw, every time I need it."

"Well, goddamn it, J. O., this ain't one of the times. So keep your nose out of our business, or you'll be a sorry boy."

"Paw, I don't take kindly to being threatened, even by you."

"You don't, hey? All right, then, J. O., I'll tell you what I'm likely to do. I'm not making any *threats*, understand? I'm just telling you what I'm likely to *do*. Lately, now, I been giving some mind to what old Black Jack Eastmere went and done—"

J. O. Macleod was shocked. "You mean, *sell* everything, Paw?"

Nelse waggled his beard up and down. "Every inch of land, boy, every head of stock."

"Ah, Paw, listen, if Hannah heard you say that, she'd—"

An unpleasant smile appeared through the old man's whiskers. "*You* listen, son," he broke in. "You don't know it, but you're lucky, because this way you'll be done with Hannah. Because, come fall, you won't be elected sheriff again, that's for sure. And nobody can keep a wife when he's a ranch hand working for somebody else, which is what you'll be, and drawing down all of thirty dollars a month, which is about what you'll be getting. Yep, before many more days've passed, your little Hannah'll have to—to—to go in the *circus*, by God! with the rest of the elephants—"

"Shhh, Paw! Maybe she's listening."

"Good."

"Hell, Paw, you know I want to keep on the good side of you, but they voted me sheriff, and I got this *job*. Especially now that

Arch Eastmere's showed up again and you went and pulled him in with you."

"Oh, you seen Arch when we come into town?"

"Ty seen him. I didn't."

"Arch'll be a right helpful man to have along."

"Now, he won't, Paw. Not now, anyway. Take a look at this." And J. O. handed old Nelse the letter from El Paso.

Nelse read it through with no change of expression:

> *El Paso, Texas*
> June 4, 1879

> J. O. Macleod, *Sheriff*
> Eastmere, Colo.

> SIR:

> On June 2, this year, John P. Rettis, of San Antonio, this State, was mortally wounded during a quarrel with A. A. Eastmere, of Eastmere, Colo., and a man whose name is believed to be Philip Tight, place of birth unknown, who is believed to have been seriously wounded in the same quarrel.

> J. P. Rettis, before he died, asserted the fatal shot was fired by Eastmere, who Rettis had followed here from Mexico, and who is believed to have committed another murder there.

> Eastmere may be known by an expensive silver saddle he rides. When last seen, he and Tight were moving in a northwesterly direction. Should these men be apprehended in your territory, please hold and advise forthwith. Yours, etc.,

> L. M. Conners, *Marshal*
> *El Paso, Texas*

Nelse Macleod carefully folded the letter and gave it back to his son. "Never heard of this Rettis," he said, "but I reckon the other one's Phil Tate. Arch sure does have his troubles now, don't he?"

"I got to pick him up, Paw." J. O. returned both letters to his breast pocket.

"If you try, son," Nelse said, "you know who they *will* be picking up, don't you?"

"Can't help it, Paw. It's my duty. And you know damned well I ain't afraid to face him down."

"Never said you was, J. O.," Nelse said gravely. "But I tell you this—if you mix with Arch, he's got nothing to lose. But me, now," he sighed, "well, I got only *one* son left and, by God, I'd sure hate to lose him."

J. O. brightened. "*Would* you now, Paw? That don't sound much like you."

"It's a fact, though," said old Nelse gruffly. "Man don't have to yell from the roof tops how he feels, does he? And so, since I'm the father of this one last son, I got to tell you right out, J. O., leave Arch alone."

"But he's in *town*, Paw."

"Hearsay evidence, boy. You ain't seen him."

"I will, though."

"Not if you ain't here. If I was you, say, I'd take Ty Quarton and head for Grant's Pass this very minute."

"And what'll be happening here while we're gone, hey?"

"Well, now, you just let your old father worry about that. I've managed pretty well around these parts so far. Reckon I ain't lost my grip yet."

"You *sure* things'll be all right, Paw?"

"Yep, J. O. My word on it."

J. O. Macleod could not help but look relieved. "I guess me and Ty'll get along down to Grant's Pass, then," he said.

"Always said you were a smart one, J. O.," said Nelse. He slapped his big son on the back.

"But—you ain't *really* figgering on doing what you said, are you, Paw? Selling everything, I mean?"

"Hell, *no*, boy!" exclaimed Nelse Macleod with a grin. "Not while I got me a fine son and heir, even if he don't knock his damned wife around the way the old sow deserves. I'll walk you to the jail, J. O."

Arch Eastmere sat at one of Smiley's two rear tables and let his hard eyes run over the words he had so laboriously put down with a pencil stub:

Phil tate

remmember how i Helped you that Day at el Passo texsas and then Arter wards wel Phil you May be now can Returen the Faver now if you wil Meat me here at Alen lacy place yrs

A Eastmere

rite Away i mean Phil if you Can now

The bar had more men drinking in it this morning than on any other morning since Smiley Brann had first thrown open the doors. Arch was slouched at one of the tables with Pace Gray and Oliver Swindon. At the other table were Drury Wynward and Jock Menzies. Three of Jock's hands, along with five of Oliver's and Nelse Macleod's half dozen, were strung, like lazy beads, along the bar. Every man jack in the room, with the exception of Arch and Pace Gray, was working his way through either a beer or a whisky. Nearest of them all to the swinging doors, a few feet from Randy Worth and Will Clough, who had moved down the bar gladly when he came in, Terry Sykes, slit-eyed and stiff-backed, stood studying a glass of beer.

The Lacy brothers had gone on ahead, each to his own spread. Mark was getting his contingent together; and Alan was preparing to receive the forty or so men who would gather at his ranch house at three that afternoon, to ready themselves for the foray into the Marias which was planned for a suitable time after sunset.

There was little conversation among the men drinking at Smiley's place. Most of them watched, with varying degrees of curiosity, as Arch Eastmere struggled with the wording of his note. They sympathized with him, too; for, to those of them who *could* write, to put down even the simplest phrases was as troublesome as it was to him. So, when Arch, after reading over what he had written, nodded to himself with silent satisfaction, many of them felt relieved. "He done it, by God," Randy muttered to Will.

Pace Gray had been trying, without success, to peer over the big hand with which Arch had shielded his scrawl. "What you writing, Arch?" he had asked before the tall, intent man had set down three words.

"Asking a favor, hoss," Arch had replied, scratching his nose with the end of the pencil.

"From who?"

"Feller I know."

Now, with the note finally written, Arch called over to Smiley Brann: "Smiley—you got something I can put this in?"

"You mean a *envelope?*" Smiley frowned and sucked in his cheeks. "Ain't used one in years. Wait a minute, though." He opened his cash drawer and rummaged in the back, finally pulling out a wrinkled gray rectangle that had once held a bill from a manufacturer of glassware. "Here's an old one come to me a while back," he said, blowing dust from each side, "only it's got my name on it. But it ain't tore."

"Don't matter," Arch said. "Much obliged." He held out his hand as Smiley limped down to the end of the bar and gave him the envelope. Arch very deliberately folded the note twice and slipped it inside. Then his eyes went to Pace Gray, and he smiled. "Reckon I'll have to ask another favor now," he said.

Pace straightened himself and leaned forward. "Sure, Arch. Anything you say."

"I'd like you to ramble on down to Divide for me, old hoss. You game to do it?"

The eagerness went out of Pace's eyes, and the corners of his mouth fell down. "Aw, Arch," he said, "I won't get back here till *tomorrow* sometime."

"That's right, hoss, you won't."

"But we're all going up in the Marias tonight. I'll miss the fun, Arch."

"What makes you think tonight's the end of it?"

"Because it *will* be, that's all." Pace seemed to be on the verge of tears.

Arch bit his lower lip. "If I figgered it would, well, I wouldn't've wrote that letter," he said steadily. "And what you'll be doing down to Divide's more important than riding up the Marias."

"I was looking forward to that ride up there, Arch."

"And I'm looking forward to you doing me this favor," Arch Eastmere said. He sounded humble.

Glumly, Pace gave in. "All right, Arch. If you want me to."

"Figgered you would, old hoss," said Arch. He handed the grimy envelope to the boy. "You know Carl Lowen's saloon down to Divide?" he asked.

"The log place there? Couple of miles the other side of town? Yep, I been past it."

"Well, you go there and tell Carl Lowen—he's a big German feller with a mustache that curls up—you tell Carl Lowen and nobody else you got a message for Phil Tate and—"

"Aw, I know Phil Tate when I see him," Pace interrupted.

"Except as how you won't see him at all, unless Carl Lowen tells you where to go," Arch went on in a quiet voice. "Phil's been feeling poorly lately, and when he's that way he likes to kind of keep out of sight, same way a cat does. But you tell Carl Lowen I sent you, and he'll show you where Phil's holed up. Then you come back up here with Phil."

"Couldn't I have just told him you wanted to see him, Arch? There wasn't any need to write a letter to him, was there?"

"Well, now, hoss, I'll tell you. I figger old Phil never got a letter from anybody in his whole life. And so when you read this one to him, it ought to pleasure him considerable, with him feeling so poor, and all."

"But if he's feeling all *that* poor, maybe he can't come. So what do I do then, Arch? Do I come back up here alone?"

Arch Eastmere thought for a moment. "Better leave that up to old Phil," he said. "But the quicker you go, old hoss, the quicker you'll be coming back."

"Sure, Arch, sure." Pace rose to his feet. "I'm going." He folded the letter and put it in the pocket of his shirt. "Don't let nothing *big* happen while I'm gone."

"*You* won't miss a thing, son," said Arch Eastmere blithely.

Pace strode outside, at precisely the right moment to bump into old Nelse Macleod, just beyond the swinging doors.

"Easy, young Pace, easy," Nelse said, annoyed, steadying himself on the boy's shoulders. "Where you rushing off to, in such a blasted hurry?"

"Doing something for Arch," Pace said. "Sorry, Mister Macleod." He hurried over to his horse. Nelse went on into Smiley's.

"Beginning to get in each other's way *already,* ain't you, by God?" Terry Sykes demanded as the old man passed him.

Nelse ignored the remark. "Shot of whisky, Mister Brann," he said to Smiley. He sat down in the chair Pace had left. "Got the boy doing something useful, Arch?" he asked casually.

"One way or another, Nelse, I reckon."

"He's gone down to get Phil Tate up here," Oliver said.

"Oh?" Nelse cocked an eyebrow at no one in particular, then reached over and took the drink Smiley Brann was extending across the bar. "We *need* Phil Tate?" he wondered mildly, as though he were asking the question of himself.

"Reckon not," Arch Eastmere admitted. "Not when you come right down to it."

"I was wondering about that myself," said Oliver Swindon. "Why there was any *call* to drag in outsiders. Unless, Arch, it was because you—"

"Ah, the more, the merrier," Drury Wynward said from the next table.

"You got any special reasons for wanting Phil, Arch?" Nelse asked.

"Can't say as I have, no," Arch said slowly. "But let's say I got some special reasons for not wanting Pace Gray."

Oliver Swindon grinned. "Yep," he said, "that's what I *figgered* was behind it, by George."

"No point in a nice young feller, like Pace, maybe getting hurt," Arch said. "I'd be the one who'd have to tell those two fine old ladies."

"Phil Tate's been sick, anyways, according to Arch," Oliver Swindon told Nelse. "He's sending Pace on a wild-goose chase,

Arch is, to keep him out of mischief. Wish somebody'd send *me* on one."

"Sick, that's too bad," Nelse said automatically, his mind on something else. He pulled his beard a few times, then fixed his beady old eyes on Arch Eastmere. "Where'd Phil get shot, Arch? Shoulder, maybe?"

Arch Eastmere showed absolutely no surprise at this unexpected question. "Near the crotch, Nelse," he said. "Pretty close to the crotch. Didn't know you'd heard. Been talking to J. O.?"

"The El Paso sheriff wrote a letter," Nelse said. "And I just chanced to see it. Must've hurt Phil Tate like hell, taking a bullet down there."

"It did, Nelse. He howled all the way till I left him. Reckon he's still howling. Just like Jack Rettis must be still talking."

"He's not talking now, Arch, he's dead."

"Oh. Good. And bad, too, I reckon."

"Whose fault was it, Arch?"

"Rettis drew first. I come in on him from the side."

"But you didn't start the trouble?"

"Rettis drew first, I said. And Phil was just turning around."

"All right, Arch. If it don't matter to you, being out in plain sight, with the word getting around the way it is."

"It don't matter to me, Nelse. *I* don't make trouble."

Nelse wagged his head and sighed wearily. "But it seems to me, Arch," he said, "that when you say you don't want the boy hurt you got it in the back of your head that they's going to be trouble here."

"I got it in the *front* of my head, too."

"You sound pretty sure."

"That's what I am. Pretty sure."

"How so?"

"Just looking around me at you fellers."

"The whole business'll end up in a lot of talk."

It was Arch Eastmere's turn to sigh. "Nelse, you're all talked out already. And now you've went and got yourselves a passel of men that don't have much to *say* about anything at all. There'll be trouble, all right, don't you ever doubt it."

"*We* won't start it."

"It's started already, Nelse. And I reckon it can't be stopped."

"Started by who? Not *us*, by God!"

Arch Eastmere let his shoulders droop. "For all you know," he said, "maybe your *mothers* started it. Don't ask *me* how things start."

Nelse Macleod leaned across the table. "Don't you *want* to go along, Arch?"

"You all hired me, Nelse. Remember?"

"Yep, we did, Arch, but just for the frosting on the cake. But I'm older'n you and I know these folks, and I also know—"

"*Nelse!*" Arch cut in, sharp and deadly. "You don't know *nothing*. You're older, sure, but I seen more in six months of my life than you'll ever see if you live to be ninety. So I'm not a man that'll *listen* to you, hear? And I don't care *how* long your dirty old beard is."

A black crepe of silence hung over the room, and every eye was fixed on the two men. Then Nelse Macleod abruptly tossed off the rest of his drink. "Yep, you could be right, Arch," he said. "You *could* be right, at that. And just in case you *are* right, well I don't know what we'll do for law around here. Seems like I talked the sheriff into taking his deputy and going down to Grant's Pass. Yep, that's what I went and did, not half an hour ago, leaving his poor, pretty goddamned wife to weep and wail on her lonely bed."

Arch Eastmere suddenly grinned and relaxed. "You're a smart old feller, and that's the truth," he said. "I should've seen you was just baiting me."

A heavy exhalation of relief came from Oliver Swindon. "Ah, now, that's a lot better," he exclaimed. "No sense in us fussing amongst ourselves, not with all these other folks we can fuss with. Hey, Smiley, drinks all around. And on *me*, too, by George."

Jock Menzies guffawed. "Watch out he don't try to pay you in Confederate money, Smiley."

"What you don't recollect, Jock," said Oliver, "is on that Confederate money I got it says it's going to be redeemed right after the peace treaty's signed between the Confederacy and that other country, whatever it's called. The *United* States. Well, there ain't been any peace treaty signed yet, that I ever heard tell on, so that money still looks *mighty* official and solid, far as I'm concerned. Good as gold, and maybe better."

"Fool's gold," said Smiley Brann.

"Only trouble is," Arch Eastmere said, "they can't seem to *find* the Confederacy anywheres, no matter how hard they look."

"Well, seeing as how I'm in the enemy camp," Oliver said cheerfully, "I'll just have to use that cheap enemy money. *Greenbacks*, goddamn 'em. Come on now, Smiley, start your pouring. It's one long, dry ride up to Juncture Valley, and the Randals've probably poisoned what little water they—"

He was cut short by a wild laugh from the cavernous throat of Terry Sykes. The noise was so startling that every head jerked in Sykes's direction, veering from there to the swinging doors just behind him, through which had come in sudden quiet the reason for such hyena laughter.

Two reasons, as a matter of fact. Hallock Randal, with a heavy pistol hung low on his hip, stood just inside the saloon, coolly looking down the bar; and beside him, unarmed and a step to the rear, was his little, long-haired brother, Luke, who was, on this Thursday, eight days a man.

CHAPTER 14

SAM WADLEY hadn't found Hallock until Wednesday's light was nearly gone, and Thursday's sun was already up before Hallock got back to the Randal ranch house, with young Luke riding beside him. He was eight hours later than he should have been. But whether the delay was a fatal one, or really made any difference at all in the outcome of things, would never be known by Hallock Randal or, indeed, by anyone else concerned.

There were various reasons for the loss of time. To begin with, Sam Wadley had not forgotten the exhaustion brought about by his Sunday gallop from the South Tine. As a result, he made no effort to press his horse. He even made a casual halt of over an hour in which he fixed himself some hot food. Then, once he got well into the Marias, he went by such odd and circuitous ways that he finally wandered into the area of Camp Number Two instead of Number Three.

There he ran into Soap Damson and Luke. The three of them had to work their way along the slopes of the Marias until, at last, they located Hallock, midway between the Tines.

The only message Sam had for Hallock was that his father wanted him home as soon as possible. Hallock, not greatly alarmed, spent a half-hour in having something to eat, after which he intended to ride to the ranch house without a halt. But then, agreeing to let the importunate Luke accompany him, he wasted another twenty minutes while his brother ate too.

Once they started out, leaving Soap Damson in charge, and with night already upon them, Hallock was forced to hold in his horse so as not to outstrip Luke, the slower and less adroit rider. The last and most serious delay was caused by a light, steady rain that blotted out the waning moon as well as all known landmarks. When the storm finally passed, Hallock discovered to his surprise that he was lost, as he rarely had been in his life; and before he was able to learn that he and Luke had blindly swung miles to the north, several more hours had been wasted. So, because of all these delays and confusions, it was after seven o'clock on Thursday morning before they got back home.

Percy Randal, who had seen them coming from his bedroom window, was waiting for them at the corral. His eyes, due to the almost sleepless night he had undergone, were sunken. He looked tired and ten years older; and Hallock, seeing this sudden change in his father, was himself shaken and moved. He was even more disturbed to hear Percy Randal give a wandering, almost incoherent account of what had taken place since Hallock and the others had left for the Marias—of Mark Lacy's wild accusations, of Pax appearing with Ellen Lacy, of Drury Wynward's sinister visit, and of the Cospatricks' flight. As Percy rambled on, however, one thing became very clear to the tired Hallock: the reins had fallen from the hands of the father, and it was now the son's duty to drive the wagon.

Percy Randal himself made that plain, as he finished his stumbling recital. "I don't know what to do, Hallock, I swear," he said. "Don't know whether I should maybe bring in the sheriff, or call you all back down here, or just *what*. So *you* better do it. Your mother's taking it real hard, too. She felt bad yesterday afternoon and went to bed, even though she don't know the whole of what's happened. So it's up to you now. It's the damnedest thing I ever saw and, well—there's just no *reason* to it, Hallock. Everybody sees there's not a bit of reason to the whole crazy mess."

"Why didn't you go in and see J. O. yourself yesterday,

Father?" Hallock, worried and somewhat exasperated, wanted to know. "Or send Pax? Why didn't you, Father?"

Percy Randal shrugged and ran his hand through his hair. "What good would it've done?" he said helplessly.

"Well, we'll see *today* what good it'll do," Hallock said. "And if it don't do any good today, there'll be trouble, by God." He looked up and saw Pax coming toward them from the house. "And trouble in *spades,* for Mister Pax," he went on. "Which won't come from Mark Lacy, neither." He felt a sudden white rage at his brother's stupidity in fetching Mark's wife away at such a critical moment.

"Howdy, Hallock," Pax said, and he jerked his head toward his father. "He told you what's going on?"

"He didn't tell me why you took Ellen Lacy," Hallock said coldly.

"Why, hell, Hallock, she needed help, that's why."

"What kind, hey?"

"Why, everybody'll tell you. Mark was—"

Hallock moved up to his brother. "Don't you lie to me, you curly-haired, rotten son of a bitch, or I'll break every bone in your body."

Pax turned pale, and his voice turned pleading. "It's the *truth,* Hallock. What do you think I *am?*"

"By God, I *wonder,*" Hallock exclaimed. "Goddamned *fool,* bringing that woman here, knowing all the time how riled up Mark was. Christ, I'd like to kill you! Where is she now?"

"Ellen? She's—why, she's in bed, I guess."

"Hers? Or yours?"

"Son, son," Percy Randal said. "The woman's a guest in my house."

"We gave her a room," Pax said hurriedly. "She's in her own room."

"You oughtn't to think those things, Hallock," Percy Randal muttered.

Hallock ignored his father. "If *you* knew what I was thinking, you yellow-haired bastard," he said to Pax, "that yellow hair of yours'd turn gray in ten minutes. Did she bring all her stuff here, or did you ride her in naked?"

"Now, you *listen,* Hallock," Pax said, bridling.

"Shut up, goddamn you, Pax, or I'll—you want to know what I'm going to do, Pax? You want to know how I'm going to handle this Ellen Lacy business?"

The fight went out of Pax all at once. "You're not going to send her back, are you, Hallock? You won't make her go *back?*"

"If Father let her stay here, she can stay. But once this whole thing's cleared up, I'm going to drag you about a mile away from this house, where nobody can hear you yell, and then I'm going to give you the beating I should've given you long ago. You won't be able to walk for a month, goddamn your whoring soul."

"You'll be sorry you said that, Hallock."

"Let's hear you stand up and say you don't deserve it."

"No, I won't, by God."

"I didn't think you would, goddamned weasel!"

"Look, Hallock, please," Pax said, "it don't matter whether I deserve anything, or even *what* I deserve. Right now we've got to work together."

"I don't even want to *talk* to you, you ten-cent son of a bitch," Hallock said. "Get out of my sight and *stay* out of it, hear? I'd be better off working with a buzzard."

Pax gazed with a hopeful desperation at his father, but Percy Randal's eyes were averted. Pax gave up and turned to Hallock. "All right," he said, his voice breaking a little, "if you want me out of your sight, I'll do *just* that, and the hell with you. You always did want to be top dog, so go ahead and bark." He spun around and ran back to the house.

"Reckon that's what *I* should've said," Percy Randal remarked looking off at the mountains. "Told the boy off long ago. Yep."

"But *when,* Father?" Hallock demanded. "And for Christ's sake, Father, why didn't you?"

"It's too late now," said Percy Randal. He ran his hand through his hair again.

"Oh, *Jee-*sus!" Hallock glanced up at the sky. "Come on, Luke, let's eat and then do what we got to."

Ann Randal watched in silence as her husband dried his hands and face and then the back of his neck, afterwards drawing a clean shirt over his hard white torso. In the corner of the room Simon, after his usual early waking, was oblivious to the presence of his parents, sodden with his first heavy doze of the day. His father, as he tucked in his shirt-tails, walked over to the cradle, and looked tenderly down at his tiny son. "By God, you're a good sight," he said.

When Hallock reached in the wardrobe for his gunbelt, Ann said: "Aren't you going to speak to your mother?"

"Let her sleep. She needs it, I reckon."

"She does that. I could hear her half the night."

"*Hear* her?" Hallock was checking the chambers of his pistol.

"Talking to your father. I had the door open. But I couldn't hear what they said."

"Why'd you have the door open?"

"In case Pax might—you know."

"All right."

"Ellen's been keeping to her room, though. Just like Cora."

"What about Cora? She behaving herself?"

"I haven't seen her, Hallock. I don't think she's even gone down to eat." She saw that her husband was ready to leave. "You know what you're going to do, dear one?"

"Going into town, that's all."

"Alone?"

"Reckon I'll take Luke along, seeing as how I've brought him this far."

"Will he be all right?"

"Pax isn't worth a damn, so Luke's going to have to grow up right fast. Anyway, I don't think there'll be any trouble in town." Hallock grinned ruefully. "Come to think of it, I don't know *what*'ll be in town, but I'm pretty sure that whatever it is, it won't be trouble. All I want to do is talk to a couple of fellers."

"And then you'll be coming back?"

"Depends." Hallock went over to Ann and put his arms

around her. "Anyway, *you* look out for things. See if you can make Father get some sleep."

"You're tired yourself."

"I'll get my sleep, sweetheart, don't you fret." He kissed his calm Ann, while her long arms held him close.

"If you think all this soft-soaping's going to stop me from seeing you off," Ann said, before she set him free, "you're very, very wrong, Hallock Randal."

"I'm very *right*," said Hallock.

A little while later, as Hallock and Luke rode off, they were watched from an upstairs window by a half-dressed Ellen Lacy, and by Pax, who, having entered her bedroom unseen, had come up behind her and slipped an arm around her willing, uncorseted waist.

Hallock and Luke were not watched, however, by the smoldering eyes of little Dolores Costa, who was just inside the open barn door, well concealed by the shadows. For the eyes of Dolores were on the bedroom window of Ellen Lacy, and as Hallock and Luke clattered away she saw her golden Pax draw the gold Lacy woman to him, kiss her with much passion and more purpose, and then pull her back from the window toward the unseen, shaded bed.

This lascivious pantomime was what finally buried the love and lost hopes of little doe-eyed Dolores.

The hyena laugh of Terry Sykes gurgled to an end.

For a good ten seconds Smiley's saloon was like a wax-works museum. Nobody spoke. Nobody moved. Some men didn't bother to breathe. The only things that stirred in the suddenly stilled air were the eyes of Hallock Randal as they flickered along the bar and down to Drury Wynward.

"Mark Lacy here?" Hallock asked. His voice was bleak.

Drury smiled cheerfully. "He's home, Hallock," he said.

"I went by his place. He's not there."

"Then maybe he's over to Alan's," said Oliver Swindon. "You go by Alan's?"

Hallock shook his head. "I went by the sheriff's office. Found the place locked up tight." He looked down at Nelse Macleod. "Where's J. O., Nelse?"

"Why, I think he said something about him and Ty Quarton riding down to Grant's Pass to look at a feller they got in the jail there."

"The *both* of 'em, Nelse? J. O. and Ty?"

"It's a nice ride down to Grant's Pass, Hallock."

"There's also no law at all in Eastmere while they're taking that nice ride down to Grant's Pass," Hallock said.

Nelse Macleod pulled at his beard. "Why, now, that's so, by God, ain't it?" he said. "I never thought of it that way, I swear. J. O. ought to know better than that, and I'll sure speak to him about it, the minute he gets back." He sighed. "Good thing Eastmere's such a lawful place, now, ain't it, Hallock?"

"I want to know what's going on, Nelse," Hallock said flatly. "*What's* going on, and *why*."

"So do we," said Oliver Swindon. "Want to tell us, Hallock?"

"Don't fool with me, Ollie, damn you!"

"Don't reckon I'm fooling, Hallock."

"Besides," old Nelse said, looking bored, "Mark Lacy's the feller you ought to see, Hallock. It was poor Mark's wife that got took away."

"The hell with Mark's wife!" Hallock said. "I'm talking about what you think we're doing up in the Marias."

"So're we, Hallock," Oliver said. "Why, hell, women're lighting out with some damn popinjay or other all the time, but what you folks're doing up there, well, that's something else again."

Hallock turned white. "You mean to sit there, Swindon," he demanded, "and tell me you think we're damming those streams?"

Oliver Swindon raised and lowered his head solemnly. "Looks like that's about what we all *do* think, Hallock," he said.

Hallock's eyes fell on Jock Menzies, who looked uncomfortable and unhappy. "How about you, Jock?" he asked, "*You* believe it, too?"

Big Jock hesitated, flushed, and stared down at his great brown hands. "Well, *say*, Hallock," he stammered, "I don't rightly know, I suppose, but—but, well, if *every*body believes something, I reckon it must be the truth. That's the way I look at it, I guess. But I don't like it much. Go*ddamn*, but I don't like it much at *all*." Jock never looked at Hallock, all the time he was talking.

"Jock, man," Hallock exclaimed, "if you don't *like* it, my God, why do you *do* it?"

But Jock would not, or could not, answer.

Nelse cleared his throat. "Nobody likes it when folks they thought was friends start getting high-and-mighty ideas," he said.

"Nelse, for God's sake, *what* ideas?" Hallock demanded. "There's no ideas except what popped into your heads when you up and swallowed a lot of crazy talk from Mark Lacy."

"Well," Nelse said slowly, "we *did* think it was a lot of crazy talk, especially when Mark was carrying on about one of you Randals and his wife. But now—" Nelse grinned crookedly. "How *is* that little beauty, anyway? Nice and peaceful at your place? Getting enough sleep?"

Hallock started to come down the bar, leaving Luke behind by the doors. "I don't give a hoot if that damned woman's asleep or dead," he said. "But, goddamn it, I *do* care when everybody in town takes as Gospel something that a—" He stopped talking and halted in his tracks as he saw, for the first time, long Arch Eastmere slouched down in the corner chair behind the bar.

Arch grinned in a friendly way and waved his hand. "Poor old Hallock," he said. "Sounds like these fellers're giving you a peck of trouble. Leastwise, it does from where I sit."

It took Hallock a moment to recover, but then he managed to bring forth a smile for Arch that was genuinely warm. "*Well*, now, Arch," he said. "When did *you* get back?"

"Few days ago, hoss."

"You should've let us know."

"Reckon I would have, in time."

"You been in Mexico all this while?"

"Every blessed minute."

"You don't look none the worse for it."

"Don't feel none the better, though."

"Didn't get rich, did you?"

"Not yet, old hoss."

"Well—" The present situation tore Hallock from the amenities. "You got back just at the wrong time, looks like."

"It does seem that way, don't it? But—a man never knows. How's your father?"

"Pretty good, till this thing come along." Hallock made a gesture that took in everyone at the two tables. "You in with these fellers, Arch?"

"Afraid so, Hallock."

"Why?"

"Oh, sort of returning a favor, you might call it."

"*You* think we're building dams? Trying to force people out?"

"Reckon I don't have much choice what I think, Hallock, seeing as how I'm returning this favor."

"But you know damned well we're not, don't you, Arch?"

Arch Eastmere made a careful study of the ceiling. "Ah, it might hurt these men's feelings if I said something like that."

"Arch, for God's *sake!*" Hallock exclaimed.

The hard eyes of Arch Eastmere went straight and steady to meet those of Hallock Randal. "I'm not driving this herd, hoss," he said. "You better talk to the Lacys."

"I'm talking to *you*," Hallock said. "And you, Nelse. Drury. Oliver. *Every*body." He looked back over his shoulder along the bar. "The Lacys don't mean a pinch of snuff without you behind 'em. They tell you we're damming up the Tines, and I say it's a crazy lie. And if you don't believe me, well, then the only way to find out for sure is to go and see for yourselves."

"Yep," Nelse agreed. "The *only* way, by God."

"All right, then," Hallock said. "So I say, if you want to find out exactly *what's* happening up there, just you come along with me, and I'll sure show you."

"How many of us?" Oliver asked.

"One. Two. The whole lot. It don't matter to me. I just want to get this mess straightened out, once and for all."

"I reckon the lot of us'll come," Nelse Macleod said.

Hallock took a deep breath. "Well, then, let's us get going."

"I said, the *lot* of us, Hallock. We're not all of us here right now."

"Damn it, then, when you're all together. When'll *that* be?"

Nelse Macleod glanced over at Arch Eastmere, but Arch's eyes were closed. "Oh, we'll let you know," he said.

"When, Nelse?"

Nelse's reply was a grin.

Arch Eastmere's eyelids rose lazily. "I reckon when you least expect it, Hallock," he said in an offhand way. "I reckon that's what old Nelse here means."

Under his beard Nelse Macleod let the grin grow broader. "That's what old Nelse means, sure as hell," he said.

Once more, and out of pure tension, the saloon became a wax-works museum. "Nobody can say I didn't try," Hallock said bitterly.

"We're obliged to you, Hallock," Jock Menzies muttered. "*I* am, leastwise."

"You won't be," Hallock told him. His frigid eyes swept across the men at the tables. "Because if you won't none of you *look*, then you can't nowise *see*. So I'm telling all of you right now— stay *off* the Randal land. That's five simple words you all of you can remember. *Stay off the Randal land.*"

"And if we don't?" Drury drawled.

"I'll let *you* know," Hallock answered, in an echo of what Nelse had said. He walked back to the doors, said "Come on, Luke," to his brother, and left the saloon, young Luke at his heels.

The renewed hyena laugh of Terry Sykes followed them to their horses.

Arch Eastmere swung himself to his feet and moved down the bar. "Just everybody stay right here," he said to the men lined along it. Then he went through the swinging doors and out on the plank sidewalk. "Hallock," he said in an ordinary voice.

The brothers were on the point of mounting their horses, tethered beside Arch Eastmere's own mount. Luke stared incuriously at Arch, then climbed into his saddle; Hallock, however, turned and came back to where Arch was standing. He seemed to have left his anger behind in the saloon; now he looked tired and troubled. "What is it now, Arch?" he asked.

"I wanted you to know I'm sorry, that's all. I don't know what's gotten into those fellers, and that's the truth."

"You're with 'em, Arch. What's gotten into *you?*"

"Well—I needed some money."

"You could've come to me."

"Reckon I wouldn't want to. Not the way things are."

"Because of *this?*" Hallock jerked a thumb in the direction of Smiley's.

"Naw, Hallock, not exactly. Other things, let's say. And you might not've got that money back. You and me, we always got along too well together for something like that to happen between us."

"Looks like something's happening between us now," Hallock said. He sounded sad.

"Well, now, nothing's happened yet, hoss. So let's us just wait and see. Maybe things'll straighten themselves out before folks get to spitting in each others' eyes."

"Not the way Nelse and them're talking, they won't."

"Talking's one thing, hoss, and doing's another. Maybe I can do something that'll stop the talking."

"By God, Arch, I wish you could. You believed me, didn't you, when I told 'em it was all a pack of lies?"

"Always *have* believed you, hoss, and I sure don't see any reason to change my mind. Reckon you ain't putting up any dams. Reckon no wife-stealing's been going on, neither."

"Those bastards think that's what's going on."

"Well, now, hoss, I don't rightly know just *how,* but I figger I can come up with something that'll break up the game." He put his arm around Hallock's neck and walked with him to his horse. "All right, now, Hallock?"

"I'm obliged to you, Arch."

"We had too many good times together, hoss, to let a passel of fools go and spoil it now."

"You're right, Arch, by God," said Hallock Randal. "But until I know for sure, I won't be taking any chances." He swung up on his horse.

"Neither would I," Arch told him. "Can't say as I blame you, hoss." He grinned up at Luke, who was gazing at Arch's silver saddle with admiration. "Well, Mister Luke," he said. "I hear you're finally a growed man, after forty or so years."

Luke giggled. "That's what it seemed like, Mister Eastmere," he said. "All that, and more."

"Time'll run fast enough for you from now on, though," Hallock told him. "Wait and see."

"That it will," said Arch Eastmere. "Like that saddle of mine, Luke?"

"She's a beauty, Mister Eastmere. I never saw one that pretty, I swear."

"Never did myself. Found that saddle in a field, just outside Guadalajara, all by itself in a field. Nobody seemed to know who it belonged to, so I toted it along with me." He stepped back on the planking. "You'll hear from me, Hallock," he said.

Hallock gave him a broad smile. "I'll be up above Juncture Valley," he said. "Trying to find a goddamned river."

Arch Eastmere watched them start north along the dusty street at a trot; then, as first Hallock, then Luke, broke into an easy gallop, he realized that Nelse Macleod was standing at his shoulder.

"What was all the talk about?" Nelse wanted to know.

"Nothing much," Arch said. "I'm still here, ain't I?"

"Yep, yep, so you are," said old Nelse. "Hallock go away mad?"

"I tell you," Arch said, leaving the question unanswered, "I never in my life saw a finer hand with a horse than Hallock Randal. It's a pleasure to watch him, I do declare."

"You reckon they're going by Alan's now?" Nelse asked.

"Not if I know Hallock, they ain't."

"Where, then?"

"Can't rightly say, Nelse. But I got a hankering to ride after 'em and see."

"They may just be going back home."

"That could happen." Arch Eastmere started toward his silver-saddled horse. "But Hallock's got me *real* curious, and that's the truth."

"We're all of us supposed to be out at Alan's at three o'clock," Nelse called after him.

Arch answered without turning around. "Don't get yourself all aroused, old man," he said.

Drury Wynward came out on the planks and saw Arch riding off. "Where's he headed for now, Nelse?" he asked.

"For hell, I suppose, one of these fine days," said old Nelse Macleod, with his jaw set. "But in his own good *time*, goddamn him."

At Lacy's Ford the Forkhandle River made a long curve over a hardrock bed.

This, to a rider approaching the Randal ranch in a north-easterly direction, offered the best approach to Randal land, save for the bridge that lay ten miles to the east and another two miles below the ranch house. A trail, well-traveled and clearly discernible, led across the river into the vast acreage of Percy Randal. Perhaps a quarter mile above Lacy's Ford this trail ran between a pair of tree-surmounted outcroppings of rock, so placed as to make the fifty yards of mountain meadow that separated them the only feasible passageway to the foothills of the Marias beyond.

It was here, between these outcroppings, that Hallock Randal drew rein. Luke, a little behind him, also pulled up. "What's the matter, Hallock?" he asked.

"Wait a minute," Hallock said. He studied the terrain for a moment, then drew his saddle carbine from its scabbard and passed it over to his brother. "I want you to settle yourself up there," he said, pointing to the crown of spruce trees that topped the rocks to their left. "And if you sight anybody coming onto our land this way, you fire three shots, understand me?"

"Sure, Hallock," Luke said. "But where'll *you* be?"

"Up ahead, don't worry. And I'll hear you, don't you fret about that, neither. Me or Soap or somebody, we'll hear you."

"Just shoot in the *air*, that's all?"

"God, yes, Luke. You want to go killing somebody? But

tether your horse where you can get to it in a hurry, if things should come down to running."

"How long you want me to stay, Hallock?"

"Just till somebody comes to get you. Me, that is, or probably Soap. I'll see about just which, once I get back up there. And in the meanwhile, you stay awake, hear? I know you're tired, hell, I'm tired, too, but we'll both of us get lots of rest later."

"I'll stay awake. You want three shots, one right after the other?"

"Fast as ever you can work that lever. Reckon you'll be all right?"

"Don't be too long, that's all."

Hallock had to smile. "Thought you *liked* being off by yourself."

"I do, mostly, dang it. But right now, well, I wouldn't mind a bit of company."

"Don't worry," Hallock said, still holding the smile, "you'll get it before long. But don't go firing three shots for a rabbit or something, hear? Just for somebody going by who ought to be someplace else." Hallock touched his heels to his horse's flanks and went clopping off to the north.

Luke watched until his brother had circled a patch of spruce and was lost to sight, already more than half a mile away. Then Luke walked his own horse toward the place where he had been stationed, holding the carbine with its muzzle pointed haphazardly toward the sky, its butt resting on his left hip.

There seemed to be no good reason to think so, but the little carbine struck him as being more of a weight than a weapon.

Tall Arch Eastmere rode toward the noonday. The birds of the morning were loud around him. They sang in the grass and from the tree branches. They cried in their passage through the air. The birds of the field were loud on the gray rock. The birds of the high places spoke from the spruce. Their roof was the cloud, and their path was a broad one.

Arch Eastmere was a tall man. His path led nowhere. Beneath the high sun it led but to darkness. He followed it northward beneath the high sun. He followed two men on a path to the north. A mile was between them, beyond them was nowhere. Under the high sun he had a bright saddle.

The eyes of Arch Eastmere were as winter in the land. Beneath the high sun they were white and blue, as the ice of the mountains beneath the high sun. They were colder than silver. They were colder than caves.

Tall Arch Eastmere rode the high meadows. He moved among groves in the mountain places. The cattle lowed as he passed by them. They paused in their browsing to watch his passage. The cattle were fat and they covered the grasses. The land was rich with the cattle on it. They bent their heads and forgot tall Arch

Eastmere. His thighs curved over a saddle of silver. His saddle had sounds of silver and leather.

Arch Eastmere was a tall man abroad on the earth. As he wandered the earth he was long and lonely. He could teach the tiger to be more deadly. The crouching lion would flee his face. He rode as a king on a saddle of silver. He held, as he should have, a dead man's seat. He talked through the pistol that lived on his thigh. The tongue of the pistol spoke words none might answer.

The heart of Arch Eastmere was as winter in his breast. It beat as a drum that was wet with water. It drove the blood through his tired long body. It drove the blood as an old man walks. This heart had forgotten many secrets. It had forgotten how blood should go. It heaved like a knife poised to kill Arch Eastmere. It drove him in fear, like a murderer's knife.

Tall Arch Eastmere stood six feet three. The years of his life were forty-two. A big old Colt hung low on his hip. He sat on a saddle of Mexican silver. His body was that of a jaguar stalking. His grace was the grace of a catamountain. His eyes were ice beneath the high sun. But his mouth was as a remembered childhood.

Arch Eastmere rode toward the fate of noonday. He moved like a king on the earth's green carpet. His face had the cruel smooth lines of a cat. Yet his mouth was as a remembered childhood. He rode toward the death of many men. He rode toward the death of tall Arch Eastmere.

For, after other deaths, *he* must die.

Arch suddenly realized, with some embarrassment, that he was humming a tune that he knew well. The words, however, and even the song's name, had gone completely out of his mind. His inability to remember the song annoyed him briefly, and then this annoyance was replaced by a dragging curiosity as to just *why* he should be humming in the first place.

A man usually went in for humming when he was feeling pretty good; and if he felt *real* good, and happened to be well out of other folks' hearing, well, *then* a man might sing his old fool head off. It was a long time since Arch had done that—not, he guessed, since just after he had crossed the Border two years ago, on his weary way down into Mexico. He had felt right then, as though he'd been reborn. All the bad old things were being wiped out, and a lot of good new ones were just beginning.

"Easy," he said to his horse. In spite of the weight of the saddle, the great beast wanted to run.

Arch had been wrong, of course, about replacing the bad things with the good. It seemed as though he was always wrong, every time he tried to make a new start, to set his life for once on a straight line. He knew that all he had ever done had turned out that way, and yet he had never given up. But why hadn't he—and especially now? Why should Arch Eastmere be feeling pretty good *now*, with all the troubles he had?

"Easy, you, easy," he said, holding his snorting mount in. "We know where they're going. Let's not go running right over 'em." The horse steadied.

What he ought to do, Arch thought, looking across to the old peaks that loomed to his left and cut off the west—what he ought to do was head up in the hills somewhere and then keep right on going, until the country got wild enough and rough enough to hide him forever.

That trouble in El Paso had turned out mighty bad. He'd never thought that Jack Rettis, with two holes like that in him, would live long enough even to roll over and die, let alone shoot off his mouth the way he must've done. It wasn't as though Arch hadn't come by that saddle fair and square, because he had. One way or another, he'd earned every ounce of it. But Jack Rettis had been plumb crazy to follow him all the way back to Texas, thinking he had a chance at some fancy silver. And, to make things worse, Jack had to go and kick up a fuss with old Phil Tate, who had never been in Mexico in his life—and only because he saw Arch talking to him. All Arch had been saying to Phil was that he was surprised to see him so far south of Divide, especially since nothing made Phil Tate happier than to go a couple of years without speaking to a living man, and—as somebody once said—precious few dead ones.

The thing was done now, though. Jack Rettis was dead as

mutton, and they were looking for Archie Eastmere, to fix it so he'd join old mutton-dead Jack. And they would, too—once they caught him. Arch knew only too well that, with his record and reputation, he wouldn't be able to twist his neck free of this particular noose. Once they *caught* him, that is.

Still, if they hoped to catch him, they might have to move pretty fast, or his heart'd get him before they did. If what Phil Hyssop had said was true—and Arch gathered that it was—the day would come, and probably sooner than later, when he would make a slip and find himself doing one of the things Phil had told him not to do. Then, almost before he'd know what had hit him, the coffin lid would be shut on Arch Eastmere. And he might even have his boots off when it happened, too.

Arch had been good and careful up to now, though. He hadn't had a drink. He hadn't fooled around with Maudie Fletcher, neither, though it was all he could do to hold himself back, with her running around half naked or better most of the time and teasing him something terrible, poor little lonely Maudie. And he hadn't even lost his temper. The closest he'd come to getting downright mad had been this morning, when Nelse Macleod, the old fool, had grated on him for no reason at all. And even then Arch had held himself in check, in a way he wouldn't've done, say, a month or six weeks ago.

His horse splashed across Lacy's Ford.

Phil Hyssop had said Arch had maybe forty years left if he watched his step, and maybe ten minutes if he didn't. But Arch Eastmere wanted neither the forty years nor the ten minutes. One was too much, the other not enough. How much *did* he want, then? As much as he could *get?* Or as much as he *deserved?*

No, not as much as he deserved. If he'd gotten that, well, by now he would have been dead twenty-eight long years, at least.

What he really wanted, he supposed, was a *few* years more, four or five, say—enough time in which to get together a little honest money with which he could give poor little Maudie a hand, and Pace too, if the boy wanted or needed a stake. That was it: a few years, in which Arch Eastmere might do a little good for a change, a few years in which he might finally get on

that straight road he'd been looking for all his unlucky life, a few
honestly dealt hands where for once the cards'd fall right for
him. It wasn't too much to ask, considering all the years of failure
he'd had, and what those sad years had cost. And all he'd have to
do, to make the hopes of these next four or five years become a
reality, would be to take it very *very* easy and keep his head
about him—but away from *here*, away from the Forkhandle
country. He might go somewhere north of Denver, or California,
perhaps, or even Oregon.

Ah, that's what he'd wanted all along, deep inside himself.
What he couldn't understand, though, was why he hadn't realized
all these truths before. If he had, certainly, he wouldn't have let
Mark and Alan Lacy and the rest of them argue him into this
crazy fuss with the Randals. Or perhaps he would have, after all.
There was that matter of $100 in gold, which Alan Lacy had
given him right then and there, down at the Pace ladies' place,
and which he had in turn handed over to Maudie Fletcher on his
way back up to Eastmere. And the debt he owed Mark was canceled, too. A man would do much for money. Except, he guessed,
be a man.

And as far as this mix-up with the Randals was concerned,
Arch knew exactly what would happen, no matter how long and
how loud they all yelled about how there wouldn't be any trouble.
What would happen was that the Lacys and their people would
come together with the Randals and their people, and there'd be
words, and the next thing you knew there'd be gunplay, and the
last thing you knew there'd be three or four good men lying
around, as dead as men could get. That was the way these things
always ended, no matter how simple their beginnings might be.
It was a plumb easy thing to start a big rock rolling down hill,
but once it was given that first shove, no man alive could stop it.
A wall of dead men might, though.

This Randal foolishness was a big mess now, but before it was
finished it would be a lot bigger. And yet here was old catamountain Arch Eastmere, who used to have eight or nine lives, right
smack in the path of that big rolling rock, with no time to get
out of the way with his ruin of a heart, and no place to get to if
he *did* have time. If he wanted to commit suicide, Arch rea-

soned with himself, why didn't he put the muzzle of that old, worn Colt in his mouth and pull the trigger? Or hadn't the scare he'd had on Maude Fletcher's bed been enough to—?

Wait just a minute now.

"Well, *sure*," Arch said aloud, in delight. "I swear I should've seen it all *along*."

The knowledge of what he was doing burst in his head, like a thousand bright rockets—and yet he had been aware of what he was about ever since he'd watched Hallock Randal and Luke ride off from Smiley's. The rock that he'd been so worried about was *still* balanced there on top of the hill, and he, Arch Eastmere, was going to see that nobody, nobody at *all*, was going to give it the kick that would start it on its deadly, man-killing course.

Last Sunday—*was* it last Sunday?—sure, that was when it had been: last Sunday he'd thought of Hallock and himself laughing about something they'd done together, and he knew it had been just before the War that they'd done it, but for the life of him he couldn't remember what it had been. *Now* he could, though. Perhaps the sight of young Luke had reminded him.

It had been right around this time of year, too, so it must've been in '60, because by June of '61 he and Hallock were both in the War. Yep, it would've been in May or June of '60 when they had Luke thinking they were going to sell him.

Arch Eastmere threw back his head and laughed as the scene re-entered his mind.

Darius Oliphant had a first-rate stallion he had announced he was willing to part with, and Hallock and Arch had gone around to have a look at the animal. Not to buy, but just to look. Hallock, for some reason, had little Luke with him. At the time Luke couldn't have been much more than three years old.

"He's a beauty, Mister Oliphant," Hallock had said, after they'd gone over the stallion carefully, point by point. "I sure wish I could afford him."

"I'll bet you we could arrange some kind of a loan so you could," Oliphant had replied.

But Hallock was against the idea. "That'd take it out of my hands and put it in Father's," he said. "And if I can't afford him with my own money, well, I guess I'll just have to do without.

Still—" He'd looked at little Luke, and then winked at Arch. "Tell you what I'll do, Mister Oliphant. I'll swap you my brother Luke here for him."

Oliphant, to give the devil his due, had gone along with the joke, while the terrified Luke had gaped in disbelief. "Is young Luke sound in wind and limb?" the banker had asked, reaching for the child's mouth as though he intended to inspect his teeth.

Luke had jerked away and started to bawl.

"Sound in wind, anyway," Hallock had said wryly.

"Probably in limb, too," Oliphant had remarked, "considering how fast he ducked just then. It's a fair trade, Hallock, a fair trade."

"Now, just a minute," Arch had said. "I reckon I got a right to half that stallion, Hallock, because I been standing here appreciating him just as much as you have, and maybe a little more."

"Could be, Arch," Hallock had admitted. "But I got the brother here to swap for him. I don't see any little brothers hanging around you."

"Then there's only one thing to do, Mister Brother-Seller."

"I'm listening with every ear I got, Mister Brotherless."

"You've got to sell me half of *your* brother here," Arch had continued. "And that'll be *my* half of Mister Oliphant's horse."

"I'm open to any reasonable offer, sir," Hallock had said. "Stop that damn howling, Luke, or I'll swap you for a sick pig."

"Will a nickel swing it, Mister Randal?"

"Just about, Mister Eastmere," Hallock had answered.

Gravely, then, Arch had handed Hallock a five-cent piece. Luke had broken off his bawling long enough to watch the money change hands, then he had started to kick Arch in the shins with all his strength, screaming: "I'm worth a *dime!* I'm worth a *dime!*"

Arch and Hallock and even testy Darius had doubled over with laughter; and for weeks afterward *I'm worth a dime,* said by either Arch or Hallock, was all it took to set them roaring like a pair of big ninnys.

Ah, it was *better* then.

Arch found himself chuckling even now at the scene he had just relived. No *wonder* I was humming back there, he said to himself. Blowed if I'm not feeling mighty good and peaceful.

And I know why, indeed I do. I'm feeling mighty good and peaceful because I'm going to ride up in the Marias, and I'm going to find that old hoss, Hallock, and he's going to show me what's happened up there, and I know it's going to turn out to be not what the Lacys and the rest of them think, at all. And then I'm coming back down the Marias, and I'm going to meet 'em all at Alan's, and I'm going to tell 'em they're all making fools of themselves, and tell 'em to all go home and shut up. And if Mark Lacy wants to make any fuss about Lacy money, either the borrowed or the given, well, dang it, *I'm* worth a dime—even if all I did was keep 'em from seeing the elephant, man and boy.

Grinning to himself, feeling happy inside, Arch Eastmere rode on across Randal land. He found that he was starting to hum again, but this time he knew the tune. It was "We Are Coming, Father Abraham, Three Hundred Thousand More."

The way they were going by, they seemed like an army with banners.

Luke Randal, his hat off, his hair hanging down along his cheeks, lay on his stomach and studied the ants. His eyes were no more than a foot above them. In an endless line they scurried over the hump of the rounded, spruce-topped outcropping. Perhaps one ant in ten carried in its jaws a bit of green leaf that, however small it might be, still dwarfed the insect that bore it, and these bright fragments they moved with looked like nothing so much as minute green flags. They even seemed to have been cut in a roughly rectangular shape. Other ants carried the tiny cream ovals that Luke recognized as eggs. Here and there, too, he could pick out a queen, guarded by ten or a dozen soldiers as she lumbered along, slowed by the drag of a great, swollen abdomen.

Perhaps a thousand times in his short life Luke had lain like this and watched a myriad purposeful ants on their way to a new nest. The sight never failed to fill him with wonder. So many things about these migrations had always been a mystery to him. He couldn't say, for instance, whether the bits of leaf had been cut for the purpose of lining their underground chambers or to be used as food by the insects themselves. Why, for all Luke could tell, they might even let the cuttings of old leaves decay and ferment, finally turning the stuff into liquor. Ants were pretty smart, he reckoned, and a man couldn't rightly say just *what* they did down there in the dark. Maybe, Luke thought with a sleepy half-smile, maybe they live in a place like Smiley Brann's, only with no lights at all, and every night the lot of them get drunk.

And the eggs they were carrying—Luke didn't understand about those, either. Birds' eggs, he knew, had to be kept warm, and if the mother bird left them for too long the unborn babies would die of the cold. Yet coldness didn't seem to bother ants at all. Luke guessed that *nothing* bothered their eggs, because they sure hatched out ants by the millions. Why, if birds hatched as many eggs as ants did, in a little while there'd be so many birds crammed in the air that there wouldn't be any air left for human beings to breathe. Or birds either, for that matter. But ants were so *very* tiny, well, the earth had lots of room for ants.

What Luke would like to do best in all the world, he decided, would be to find out just how the ants lived down there under the ground, where it was dark and quiet and cool. But he couldn't figure a single way by which he could realize this desire. He'd certainly never be able to dig down through the nest. That would merely scatter and confuse them.

It was all a question of size, that was the whole trouble. The ants were so small he could hardly see them. Luke Randal, on the other hand, was so big that they probably couldn't see *him* at all—the way folks couldn't see God, who was big enough to be everywhere, ever.

Luke sighed, the way his mother did sometimes. Then he yawned.

The endless, steady parade of ants had a hypnotic effect on him, drowsy as he already was after the rigors of the night now passed. It became harder and harder for him to hold his guileless eyes open while they clung, with a fixed and glazing focus, to the flow of minute bodies along the mold below his face.

His head sagged forward. His neck sank down between his shoulder blades. The world around Luke Randal darkened, and the various noises, drawn from the inhabitants of meadow and tree, blended indifferently into a low monotony of sound.

Plunged in this cotton suspension, disembodied as a dream, Luke heard a horse cantering in some other country, a country a thousand miles away. A horse was cantering somewhere, across an ocean, across some wide water, and its hooves were made of water, too, of water drumming like rain on a tight roof. But then it was much too loud to be rain beating. It was loud enough to be a flash flood, bearing whole forests before it, sweeping Luke Randal away—

He lifted his head: he returned to his last truth.

The horseman had nearly reached the outcropping on which Luke was sprawled. "Oh, won't Hallock be *mad!*" was what came to the mind of Luke Randal, eight days a man, as he grabbed his brother's carbine and scrambled to his feet.

He pointed the carbine's muzzle at a patch of sky between the spruce tops and fired, then brought the weapon down and shoved the lever forward to throw another cartridge into the chamber.

Only half of the cartridge got there. The carbine promptly jammed.

The shot had been so unexpected and so close that Arch Eastmere acted mindlessly and by instinct. As he reined up his horse with his left hand, his right was already hauling the worn old Colt out of its holster, and his body was twisting itself toward the outcropping of rock from which the noise had come.

A little above him and perhaps ninety feet away, Arch made out the indistinct figure of a man. Whoever it was, he was struggling with the lever of a carbine, bending over the gun and obviously having some trouble in reloading. At this unlucky shadow Arch snapped off a shot. Just one.

It was enough.

It was the best, or the worst, shooting Arch had ever done in his life. He had not really aimed; and ninety feet is long range for a pistol, even under the best of conditions. The big lead slug, however, caught the man with the carbine square in the belly and jackknifed him backward against a tree.

The carbine went slithering along the smooth outcrop of rock until it reached the floor of the meadow, half again a tall man's height below. The man he had shot looked at Arch in wonder and surprise, and Arch knew with abrupt surprise himself that it was Luke Randal who now had his bullet in him.

Luke took a tentative step away from the tree that had propped him, collapsed with an astonished grunt, and then went tumbling down after the jammed carbine that had been his ruination. He ended up on the floor of the meadow, his legs sprawled out toward Arch and his head and back supported by the outcropping's flank, so that he was in a half-reclining position. His mouth was slightly open, and his gaze was fixed on Arch Eastmere, who seemed to be frozen out there on his silver saddle.

Arch's mouth was open, too, and on his face was a look of blank expectancy. He was waiting for the heart in his breast to kill him. He *wanted* that sick heart to kill him for what he had just now done.

He could feel it swelling against his ribs. He was sure that it was about to explode like a shell in the hold of his body, turning him into a hulk full of blood. He held his breath and hoped he'd go under all at once, before the pain grew as bad as it had before. He wished he were lying down, like Luke. He wished he were dead already.

The smoke of his powder dissolved in the still air. He waited. So did his perilous heart.

Luke continued to stare at him, almost as though he, too, waited for Arch Eastmere's death. But the heart seemed set on betraying them both.

It let the thunder of its throbbing fade.

Arch Eastmere realized by degrees that the dog of death must have lost his scent again, at least for the moment—though, for all he knew, the live shell buried so deep in his body had a delayed fuze that was set to shatter him, say, ten minutes from now, the ten minutes that Doctor Phil Hyssop had told him he might expect, if ever he did anything to—

But he *had* done something, and yet here he was, still among the living. And if there were only ten minutes left to him, well, he'd take those ten minutes for what they were worth.

He glanced along the trail, listening for the sound of a horse or a man. Then, satisfied that Hallock must have ridden far ahead, he swung off his horse and walked over to Luke. The big Colt hung loose in his hand.

The eyes of Luke never left the man who had brought him down, neither while Arch moved toward the wounded boy nor after he stood tall above him. There was no anger in Luke's expression. He seemed more like a puppy who had been whipped for no reason; nor did he seem in pain. Not as yet, anyway, for Luke was in shock. The pain would come later, pretty soon now. And, Arch Eastmere knew, there would be a *lot* of pain.

Blood was welling from the hole that had been made in Luke's belly. It was seeping through the wool of his trousers and running down his groin. In a while the earth would be drenched with it.

There would be more pain, Arch thought with great sadness, than Luke could ever stand. He wouldn't be able to keep his pride and manhood for the sheer agony of it. It would tear at his guts until he died screaming. During the War Arch had seen more gut-shot men than he liked to remember, but he had never known a gut-shot man who recovered. Before the poor devils had cashed in their chips they had shrieked like rabbits and howled like dogs, stinking to high heaven, clutching their bellies, cursing the mothers that bore them, and begging their comrades to blow out their brains. To these gut-shot men, death had become more merciful than feared. And it at last had taken them all, but only after it had changed each one from a man in his strong prime to a writhing worm of tortured flesh.

And now here was another. Poor Luke Randal.

"You didn't have to shoot me like that, Mister Eastmere." Luke's voice was weak, but steady enough. "I wasn't fixing to harm you."

"You took a shot at me, Luke," Arch said mildly, blinking. "Reckon I had to do something right quick."

"I didn't take a shot at you, Mister Eastmere."

"You saw me riding up, didn't you?"

"I—I was watching the ants."

"The *ants?*"

"That's all I was doing. They're making this new nest, and I was watching 'em."

"So you took a shot at me. Just because you were watching the ants."

"No, I didn't, Mister Eastmere, honest. I was just doing what Hallock told me to. Hallock said if I saw anybody coming, then fire three shots off real quick. In the air, Mister Eastmere."

"Didn't look much like that to me, Luke."

"The gun jammed. I don't know much about guns."

Arch Eastmere saw the carbine lying a few feet away. The lever was down, and the chamber was open. He could see the cartridge jammed in the chamber.

"Never did like those saddle guns much," Arch said. "And if that's the way it was, Luke, then I'm a sorry man. I sure wish I'd known what you were up to. And I'm sure sorry, Luke." He dropped to his knees beside the wounded boy. "Sure sorry."

"It's all right, Mister Eastmere. I'd've done the same thing you did, probably. Hallock would, too, I reckon."

"What about Hallock?" Arch asked.

"He'll be back," Luke said. "There was only two shots, but he'll be back anyways."

"Reckon he will," said Arch Eastmere. "You hurting, Luke?"

He asked the question in a very gentle voice, for Luke, frowning, had shut his eyes tight. Now, however, he opened them again, shook his head, and managed a faint smile. "I suppose I will pretty soon, though, won't I?" he asked.

"That's the way of it, Luke," Arch Eastmere said.

"Hallock'll be able to get me back to the house, though, won't he?"

"Oh, he'll get you back to the house, all right."

There was a note of flatness and finality in Arch Eastmere's voice that he hadn't intended to be there. Luke caught it, though, and he knew what it meant. His eyes widened. "But I won't be alive when we get there," he said.

"I didn't say that, old hoss."

"But you *think* it."

"No, I don't. You'll be alive, Luke. Sure you will."

But Luke refused to believe him. He tried to sit up, his mouth twisted by terror, and then sank back again with a groan. "Mister Eastmere—*Arch*—listen," he whispered. "I don't *want* to die. My God, I just started to live my life. I haven't even *done* anything yet—only *little* things. I haven't been anyplace or seen anything. I got a right to live, like all the other men, and love somebody and get married and have a family and be happy, like everybody else—"

"I didn't," Arch said heavily. "Lots of things that you think matter, they just don't matter at all."

"But I'm *me!*" said Luke in fear. "And I'm *scared* to die. I don't want to. I'm scared, my God, Arch, Mister *East*mere, oh, God, I'm *scared*. . . ."

He closed his eyes again, as if he could shut out his death. And as he did so, Arch Eastmere, with the slightest of efforts, shot him through the heart, dead center.

Luke looked at his killer for one last time. He tried to speak and failed, as his black fear became his white peace. Then his pale-lashed lids lost all power, and heavily they fell around his eyes. So, with a sigh for the small things he had loved and an unimportant tremor of his mouth, he went to silence in a sleep of lead.

Arch Eastmere spoke aloud to the body. "Least I could do," he said. "You *got* to believe me, Luke, because nobody else in this world will. I didn't mean for none of this to happen." After speaking, he sighed, then rose unsteadily to his feet.

He had, he believed, saved the Randal family many griefs, except this very first one. But they wouldn't thank him, nor should they. And nobody could ever give these last few minutes back to either Luke or Arch. Especially to Arch Eastmere—alas, still alive—he who had once been his mother's only joy, and who had learned how to die the hard way, by watching others do it.

"*Ants*," he said. "Luke, you're worth *more'*n a dime."

He stood above the body for another minute, full of self-loathing and despair, while he prayed for the thing that had once been his heart to kill him dead as Luke.

But nothing happened, except to his soul—and of this change he was not yet aware.

Nor was he aware, when he walked back to his grass-cropping horse, that he was weeping from his hard eyes.

Later, Dolores saw the horse, as it nuzzled more grass by an aspen grove. On its back was a saddle of silver that gleamed, like white fire, in the afternoon sun, taking her breath away. It was, she was sure, the kind of saddle that the saints used when they rode their winged horses along the streets of Heaven. The sight of it almost made her forget her own sorrows and the cruel way in which her love had been betrayed. Almost, but not quite.

Until she saw the man, that is; then she nearly forgot her own name. He was the sort of man she had always imagined her father must've been. He was big, as tall as anyone she'd ever seen; she could tell how tall he was, even though he was sitting on the ground by an aspen, his huge hands clasped around the calves of his legs and his head hung forward, resting on his knees. There was something about the man's size, as well as the position he was in, that made her want to take him in her arms, comfort him, and—well, she didn't know what all.

Oh, if *only* it hadn't been for Pax Randal!

She was about to go on past the grove when the big man raised his head and looked at her. That was *all* he did, too. He didn't speak. He didn't get up. He simply sat there and looked at her. And she was close enough to him, and close enough to tears herself, to know that he had been crying. Long and hard, from the looks of him. Suddenly she didn't want to leave there.

"Hello," she said.

"Thanks," the man told her. "Thank you."

"What for?"

"Well, saying hello, like that."

She came closer to him. "Shouldn't I have said hello?"

"I reckon so. But—" He lowered his eyes.

She was so near to him now that she knew who he was, even though she hadn't seen him since she had been much younger and sillier than she was this afternoon. Some folks said he was a bad man. He didn't look bad, though. He looked just as lonely and just as unhappy as Dolores did herself. He must have a terrible sorrow in him, for somebody or something. "What're you crying about?" she asked.

The man looked up sharply. "Who?" he said.

"You were crying."

"Reckon I just *look* like I was."

"*I* can tell."

"What's your name, Miss *I*-Can-Tell?"

"Dolores. And you *were* crying."

"Tell you what, Dolores. Men find themselves doing a lot of mighty peculiar things from time to time."

"Women don't."

"That's nice. You a woman?"

She hesitated, then said: "More than I look."

He seemed to understand what she meant. "You live around here, Dolores? Because if you don't, you're a far piece from home."

"I—I used to live around here," she said after a moment's hesitation.

"Where do you live now?"

She turned her face away. "I don't know yet."

"Now, just what does *that* mean?"

"I did a bad thing," she said, her face still averted. "And now I've got to go away someplace." She was ready to cry herself.

The tall man saw this. He studied her fresh, dark beauty, and, as he did so, he felt, for some inexplicable reason, closer and more attuned to this tiny dark girl than with anybody else for a long time indeed. Perhaps not since the day when he had stood at somebody's deathbed somewhere.

"Well, now, *I* might've gone and done a bad thing, too," Arch Eastmere said quietly. "But me, I can't go anyplace at all. So you come over here and sit down beside me, Dolores. I reckon you and me maybe need each other a little."

Meekly, Dolores sat by him, and for a time they talked in dim voices together. And after a while they laid themselves down, there on the grass in the aspen grove.

"Far as I'm concerned," Randy Worth said, "I don't care if Arch Eastmere *never* shows up. Then we all can just go on waiting for him. I sure do love these easy afternoons."

"You ought to've brung your banjo," said Will Clough.

"By God, if I'd've knowed we was going to laze it like this, that's what I'd've brung, all right."

The two of them were sitting on the top rail of Alan Lacy's corral, smoking two of Alan Lacy's cigars, and lethargically blowing blue smoke toward Alan Lacy's ranch house. All around them men were gathered in small groups, talking quietly together. It was nearly five-thirty, and they had been waiting for Arch Eastmere since three o'clock.

"Where do you reckon that big bugger went to?" Will Clough seemed disinterested, and as he asked the question he knocked the ash off the end of his cigar.

"Back to Maudie Fletcher's," Randy Worth said. "Same as *I* would, if I had the money."

"*And* the strength," said Will.

"Hell, if I had as much money as I got *strength*, I'd own the whole United States. Lock, stock and barrel."

"Well, now," Will said, "if you could get old Macleod to pay you, say, fifty cents more a month, then you'd have as much money as you got strength, by God. And maybe more."

"He *is* a cheap old bastard," Randy said, "and that's a fact."

"Jock Menzies's paying his boys two dollars extra."

Randy Worth's eyebrows went high. "For just riding up in the Marias with this bunch?" he wanted to know.

Will Clough chewed the end of his nearly finished cigar. His eyes were on the far mountains. "For just sitting here on the fence, looks like," he said.

"I'll be damned. Wonder if Jock needs any more hands."

"Not right now, I don't think. Maybe come fall."

"Come fall, we'll still be sitting right here."

"No such luck, Randy. We'll be up the Marias tonight, you wait."

"Even if Arch don't show?"

Will Clough nodded. "We *got* to. The Lacys've put so much in the pot, by God, they don't dare try bluffing now."

"How about the Randals? You seen Hallock when he come into Smiley's, didn't you?"

"Damn right. He weren't bluffing, neither."

"And he said to stay off the Randal land, didn't he?"

"That's what he said, yep."

"But he didn't say what'd happen *if* we went on it."

"Nope." Will Clough sounded very cheerful.

But Randy Worth's brow was furrowed by a frown. "Well, I reckon *I* know what'll happen," he said. "Old Hallock'll be waiting for us with every damn short gun he can dig up."

"Probably," Will Clough agreed.

Randy was annoyed by his casual tone. "By God, Will, you must be mighty stupid, if *that* idea don't faze you."

"Well, I'll tell you," Will said easily. "The Randals've got themselves a powerful lot of land up there across the Forkhandle, so I figger they'll have a hell of a time finding us in the dark."

Randy Worth looked up at the blank blue sky. "It won't be *that* dark," he said. "There'll be plenty of stars, and the moon'll be good and bright."

"It's still a powerful lot of land up there," Will said. "They'd need a thousand men to cover it all. Of course," he went on, studying the now-dead stub of his cigar, "we got *one* thing against us, before we ever start out."

"What's that, Will?"

"Them." Will flipped the cigar butt toward Terry Sykes and Charley Samuels. They were sitting apart from everyone else, leaning their backs against a tree, newly dead this same spring, which Alan Lacy hadn't yet cut down. "Those two ugly buzzards'd be bad luck for any man."

"By God, that's so," said Randy. "Keeping old First'n'second Samuels around sure didn't do Mark Lacy any good."

"Keeping old Terry Sykes around ain't done *no*body any good," Will said. "Say, Randy, I wonder if that tree they're scratching their backs on was alive when they sat down there."

"I reckon it was," said Randy.

"Poor goddamned tree," said Will.

Mark Lacy had been running from one window to another for nearly two hours, peering out in annoyance and never seeing what he wanted to see. The six ranch-owners had eaten together; but now, as the fretful day waned, only Alan and Nelse Macleod sat in the main room of Alan's ranch house, counting the passing minutes and watching the restless Mark. Drury and Jock and Oliver Swindon had wandered off somewhere among the ranch buildings.

Alan Lacy watched his brother change windows for at least the thirtieth time. "If I thought a slug of whisky'd quiet you down," he remarked, "I'd sure have Liddie in here with a bottle damned fast."

Mark hadn't had a drink of anything but water in two days, not since he had heard Charley Samuels say his wife had run off. "Only thing that'll quiet me," he said, "is for that Eastmere to show up. God *damn* him, anyways."

"Seems to me you was mighty anxious to have him," old Nelse said.

"I *still* am," Mark said. "But where the hell is he?"

"We can get along without Arch Eastmere," Alan Lacy said.

"We can, by God," said Nelse, "we sure can."

"Not after what I paid him," Mark said. He came away from the window, sat down in a chair, then immediately rose and went to a window opposite the one he'd just left.

"Ah, hell," Nelse said. "I'm getting dizzy spells watching you jumping-jack around this way." He heaved himself up and went out of the house.

Alan waited until the old man had gone before speaking again to his brother. "It was *my* hundred dollars," he said. "I don't know where you get that talk about what *you* paid him."

"That five hundred dollars he was lent was mine," Mark said angrily. "Just don't go forgetting that."

"Hell," Alan said with a snort, "I figgered you'd *never* get that back. And so did *you*, by God. I heard you say so, half-a-dozen times."

"Well, I'm not saying it now."

"You might, Mark boy, if you'd just simmer down a bit."

"How the hell can I simmer down?" Mark began to walk rapidly back and forth past his elder brother. "I want to get this thing over with."

Alan's eyebrows went up. "After all the trouble you went through to get it started? Why, Mark boy, I'd've thought you'd want to drag it out as long as you could, and then some."

"I don't, hear?"

"Maybe *I* do, then," Alan Lacy said evenly.

Mark stopped at the far wall and surveyed Alan for several seconds through veiled eyes. "I take it you're driving the herd now," he said guardedly.

Alan nodded. "I *am* driving it," he said. "What made you think I wasn't, for Christ's sake?"

"Nothing." Mark turned away bitterly and stared out yet another window. "That's the way it's always been. I start something, and then you take it out of my hands."

"You're crazy as a bedbug," Alan said sharply. "You never get around to finishing *anything* you start. By God, all my life I've always had to end up burying my little brother's goddamned dead for him. Ever since I can *remember,* that's what I've had to do."

"Suit yourself," Mark said heavily. He crossed to a chair and dropped into it. "You're the boss."

"I sure *am* the boss," Alan said. "And, in case you want to know, I'm beginning to fancy this little excursion, whether Arch Eastmere's run off or he hasn't."

"*I'm* not, by God," Mark murmured.

"Go along home, then," Alan said. "We all can get along without *you*, too."

Mark looked up unhappily at his brother. "Ah, I don't like being alone in that house," he said. "Didn't think I'd ever have to tell you that."

If this were a plea for sympathy, Alan Lacy wanted no part of it; he had come too far to retreat even a single compassionate inch. "Well, damn your soul, Mark Lacy," he cried, "you'd best start liking it *here*, then. There's more than forty men come together on account of you, and, by God, you better not try to weasel out now."

"Hey, Alan! Mark!" Drury Wynward was calling their names as he threw open the door and hurried into the room. "Archie Eastmere's riding in, and he's got the prettiest little filly you ever did see swung up behind him." Drury grinned wickedly. "For a while there, by God, Mark, we all figgered it was Pax Randal, bringing back what's-her-name—Ellen Zane Lacy—if it hadn't been for that silver saddle, and this filly being a mite younger than your wife was. *Is*, I mean."

Mark Lacy, pallid, leaped to his feet. "Shut your goddamned mouth!" he exclaimed.

"Sure," said Drury cheerfully. "Sure I will, Mark *boy*." He pointed toward the north end of the room, where there was a fireplace but no window at all. "He's coming in from there, or don't it matter? I'd like another one of those cigars, Alan, if you've got another one of 'em to spare."

Later Arch Eastmere faced them all in the main room of the ranch house.

Dolores hadn't wanted to leave him, and she'd very nearly

made a spectacle of herself in front of most of the men outside,
until Arch had said something in her ear that had quieted her
and sent her off smiling with Lydia Lacy, to get a bite to eat in
the kitchen. But until Arch was out of her sight she had blown
him kiss after kiss.

As he stood in the main room, Arch seemed unaware that his
return had caused an odd tenseness and discomfort to come over
the six ranch-owners. He himself felt relaxed, almost placid—on
the surface, at least. What was seething deeper in him was still,
for the time being, his own affair.

"Where you *been* all this time, Arch?" Alan Lacy asked. The
question had been asked before, but not in such earnest. Until
now, except for that exchange with Nelse in Smiley's, all the talk
in which Arch had joined had been jocular and amiable. He
wasn't too pleased with Alan's brusqueness.

"Oh, here and there," he said. "No place special."

"But *doing* anything special?" Alan continued.

"Oh, maybe finding things, I'd say," Arch told him.

"Where'd you find the girl?" Nelse wanted to know.

"Let *me* do the asking, Nelse, if it's all the same," Alan said
sharply.

Old Nelse looked at him in hurt surprise, then grunted. "Ask
away, and be damned to you," he said edgily, tugging at his
beard. "Just so's I got your permission to *listen.*"

"Hell, Nelse," Alan said in a more gentle tone, "it's only that
if *one* man does the asking it'll maybe take less time."

"There's plenty of time," Drury said.

"The hell there is," Mark muttered.

"You fellers still interested in where I found the girl?" Arch
Eastmere asked. "Well, she come on me when I was sitting under
this here aspen tree."

"Where was that?" Alan said.

"I don't rightly know, offhand, Alan. I didn't have any maps
with me."

"You know who the girl is, though?"

"Sure," Arch said with a smile. "Name's Dolores. That's a Mexican word that means 'sorrows,' and there never was a young lady

prettier named or more rightly so. Dolores and me, we found we had plenty of sorrows to talk about."

"How old you think she is, Arch?"

"Oh, I reckon about the age we all wish we was."

"Didn't she tell you anything?"

"Not even her last name. Guess I'll have to get *that* later."

"Her name's Dolores Costa," Alan said. "She's one of the daughters of the Randals' cook. The *youngest* daughter. She can't be much over fourteen, if that.

"Sixteen," Arch said.

"Sixteen, then."

"That's fine with me, Alan. It bother *you?*"

"It's got me thinking you maybe ran into her on Randal land."

"Well, now, Alan, I might've done that."

Alan Lacy looked relieved. "You *were* on Randal land, then?"

"Might've wandered around there a bit, yep."

"What'd you see, Arch?"

"Nothing I hadn't seen before. Except my friend Dolores."

"You didn't see anybody else? You didn't have any trouble?"

"Depends on what *you* call trouble, Alan." Arch Eastmere's voice was almost too casual, and he was no longer smiling.

"I call it same as you, I reckon."

Arch Eastmere shook his head slowly from side to side. "Nope, I don't expect you do," he said. "Because what *I* call trouble is standing here being asked a lot of fool questions about things that's the most of 'em none of your business."

Alan held up his hand as though he were having a palaver with an Indian. "Now, no sense in getting mad, Arch," he said placatingly. "I wasn't meaning to rile you."

"You didn't," Arch said, "and I ain't mad. I'm just telling you how I feel."

"Sure," Alan said. "So let's us all forget it. You got back late but, hell, there's no real harm done. We won't be heading up there till after dark, anyways."

"Yeh, there's still lots of time," Arch Eastmere agreed. "And I want to let my friend Dolores get a couple of hours' sleep or so, before we get started out. And I reckon I'll need another pony for her, too, Alan. I'd be much obliged if you could let her have one."

Alan stared at him in disbelief. "Now, wait a minute," he said. "Don't tell me you're figgering on bringing the girl along with you?"

"Sure, why not?" Arch said. "We get along right fine together, and we all might be spending two, three cold nights up there. Me and Dolores, now, we'll keep each other warm."

"The hell you will!" exclaimed Mark Lacy.

Arch Eastmere narrowed the lids of his hard eyes. "You and me might just as well keep on the good side of each other, Mark," he said. "You and your brother paid me to come along, and I didn't take to the idea much, don't forget, even with the money."

"We paid you enough," Mark said.

"You'll get your money's worth," Arch replied.

"What we *did*n't pay you for was to go on a whoring bee," Mark said.

"That's talk that don't pleasure me much," Arch said. "So let's us make-believe you never said it, hear?"

"All right," Mark said glumly. "But I reckon you get what I mean."

"Let's say I don't get that, neither," Arch remarked. He turned to Alan once more. "*You* got any objections to me taking my friend Dolores along?"

"I think she better stay here, Arch. Liddie'll look after her."

"You got a good reason why she better stay here, Alan? Because if you have, I sure want to hear it. And it *better* be a good one."

Alan Lacy hesitated a moment before replying. "The reason is that I'm driving this herd," he said, "and *I* don't want her along. That maybe's not good enough for you, Arch, but it'll damned well have to do."

"Fine, then," said Arch Eastmere. "*I* don't go, neither."

"Nobody's making you, Arch," Alan Lacy said. "And if you want to go about your business, well, then just hand over that hundred dollars I gave you—and don't forget you owe Mark another five hundred."

Arch Eastmere hesitated. "I turned that hundred dollars over to Maudie Fletcher," he said. "Reckon I can't ask her to give it back. I'll have to owe the two of you six hundred, I guess."

"We made a deal, Arch," Alan Lacy said sadly. "But I'd never've put you down for a man that'd go back on an obligation, just because you had to leave some fool girl by herself for a couple of days. My God, Arch, you left Maudie Fletcher alone for two years."

"My friend Dolores ain't the same as Maudie Fletcher," Arch said. "It ain't the same kind of thing at all. And, besides, these might turn out to be the couple of days we need each other the most."

Alan was standing by his guns. "I'm sorry, Arch," he said with great firmness, "but you're not going to take her up the Marias with you—not with this bunch along, anyway. It's not even a place for a woman up there, let alone a little girl."

"*Little,*" Arch said, closing his eyes momentarily. He opened them again and stared down at the floor. "That's all you got to say?" he asked. "The last word?"

"Afraid so, Arch."

"That's it, then. You can keep my friend Dolores here until I'm ready to take her." Arch started to leave the room. He had his hand on the doorknob when he heard Nelse Macleod say: "Hell, we don't need him, anyways. Never did."

Arch Eastmere stood motionless a moment, then turned to face the others, viewing them not as single men, but as a group of vague faces. His own face was bland, his voice controlled. "Before I go," he said, "I reckon I maybe ought to clear up a couple of things for you. Maybe you figgered I'd be mad and blow up, being treated this way and all, but I'm not mad a bit, and that's the truth. I might've been once, if the same thing'd took place, but not now. Not any more."

"We're the ones ought to be mad," Alan said with some heat. "After all, we reckoned on you being with us. But because you figger you've got to take this girl—"

"Maybe so," Arch said. "Maybe you're the ones ought to be mad. And if you ain't now, well, you're going to be. And the reason I know is, you started pumping me before I even had a chance to tell you anything myself. Anything about *anything.*"

"Tell us *what*, Arch?" Oliver Swindon asked. "And *about* what? I'm game to listen, if nobody else is."

"Me, too," said Jock Menzies.

"It don't matter now," Arch said. "And maybe it wouldn't've mattered if I'd told you before. You'll run into trouble, anyway, soon's you cross over onto Randal land."

"Now, that's what I wanted you to say in the first place, Arch," said Alan Lacy. "What kind of trouble?"

"You're going to have to work your own way out of it," Arch Eastmere told him. "I recollect you all thought you wouldn't have *any* trouble up there, but now I sure hope you're all men enough to handle what you're going to get. Because you sure *are* going to get it, and then some. I didn't even get a chance to tell you I run into a little trouble myself. I did, though, even though it wasn't anything of my own making, any more than it ever is."

"What trouble's that?" Nelse demanded.

"You'll learn," Arch said. "They must've found him long since."

"Found who?" Mark, frowning, wanted to know.

"Young Luke Randal," Arch Eastmere said. "Somebody shot him to death."

The room was instantly as silent and seemingly airless as a vacuum. The six men looked dead themselves, as they gazed open-mouthed at Arch Eastmere. "Somebody shot—Luke—Randal —?" Alan finally was able to say.

"Somebody *did*," Arch said. "Feller by the name of Arch Eastmere, not that he meant to do it, not by any means. It was pure accident, hear? Only trouble is, nobody knows that except Luke, and he's dead, and Arch Eastmere himself—and he just quit working for you."

He loped through the door, closed it quietly behind him, and left them to the future.

PART THREE

Then Were
the Horsehoofs Broken

THEY brought Luke Randal home draped over his own saddle, lashed to it so he wouldn't fall off, his long hair hanging across his face.

It had been late in the afternoon when Hallock and Soap Damson found him. Hallock had been wrong when he'd told Luke that someone would hear the shots, should he have to fire—for, due to some trick of the air or perhaps a juxtaposition of muffling hills, neither the carbine nor Arch Eastmere's answering pistol had been heard by anyone at all. And so Hallock, innocent of any knowledge of what had happened to Luke, had continued on up into the Marias.

There, between Camps Two and Three, he had rounded up all the hands. As much as he hoped Arch could do something to stave off a showdown, he wasn't going to let his wishes interfere with his plans. He told them that every rancher seemed to have gone plumb out of his mind, and that a slew of crazy men might shortly be riding across Randal land, in search of the dams they believed were being thrown across the Tines. "And maybe I'm just taking a chance," Hallock had said, "but I've got this feeling in me they're all going to make for Juncture Valley and start tracing the South Tine up from there. Leastwise, that's what I'd do if I was crazy enough to be in their boots. So *that's* where we're going to wait for 'em."

The whole group spent part of the afternoon moving down the slopes into Juncture Valley. Then Hallock, leaving Jim Good in charge of things, went off with Soap Damson to pick up Luke.

Hallock was dead tired, and his eyes were darkly ringed; below them his skin looked loose and soft. For thirty-six hours he had been without sleep, and he was beginning to have occasional moments of lightheadedness. As he rode along next to Soap, who was phlegmatically chewing tobacco, Hallock once or twice found himself dozing off in the saddle, and each time he came awake with a start. Soap, however, seemed not to notice.

"Damned if I can make out why Arch Eastmere'd go join up with those damned fools," Soap said. "Always knew Arch had a little too much damnation in him, but I always put him down as having a mite more sense than he's showing now. Son of a bitch ought to've *stayed* down in Mexico. They're all of 'em crazy down there."

"Matter of fact," Hallock said wearily, "I gathered he didn't much like being in with that bunch."

"How so?"

"Oh, just from the way he run on. We'll see."

"How'd he look? Mean as ever?"

"About the same. Little peaked, come to think of it."

Soap spat out some tobacco juice. "Plenty of gold down there in Mexico. Wonder how much of it stuck to Arch?"

"He said he didn't do good at all." Hallock could no longer suppress a yawn. "But this big horse of his was outside Smiley's with one of these fancy silver Mex saddles on. Looked like it weighed nigh enough to break the critter's back."

"Yep, yep, the son of a bitch," Soap said dispassionately. "That's the kind of thing he'd bring back." He glanced quickly over at Hallock. "You're kind of tuckered, looks like. Better bed down, hadn't you, before very long?"

"When I can, Soap, when I can."

They cantered around a finger of spruce that ran out into a narrow meadow. Three hundred yards away they could see the pair of outcroppings where Hallock had left Luke. At the foot of the one to their right was Luke himself, stretched out.

Soap pointed ahead at the sprawled form. "Looks like Luke went and hit the hay early," he said. "A sight smarter than his big brother."

A surge of anger carried Hallock up from his exhaustion. "Well, goddamn him!" he exclaimed. "He might at least wake up when he *hears* us."

"Aw, hell," Soap said, "these young fellers're always either tomcatting around or snoring their guts out. Though Luke ain't got around to the tomcat part quite yet."

"I told him to look lively," Hallock said. "My God, back in the War, he could've been shot for sleeping on post."

"Kick him in the tail a couple of times," Soap said placidly. "That ought to do the—"

"Wait a minute, Soap." They were close enough to Luke now for him to get a good look at his brother. Hallock had seen too many men, on too many battlefields, lying the same way as Luke, to delude himself any longer that the boy was asleep. Then he saw the red-brown stains that encompassed Luke's breast and stomach. "Hell!" he said under his breath, and galloped on to the outcropping.

Even before he reined up by the body, Hallock knew that nothing more would ever be done in this life for Luke Randal, eight days a man. Hard-faced, he waited for Soap to come up, and together they dismounted without any words and stood looking at Luke. The blood on his shirt and trousers was lusterless and dried, and blue-green flies crawled across the stained cloth. One fly was preening itself on Luke's right eyelid.

"Well," Soap Damson finally said, "*that's* bust it, for sure."

Hallock went over, picked up the carbine, and saw that it was jammed. "The dirty bastards," he said in his usual tone. Then he took the gun by the barrel and heaved it into the spruces on the outcropping. Luke's horse, still tethered where the boy had left her, shied and whinnied as the weapon fell noisily through the trees.

Hallock came back to where Luke was sprawled and sat down beside him on the meadow floor, brushing the flies away from the body in an abstracted way. He seemed helpless and drained of all energy. He let his head hang.

Embarrassed, Soap turned away, spat out all the tobacco juice he had left in his mouth, and lumbered off into the open grass between the two outcroppings. He kept his eyes on the earth, and he missed very little of the terrain he covered. Two or three times he stopped, and once he bent to pick up something. Then, after he had spent nearly twenty minutes in this fashion, he returned to where Hallock still sat dumbly by Luke.

"You all right yourself, son?" he asked, awkward and gentle.

Hallock slowly raised his head, compressing his lips. "Reckon I'll do," he said. "I better get Luke back home." And he climbed to his feet.

"It was only *one* dirty bastard done it," Soap said.

Hallock's face was expressionless. "You sure?"

Soap nodded. "I went over the ground pretty careful," he said. "They was signs of three horses, that's all. Two of 'em was yours and Luke's, I reckon. And they was also signs of one feller that left his horse out there and walked in here. He was the goddamned son of a bitch that done it. A *big* feller."

"I'm obliged to you, Soap," Hallock said. "Now all we've got to do is find out which one of 'em was *big* enough."

"I done that, too," Soap said, and he held out his open hand. "Picked *this* doo-dad up out there."

In his palm was a silver rosette, the size of a twenty-five-cent piece.

Hallock took it and turned it over and over with his fingers. "Silver," he said finally.

"Yep."

"Mexican."

"Yep."

"Arch Eastmere."

"That's him, the goddamned murdering bastard."

Hallock lifted his eyes from the rosette and turned his gaze to the south—toward Lacy's Ford, toward Alan Lacy's ranch, toward Smiley Brann's place, down in the direction where, *some-where*, Arch Eastmere could be found. Soap Damson noticed that a vein on Hallock's temple was throbbing and that the one eye he could see from where he stood was narrowed and slitted. Bad signs.

"Whatever you got on your mind, Hallock," he said, "don't you go trying it. Not right now, you hear?"

Hallock expelled all the air from his lungs, took a deep breath, and dropped the rosette in his pocket. "No," he said, "I better get Luke home."

"You and me, we'll do it."

"Soap, maybe you ought to get back up there with Jim Good and the rest of 'em, before they start to worry. Next thing you know, they'll all be coming along here, looking for us."

"Ah, they'll stay put where they are," Soap said. "Jim Good ain't one to move till he's told." He knelt beside the body. "Come on, now, let's us get old Luke on his horse."

The body was stiff and unwieldy. It was neither an easy job, nor a pleasant one. Together, however, they got it done.

They rode in silence. The sun had gone under, and the air was mauve. Soap, who was leading Luke's horse, occasionally looked around to see if everything was in order. Hallock paid no attention to the body. He had been staring straight ahead ever since they'd started out, holding the reins listlessly, letting his mount keep her own pace and direction alongside Soap Damson's horse.

Then, when they were more than halfway to the Randal ranch house, Hallock, who had allowed himself to sag forward, came to life. He straightened his back and squared his shoulders. He rubbed his eyes with his free hand. "*God,* I'm tired," he said.

"Figgers," Soap said. His mouth was very dry, and he would have liked nothing better than to have a big chaw in it. But he didn't guess this was any goddamned time for a man to be chomping tobacco.

"*Why?*—that's what *I* want to know," Hallock said, speaking louder than usual.

Soap looked at him with surprise. "No sleep," he said. "What else?"

"Why should Arch Eastmere kill my *brother?*" Hallock went on, as though he hadn't heard Soap's words.

Soap shrugged: he had no answer for that; not at the moment, anyway. "Mean son of a bitch," was the only reply he could give.

"A kid like Luke, my *God!*" Hallock said. "Never hurt a fly in his life. Why, Arch even *liked* him. We *both* of us used to have fun with Luke."

"Sure," Soap said. He glanced over his shoulder at the body.

"Arch maybe's done some bad things in his day," Hallock said, "worse than the rest of us, far as that goes, but—but, *Christ!* how could he go and gun down my little brother? What in God's name got *into* him?"

"Nothing," Soap said. "Nothing that ain't *always* been in the big son of a bitch."

"It's like everybody's gone crazy."

"No *like* about it. That's what they've all *gone,* by God."

"And, Jesus, Soap, my mother—"

"Poor woman, yep. What you figgering to tell her?"

"My God, I don't know, I swear. And then she's going to want to see him—."

"Well, she can't see him the way he is, and that's the truth," Soap said. "We ought to get him cleaned up a bit. Maybe we could take him into Eastmere, the hell with anybody that tried to stop us, into the undertaker's there—What's-his-name—*Hutch*inson. He could fix Luke up so she could see him."

"No, by God!" Hallock cried. "If I have anything to say about it, not *one* of us Randals, living or dead, is ever going to have *any*thing more to do with that goddamned town or the sons of bitches that use it. We'll take care of our*selves,* from now on. And *them,* too, damn their eyes, so help me God!"

"That's better, now," Soap said, nodding solemnly. "That talk about *them.*"

Hallock sucked air into his lungs. "Now, look, Soap, here's what I want us to do. It'll be good and dark by the time we get home, and when we do I want us to swing around and come in from the north, just as quiet as we can. We'll come in behind the barn, and I want you to take Luke in there while I go along up to the house myself. Lay him out as well as you can on the floor, and leave a lantern burning. Then you get back up to

Juncture, fast as you can lick it, and tell Jim Good and them we took Luke back home for a rest and that I'll be along soon's I can get a couple of hours' sleep myself. But for God's sake, Soap, *don't* tell the boys up there Luke's dead. They all know he was wore out, anyway, and that's all they'll think is the trouble. God knows what some of 'em might take it into their heads to do if they got the truth of it."

Without thinking, Soap pulled his plug of tobacco out of his pocket. "But what if the Lacys and those other bastards try to get through Juncture, and you ain't there?"

"Well, I don't reckon they will, but if they just might happen to, you fellers go right ahead and shoot the living hell out of 'em."

"By God," Soap said fervently, "won't we *just!*" And he wrestled off a big, brown chaw.

As Hallock went up to the house from the barn he heard the sound of a woman weeping.

Then, much to his surprise, he found Percy Randal, Pax, Ann, and lovely Ellen Lacy having supper together in the kitchen. It was unusual for the family to eat so late, and it was equally unusual for neither Luisa Costa nor any of her daughters to be in evidence. All the people at the table, too, looked down in the mouth, although Hallock's entrance brightened the faces of at least his father and his wife.

"You came home mighty quiet," Percy Randal said mildly.

"What's wrong?" Hallock wanted to know. "Mother all right?"

Ann came quickly to him and kissed him. "She's asleep, I think, dear heart," she said. "And so *you* ought to be. I never saw you looking so tired." She held him at arms' length and frowned at him.

"It's Luisa," Pax said, jerking his head toward the kitchen. "She's been yelling her head off all afternoon."

Hallock nodded; he had already pinpointed the weeping. "What's troubling *her?*"

"Dolores went and run off, it looks like," Percy Randal said.

"You haven't seen her anywhere, have you?" Ann asked.

"Where would *I* see her, honey, up in the mountains?"

"We thought, maybe in town," said his father.

"I didn't see her in town." Hallock went over to the table, picked up a cold slab of beef from a plate, and was about to take a bite from it. Then he changed his mind and put the slice of meat back. "Sorry," he said. "I've been taught better than that."

"Sit down, and I'll fix you something hot," Ann told him.

Ellen Lacy rose to her feet. "You can take my place, Hallock," she said. "I'm not hungry at all, I don't think."

Hallock ignored Ellen. "Bring me something up to the bedroom, will you?" he said to Ann. "I'll have it up there in a little while." Then he turned to Percy Randal. "Father, I'd like for you to come out in the barn with me, if you would, please."

"Right now, Hallock?"

"Yes, sir, if you'd be so kind."

Percy Randal stood up. "Anything you say, son."

Hallock looked over at his brother. "You too, Pax."

"What for?" Pax said sulkily.

"I want to talk to you. Father and you."

Pax made no effort to rise. "What about?"

"You'll learn, soon enough."

"Can't we all talk in the other room?" Pax asked, with a sidelong glance at Ellen.

"I said, in the barn, God *damn* you!" Hallock exclaimed.

Startled, Pax jumped to his feet. "All right, all right, Mister Randal," he said. "All you had to do was ask."

"I'll be upstairs in half an hour," Hallock told Ann. Percy Randal was already out of the room, and Hallock strode fast to catch up with him. Pax slouched along behind.

Hallock and his father walked slowly down to the barn, side by side. After them came Pax, still keeping to his own grudging pace.

"Anything happen in town?" Percy Randal asked.

"Talked to a slew of 'em. Nothing much else."

"You get any idea what they got up their sleeves?"

"Not right then, I didn't," Hallock said. "But I got a pretty good sample this afternoon."

"How so?"

"That's why I wanted you down here." They had reached a side door of the barn and stopped. Hallock put his hand on the latch. "Luke's inside."

"*Luke?* What'd they do to Luke?"

"They went and killed him, Father," Hallock said quietly.

Percy Randal sighed, swayed, and closed his eyes. But Pax, who had come up to them in time to hear the last few words, cried: "They killed our *Luke?*"

"Keep your goddamned *voice* down!" Hallock said.

Percy Randal opened his eyes again. "Gunshot?" he asked very softly.

Hallock nodded. "But I don't think he suffered," he said. "Judging from the look of him."

"Good God, *Luke,*" Pax muttered. "Little Luke Randal."

Hallock opened the door and let his father walk into the barn. Pax looked blankly at his older brother, then followed Percy. Hallock, stepping in after them, shut the door against the world outside.

A lantern was hanging halfway up a vertical beam in the middle of the barn and, stretched out beneath it, lying on one blanket and covered with another, was the body of Luke Randal. Soap Damson had worked fast and well, in the little time he'd been given. Luke's horse was tethered to another beam, a dozen feet away.

Percy Randal and the white-faced Pax walked across to the body and stood looking at the covered form, confused and somehow embarrassed. Pax gave a faint groan as Hallock bent over and drew the blanket down. The human mask behind which Luke Randal had lived seemed very placid and relaxed; in the dim light anyone might have thought him a pleasant-faced young man, on the verge of waking up after a most refreshing sleep.

Pax stared at what but a few hours ago had been his little brother, and the corners of his mouth dragged themselves down in grief. "Luke," he was whispering, "little Luke, Lukie." Suddenly he turned to Hallock. "Who did it?" he demanded.

"Pax Randal did it," said Hallock. "As much as any man

else." He watched coldly as Pax turned his ashen face away.

"Hattie loved her Luke more than her own life," Percy Randal said. "The way she is now, this might kill her, too."

"She's not going to know about it," Hallock said. "That's why I brought the two of you out here. *None* of us're going to tell her what happened to Luke till she's more like herself. I know *you* won't, Father—and *I* won't—and by the Almighty God, neither will *you*, Pax, not her nor anybody else, or I'll kill you where you stand."

Pax's only response was to shake his head back and forth.

"We can't leave the boy here," Percy Randal said.

"We won't," Hallock said. "He's going to be buried tonight. Tonight we're going to start us a family burial plot, where we all can end up when our time comes. And Pax is going to dig this first grave. His own dead brother's grave."

"*Me?*" Pax said hollowly.

"You," Hallock told him. "All by yourself, alone. And I want it dug, and Luke in it, and all covered up, by daybreak, hear?"

"I don't know if I can, alone," Pax mumbled.

"You'd *better*," Hallock said. "Because if you don't, I swear to God I'll put you in it with him." Abruptly Hallock turned to Percy Randal. "I'm going to get some sleep, Father," he continued in a more rational tone. "Then I intend to get me back up to Juncture, where everybody else is. And if you don't hear from me for a day or so, don't fret yourself. We can handle anything that might come along." Then on an impulse he threw his arm around his father's shoulders, hugged him quickly, and left the barn.

For several minutes, after Hallock had gone, Percy Randal and Pax stood silent above the body. Then the old man dropped to his knees and caressed the dead cheek of young Luke Randal, eight days a man, eight hours a corpse. He shivered.

"Don't, Father," Pax whispered hoarsely.

Randal gazed up at his living son. His wet eyes shone in the light of the lamp. "I'll give you a hand with the burying, boy," he said. "Reckon I had as much to do with killing him as you did."

Upstairs, Hallock discovered that he was too tired to eat. After he had forced himself to swallow a few mouthfuls, watched by his wife, he pushed the plate away and threw himself down on the bed without even bothering to remove his boots. "Sorry," he said, smiling drowsily at the patient Ann.

She came and sat beside him on the bed and brushed his matted hair back from his forehead. Then she began to unbutton his shirt. Half asleep, he tried to push her hand away. "Don't need help," he murmured, his eyes closed. "Just want to get up in two hours. Two—"

But Ann Randal's hand had brushed across a stiff stain near her husband's belt buckle, and instantly she knew it for the dried blood that it was. She blanched and shook him. "Hallock!" she said with great urgency, "*Hallock!*"

"Uh?"

"What happened out there in the barn?"

"Barn? Nothing. Nothing happened out there."

"There's blood on your shirt. Dry *blood.*"

"Oh." He was again, though only briefly, wide awake. "It wouldn't've dried between here and the barn."

"Then—then what happened this afternoon? Today?"

He looked into her earnest eyes, then sighed. "You'd best know too, I reckon, Ann. Just Father and Pax and you. But, for God's sake, don't tell Mother or Cora. You won't do that, will you, now?"

"I won't. You know I won't."

"Luke was—" He swallowed. "Luke was shot."

Ann gave a gasp. "Oh, *no!* But not badly, Hallock, not too *badly.*"

"He's dead, Ann. I'm sorry."

"Oh, *God,* Hallock! Who did it?"

"Arch Eastmere." His eyes were closing again. "In two hours, dear one, remember."

He went to sleep on the instant.

Two hours later to the minute she shook him awake.

He felt befogged for a space and then, knowing himself much refreshed, he swung his legs off the bed and sat upright, yawning and stretching.

Ann, who had sat stiffly on a chair near the bed during the whole time he slept, studied her husband's rested face: the eyes were much clearer, and the skin below them had lost its loose waxen appearance. She moved over to him and kissed his forehead. "You look much better, dear heart," she said. "I'm glad."

"Feel better, too," Hallock told her. He went to the commode, poured some cold water into the basin, and washed his face.

Ann handed him a towel. "What about Arch Eastmere?" she asked, as steadily as she was able. "What action'll be taken against him?"

Hallock, his washing completed, handed her back the towel. "I'm going to kill Arch Eastmere," he said, "first chance I get."

"Yes," said Ann Randal quietly, "yes, I think that's what you'd better do."

CHAPTER 18

THE TIME: *3:00 a.m.*
THE PLACE: *Alan Lacy's ranch house*
THE PEOPLE: *Mark and Alan Lacy*

A‌LAN—?"

"What is it now?"

"A man's got a right to get his wife back, that's all I wanted. I didn't mean for nobody to get killed. There's other ways of handling things."

"Sure, Mark boy. Other ways than dragging in Arch Eastmere."

"Jesus, Alan, we could've rode up there and talked to 'em reasonable, Perce and the rest of 'em, without it coming down to shooting kids or anything like that."

"How long ago'd you figger *that* out?"

"Reckon it's always been in the back of my head."

"Tell you something, Mark. I don't think you know just *what* you got in your head. And what*ever* it is, it sure makes you act different."

"Now, *that's* a damned lie. Any other man that'd had his wife stole would act just like me."

"*I* wouldn't."

"Nobody's stole your wife."

"For Christ's sake, Mark, I don't give a damn if Ellen run out on you or not, and nobody else does, neither. You think all these men've come together because Pax took her off? Well, by God, they didn't. They come together because of what Perce Randal's doing with the Forkhandle and—"

"And he's *still* doing it, too, and you keep forty men lying around here, not lifting a goddamned finger, while that Eastmere bastard rides out and kills Luke Randal for himself, and now there's going to be bad trouble, for sure, when if we'd only gone and—"

"You reckon so, Mark boy?"

"You're damned right I do. And that's not the only thing that's come to my mind. Take, for instance, what *you'd*'ve done if Lydia'd run off with somebody."

"I'd go and kill whoever it was."

"And Lydia, too?"

"The hell with Liddie. I wouldn't want her after."

"Trouble with you, Alan, you've let Arch Eastmere have all the rope he wanted, hand over fist, enough goddamned rope to hang us all, while you just lazed around and let those Randal bastards work. And now, by Jesus, there's this dead kid up there, and before you know it there's going to be more law and damnation around here than you ever heard tell on. We'll be lucky, by God, if prison's all they give us, once they start to move."

"Just listen here, Mark boy, what makes you think Luke Randal got killed?"

"What *makes* me? Jesus *Christ*, Alan, Arch Eastmere stood right here in this room and *said* he killed him. *That's* what makes me, you goddamned fool."

"Now, by God, Mark, it looks like something has to be showed you real slow and careful, just like a babe in arms. So tell me one thing. You seen any *body*? Did Arch come back here dragging Luke by the heels and say: 'Boys, I'm sorry, but look what I went and done'?"

"He didn't have to. He said he killed him, and that's enough for me."

"Well, it's not enough for me, by God. I don't think Arch Eastmere killed *any*body, hear? Not Luke Randal. Not *any*body. Now what do you think of that?"

"——"

"Surprised, hey? I thought so. And, I was, too, when he stood up here and said he shot Luke. By God, I felt like he'd pulled the floor right out from under me. But then I got to thinking and not five minutes later it come to my mind that Arch was lying his damned head off."

"Now, why—wait, why should he lie about a thing like that? I never heard tell Arch took kindly to lying. Give the goddamned devil his due."

"Anybody can start a habit, anytime. And if Arch Eastmere ever had any good points about him, well, he's sure managed to wear 'em down to the nub over the past twenty years."

"You can think what you want, Alan, but I believed him when he said he killed Luke Randal and, by God, I believe him now."

"Well, you weren't alone then, Mark boy, because everybody else did, too, with him standing up here cool as you please and giving us all that talk about the trouble we were in, and then sashaying out of here. After I thought about it awhile, I figgered the only feller who'd been in trouble was Arch Eastmere, and damned little trouble at that. Arch made up what he said out of the whole cloth. Mark boy, you know as well as I do, if he'd shot Luke Randal, Hallock and the whole passel of 'em would've been down on us by now. No, sir, Arch Eastmere didn't kill *any*body. All he killed was an afternoon."

"But for Christ's sake, Alan, why should he *say* he killed the kid?"

"Mark boy, he decided he didn't want any part of what we were doing, and saying that was his ace in the hole. I tell you what I reckon he did after he left Nelse and the boys at Smiley's. He rode after Hallock and Luke awhile, and then he got to thinking maybe it wasn't such a good idea, him joining up with us. Nelse said Arch was talking to Hallock outside, remember, and I don't know what they said to each other, but they always was pretty good friends. Anyway, Arch figgered he didn't want to mess with the whole business, so he pulled up under some trees somewheres, and set out to take a nap. Then along come this little Costa girl, and maybe she reminded him of one of those *señoritas* down in Mexico, so he fooled around with her a bit and then decided he could use her to break himself away from us. So he started this talk about not wanting to go up in the mountains unless he could take her along. But when he found out I wasn't having any, he turned over his hole card and said he'd gunned down Luke Randal. Hell, he thought he could weasel out himself, and at the same time scare us off from what we figgered to do. Well, far's I'm concerned, he's weaseled out, sure enough, but he ain't scared me off, not by a long shot. But he kept us from going up the Marias tonight, because I had to make sure he was lying. If he hadn't been lying like hell, the Randals would've been down here long ago, don't you think they wouldn't. But he *was* lying, by God, and Hallock Randal's still up there, and that's where we'll be heading in about eighteen hours from now. Anything else you want to know, Mark boy?"

"——."

"What's the matter?"

"Nothing. Just letting it sink in."

"You *believe* me?"

"I reckon I do, Alan. I might as well."

THE TIME:	*3:18 a.m.*
THE PLACE:	*A shack in the hills below Divide*
THE PEOPLE:	*Pace Gray, Phil Tate*

"Urrr—gh—"

"You all *right*, Mister Tate?"

"Huh? Hell, son, didn't mean to wake you up, sorry. Reckon I'm worse'n half-a-dozen women, grunting and groaning and carrying on this way. Sorry as hell, son, bless your heart."

"Anything I can do to ease you?"

"Naw, son. I just rolled over wrong. I was asleep, too. Woke myself up with my own noise, God *damn* Jack Rettis anyhow, I hope he dies three times over."

"You bleeding?"

"Lord love you, no. She's pulled together fine now. It's just that I still got that lead in me, and it ain't found a proper home yet."

"Can't you get somebody to take it out?"

"No point in it now, bless your heart. Sooner or later it'll work itself around someplace and show up right under the skin. Then I'll flick it out myself."

"That might take quite a while."

"Most things do, son. Come to think of it, you might give me a heft of that jug on the table."

"Yes, sir.—Here you go."

"Now, that's what I call *easing*. Have some yourself."

"Thank you, Mister Tate."

"Yep, I'm sure sorry to've waked you that way, bless you, boy, a young feller that's ridden all that far and's got to ride back again."

"I don't mind."

"Well, son, *I* do. Lord, Lord, Archie must think I'm tougher'n leather judgment, wanting me to ride up there to lend him a hand."

"Reckon he needed you pretty bad, Mister Tate, or he wouldn't've asked."

"Why, now, bless you, son, I guess he figgers he *does* need me and that old repeater of mine, else he wouldn't've went and put you to all this trouble, knowing what I've went through the past two weeks. But from what you told me about what's going on up there, I swear I don't see how I can be any help."

"Well, Mister Tate, I told you all I know, and all Arch told me."

"Know you did, son, Lord love you, know you did. But I'll be blistered if I can figger what's best to do. I can ride all right if I have to, but—"

"Maybe I better get back up there and tell Arch you don't feel fit yet, Mister Tate. You reckon I ought to do that?"

"You sure are one to chafe at the bit, ain't you, son? You been itching to leave since the minute you got here."

"Well, I ought to get back to Arch."

"He need you that bad?"

"Reckon he does, Mister Tate. Reckon he needs the both of us."

"Well, sure. But I can't move as fast as you. Might take me a couple of days to get up there."

"You have to ride *that* slow, Mister Tate?"

"It's *that*, yep, and then it's a case of sort of keeping to the quiet country along the way. I don't cotton to the idea of stopping on the road and talking to folks I don't know from Adam. They got nothing I want to hear, and I sure got nothing I want to say. To strangers, that is. Don't mind chattering away to a nice young feller like you, though."

"Well, uh—don't you reckon it'd be smart if I went on ahead and told Arch you was coming? It'd sure take a load off his mind."

"And *yours*, too, hey?"

"Yes, sir, I'm getting mighty fidgety, trying to figger what's going on back up there."

"Used to be the same way myself, in my younger days."

"Why, you're not old, Mister Tate."

"Son, I'm younger than I look, and that means I'm older in something besides years. Well, come first light, Lord love you, you ride on up to Archie, and tell him Phil Tate's on his way, and bringing his shiny old repeater along with him."

"Hell, Mister Tate, I can leave right now."

"Well, by God, if you *ain't* the jumpy one. Well, then, git, son, bless your heart. But leave that jug by me, if you please. And watch yourself, hear, riding in the dark."

"Always have, always will."

"That's the way, Lord love you, that's the way—always look at what's up ahead. What'd you say your name was, son?"

"Gray. Pace Gray."

"Why, *sure*, now. You'd think I didn't hear people when they tell me things. Pace *Gray*. I knowed your two aunts as a small child. Dorrie and Sallie Pace. And right pretty girls they was, too."

"I'll tell 'em I saw you, Mister Tate."

"Why, bless your heart, boy, they wouldn't remember old Phil Tate. It's been forty years, and more."

"They remember every single little *thing*, Mister Tate, I swear they do. I never knew folks could recollect so much. And they'll remember *you*, too, don't you think they won't."

"Son, son, don't you trouble to tell 'em you met me. Because they'll start talking about a feller *you* never saw, and one I ain't seen myself for a good long time. Git along back to Archie now, God love you, boy."

THE TIME: *3:49 a.m.*
THE PLACE: *Maude Fletcher's bedroom*
THE PEOPLE: *Arch Eastmere, Maude Fletcher*

"God *damn* you, Archie, you can't keep it up, you can't go on drinking that way, you've put away almost a gallon."

"Just getting myself warmed up, Maudie honey."

"Warmed up for *what?* damned old catamount, not for me, that's for sure, not for Maudie."

"I'm cold inside, little Maudie, real cold, and the booze makes me warm all over."

"You're sick all over and you're making it worse, that's what you're doing, Archie. You haven't been drinking and you shouldn't be drinking and you ought to be lying right here beside me asleep, damn you, instead of walking like in a cage. Big sick old cat, you, come to bed, come and lie down and let Maudie hold you."

"I'll get to lie down, Maudie honey, but not right now, not while I'm cold."

"I'll keep you warm, hear? Archie, warmer than you've ever been yet, warmer than you reckoned you could be."

"It's a different kind of cold, Maudie, nobody's arms can help it much. It's a grave cold, Maudie, a casket kind of cold."

"Oh, God, Archie, don't *talk* that way, it's getting on to morning, you need sleep."

"I've had lots of sleep in my life, Maudie, and there's plenty more to come. A man always ends up with more sleep than he wanted."

"Ah, Archie, it hurts me, I love you so."

"Now, little Maudie, Mrs. Maude Fletcher, there's no point in crying, so wipe off those tears. Old Archie's just making up for a little lost time, those few days he didn't touch a drop, real *tee-total* old Archie was, but pretty soon it'll balance out."

"You'll make yourself sick again, oh, damn you, Archie, as easy as you make me cry."

"Who's making you cry, shiny little Maudie, with your pretty skin shining there in the moonlight? There's nothing to cry about, Maudie honey, in a man drinking and a woman lying alone, not when they're in the same room and talking to one another."

"What started you drinking, Archie, damn you? Ever since you come home you've been tilting that jug till your long old arm must be aching."

"Did I come home, little Maudie?"

"This is your home and you know it, Arch Eastmere, the only home you got, and the only woman you got, and my God, it makes me cry just to think how much I love you, you walking back and forth there, tilting that jug and holding your tongue and with your head all full of God knows what about God knows who."

"Is that what my head's full of, Maudie?"

"Big old cat, you're not thinking of me, you're a million miles away, you long-legged devil, what happened with the Lacys to set you off?"

"I ain't set off, Maudie honey, you know I ain't set off."

"It's a different man than went away, Archie Eastmere, and ah! you know it, old longshanks you."

"I grew a day older, that's all, little Maudie, and the jug's nearly empty, now look at how light it is."

"Will you come and lie down when it's empty, Archie?"

"There's another jug to go, little Maudie, another jug, and then I'll lie down. Another jug'll make me warm, it'll make me sleep, another jug will."

"Ah, no, dear Archie, sweet Archie, don't drink any more, damn you, *please* don't, Archie, I want to hold you and sleep at your side."

"Too many thoughts to let me sleep, Maudie."

"Thoughts about *what*, Archie, thoughts about *who?* My God, it kills me to see you suffer."

"No suffering here, Maudie, none at all, I'm peaceful in my mind."

"Where did you go, old wandering cat, what did you do and where did you go?"

"Upcountry, little Maudie, saw some sights, saw some people."

"What people, what sights?"

"Live people, dead people, live sights, dead sights."

"Ah, tell me true, Archie, where did you go, where did you go and why?"

"Had the world in the palm of my hand, little Maudie, it weren't no bigger than that, saw myself on it, small as a flea, saw a lot of people betwixt and between, talked to a woman, talked to some men."

"What woman, damn you, Archie, who, *who* was the woman you talked with?"

"Had a few words with my mother, Maudie."

"Ah, now, old drunk Archie, tell me true, who was the woman you talked with?"

"She asked me, was anything she could do for to help me, Maudie honey, and I told her no, I reckoned not, not after forty-two years. But that was afterwards, after the other, long, long afterwards, Maudie."

"Archie, you're good and drunk, damn you to hell, long after *what?*"

"After I went and got born, little Maudie, after all that and then some."

"Oh Jesus, Archie, come down on the bed before you pitch on your face, please, darling, come down here with Maudie, and let her hold you tight, I don't want to cry, but I've got to, I hate to see you like this, you're the best of the lot and it hurts me, ah! come down on the bed and rest, dear one, dear sweet tired Archie."

"I'll know when it's time to, pale little Maudie, so you sleep now and let me alone, hear? because when it's time I'll just float down, so soft you won't even know I'm beside you, and then,

Maudie honey, I'll sleep the sleep, maybe a whole day, even."

"If I could believe you, Archie honey——"

"I only lie to myself, you know that, just to myself, not my Maudie."

"Don't fall, long old catamountain."

"I fell a dozen times in my life, and never once did you hear me."

CHAPTER 19

IT HAD been dark when he started. Now, as Pace Gray was ending his long ride to Alan Lacy's place, the sun was beginning the longer descent from the apex of its own journey. Pace's horse was showing signs of exhaustion, but he himself was kicking-fresh, bright with a barely suppressed elation and buoyed by his own eager days.

Pace had set a crow-flight course for Alan's, bypassing Eastmere entirely, aiming straight for the target of his excitement and hope. Yet, for all his high expectation, he had known fogged doubting moments as he rode, vaporous wisps of thought that told him he would arrive too late, that the men would have gone up into the Marias and returned, and that the action of which he so longed to be part had already taken place.

But when he was within sight of Alan Lacy's ranch house and could make out human figures moving around it Pace knew that nothing had happened during the restless hours he had spent on his trip to Divide. None of these men, he was certain, had been in the mountains last night. He couldn't have said how he knew this, because he was still too far away to distinguish individual figures, let alone individual faces—but somehow he *did* know it. With a happy yelp, he spurred his horse to a last tired effort, clopping up to the ranch house in triumph and dust.

As he dismounted a number of men studied him with exaggerated disinterest, with the exception of Randy Worth, who, sitting on the top rail of the corral, spat wearily into the dirt and muttered: "Son, there just ain't that much rush."

Drury Wynward, an unlit cigar jutting blackly from his white, even teeth, sprawled alone on the top of the porch steps, whittling at a stick. His hat was shoved back on his head, and his eyes were sleepily lidded. The grin he gave Pace was sleepy, too. "Well, now," said Drury, "if you ain't just what the doctor ordered. Lose one, get one. Why all the dash, now, Pace?"

"Got here in time, didn't I?" Pace, out of breath, spoke jerkily.

"Time for what?"

"Well, none of you've went up there yet, have you?"

"Oh." Drury brushed some shavings from his thigh, frowning. "Nope, can't say as we have. Lot of us got sore jaws, though, what with all the fat that's been chewed hereabouts."

"Where's Arch? Inside, huh?"

"I don't rightly know where Arch went. Maude Fletcher's, maybe."

Pace knitted his brows and ran his tongue over his dry lips. "What the hell's he doing down at Maudie's?"

"Probably the very same thing they wouldn't let him do around here."

"I don't get your drift, Drury. Damned if I do."

"Don't get it myself, half the time," Drury said blandly. He started to whittle again. "Reckon you better talk to Alan. He's holed up inside."

In the main room of the ranch house Pace found the Lacy brothers and Nelse Macleod. "Where's Arch?" he demanded.

They all stared at him with calm faces. "Well, now," Nelse said finally, "you back?"

Pace nodded curtly. "Yes, sir," he said. "And Phil Tate's on his way, same as Arch wanted."

Nelse Macleod seemed surprised. "Can he *ride?*"

"He'll be here," said Pace. "Tomorrow, like as not."

"Out of the goddamned frying-pan," Mark Lacy said.

"Not so's you'd notice it," Alan said patiently.

"Where's Arch, anyways?" Pace asked.

"Gone," Mark said.

"That's right, son," Alan said. "Arch saw things a little bit different than we did. So we all kind of parted company."

Pace was confused, and confusion made him tongue-tied. "Why'd he—that's a, now, *hell* of a thing," he managed to say.

"You're damned right it is," Nelse said. "He went and killed Luke Randal."

Pace let his jaw drop. "He went and *what?*"

"Murdered little Luke Randal," said Nelse Macleod. "Never give the poor lad a chance."

Under Pace's tan, white crescents appeared on each side of his mouth. "By God, now, that's a lie!" he exclaimed.

"Show a little respect, you," Nelse said through his worn teeth, "or I'll fetch you a backhander that'll knock you clear across this room."

Pace leaned toward the old man, straddle-legged. "Try it, you dried-up bastard," he said. "Go on and try it, you long-beard son of a bitch."

"All right, now, that's enough," Alan Lacy said sharply. "Now, you listen to me, young Pace. Arch Eastmere stood right here in this room yesterday afternoon and told us how he shot Luke. Right here in this room, about where you're standing."

"He *told* you he shot Luke?"

Alan nodded. "That's what he told us, all right."

"With his own goddamned mouth," said Mark.

Pace looked as though he were in physical pain. "Why?" he asked. "Why'd he shoot Luke?"

"He didn't trouble to say," Alan told him.

"Didn't have to," Nelse grumbled. "All you got to do is look at him to know the feller'd shoot you soon as look at you."

"Anything Arch ever done he was driven to," Pace said, feeling like a man on a runaway horse.

Nelse Macleod tugged gently at his beard. "Yep, yep," he said, nodding.

"Anyways, what with one thing and another," Alan Lacy said, "he didn't stay around."

"Where'd he go, then?" Pace demanded.

"Nobody asked him," said Mark. "Nobody give a damn."

"Back to Maudie Fletcher's, most like," Alan said. "Didn't you see any sign of him there when you rode by?"

"Didn't come that road," Pace said heavily.

"Well," Nelse Macleod said, "if Arch Eastmere's got any brains left at all, he won't tuck in at Mrs. Fletcher's, or any other place where a human ear'd hear him. Seems like a whole passel of people're fixing to get him hung."

"Just because *you* say he shot Luke Randal?" Pace said.

"Maybe just because he's Arch Eastmere," said Mark.

"We didn't say it, Pace," Alan said in a mild voice. "*He* said it."

"Damned good thing a feller can go and get himself hung only once," Nelse muttered. "Because otherwise *that* one'd have a mighty sore neck."

"But don't you worry about it, Pace boy," Alan said, smiling faintly. "Everything'll turn out fine."

Frowning, Pace put his hand up and rubbed the back of his neck. Then he realized that Alan was smiling at him. He looked uncertainly at the other man for a moment, and finally he managed a wan smile of his own. "You been pulling my leg," he said flatly.

"Sure, Pace, pulling your leg," Alan said.

"I should've known."

Nelse Macleod glanced over at Alan, then sniffed. "You sure should've, boy," he said, "and that's a fact."

"Same way Arch pulled our legs," Mark said.

"Then he never shot Luke at all," Pace said. He felt almost dizzy with relief.

"That's about the size of it, I reckon," Alan said.

"Wonder why old Arch'd say a thing like that?" Pace said.

"Well, now, you know Arch," said Alan.

"Reckon I do," Pace said dubiously. "Most of the time, anyway. You all figger he's down to Maudie's now?"

"Why, sure," Nelse said. "Same as I'd be, if I was a year or so younger."

Pace turned to face the old man. "What'd you mean by that, Mister Macleod, saying a lot of people're fixing to hang Arch?"

"Well, now, son, when you come right down to it, everybody's always fixing to hang everybody else. That's the way life's lived, as you'll find out, once you've lived it a little bit longer."

"Hell, I guess I know *that* now," Pace said. He turned back to Alan. "You all going up in the Marias tonight?"

"Tonight," Alan said.

"Can I still come, too?"

"Don't see why not."

"Guess I got time to ride down to Maudie's, though," Pace said. "Got to tell Arch about Phil coming along."

"Yep, yep," Nelse said. "You *do* that."

"You want a fresh pony?" Alan asked.

"That's right nice of you," Pace said, "but the one I'm on ought to do fine."

"Well, go on out in the kitchen and tell Liddie I said to give you something to eat," Alan said.

"Now, that's one thing I *will* do," Pace said. "Much obliged." He went to the door and turned back, his eyes grave. "Mister Macleod, I'm right sorry I took on that way. I got no call to say such things to a man of your years."

"Never you mind, boy," Nelse said. "I heard worse in my day. And *give* worse, too. And will again, by God, if the weather holds."

The three men watched Pace leave the room. He shut the door behind him as he went through to the kitchen.

"Damned snot-nosed little fool," Nelse said. "Pity nobody never got around to shooting *him.*"

"Jesus," Mark Lacy muttered, heavy-throated. "*Jee*-sus Christ, Phil *Tate.*"

"Takes more than an old Henry rifle to blow up a dam," said Alan. "Which I'll tell Tate if he comes around here with that repeater of his. Except I don't reckon he will, not if he stops off at Maude Fletcher's first."

There was a beautiful little Mexican girl in the Lacy kitchen who fried up three eggs and a slab of bacon for Pace Gray. Her eyes were sad and her mouth was sullen; and Pace was sure he'd seen her before—but for the life of him, keyed up the way he was and eager to get along to Arch, he couldn't remember where he'd run into that troubled olive face. She was moping around, though, Pace thought, as if she'd lost her last friend, or as if she'd been sent for and couldn't go. And so, he decided, as he ate with a dog's impatience, was Mrs. Alan Lacy.

Lydia Lacy, indeed, looked worn and drawn, and a variety of dark shadows that had no business there hung around her brows. She did not mope, however; on the contrary, she was acting as nervous as a cat on a battlefield. She hovered around Pace while he ate, skipped out of the kitchen, came back, stared out of a window, patted her hair half-a-dozen times, and seemed to Pace to be keeping one part or another of herself in continual, pointless motion.

While Pace was drinking his second cup of coffee the lovely little Mexican girl left the room, and immediately Lydia Lacy came over to him. "Pace, are you going into Eastmere?" she wanted to know.

"Riding through there, ma'am."

"But not stopping?"

"No, ma'am."

"But could you stop for just a minute? Leave a message for me?"

"Glad to." Pace drank the last of the coffee and rose to his feet.

Lydia, instantly composed, gave him a smile of great warmth. "That's *very* kind of you, Pace. I just didn't know who I could ask. Why, since all these men came here, I don't think I've been out of the kitchen ten minutes at a time or had ten minutes' peace."

"Reckon not," Pace said. "Who's the message for, ma'am?"

"George Throstle," Lydia said. "Tell him Mrs. Lacy said she'd be in tonight."

"Tell George Throstle you'll be in tonight," Pace said, as though trying to memorize the words.

Lydia Lacy reddened. "No, not *me*," she said, her hair fluttering as she shook her head. "The *girl* there. Dolores. You saw her." She pointed at the door through which Dolores had gone.

"I sure did," Pace said happily. "Yes, in*deed*."

"Well, Mister Throstle was saying, just last Sunday, at the Randals, you know, just how much he wished he had a young woman to help him around the store, and she's—well, tell him I've got just the thing for him."

"Now, that's the truth, Mrs. Lacy," Pace said, and he grinned. "With what's-her-name—little Miss Dolores—giving old George a hand, I reckon I'll maybe be dropping in to buy some dry goods myself. Once I get the chance, that is. Not right today, though." He put his hat on. "Much obliged for the grub, Mrs. Lacy, I'll stop by George's place, first thing."

Three quarters of an hour later Pace faced George Throstle across the counter of the Dry Goods Emporium: "Mrs. Lacy says to tell you she'll be in tonight."

"She said *what?*" George Throstle, aghast, nearly dropped the bolt of taffeta he was about to put back on the shelf.

Pace winked at him. "You been wanting a female, ain't you? Well, to hear Mrs. Lacy tell it, she's got just the thing you need. Wait'll you *see* it, George. Wow!"

The boy left the store without another word, leaving poor George Throstle with shaking hands and a shaken mind: what in God's name had Lydia been *saying?*

And Pace, on his own part, was already out of Eastmere before he was able to connect Dolores with the Randals and remembered that she was the daughter of their cook, Luisa Costa. *One* of the cook's daughters, he thought; Luisa had two or three more, come to think of it. But he had so many other matters on his mind that it never occurred to him to wonder what she was doing at the Lacy ranch, or why whe was being apprenticed, if that was the word, to a stallion like sleek George Throstle.

It was only later that he discovered he couldn't forget her dark trapped face, in itself such a lovely entrapment.

Maude Fletcher sat on her rickety porch in the still heat of the afternoon, her skin more dun than ever, and her cheeks, like the roof of the porch above her, sunken.

She felt wrung out, and bewilderment lived in her eyes. She stared blindly at the long shadows of things, shadows lengthier by far than they had been when, unkempt and uncomprehending, she had left her bed and the snores of Arch Eastmere, to try and draw herself together in the poor shade of her porch.

The sun was well up before Arch had finally drunk enough to stun him and then, unseeing, had sought her sheets. He had talked the night away, growing more and more incoherent, until it sounded as though he were Talking in Tongues, making no sense at all, shouting sometimes, sometimes almost crooning, until at last, with the whisky-heavy air of the bedroom flushed by first light, he had fallen into a sullen silence, aware neither of her importunate pleas nor, for that matter, of anything else except the jug between his feet, the jug which he heaved, now and again, up to his slackened mouth. And then, on the sudden, he had risen and thrown himself across the bed and Maudie Fletcher, nearly crushing her naked chest with his weight, swept down by the whisky to oblivion and bewildered deeps.

She had freed herself from his heaviness and had pressed herself close to him. She had even dozed for a few uncomfortable hours herself, waking more weary and wasted than before, with her thin right arm asleep under unconscious Arch Eastmere, who had neither stirred nor murmured since his first falling down. Almost in tears, her arm tingling, she had left the sweaty bed, pulled off Arch's boots, and covered him with a blanket, drawn an old wrapper around her, and wandered, disconsolate, out to the porch. There she sat in the battered rocking-chair, careful not to make it creak for fear of waking Arch.

Maudie felt helpless and small and exhausted and more than a little scared. The last time she had seen Arch was when he had come by with Pace Gray to leave her that hundred dollars, five double eagles, and those other men had waited for him down the road from the house, Drury and old Nelse Macleod and the Lacys and Oliver Swindon. Arch had been just the same as always then, big damned gentle old catamountain, giving her the money that way, and saying the best things ever, but he wouldn't tell her where he was going or why or for how long. And then he had

come back, looking the same outside, but inside different somehow, wanting a lot of whisky, putting enough whisky down his
throat to float a Mississippi River gunboat, and talking more
tomfoolery than she'd ever thought he had in him. But not,
goddamn him, talking about what she wanted to hear, not
answering one of her questions, just pulling away at a jug until
he drowned in Whisky Bottom, the damned old long-legged
devil.

It wasn't because he knew he was sick. Arch wasn't the kind
to kill himself, and he must've had a pretty good idea that whisky
could kill a sick man even quicker than some of those hairy-face
doctors could. But Arch *was* sick. Maudie Fletcher knew it
better than he did, even; and to see him punish himself that way
was like to be the death of *her* before it was of him. She'd begged
him to stop, cried even, and it hadn't done a bit of good. Nor had
it done anything else, except maybe make him talk a little wilder,
and then finally to start him on that awful brooding that scared
her even more than all the crazy talk he'd come up with before,
hour after hour, the whole lost night through.

But Arch was back with her now, no matter how he carried
on, and she wasn't going to lose him again, ever—not to any sickness and certainly not to those other people, whatever they
wanted from him. They'd get out of here, both of them, little
Maudie Fletcher and her long tall Arch. They'd go east, maybe,
yes *east*, where it weren't so lonely and a lady could hold her
head up and take care of her man and live in a real whitewashed
house and buy pretty things, ready-made, in the stores. Why,
when sweet old Arch came out of it, once he woke up, with that
crazy night behind him, he'd feel so awful and so ashamed that
he'd up and do every last thing she wanted. And the hundred
dollars would take the two of them just as far as ever they had to
go, yes.

It was a fine dream, and it was opening, petal after petal, in
her mind when she realized, with a start that made the rocker
creak, that a horseman was coming toward her, a man on a bone-
weary, unsteady horse. Annoyed by this intrusion on her mental
flight to the east, and at the same time alarmed that Arch might

be disturbed by clatter and talk, she came down off the porch and trotted toward the approaching rider, frantically waving him down.

As he reined up and waited for her she saw that it was Pace Gray. This relieved her, to a certain extent. Her first thought had been that whoever was coming would want a little afternoon roly-poly, not knowing that she belonged to Arch all the time now—and her second thought had been that it was one of the Lacys or Nelse Macleod or somebody, come to drag Arch back to whatever it was they had dragged him off to in the first place. But Pace Gray—well, Pace was one she could handle. And, too, he ought to be able to tell her what had gone on, what had started her poor, sick Archie, goddamn him, to drinking so hard.

Pace sat on his hung-head horse, fifty yards or so from her shack, and as she came up to him he swung himself from the saddle to the ground. "What's the trouble, Maudie?" he asked.

"Arch's sleeping." Maude glanced quickly back at the house.

"This time of day?"

"We were up all night."

Pace grinned. "Oh."

"No, now, not what you think, hear? Archie was drinking something awful, damn him to hell."

The grin faded away. "All night *long?*"

"And then some. What happened yesterday, Pace? To set him drinking like that, I mean?"

Pace hesitated. The thought that Arch really had shot Luke Randal dropped, a meteor, through the dark of his mind. It burned out instantly, however, upon contact with the atmosphere of reason: that was *one* thing Arch'd never do. And besides, Alan Lacy had said they'd been pulling his leg. What it was, probably, was that, as Alan had said at first, they'd had some kind of argument about how to do things, and Arch had gotten his dander up and walked out on them. But without giving back the hundred dollars—that was it. He *couldn't* give back the hundred dollars, and it must've galled him like hell. So it set him to drinking, same as it would anybody else with any feelings at all. "I don't rightly know, Maudie," Pace said with deliberation. "I wasn't around."

"You left with 'em."

"Yep, but I had a little business down to Divide."

"For who?"

"Why, my aunts, who else? And I just got back, too. Look at this poor critter," Pace said, slapping his horse. "Like to drop in her tracks."

"Take her in the shed, Pace. Out of this goddamned sun."

"Reckon I better, Maudie, thank you."

They walked together to the shed, the spent mare between them. Arch's own horse was in one of the stalls. The saddle of Mexican silver rested on a bale of hay in a corner.

Maude sat down by the silver saddle. "When did you see Arch last?" she asked.

"Wait a minute, now," Pace told her. "Just let me ease this critter a bit."

He removed the saddle from his pony. As he worked, Maude Fletcher never took her eyes from him. Arch Eastmere's big horse, also watching, became restless. It whinnied softly and began to hit its right forefoot against the earthen floor.

"Be still, you," Pace said indifferently. He finished taking care of his own mount and went over to Maude. "Last time was in Smiley Brann's," he said, letting his hand run lovingly over the silver saddle. "Everything was fine, then."

"Where did he go after that, goddamn him?" Maude's voice was listless.

"Reckon he went with Alan Lacy and them."

"What for? What's the truth of why they wanted him?"

"For a job. Working for Alan."

The pink lips of Maude Fletcher grew thin. "That's what he told me, when he gave me that money," she said with some bitterness. "But that's a goddamned lot of money to hand a man, especially before the man's even started to work for you."

"Reckon it depends on how bad you need the man."

"Well, *I'm* the only soul around here that needs Archie Eastmere that bad. And when he comes back here the way he done, well, I've got a right to know what they did to him."

"Listen, Maudie," Pace said with increasing impatience, "I don't know what went on, and if Arch didn't tell you, how in God's name do you expect *me* to be able to? Hell, all it was, probably, is that they had some kind of a fuss and he walked out on 'em."

Maude Fletcher stared down at the straw-matted ground. "Will they want their hundred dollars back?"

"I don't know that, neither."

"I got to find out, Pace, one way or another."

"Reckon you will, once Arch comes out of it."

She shook her head. "No, I won't. He won't tell me, the long old bastard. And he'll maybe start drinking all over again."

Pace's eyes were on the marvelous saddle. He caressed it, dreamily, as he might a girl like Dolores Costa. "Tell you what, Maudie," he said. "I'll find out for you. I'm on my way to Alan's right now."

She brightened. "Oh, Pace, I'd be right grateful if you would, you promise you will, promise?"

"Yep," Pace said, with a faraway smile. "Only thing is, I better take Arch's horse."

Maude put her hand on his sleeve, and the brief glow left her. "He wouldn't like that, Pace. Don't take his things."

"I'll ask him."

"No. Don't."

"But my horse is plumb wore out." Pace pulled his arm away. "My God, you can *see* that, Maudie."

"Arch won't wake up. I don't want him woke up, Pace, hear?"

"He can wake up enough to tell me 'yes,' " Pace said. He moved toward the door.

"Stay out of our house, goddamn it, Pace, *please*," Maude said.

But there was no real strength behind her words, and Pace turned to glare angrily at her. "Leave me be, please, now, Mrs. Fletcher," he said.

She let him be. He walked out of the shed, into the shack, into the bedroom, and stood above the tall man who was sprawled on his back across the bed. A full minute went by.

Then Pace reached down and shook the unresisting shoulder.

Arch Eastmere, nine years old and scared, was hiding somewhere deep in tall grass, hiding with little Hallock Randal, only
it wasn't grass, really, it was mostly red flowers, so high that
crouching small boys couldn't see beyond the near blossoms. And
Hallock was scared, too, and pretty soon Arch couldn't even see
Hallock any more, because all these big long-stemmed red
flowers were growing high between them.

People were hunting them down, those two, somebody was
hunting them down, poor little boys, hunting them down in the
flowers. Arch Eastmere could hear one of the horses coming
closer to the place where he was crouched. He could hear the
horse snort, and the creak of leather, and once in a while he
heard a man talking to himself, or maybe to the huge inhuman
horse he rode, weaving back and forth through the flowers, beating down the bright red blossoms, closing in on his quarry with a
jingle of iron spurs.

Little Arch Eastmere, nine years old, weaponless, frightened,
crouched down in the flowers, and the sound of his heart was
louder and louder, louder even than the noise of the walking
horse, and he could neither breathe nor speak because of his
fear. Then he heard them find Hallock Randal, heard Hallock
yell and cuss, and then everything fell silent, so *very* silent that
even the horse was approaching in silence; and then began a
pounding of his heart.

He squeezed his eyelids tight together until blurred patterns
formed behind them, and he hunched down as close to the earth
as he could. But nearer and nearer came the horseman who
sought him, until at last the hooves sounded louder, heard even
over his trip-hammer heart. And then suddenly the hooves
were still again, and Arch Eastmere, found at last, heard nothing
but the horse's breathing and the tenuous echoes of the noise his
heart made.

He kept his eyes shut, and he shivered and waited for the
hand that would reach down and pull him erect. But nothing
happened, for a long time nothing happened, until at last he

could bear the tension no longer. He lifted his head and opened his eyes and looked up at the horseman who loomed over him, Black Jack Eastmere, his grandfather, bearded like Moses and angry as God.

And Arch Eastmere, nine years old, couldn't stand those two fiery eyes that were burning such holes in him, and he flinched and hid his face once more. But then he was being shaken roughly, shaken like a dead leaf on an autumn oak, so roughly that all the fear went from him, and he gazed up again at his grandfather, ready to rend Black Jack Eastmere apart, the way a cornered cat would—

Only it wasn't Black Jack Eastmere, it was Pace Gray, old hoss Pace Gray, a smile on his face, all red as the flowers, and Pace was saying: "All right, Arch? All right?" And, "All right, sure," Arch Eastmere said, Arch Eastmere, forty-two years old. "Sure, Pace, old hoss, all right, sure," and the dream went out like a gutted candle.

Pace Gray loped easily back to the shed, and his stride copied that of Arch Eastmere. Maude Fletcher, tiny and tired, still sat on the bale of hay, beside the saddle of silver. "Arch said I *could*," he told her. "Horse and saddle both."

CHAPTER 20

Tʜᴇʏ made for Juncture Valley.

It was night. The moon, beginning to wane, bathed forty-odd men in an ivory glow, burying their eyes in shadow and secret beneath their hats' overhanging brims. Forty-odd men were making their move, under a pale indifferent moon.

They left Alan's place at a gallop, crossed Lacy's Ford at a trot, and walked their horses along the bank sinister of the Forkhandle. Steady they went, forty-some men, silent and strained, beginning at last their fated course. And yet, save for four unusual items, they might have been setting out on a roundup, getting an early start. But these unusual items meant destruction and wreck, four small barrels of gunpowder, lashed to four separate saddles. Alan Lacy had one, Mark had another, Nelse Macleod the third, and Charley Samuels, who had fetched the barrels to begin with, took care of the fourth.

The group, in a long line, moved over grasses, the riders swaying negligently with the rhythm of their mounts. To their right the shrunken river gurgled around the larger stones, so newly exposed, of its bed. Beyond the low water, and even nearer on their left, groves of aspen and spruce, jutting out from larger masses, pointed dark accusing fingers at the column. They had long since passed the place where young Luke Randal had died. Here and there cattle, huddled together, stared dimly at them with moist and impassive eyes. A hawk, swooping from beyond a concealing wall of spruce, came upon the unexpected concourse and, giving a harsh, startled cry, veered like its own awkward fledgling and pounded away to the south. An occasional rabbit leaped obliquely before them. Once in a while a night bird spoke.

Hundreds of wild ears, close to the earth, heard the beat of many hooves and paused in their feeding, briefly alert but unalarmed, for death approaches ruminating beasts more quietly than clouds do. Of a clatter of horses they had no fear.

And, along the line of horses, the riders, too, were not in the pure sense fearful. Each one had convinced himself that he knew where he was going and what he would find there, what he must do and how he should do it. They were, each believed, undertaking a job of work, a job of work no more dangerous than a dozen others that fell to a man's daily lot. Yet, as the matter with which they were concerned was so removed from their ordinary and casual expectations, every rider found himself, for all that, somehow unwillingly troubled in mind, pregnant with an ill-formed confusion and, despite a full confidence in his cause, puzzled as to his own presence among such seemingly determined men. And there was a heavy dissatisfaction in the hearts of these forty-odd, denied perhaps by their conscious selves, but plunging, like a leaden ball, to green, unplumbed depths in their souls—and, as it fell, it splashed with burning drops the undefined edge of their guilt. Thus, while they were, in their bodies, on the way to Juncture Valley, their thoughts, like marsh birds startled by stirred water, took quick wing from them, shaken.

So it was night. So the cool moon, whitely beginning to wane, puffed out the pillow of their visions, and the air of the high meadows became their gossamer quilt. And so each man unknowingly formed in this protective air a focus for his imagination, each one of them shaping, from its peace and pallor, a phantom or a fragment of his life.

They arrived at Juncture Valley.

When they came to where the river forked—with, to the left, the bed of the South Tine, dry and stony; and, swerving off to the right, the North Tine, deep as ever it was—Alan Lacy raised his hand and pulled up.

Behind him the others halted, too. They formed jaggedly along the South Tine's deserted course, by rocks showing gray in the moonlight. For nearly a minute they studied the landscape, in a silence broken only by creaking leather, a horse snorting gently, a shifted hoof.

Thick spruce reared above the shadowed arrowhead of forest that the blending streams had formed and, tier on invisible tier beyond this opaque nadir of the valley, slopes equally wooded rose black against the star-enjeweled sky. The pale scar of what had been the South Tine was dappled where it curved along the west side of the valley, cut off at last behind a treetrunk curtain, two thousand feet or more beyond.

"I was right, by God," Nelse Macleod said. "Old Perce went and put up a dam, sure as shooting. Reckon she's half, three quarters of a mile along, up beyond the bend there." His voice was low, and it quavered. His finger, too, was shaking as he pointed toward the far bend.

"I don't guess they started on the North Tine yet," Alan Lacy said. "She seems high as ever."

Old Nelse tugged nervously at his beard. "They could have," he said. "They could have. Depends."

"Maybe we better split up," said Mark. "Take 'em both."

"One at a time, Mark boy," said Alan. "One at a goddamned time."

"Way I see it," Oliver Swindon said, "if they're finished with the South Tine dam, they're probably camped over by the one that's a-building."

"Figgers," said Nelse.

"They're bound to leave a guard by the South one, though," Alan said. "Just in case. They know how folks feel about what they're doing, the bastards."

"One or two men, maybe," Oliver said. "And *they*'ll high-tail it, soon's they get a look at us."

"How far you reckon it'll be across the valley up there, Nelse?" Mark asked. "Between the first dam and their camp, I mean."

"Oh, maybe a half-mile or so. This goddamned Juncture widens considerable once you get into it."

Mark frowned. "I can see a hell of a mix-up once we try to get across through those trees. You can't keep any kind of touch at night in country like that."

"Nobody said we figgered to go across to their camp," Alan said. "Nobody I heard, anyway. And *I* sure don't figger to."

"Far as that goes, by George, there's no need," Oliver Swindon said. "We'll blow the one dam higher than they hung Haman, then beat it back out of harm's way."

"Hell for leather," Drury Wynward said cheerfully. He slapped the next man to him, big Jock Menzies, on the shoulder. "Race me home for a dollar, Jock?"

But Jock who, with lowered eyes, was rubbing the pommel of his saddle with a forefinger the size of a broomstick, shook his head and said nothing.

"And them hell for leather after us," Mark said. "That's when they hurt you, running away."

"You ought to know, Mark boy," said Drury, under his breath and unheard.

"Hell," Nelse said, "time those fellers even get through the woods, we all'll be back home asleep."

"Just about," Alan Lacy said with a nod. "Let's go."

He spurred his horse into the dried-up stream, and the rest of them came behind him. Without anyone's suggesting it, they formed themselves into a solid mass, riding more or less six abreast, with Alan Lacy ahead.

It was difficult going, that advance, difficult and noisy, the hooves of the horses striking their iron against the smooth stones of the bed and sending the smaller ones scattering roundabout with a clatter that racked men's nerves.

The moon had dropped more deeply down the sky, and the stars were all the brighter for this falling. In another hour or less it would be gone for good. The shadows were changing, becoming grotesque, giving birth to odd twisted shapes beyond the outermost spruce. Now the trees came quite to the edge of the South Tine's bank sinister, and that side of the valley began to be more precipitous.

They rode around the bend, cutting themselves off from the open end of the valley, the place where the Tines came together, and the trail that had brought them to where they were. But beyond them still the ribbon of rough gray stone stretched on. There was no dam to be seen.

Frowning, annoyed, Alan Lacy led them on for another hundred yards, then reined up. They moved in around him. "Now, where's this dam you were talking about, Nelse?" he demanded. "Here's the place you said it would be, for Christ's sake, but I don't see hide nor hair of any dam."

Nelse's mare was becoming skittish, and it was all the old man could do to steady her. He looked off ahead, chewing his bottom lip. "Hell, I never told you it'd be right *here*," he answered. "What I said was, if *I* was damming these streams, this'd be more or less the place I'd do it."

"Looks like you and Perce Randal think different," Alan said.

"Well, we'd best go on some more," said Nelse.

"Ah, hell," Mark exclaimed, "let's forget the whole thing. Let's some of us see Perce tomorrow and settle the matter like sensible men. We've got no more business being up here than—"

"Than your Ellen's got being where *she* is," Alan Lacy broke in. "My God in Heaven, listen to who's talking. And who *started* this whole thing anyways, Mark boy?"

"I don't *care* who started it, by Jesus," Mark said loudly. "Let's turn around and get off this goddamned Randal land before somebody takes it into his head to—"

Will Clough was beginning to fall from his horse, already dead, a bullet hole above his right ear, when they heard the near, flat voice of Soap Damson's carbine, the weapon that killed him, speaking.

There were fifteen men of the Randal ranch along that part
of the South Tine, split into two equal bands. West of the dry
bed were Soap Damson and Jim Good with six of the hands; east
was Hallock with a half dozen more.

"When they come along here," Hallock had said, "—and they
will—wait till they're past us before you fire. We can rake 'em
again when they try to get back."

But Soap Damson hadn't been able to wait. He had heard
them coming almost from the time they started along the dry
South Tine—leather creak, crunch of rock, thud of hoof, and
scrape of shoe. And as he stood there, leaning his left shoulder
against a rough tree bole, with Jim Good on one side of him,
Sam Wadley on the other, and the remaining five hands spread
out ten feet apart among the spruces that rimmed the spent
stream, it seemed to Soap that the time it took for the riders to
come, at last, swinging around the bend, was the longest time he
had ever spent in his life. "Jesus," he muttered to himself, "I won't
even be dead *this* long." Then: "Come on, fellers, come on and
get it. Come on, Arch Eastmere, you murdering bastard. Come
on, the goddamned lot of you."

Then, when an eternity of sweat and impatience had passed
for tough old Soap Damson, when his eyes had narrowed and
narrowed and were nothing but hair-thick slits, there they came
around the bend in a solid body, forty-odd riders huddled together, old Soap thought, like goddamned sheep in a blow. And,
though the light was too poor to see men's faces clearly, his eyes
became fixed on a silver saddle that *had* to be under Arch Eastmere.

Soap licked his lips and grinned like a panting dog. He
brought the carbine up against his shoulder until the big buck-
horn sight hung under the belly of that silver-saddled son of a
bitch, and as he rode forward Soap swung the sight, unwavering,
with him. But then, abruptly, the whole bunch of them stopped
and started milling around and jawing among themselves, and
he'd lost his man in the middle somewhere. He glanced over at
Jim Good and Jim glanced at him, shaking his head, his eyes

angry, and Soap knew that Jim, too, had drawn a bead on that Eastmere bastard. Both of them, then, after this silent exchange of information and regret, turned back to the matter at hand.

Down on the South Tine stones the voices held more impatience, more wrath. And, ready against his tree, Soap went on waiting, until finally he was fit to bust with all the bile that had filled him since they'd found Luke Randal dead. He could wait no longer, then. To hell with this holding back till they passed by; the bastards might argue there all night long.

He saw a rider's head outlined against a boulder across the stream bed. Up came the muzzle. It steadied, level. Soap took a short breath, held it. Then he squeezed off.

Will Clough never knew what hit him. Or who. Or, for the life of him, why.

On the instant, gun muzzles flared by a dozen trees. The men who were gathered in bewilderment and rage on the stones of the South Tine fanned at all points outward, like the petals of a flower that feels the first heat of the morning sun, but with far less purpose and far more confusion. Juncture Valley itself seemed to roar like a rutting bull.

Accuracy was out of the question. The men on the frantic, cavorting horses could only snap off shots at the spitting tongues of fire among the trees. Invariably they aimed too high, and their slugs went whining away or thudded into yielding wood. The men in the spruce, on the other hand, were lost, for the most part, when it came to hitting a target that moved, especially when it sat on a horse. For none of them wanted to kill a horse. So, on both sides, a great deal of ammunition was being used, with a great lack of success.

Yet, in spite of this, in fifteen seconds everything was over.

Alan Lacy was yelling for them to charge the trees, but no one heard him. Charley Samuels kept screaming for the righteous to smite the Philistine hip and thigh, but no one heard him, either. Pace Gray, seized by black, unexpected fear, began to howl in helpless fury as Arch Eastmere's horse turned and turned, dancing around in a circle no wider than its own length, ignoring his wild tugs at the reins and refusing to take him out of there, to the safety he wanted so much.

Pace's life was for all of ten seconds charmed. Hallock Randal had never lost sight of that silver-mounted saddle. Three times he had fired at what he thought was Arch Eastmere, and three times he had missed. The damned horse would never hold still. At last, then, full of red wrath and forgetful of the danger he ran by showing himself, he burst out of the eastern fringe of trees, darting along the Tine stones.

"*Eastmere!*" he bellowed. And he was heard. The man on the silver saddle turned.

As he spoke, Hallock had brought up his pistol, and he was on the point of pulling the trigger when he realized that he was looking not at hard-eyed Arch Eastmere, but into the terrorized face of Pace Gray.

He managed to hold his fire.

Jim Good, however, forty feet away, did not. And even as Hallock started to lower his six-gun, Pace Gray, staring at him with shock and surprise, started to tilt in his saddle. Arch Eastmere's horse had been still just long enough for Jim to fill Pace Gray's chest with a small piece of lead and a great hemorrhage of blood. And in that same moment Hallock saw, like a tableau of wax figures, Terry Sykes sneering at him and, just beyond Pace Gray, Jock Menzies fixing him with an agonized stare. Then Sykes, still sneering, making no effort to fire at him, veered his horse away—and Jock Menzies, with that tortured expression still distorting his features, moved in on Pace and propped the boy's drooping body against his own. He lifted Pace out of the silver-mounted saddle as lightly as though he were a feather-filled pillow. Arch Eastmere's horse, unburdened of its unfamiliar rider, went snorting at a gallop up the bed of the stream.

Hallock turned to dash back to the safety of the trees. Before he had gone two steps, however, he was knocked flat on his face, stunned, his forehead bruised by a stone it hit. Hallock's light went out in a thunderclap.

Charley Samuels had blown up behind him.

A bullet, chance or aimed, had struck the iron rim of the gun-powder keg he carried, carrying sparks along with it as it bored on into the black grains. The explosion tore Charley Samuels to pieces, ripped his pony apart, shook the trees, sent stones big as

fists flying through the air, and further crazed the already dis-
tracted horses. Men were, an hour later, still half deaf from that
monument of sound.

But then, as the man-wrecking noise subsided, and before its
echoes began, there was an astonished silence, followed by what
might have been hail crashing down through the trees. Soap
Damson, who had been staggered back by the blast, came forward again, the tough old bastard; and there was Sam Wadley
standing erect againt a spruce trunk, his whole spinal column
pressed tight against the bark, and even his round little gut
sucked in. He might have been watching the melee below, but
somehow Soap knew he wasn't.

"You all right, Sam?" he asked.

Sam didn't seem to hear, and Soap started to walk toward
him. But as he did so Sam himself began to stumble forward in
an amble of jerks and spasms, for all the world like a doll under
the control of an incompetent puppet-master. He took a few
jiggling steps along the South Tine's gray stones and then pitched,
like some boneless thing, forward.

"Ah, what the hell," Soap said, in annoyance.

He moved unhurriedly to where Sam was lying, got down on
one knee, and began to roll him over.

"What the hell," Soap said again. His tone was level, but he
spoke with a calm brought on by shock.

A narrow, triangular sliver of barrel stave, six inches long,
stuck out from the wet red glue and void that had been Sam
Wadley's right eye. And judging from the shape of the wood, considerably more of the barrel stave, a good four inches of it at
least, was inside Sam Wadley's damp skull, reaching better than
halfway to the back of his head, scrambling his brain like a big
gray egg.

Soap Damson let the body fall face down again, staring empty-
eyed at the worn vest that covered Sam Wadley's back. Then, in
an absent fashion, he became aware of a set of horse's legs, standing motionless a few feet away. Without thinking, his mind for
the moment as blank as his gaze, Soap looked up at the man who
rode the horse. "That's a hell of a thing, now, ain't it?" he said.

Randy Worth, on the horse, had his short gun out, and he was grinning—but with his mouth only. His eyes held a long-impounded hate. "Old *Soap*," he said, very casually. He shot old Soap in the chest.

The slug knocked Soap back into a sitting position. "Yeh, old Soap," Randy Worth said again. "Old Short Gun Soap." He aimed his pistol for another shot.

But he never got it off, nor did he ever leave Juncture Valley. For at that moment Jim Good, twenty feet away, steadying his rifle against a tree, put a bullet through Randy Worth's ear.

And that was the last shot fired. Alan Lacy and everyone else who had come with him were already booting it around the bend for home, scared but still in one piece, as fast as they could lick it.

Last of them all rode big Jock Menzies. He was slowed by the boy who hung jackknifed in the crook of his right arm, by the dead weight of Pace Gray, once young.

The disembodied head of Charley Samuels, heavy-lidded and drained of blood, the biggest chunk of Charley that would ever be found again, had been blown a hundred feet upstream and was jammed there between two boulders. Oddly enough, it still wore a hat, red flecked and tilted over the milky eyes.

As the clatter of hooves faded out to the south, the Randal ranch hands, one by one, came down on the stones from the shelter of the trees, treading carefully, as though they were barefoot amid broken glass. Two of them, Pete Adams and Josh Clyde, saw Hallock getting unsteadily to his feet and went over to help him, each one grasping an arm until Hallock, at last erect, groggily pulled himself free. "You all right, Mister Randal?" Pete Adams asked.

Hallock nodded. Things were coming back into focus.

"Banged your head," Josh Clyde told him.

Hallock placed a hand on a tender place on his throbbing brow and brought away bloody fingers. "Reckon I did," he said thickly. Behind his eyes, at first, a mass of fireflies and stinging wasps flickered and burned; then, as he returned to an awareness of himself and his surroundings, the fireflies dwindled to darkness and the stinging of the wasps was less. He shook his head, clearing it further, while briefly increasing the painful pound of blood there. "Much obliged to you, Pete," he said. "Josh."

Leaving him, then, they walked over and stood by a body he recognized as Will Clough's, even though one side of the face had been mangled by iron-shod frantic horses. The hooves had broken Will's left thigh bone, too, so that the corpse's leg formed the letter S in flesh. Hallock licked dry lips and let his gaze range beyond Will to where a dead horse's belly lay rounded on the rocks. "Hey, Mister Randal!" someone called.

Across the dry stream a lot of men were gathered where Soap Damson was sitting down and Jim Good was kneeling beside him. Two other men were sprawled on the stones. A few feet below the group a riderless horse was calmly cropping grass along the bank. Jim Good beckoned to Hallock. "Over here, Mister Randal," he said. "Soap's been hit."

Hallock, still groggy, somewhat unsure of his footing, stumbled across the stones, followed by Adams and Clyde. As though unaware of Soap, he gaped stupidly at one of the dead men, then at the other. "What about these fellers?" he mumbled. Then, dimly aware that his voice rang, like a cracked bell, in his ears, he jerked his head from side to side. It seemed as though he would shake his brain loose from its hinges, but the effort brought him around.

"Knocked myself out, back there," he muttered.

Jim, who had been watching him anxiously, relaxed the muscles of his face and gestured at the nearest body. "Sam Wadley's dead, poor devil," he said. "And Randy Worth, that's him over there, he's a goner, too. He's the one that shot Soap."

"Bastard son of a bitch," Soap said to no one in particular. "Goddamned bastard Randy Worth bastard."

"And I'm the one that shot Randy," Jim Good went on. "Right after."

Hallock took a deep breath, then another. The air, so eagerly sucked in, gave him a moment of dizziness, but after his second exhalation he felt much more alert. For the first time since he'd recovered consciousness he was aware that he was smelling an odor familiar from days long past, yet an odor unforgotten. It was —yes, powder smoke, scent of a battlefield, bitter musk of burned powder, hanging heavy and still in the windless trap of the valley. But had they fired *that* many rounds? The crack on the head must have sharpened his nose somehow.

He dropped on his knees next to Soap, staring first at the dark blood soaking through the vest below the left shoulder, then peering into the dulled eyes. "Soap?" he said softly, and got no answer. Then: "How is it, Soap?"

"Bastard Randy," Soap said, speaking not to Hallock but to himself. "Son of a Randy bitch Worth."

"Let's us take a look at it," Hallock said to Jim Good.

Together they slipped off Soap's vest. Hallock chanced to lay one hand lightly on Soap's shoulder behind, and again his fingers were reddened with blood. "Slug went clean through," he told Jim.

"We won't have to dig for it, hey?" Jim Good said.

"Lucky," said Hallock.

Until they had stripped Soap's grizzled body to the waist, the wounded man's arms dangled limply at his sides. Then the cold night air, curling around his belly, brought him abruptly out of his state of shock. He gasped and glared at Jim Good. "What the goddamned hell?" he yelped. Immediately, however, he realized what was going on. Growling and snorting, he tried to warm his stomach with both hands, wincing at the pain in his left shoulder that the sudden movement caused.

"Easy, now, Soap, take it easy," Hallock said.

"Easy, my arse," Soap snarled, "not with my own damned guts. Look at that goddamned dead son of a bitch of a Randy Worth over there, him and his, for Christ's sake, short gun, waiting around three years to plug me, God *damn* his short gunned soul, and me not never knowing what the bastard was minded to do. I wish to Christ he was only half dead, by God, so's I could take him the rest of the way along. *Take* him there? Hell I'd *kick* him there, God *damn* him and damn all, and stoke up the fires myself. You blame me, boys? Anybody *blame* me?"

None of the watching men answered, but several of them grinned. Hallock paid no attention to the outburst. He studied the wound, back and front, as well as he could in the light of the failing moon. "How you feeling inside, Soap?" he wanted to know. "Feel clear in the lungs?"

"Colder than a witch's tit," Soap said. "That's how I feel, by God."

"How about the shoulder?"

"It hurts like hell, for Christ's sake," Soap snarled. "What the hell'd you expect?"

"I expected worse than I'm getting," Hallock said. "It's nice and neat, in one end and out the other."

"I know that, God damn it, Hallock. I can feel both the by God holes. I can't figger how the hell I can feel 'em, though, because I'm damn nigh numb and froze to death. Now look here, Jim, you take this shirt of mine here and tear it up and twine it around my goddamned shoulder. And *you*, Tim Bannerman—" He pointed a gnarled finger at the nearest ranch hand. "I got me another shirt tucked in my blanket roll, so you go get that other shirt of mine to cover my guts with, before I chatter my goddamned teeth right out of my gums. *Quick* with you, now!"

Tim Bannerman, a scrawny young fellow with an equally scrawny brown mustache, hurried off toward Soap's horse, tethered in the trees somewhere on the other side of the South Tine. Jim Good picked up the flannel shirt he and Hallock had eased off Soap's upper body and ripped it down the middle, tossing the bloodstained section aside. "I'll take care of this, Mister Randal," he said. "Reckon you got other things to do." He began to tear the piece he held into strips.

"Reckon so," Hallock said flatly. He stood up, went over to Randy Worth's body and prodded the foot with his toe. "Anybody else get hurt?" he asked the faces around him.

"One of them blowed hisself up," Jim said. "I don't know which."

"Yeh, yeh," one of the hands said excitedly. "All to pieces. Damned near knocked me over."

"It was Charley Samuels," Josh Clyde said. "Old First'n'second Samuels, gone to Glory, amen."

"That's old Charley's horse out there," said Pete Adams, "split nigh in two."

Hallock, looking again at the dead horse, could see, from this angle, the gaping hole where the saddle had been. "So *that's* what it was," he said calmly. "I figgered I'd been kicked in the back."

"Hallock?" Soap was peering up at him. "We going down there and get those bastards?"

"Reckon not, Soap. And you're out of it, anyway."

"The hell I am. You reckon Arch *East*mere's out of it?"

"I don't know what's happened to Arch."

"Somebody shot the son of a bitch, that's what happened, by God. And somebody else picked the bastard right out of his silver goddamned saddle and lugged him away with the rest of 'em."

"That was Pace Gray got shot," Hallock said.

Jim Good stared up at him in surprise. "Hell!" he exclaimed. "You *sure* of that, Mister Randal?"

Hallock nodded. "I was set to shoot him myself. Then I seen it was Pace."

"Might as well've pulled the trigger, anyways," Soap said. "Him or Arch Eastmere, it's six of one and half a dozen of the other."

"Soap, you know a damned sight better than that," Hallock said.

"Maybe so," Soap said grimly, "but it would've made one less of 'em."

"I don't want Pace," Hallock told him.

Jim Good sadly continued to bandage Soap's shoulder. "Now, I'll be goddamned," he said. "I could've swore that was Arch I plugged."

"You're the one that shot Pace?" Hallock asked. His voice, too, was sad.

"I'm the one knocked whoever it was off that silver saddle," Jim said. "I'll be damned. Little Pace Gray *had* to run around with the growed-up men. I'll be damned." He made a snorting sound.

"I'd just as soon it'd been Mark Lacy," Hallock said thoughtfully. "I'd sure as hell've shot *him*, and damned quick, too." He sighed. "Those aunts of Pace's are going to be real upset if he's —you got any idea where you hit him, Jim?"

"Nope," said Jim. "But if I hit him where I was aiming for, by God, his aunts'll be weeping and wailing tomorrow."

"Ah, the little bastard had no business up here, nohow." Soap said. "Trying to act like a man, with his nose still dripping snot. God *damn* you, Jim, hurry up, will you?"

"Just about done," said Jim.

"Nobody's got any business up here," Hallock said. "Not even us."

"We're the *only* ones that has, by God," Soap said.

"Ah, this all might've been stopped someplace," Hallock said. "Sometime before it got out of hand."

"Where?" Soap wanted to know. "And how? And, for Christ's sake, by who?"

But Hallock had no answer for this and, shaking his head in sorrow and bewilderment, he started to walk away. He paused, however, as he passed Pete Adams. "See if you and Josh can find that horse of Arch's, will you? It was heading upstream, last I knew. And the rest of you fellers—" He faced around. "—you better get your horses and gear together. I want to get back across the North Tine while the moon's still up." Midway across the bed of the stream he met Tim Bannerman, carrying Soap's spare shirt.

Jim Good and Bannerman, between them, and in spite of the wounded man's monumental curses, finally got Soap dressed and on his feet. He insisted on wearing his bloody vest, and when the time came to leave he wouldn't let himself be helped on his horse. "With one bad arm, by God, I'm still the best goddamned rooster ever," he crowed, and he swung himself unaided into the saddle.

And when the time came to cross the North Tine, he didn't need help there, either.

Ten minutes after they were east of the stream the moon went under the hills for good. Under the stars' weaker glow they made a compact group, rounded out by three dead men lashed over their own saddles, and one riderless horse. Charley Samuels's horse had been left as it was, a gift for the eaters of carrion. And none of them had even seen Charley's head nor, even if they all had, would they have bothered much with that grisly relic, except perhaps to be surprised that it still had its hat on.

Hallock Randal, from the moment he'd settled in the silver saddle, had trouble with Arch's horse. The beast, although it was too weary to try to throw him, was skittish and spooky. It had never before known any other rider than Arch, and here in one night two strangers had settled across its broad back. Too, Hallock's hand lacked its usual skill. His head ached, and he was undergoing a depression, a despair and sense of loss that stemmed from the recent violence. He kept the horse more or less steady, but occasionally it shied or danced sideways, until at last he gave up all hope of soothing the great gelding, in that place and in their present condition.

Soap, on the contrary, seemed elated by his wound. He let the reins dangle around the pommel while he felt, with his good hand, in every pocket of his vest. Then, with a grunt of anger, he swung around and glared at Jim Good. "God damn you, Jim," he said. "You let my terbaccer fall out back there."

"Now, that's a real shame," Jim said casually. "Reckon I was too busy keeping the claret in you from doing the same thing. Want a chaw of mine?"

"Hell, no," exclaimed Soap. "God only knows where you had your mouth before you bit into that plug."

"Easy! *Hi!* Easy, *easy*—" Hallock's horse was cavorting.

"Real fiery critter, ain't it?" Soap said. Then, as the beast calmed down again: "I swallered a mouthful of juice back there in the fight."

Hallock half heard him. "That so?" he said listlessly.

"And damned if I know when," Soap went on. "Sometime I did, though, by God. Lots of things was happening."

"Yeh," said Hallock.

Soap fell silent, and for a while Hallock, his head drooping, was caught up in a confusion of thoughts, trying without success to put them in some order, to evaluate the past and to lay some plans for what must now be done. But he couldn't even decide what he should do immediately after he got back to the ranch house. No, not even that. He could see himself dismounting, but an impenetrable veil hung over everything beyond that one simple motion. It was hard to visualize, even, the dear faces that he would see there.

Hallock sighed deeply, much like his mother would, and Soap, hearing the sigh, glanced over at the younger man with as much gentleness as his tough old eyes could manage. "I'm sorry about it, Hallock," he said, the grizzled old rooster. "Reckon you know that."

"I'm sorry you got yourself shot that way," Hallock said, keeping his eyes on his horse's mane.

"Hell," Soap said, "if I'd known this was all they was to it, I'd get myself shot every goddamned week."

"Not like this," said Hallock glumly. "Not for such damned foolishness as this."

The gentleness left Soap's face. "What happened to Luke weren't foolishness," he said.

Hallock's voice was low. "No, it wasn't. Christ, I don't know what it was."

"What you figgering on doing now?"

Hallock raised his head and looked off into the dark. "Can't say, as yet," he replied. "But something."

"I'd go after 'em."

"Don't you fret yourself, Soap. I don't figger to stand around and wait for the wind to blow me."

"*They* won't, neither," Soap told him.

"Reckon not," Hallock said. He looked up at the host of dispassionate stars. "But right now, I reckon, they're cooled off considerable. *Hi!* Easy, *e-e-easy*, there."

The horse was spooking again.

For a long time after they had pounded, pell-mell, away from Juncture Valley, the men who rode with Alan Lacy were, indeed, cooled off. But before they saw the lights of the ranch house flickering in the distance, they were all well heated again, seething with jealousy and bleak anger, distrustful, bitter, bursting with accusations, eager and begging to quarrel.

It still lacked two hours to dawn as they swung in through the open gates of Alan's big corral and, tight-mouthed and tired, climbed from their weary mounts.

The cowhands whom Alan had left behind came tumbling sleepily out of the bunkhouse, prepared to take care of the exhausted horses. Little Dolores Costa, too, who had been dozing fitfully in the kitchen, sitting at the table with her lovely young head resting in the cradle of her olive arms—she, too, aroused by the noise of their arrival, came out and stood, unsteady and nervous, in the shadows close to the ranch house.

Big Jock Menzies, unaware of the stinging sweat in his eyes, unaware that his right arm had gone numb from the dead weight of Pace Gray's body, borne all this long way by old ox Jock, was nearly half a mile behind the other riders. He came trotting in just as Alan Lacy and Nelse Macleod, with Terry Sykes at their heels, were leaving the corral on their way to the main building. The three of them halted as Jock reined up and stared blankly at them, as though he were waiting for orders of some sort. Alan Lacy's eyes smoldered in rage, and his jaw muscles rippled under his cheeks. Terry Sykes's eyes burned red, and his pale face was mottled strangely. Nelse Macleod's old eyes were charcoal, and, his mouth hung open, like that of a fish drowning in air. He jerked his thumb toward Pace. "That kid dead?" he demanded. He was hoarse from fatigue.

Jock managed to nod, dumbly. Then, with an effort, he found his own voice. "Died right off," he whispered. "Almost right off."

"Should've dropped him, then," Nelse said. "Only a damned fool'd tote him this far."

"That's what toted him, sure enough," said Terry Sykes.

Jock's dull gaze was fixed on the drooping head of his horse; he didn't seem to have heard Sykes at all. "Couldn't leave Pace up there," he muttered. "Animals'd get him up there."

"Well, you can't leave him here, neither, by God," Alan Lacy said angrily. "I don't want any fool kid's carcass around here. Sashaying around on that fancy saddle, goddamn it, no wonder he got himself killed."

"Reckon Hallock Randal's got that saddle now," said Terry Sykes. "Or maybe that goddamned Pax has."

"Alan—" Jock was mumbling, "what'll I do with him, Alan?"

"You toted him this far," Alan said, "might as well tote him the rest of the way. Take him home to his aunts."

"Take him to that Eastmere son of a bitch," Terry Sykes said. "He's the one loves him so much."

Oliver Swindon, Mark Lacy, and Drury Wynward, along with several other men, had come out of the corral and joined the group in time to hear Alan's suggestion and Terry Sykes's echoing remark. "Shut your filthy mouth, Sykes," Oliver snapped, "before I tear it open to your ears. That's one thing I'm fair primed to do, by George."

"I got to take him somewheres," Jock said. "But it'd like to kill Arch to see him."

"Good," Mark Lacy said.

"Now, wait a minute," said Drury. "Seems to me it'd be a lot smarter to take him over to Maudie Fletcher's and leave him there with Arch. I figger Arch won't start bawling, just because Pace here got killed. And he can break it to the boy's aunts when the time comes."

"I don't want to have anything more to do with Arch East-mere," Alan said, "in any way, at *all*."

"Nobody does," said Mark.

"I suppose you bastards'd like for Jock here to toss Pace at his aunts' feet and then high-tail it home," Drury exclaimed. He was getting mad.

"I don't give a damn *what* he does," Alan said. "Just so long as he does it someplace away from here."

"I will, by God, and everything else, too," Jock said heavily. "And I won't be back, neither, not any more. I'm going on home. Soon as I leave Pace, I'm going on home. And you tell my boys to go on home, too."

"I'll tell 'em, Jock," said Oliver. "Don't you worry about it."

"You'd best take Pace along to Arch," Drury said. "That's the best thing, Jock."

"All right, if you say so," Jock said. "Arch's all right."

"By George," Oliver said, "that arm of yours ought to be mighty sore by now."

"Feels dead, is all," said Jock. "Real gone-to-sleep."

"Better lash him on another pony," Oliver said. "You carried him far enough that way."

"Give him a wagon, Alan, for Christ's sake," Drury said. "Let him take him to Arch laid out decent in a wagon."

"My boys've got enough to do with all these horses," Alan said. "They don't have any time for harnessing up wagons."

"Me, I'll do it," Terry Sykes said suddenly. "And I'll drive the damned rig, too."

"I don't need you along," Jock said in a thick voice. "I don't like you, Sykes, goddamn you."

"If you're not coming back here, by God, you'll need him along," Alan Lacy said. "Because I'll be wanting that wagon back. I don't figger to have to go traipsing down to Maude Fletcher's after it, hear?"

"Oh, hell," Jock said glumly. "All right. I don't care. I just want to—" He let the words trail off. He touched spurs to his horse. The group parted as he rode through it on his way to the barn. Terry Sykes followed him. Little Dolores, who had been shocked by the cold-blooded talk of the men, shrank deeper into the shadows as they passed her. She avoided being seen, but she could not herself avoid seeing the lolling head of Pace Gray, that nice-looking boy to whom she had served such a big breakfast not so long ago. She ran around the corner of the ranch house and into the kitchen where, once again, she buried her trembling head in her soft olive arms.

"Wonder which one Arch'll miss the most?" Alan Lacy asked. He was walking toward the main building with Mark and Nelse, Drury and Oliver. "Pace, or that damned greaser saddle?"

"Neither one, by God," said Nelse Macleod. "Not if I know Arch Eastmere."

"At least, he could have *rid* on the saddle," said Oliver.

"He can always ride Maudie Fletcher," said Drury.

Nobody laughed. At the door of the ranch house Alan looked back at the men who were gathering around the corral gates. "I'll send you all out some coffee in a minute," he called.

The five of them entered the main room. Drury immediately threw himself down on the sofa, and Mark, Nelse, and Oliver Swindon sat on chairs, all of them jumpy and ill at ease. Alan Lacy, however, remained standing. "Liddie!" he shouted. "Hey, Liddie!" There was no answer, and the anger on his face thickened. "God *damn* the woman," he exclaimed. "Where the hell's she gone to?"

He went into the bedroom. The bed was not only empty; it had not even been slept in. "Liddie!" he bawled again, then strode out to the kitchen.

Dolores lifted her head as he came clomping in, but Alan Lacy ignored her trembling lips and stained cheeks. "Where's my wife?" he demanded.

"I—I don't know, Mister Lacy. She went away—someplace away."

"When?"

"Right after you—all the *men* did. After you all went away."

"*Where*, goddamn it?"

"She didn't tell me. But maybe—into town, I guess."

"Well, you, whatever your name is, *you* fix just as much coffee as you can make. And damned quick, hear? There's a lot of tired men want some coffee."

She nodded, frightened, but he didn't see her nod, because he had already turned on his heel and stamped back into the main room. "Liddie went and skittered, the bitch," he told them.

Drury Wynward couldn't help himself. He threw back his head and laughed. "By God, now, it runs in the family," he cried. "First, Mark's wife skitters, and now yours."

Nelse and Oliver had to chuckle, too, in spite of their taut nerves, or perhaps for precisely that reason. Mark Lacy, however, whitened and leaped to his feet. "You've carried that talk to the limit now, damn you," he told Drury. "But there's the *two* of us against you now, and *I'm* sure itching to get at somebody, even if Alan ain't."

Drury looked calmly at Mark, laughed some more, and then calmed down. "Reckon you are, Mark boy," he said casually. "Reckon you damned well are." His voice grew flat. "But not *me*, hear, Mark boy? Don't start itching to get at me, or you're like to get your itching scratched hard, and some of your hide along with it."

"Ah, go ahead," said old Nelse. "I'd like to see the lot of you have a go at each other. They's not much else left for you."

"Sit down, Mark, sit down," Alan Lacy said, his voice now mild and controlled. "All the damned fool woman's done is get scared and run into town. She's at the Oliphants, like as not. But, hell, she oughtn't to've spooked for no reason, that way. She knew we'd be wanting some grub once we got back here."

"I don't want any grub," Oliver said. "I've been eating your dust all night long."

"Well, now, since we're on *that*," Alan said, "if you'd done what I told you up there, you'd right now be washing down any dust you ate with South Tine water."

"Can't say as I recollect you telling me to do anything up there," Oliver said.

"For Christ's *sake*, Ollie, I was yelling my damned head off, for everybody to get off there in the trees and ride those bastards *down.*"

"*Every*body?" Drury drawled. "Not me, you didn't."

"Me neither," said Oliver Swindon.

"You didn't *want* to hear me, goddamn you," Alan said in a fury. "All you wanted to do was get yourselves out of there."

"Well, when I started to lick it out of there, by God, Alan," Drury said, "I seen *you* up ahead of me."

"I been shot at by fellers that could *shoot,*" Oliver said. "And I reckoned there wasn't any damned point in getting killed by somebody that don't rightly know one end of a gun from the other."

"They was too many of 'em, anyway," Nelse Macleod said.

"Too *many* of 'em?" Alan looked at the old man with astonishment. "Why, my God, Nelse, there weren't more than twenty of 'em up there, I swear. Not twenty, by God, if that."

"Made enough noise for sixty," Nelse said, tugging at his matted beard.

"Noise, hell, don't mean a thing," said Alan. "Just because Charley Samuels went and got himself blow—"

"By *God,* now, Alan," cried Nelse Macleod. "I'm plumb glad that psalm-singing son of a bitch got blowed to kingdom come. Because if he hadn't we all might *still* be up there shooting at each other, and that's one place I'm sure pleased to be away from—and I don't give a damn who knows it."

"That's the way I feel, too," said Drury Wynward. "We didn't handle it good."

"All right," Alan said flatly. "When we go up there again, just how would you say to handle it?"

"I wouldn't," Drury said. "Because I ain't figgering to go up there again." He sat up on the sofa, picked up the antimacassar that Lydia Lacy had placed there, and started to roll it up.

"Suit yourself," said Alan. "We don't need all the men we got, anyway."

"I ain't going up there again, neither, if it's all the same," said Nelse. "Looks like the best thing to do now is wait for J. O. to get back from Grant's Pass and let him handle it. He wanted to in the first place, by God, and, like a damned old fool, I went and scared him off."

"He'll handle the lot of us right into jail," Oliver Swindon said. "That's what J. O. Macleod'll do."

"Not me, he won't," said Drury. "I didn't kill nobody."

"There's dead men," Oliver said. He counted them off on his fingers. "Charley Samuels, Pace Gray, Will Clough probably, and probably Randy Worth. Four of 'em. And we're all guilty, the lot of us."

Alan Lacy was looking at Drury Wynward. "You shoot into the trees at all, Drury?"

"Four times. And at nothing, hear? Just in the trees."

"You could've shot *some*body, for all you know. We can't rightly tell whether we hit anybody or not." Alan swung around to Oliver Swindon. "But it don't matter, one way or another, because you ought to've counted *five*. They can lay Luke Randal to us. And none of you can go pulling out, because the minute Luke Randal got killed, every man jack of us was guilty of killing him."

Mark Lacy had leaped to his feet again. "For Christ's sake, Alan!" he cried. "You told me—you told *everybody*—that Arch Eastmere was lying about that. Goddamn it, you said he never killed Luke at all."

The others had suddenly become equally intent, equally alarmed. Nelse's fingers were frozen in his beard, and Drury let the rolled-up antimacassar fall to the floor. Alan's eyes drifted from man to man. "If Arch Eastmere hadn't killed Luke," he said with slow deliberation, "those people wouldn't've been waiting for us up there the way they did tonight. Hallock's running the show, and he must've figgered we had considerable more men than *he* did, so he waited for us in Juncture Valley. Otherwise, by God, he'd've come down here like a thunderclap."

Silence held for a few moments. "Maybe he will *now*," Drury said finally. "And if Arch went and killed his little brother—well, by God, I wouldn't blame Hallock."

"I reckon you knew all the time that Luke was dead," Oliver said. "But you figgered you'd keep your mouth shut, is that it, Alan, in case maybe some of us might've backed down?"

"No, by God, I didn't know," Alan said. "I could've *swore* Arch Eastmere was lying. I believed he was, I swear."

"Too goddamned much *believing* been going on around here," old Nelse said glumly, his eyes on the floor.

"Too much something," said Drury, "and that's the truth."

"Well, whatever," Alan said. "We can't none of us pull out now, because we're all of us in up to our necks. Maybe it'll get straightened out in the end somehow. Maybe the fellers that got killed'll cancel each other out. I don't rightly know. But in the meanwhile, we all've got to keep going with what we started."

"I'm not intending to," said Nelse. "Figgered that had sunk in by now, Alan."

"You got any idea what'll happen, Nelse," Alan demanded, "if we leave off now? You all cut and run tonight, and Hallock saw you do it. So maybe he's figgering that we had all we wanted of the whole business, and that we'll split up now. But Luke Randal's still good and dead, and Hallock's still good and mad about it. But he don't know which one of us did it, so he'll be coming after us one at a time, him and Pax both, most like. Now I wouldn't want to tangle with Hallock Randal alone, and I sure as hell'd hate to have that goddamned Pax plugging me with his saddle gun from half a mile away—which is what they'll be doing, one or the other of 'em, to every last man of us. You fellers see what I mean?"

Evidently they did, for none of them spoke or tried any further rebuttal as Alan studied each man in turn. "All right, then," he said. He wandered restlessly over to a window and stared out into the night. "Damned bitch of a woman," he muttered to himself. "For once in her life I wanted her around. But she had to go *visiting* someplace."

The visit that Lydia Lacy was making had now reached that satiate point where her rounded body lay curled, childlike in languorous sleep, in George Throstle's big featherbed. Her unbound red hair, spread over the pillow, glowed like fire around her surfeited face.

George Throstle, his nostrils drawing in an odor that mingled present perspiration with a memory of pomade, his body pulled up against the headboard in a semi-reclining position, his night vision excellent after so many hours and acts of darkness, studied the statuesque woman beside him. A certain amount of starlight came in through the open windows of his bedroom above the Dry Goods Emporium; enough, indeed, to allow him to take even further pleasure in viewing this, his latest conquest. For he was sure, and despite his earlier doubts, that the conquest belonged, not to Lydia Lacy, but to George Throstle himself. And such had been the satisfactions of the night that not once had he thought of Ellen Lacy's golden beauty nor, for that matter, of anything or anyone else save this marvelously gyrating creature who had become, so unexpectedly, his.

Red-haired Lydia had at last, and in spite of herself, gone to sleep, leaving Throstle, not yet exhausted, proud master of the white field. And he had lain awake, watching her, for—he peered at his watch, on the table at his side of the bed, and saw that it had just turned four o'clock—watching her for more than two pensive hours. But two pensive years, even two thoughtful decades, seemed hardly enough time, as far as George Throstle was concerned, to enjoy that face and body beside him. He had known—ever since 12:37 a.m., to be exact—that this was the woman he had been awaiting all his passionate life. The glass cases in his museum were broken, and the museum itself was dust: it hadn't taken a bedding of Ellen Lacy to destroy it, after all. For it had been exactly 12:37 a.m., while his arms were twined around the pale trellis of her body, during one of the minor respites from their major exertions, that Lydia Lacy had told him she hated her husband and loved George Throstle alone.

Thus it was that now, lying sleepless against her firm flank, warmed and inflamed by hope, George Throstle was prepared to become a general conflagration and holocaust of love, if only he and Lydia Lacy might remain among the resultant ashes, lost in each other and their eternal joy.

A wagon lumbered along the street below. One of its wheels, ungreased, squealed like a dying rabbit with every revolution. A frown spread across Lydia's face, and then her eyes fluttered sleepily open. As she saw George Throstle the frown went away. The ends of her full lips bent upward. "I thought I was home," she said in a husky whisper. "One of Alan's wagons sounds like that. Another thing he's neglected."

"You're home," George Throstle murmured. "Darling." He drew himself away from the headboard, put his arms around her, and pulled her to him.

"Yes," she said, "I can tell." Her voice was drowsy. "Good morning."

Somewhat later, when the maddening sound of the wheel had long since faded away, Lydia stirred in his still-encompassing arms and asked: "What time is it now?"

"Almost sunup."

"Oh." Her lips pressed lightly against his throat. "I *ought* to get up. I ought to be back before—"

"No. Please."

"Why not?"

"Because you're Lydia and I love you and I don't want you to go. *Ever*."

"That's one other thing I love about you. You call me 'Lydia.' *He* always calls me 'Liddie.' I hate it."

"I'll call you 'Lydia' all my life. Nothing but 'Lydia.'"

"Yes, I think you will. Darling. George. George *Throstle*. I like your name."

"It's yours. I want you to keep it always. Lydia Throstle. Stay here with our two names, Lydia Throstle."

"For how long?"

"For all time."

"I can't stay here for all time."

"Till tonight, then. We'll leave town together tonight."

"And your store? You can't take the store."

"I'll talk to Darius this afternoon, tell him to sell it for me."

"And where will we go, darling? Do what? Live how?"

"I can take care of us."

She raised her head from his neck. "I won't be like Ellen. I won't run away. But—" She was very awake now, and looking somberly into his eyes. "Perhaps we won't have to run anywhere. Perhaps this *had* to happen just now. Will you help me, George

Throstle, if I need you? Even if it meant that—" She broke off, yet her gaze was still fixed on him.

"You know I will."

"*Whatever* I need you for?"

"Whatever you need me for. As long as we're together."

"We will be, darling." She sighed and let her eyes wander to the window. "I love it here in the Forkhandle country. I don't want to leave it, ever."

"And I don't want to lose you."

"You won't, darling, you won't." She moved in, and her flesh was hot against him. "And we couldn't have picked a better time," she whispered in his ear. "There never was a better time for me to come to you the way I've done, and never a better time to—" Again she cut herself off in the middle of a sentence, and again she heaved a sigh. Then she began to nibble his ear, her teeth barely scraping the lobe.

"To do *what*, darling? Time to do what, dearest Lydia?" His fingers, leading their own tactile life, were caressing the small of her back.

"This," she hissed softly into his ear, "—for *now*, anyway," and she brought her mouth, open, against his.

"You're a passel of fools," Terry Sykes was saying, "the whole goddamned lot of you." He sat on the wagon that bore Pace Gray's body, and he was speaking to Jock Menzies, who rode his bone-weary horse alongside, bone-weary himself in his great bulk, and with his spent brain lost in a strange, red-streaked blackness that he had never known before, a blackness through which Terry Sykes's words fell like thrown rocks, beating a dull tattoo on a drumhead deep inside Jock Menzies.

"And *you*, you bastard, you're the biggest fool of 'em all," Sykes went on, encouraged by big Jock's silence, his mouth twisted in a sneering grin and the muscles of his flour-colored face twitching in exhaustion. "Because you ain't got the brains to stand up for yourself and beat the rest of 'em's brains out for 'em. Just a big goddamned stupid piece of beef that hasn't got any more sense than to tote a goddamned corpse all over creation, like it was your own father or something, because you don't reckon you can put it down any place. Built like a barn, by Jesus, and not enough brains to fill a thimble. Christ, I bet if I hauled off and hit you one, you'd go down like a pole-axed steer." Sykes glanced over at the big man, on the off-chance he might have maybe gone a little too far. But Jock's horse was plodding along, plodding along, and Jock Menzies was staring at nothing and looking so completely stupid that Terry was sure that he hadn't even been heard. The mean grin broadened, but Sykes was frowning, too: that goddamned squeaky wheel was beginning to get on his nerves. It didn't bother Menzies, though, the damned stupid son of a bitch. He just went on, head down, with the rising sun making his cheeks look like fat red apples, plodding even worse than the fool horse. God damn him to hell, thought Terry Sykes.

"Yeh, God damn you to hell, Menzies," he said aloud. "You're no good and you never was, neither. If I was you, and thank Christ I'm not, I'd haul out my goddamned pistol and blow the top of my head off. Why don't you do that, Menzies, hey? Why don't you go and do *just* that? Or maybe you'd do *me* a favor first. Ride back to that goddamned Alan Lacy's and kill all the rest of them bastards first. Why don't you do that, you son of a bitch? Why don't you *do* what I tell you? Go ahead, now. I'll take this Gray critter to Arch Eastmere all by myself, and maybe he'll want him to eat for breakfast. I don't reckon Maude there can even boil water. Let's us go *do* that, hey, Menzies? Or maybe you're just too goddamned stupid to know which end of a gun the bullets come out of. You didn't get off one goddamned shot up there, neither, not with that saddle gun you got or that short gun that's stuck in your holster. But, by God, if you want to know which end of a gun's which, you just hand that saddle gun over, and I'll be goddamned glad to settle all your troubles for you in jig time, goddamn you, and the jig'll be danced by you, hear?"

Jock Menzies still kept his own counsel. He heard what Sykes was saying, all right, but the words were falling one on top of another, building a terrible pyramid on the drumhead that stretched so taut within Jock Menzies. And the squeaking wheel had become a kind of music, fife music played by a madman somewhere, a madman buried somewhere in the soul of old ox Jock Menzies, and who kept old Jock plodding along.

But old ox Jock was within a few miles of the end of his plodding, on his way to the gate of the last corral that his dull, confused eyes would ever see.

Arch Eastmere had indeed slept the sleep, all through Friday and Friday night. Then, with a noise that was nearly a grunt of pleasure, he came wide awake on Saturday morning, a bare half-hour before dawn broke.

The dying stars filled the dingy bedroom with a light that was cool and clean. It even made Maudie's dun skin glow, there where she lay beside him in the bed, nearer the window than he was. Arch still wore his shirt and pants, but he was barefoot; a blanket had been thrown over him at some point. He didn't know exactly when, of course. As a matter of fact, he didn't, at the moment, know that it was Saturday morning and that dawn was about to break. His thoughts, as he lay there in the dark, did not, at first, make much sense.

He heard Maude Fletcher's faint, even snores and watched her solemnly for awhile. She looked mighty tired, poor little Maudie. It was all pretty mixed-up, but he remembered doing some drinking, and he reckoned he must've kept her up late, probably most of the night—and, thinking this, he put his big hand on her damp hair and stroked it. She stirred and mumbled, and he took his hand away. You sleep, little Maudie, you sleep.

He remembered drinking a lot, all right, but he couldn't remember how much or for how long. Till midnight, maybe? No, it couldn't've been that long—because it was still dark, and with all the booze he'd guzzled he'd've waked up with the granddaddy of all headaches, and here he was feeling fine. He stared at the gray boards of the bedroom wall, trying to bring his mind into focus. And then—in a heartbeat—he *knew*. It had been daylight when—he had a picture of himself falling down on the bed in broad daylight—

Well, now—

He rose from the bed and went to the window. The moon was

gone, and the stars seemed hesitant and overcome with that faintness that always struck them a little before dawn. Arch rubbed his jaw in disbelief. He was looking at what in a short time would be Saturday morning's sunrise. Friday, and Friday night, were gone forever from his life, unseen and never to be experienced.

Well, now, old catamountain, you sure went and got yourself some sleep—

He quietly picked up his boots and moved into the other room. He was hungry, but his thirst was even greater than his hunger. He set his boots on the table, among some dirty dishes, and went over to the stove. A big pot of cold coffee was there. He picked up three lucifer matches, stuck two of them in his shirt pocket, and opened the grate of the stove, lighting the third match as he did so. But Maudie hadn't laid a fire; the grate held nothing but ashes. Poor Maudie *must*'ve been wore out.

Arch straightened up again and blew out the match. He was too thirsty and too impatient to want to go to all the bother of getting a fire up. So he drank the coffee right from the pot, cold and bitter as it was, a whole quart of it at least. Then he took his boots from the table and went out on the porch.

He sat down on the warped boards there and pulled his boots on. After this he relaxed, stretching his long legs out as far as they would go, leaning back on his arms and sucking in lungful after lungful of the good morning air. A few noises remained from the creatures of the night, but even as he listened to them he heard, off beyond the shed toward the river, a trill from the first of the waking birds. Sharp it came to him, beautifully clear; it seemed that he had never heard a bird sing so.

He laid his hand across his chest, feeling heartbeat after heartbeat beneath his ribs. It sounded fine—steady, not too loud, exactly the way a man's heart should. And yet Phil Hyssop had said he ought to go easy—and he hadn't. And Phil had said he'd better not get mad—and he had, though maybe not as mad as he might have. And Phil had said he'd best lay off women—and he hadn't done that, neither. The girl there—Dolores—

The sky lightened briefly with the false dawn, grew dark again, then began to turn bright for good and all, with the rising

sun and the approaching day. But why had Phil told him *that?*
What did he figure to gain by telling Arch his heart was bad, and
warning him not to do all those things if he didn't want to kill
himself? Arch had gone and done them all—sure, and drank all
that liquor, too, that was even too much liquor for a man in his
prime—and yet here he was, feeling better than he had in
months. Phil sure must've made a mistake. Those doctors didn't
know everything, and that was the truth. Why, back in the War,
Arch had seen men die from wounds that were right out in the
open, when the doctors who ought to have fixed them didn't have
to work blind and by guesswork. He had half a mind to get mad
at Phil Hyssop. Why should he give Arch all that trouble, for no
good reason at all? Arch could remember how he felt just after
he'd shot poor young Luke that way, sitting there on his horse
and expecting any minute to tumble off dead himself, the way
his heart was thumping. But the thumping had stopped, and he
hadn't fallen. Yep, he *could* get mad at Phil Hyssop real easy.
Real easy—

But then he thought again of Luke lying there, and a heavy
sadness descended on him, that not even the bright rising sun
was able to lift for a while. Until he thought again about the girl
there. Dolores. Sorrows—

When his mother was dying, hadn't she said something about
sorrows? He remembered her "Little boy, little Archie, poor little
boy, I think you'll die young, too," but hadn't there been something else? Wasn't there—didn't she say—hadn't the words
been—? *Sure.* "Little boy, little Archie, poor little boy, I think
you'll die young, too, and you'll know more sorrows, poor little
Archie, than any man deserves." Sure, that was it. But his mother
—poor little Tessa Acton—she *couldn't* have said that, because
he remembered all the rest she said that last time, word for word,
and that "sorrows" thing was queer and misty in his head. Still,
sorrows—Dolores—

The piece of an afternoon that he'd spent with her had been
the nicest time he'd known, maybe ever in his life. There was
something about little Dolores that made him feel alive and lucky
and full of hope. Lying under the aspens like that, well, it was the
same as being floated across the ocean, *any* ocean, it didn't mat-

ter which one, on a smooth, lazy boat, and you knew that once
you got across there'd be a whole new life waiting for you, and no
more troubles at all. And he reckoned that she'd felt the same
way, too, and even though he hadn't mentioned it to her, he felt
pretty sure that if he asked her, she'd go with him any place he
wanted. And he *would* ask her, too, before this very day was out
—he'd ride over to Alan's and ask her right in front of the whole
bunch of them, and let's see if Alan Lacy'd dare try to stop him
from doing that. If he did, it would be a black day for Alan Lacy,
and, like as not, the last day he'd ever pass on earth. No, now,
he oughtn't to start thinking mean again. He didn't want to hurt
Alan or anybody else. All he wanted was peace, for a change,
and one last chance to get a *real* life started, and little pretty
Dolores right next to him, all the livelong time.

Maudie'd be mad, but Maudie'd watched him go away before, and she'd always managed to make out. And as soon as he
got back, things were just the way they'd always been. Of course,
this time would be different, this time he'd be going off with another female, but Maudie wouldn't know about that until later.
And when she did, maybe she'd realize that Arch *had* to go away
this time, and for good and all. This time he'd done a bad thing,
to folks he'd always liked and who had liked him, too, and he'd
never be able to face them again. His luck had plumb run out
forever in Eastmere, in the country he might have owned all by
himself if his grandfather hadn't—

He'd've done better if they hadn't caught him, him and Hallock both, that time they'd tried to run away together. He'd've
been luckier if they'd *never* found him, and Hallock might've
been, too. And Luke, poor Luke, would still be alive, if Arch
hadn't hunkered down there and—

Now, *why* was he thinking about *that?* He hadn't thought
about it for, oh, years and years now—and what he remembered
of it was mighty little. He'd been only nine years old, maybe
ten—nine years old, and already running out of luck—

And poor little Maudie, he was unlucky for her, too, going
away and coming back like a stray tomcat, and never being able
to do anything for her or help her much. Perhaps now, though, in
a year or so, he could send her back some money from wherever

it was he went to with little pretty Dolores, not saying where the
money come from, of course, and not telling who it was that
sent it. And maybe Maudie'd take it and use it to get back east
or someplace, where she could have a decent kind of life and
not have to take in—

People like Arch Eastmere? That's right, people like him.

He rose to his feet and walked out toward the shed, in order to get a better look at the rising red ball of the sun. There
was a kind of mist over in the east, and it didn't hurt his eyes
too much to watch the sun through it. And *he* knew, even if the
sun didn't, that it was going to get up there in the sky and shine
down on a wonderful day for Arch Eastmere, the most important
day perhaps that his life would ever know—outside of the day
he was born on and the one yet to come that would see him dead
—a fine, fresh day in which the old long-legged catamountain
would at last change his life for the better, and take himself
over the—

A whinnying came from the shed, pulling Arch back from his
unbridled dreams. For it was not Arch's horse that had whinnied,
and immediately he knew it. Frowning, he walked over to the
shed and went in, to stand a step inside the door, staring in amazement at Pace Gray's horse in the stall where his own should have
been, and Pace Gray's saddle lying on the earthen floor, and his
own silver saddle nowhere to be seen.

I must've slept *terrible* hard, he thought, not to have heard
him do that.

He strode back to the house and into the bedroom, bending
over Maudie and shaking her awake so hard that she sat up with
a small scream of fright. "Where'd Pace take my horse and saddle,
and *when?*" he demanded.

"Oh," she said, collecting herself and rubbing her forehead
wearily, drawing the residue of her wits back from sleep, "Oh,
it's you, Archie. You didn't have to wake me so—"

"Where'd Pace go with my horse and saddle?" he asked again.

She was fully awake now. "Didn't he tell you when you said
he could take them?" she wanted to know.

"I never said he could take anything." He stood erect beside
the bed.

"He came in here and asked you, Archie honey, and you said he could take the horse and saddle both, unless you were so fast asleep you told him 'yes,' goddamn you, poor drunk old Archie, without ever knowing what you said 'yes' to, maybe that's what you did, Archie honey."

Arch thought for a moment. Everything was still confused, but somehow he *did* seem to remember Pace looking down at him or something. Well, maybe he *had*—but he sure wouldn't have if he'd been sleeping sober, or—

"All right, Maudie," he said, "I reckon it slipped my mind, but it's coming back now, some of it. Except I can't recollect where he said he'd be going and just when he'd be back."

"He said he was going to Alan's place," Maudie Fletcher said, "and, goddamn him, he ought to've come back last night, I stayed up and waited as long as I could, I guess I might've woke you up and told you, Archie honey."

"No, it's all right, little Maudie, you go back to sleep if you want."

"I'm awake now, and I'll cook you something to eat, you must be nigh to starving, old long-legged drunk cat you."

"I'm fine, Maudie honey, I feel just fine, and I reckon I'll wait till Pace comes back, and then we'll all eat together. Go back to sleep, little Maudie."

He went back out on the porch and sat down in the rocking-chair, and started to wait for Pace Gray. He didn't think that he would have a very long wait. Pace must've gone up in the Marias with the rest of them; he gauged the distance between Juncture Valley and Alan's place and Maudie's, and knew that at that very moment Pace was probably on his way from Alan's. Arch wasn't especially worried about Pace, but he couldn't help but feel annoyed with himself that things had been so arranged that the boy finally got to go up there with the others, which Arch hadn't wanted, at all. Yet Arch was more annoyed with himself, for not staying sober and keeping his head on his shoulders. He might have been able to keep Pace out of the mountains, then. And any trouble that they might've run into up there—which would be trouble for Pace, too—was Arch Eastmere's fault, and nobody else's. He'd been a blamed fool, for certain. But there wasn't any sense in worrying about things, unless you had a good idea of just what you were worrying about. And Arch Eastmere's idea was pretty dim, take it all in all. He'd have to wait for Pace to get back. He reckoned it wouldn't be long.

And it wasn't.

Arch heard the creaking wheel before he ever saw the wagon. He didn't know what it was, at first; then the wagon came over a little rise on the road, and Arch recognized Jock Menzies riding beside it and what was his name?—Terry Sykes—handling the reins, and then he knew only too well what the wagon was, and the burden that it carried. He rose very slowly to his feet, and his body went numb all over.

He wanted to walk out to meet the approaching wagon, but he couldn't bring himself to do it. Maude Fletcher came through the open door and stood beside him, trying to hook up a dress she had put on. "There's a noisy wagon coming," she told him. She sounded scared.

"I know it," he said, staring off in fascination. "And I know what's in it, too." His voice sank to a whisper. "It's got my old hoss in it, Maudie. They done for my old hoss, Pace."

"Ah, Christ, Archie, don't say it, *no!*" She clutched his shoulder.

"That's what it is, little Maudie." His feet would carry him now, and he moved off the porch. Maude Fletcher started to follow him. "You stay where you are, little Maudie," he told her, never once turning around. And she stayed where she was, looking from Arch to the wagon, from the wagon to Arch, forgetting the hooks that she hadn't yet fastened.

Terry Sykes was pointing the wagon for the shed, and Arch Eastmere walked over there and stood, his face empty of any expression, waiting for the wagon to come up, still waiting for young Pace Gray. And then Sykes was pulling on the reins, and the nerve-grating creak of the wheel came to an end, and Jock had drawn up across the wagon from Arch, and was staring, like a drugged man, at the mane of his horse.

Arch made no effort to look in the back of the wagon, but rather his eyes sought big Jock. "Pace?" he asked quietly. "Jock, is it Pace?"

Jock nodded but did not look at him. "I'd like a drink, if you'd be so kind." he mumbled.

"In the house, Jock. In the bedroom. There's some in a jug on the floor there, I reckon. If there ain't, well, you better ask Maudie."

Jock dismounted and, letting the reins dangle, walked lurching toward the door of the house, moving very slowly. Arch turned his eyes to the back of the wagon, but he made no effort to go around there.

Terry Sykes's mouth was twisted with contempt. "Come on, goddamn you," he said to Arch, "get your breakfast meat off of there, before it begins to stink too bad. Alan Lacy wants his wagon back."

Arch continued to look at the side of the wagon. "Who killed him?" he said very softly.

"Hallock Randal, by God, who else?" Terry Sykes said. "And he got your tin saddle, too. And he'll get *you* next, by Jesus, same way he got your dead meat back there. They finally caught up with this little bastard, and with you too, goddamn you to hell, you yellow son of a bitch."

Arch's eyes remained where they were. "Come down off that wagon, you," he said in the same soft voice.

"Kiss my arse," said Terry Sykes. "And take off your goddamn meat."

It seemed almost effortless, the way he did it, the way Arch Eastmere reached up and lifted Terry Sykes from the seat of the wagon. Sykes yelled once, but it was impossible to say whether it was from anger or fright. Arch raised him high in the air, as though he were not a man but a bundle of old dirty rags, then turned and flung him against the side of the shed.

Not exactly flush with the side, though, for Arch was about three feet beyond the end of the shed when he heaved Terry Sykes away from him. Sykes had time for half a scream before the corner of the shed caught him in the small of the back. The sound, as his spine cracked in two, was heard even by Maudie Fletcher, over there on the porch, and she brought her hands up to her mouth, but not in time to stifle a scream of her own. Then she turned and fled into the house. But Jock Menzies, who had at that moment reached the porch, didn't even bother to look around. He went into the house behind Maudie.

The body of Terry Sykes sagged to the earth at the corner of the shed, and for a little while his fingers twitched, and his feet. But not for long.

Arch Eastmere paid him no more attention. Gravely he went to the back of the wagon, and tenderly he took up Pace Gray's dead body. In his arms he carried it into the shed. A moment later he came out again, but only to shut the door behind him before he returned to the cool gloom inside.

In the house, Maudie Fletcher threw herself face down on the bed, her narrow shoulders shaken by uncontrollable sobs, half of the hooks of her dress still unfastened and forgotten.

Jock Menzies came into the bedroom, too, but he paid no attention to the woman on the bed. He found the jug Arch had mentioned, sitting up in the corner, and methodically he picked it up and shook it. It still held nearly a quart of whisky.

Jock Menzies drank it as fast as he could, one swallow after another. He drank every burning drop of it down. Then, still moving like some huge automaton, he left the bedroom, left Maudie Fletcher's poor shack of a house, went out to where his tired horse, almost too tired to move, was standing, climbed into the saddle, and rode away. He saw neither the shed nor the wagon nor the body of Terry Sykes, nor did his eyes search for Arch Eastmere. For what had happened in these few violent minutes was nothing to what was building up in the breaking mind of Jock Menzies.

An hour later big Jock arrived at his own ranch house. There was no one to be seen, but there were weary horses in the corral; all Jock's hands had come back from Alan's spread and were already bedded down. Jock, however, was not concerned with anyone around his own ranch or, for that matter, with anything else but the phantoms that had gathered about him. He had translated himself to another world, one that had no existence outside his own head, yet which revolved in the dark places of Jock's mind, unbelievable in its brilliance, and blinding him to such an extent that reality was no longer a part of him, nor he a part of it.

What had happened to Jock had perhaps started in that terrible moment when Pace Gray had begun to fall from his horse. And this madness, for such it was, had swelled and deepened during the long, painful ride back to Alan's, with Pace hanging dead from big Jock's arm. And it had come at last to maturity with the aid of a shrieking wagon wheel and Terry Sykes's loathsome words. Then nearly a quart of whisky had caused it to burst into monstrous life. Nothing more remained but for poor Jock to kill it, and that was what poor ox Jock, confused for the last time, did.

He reined his horse up outside the corral and stolidly dismounted. Very calmly he drew his carbine from its scabbard by the saddle. He took a step or two backward, worked the lever to cock it, and then stared down at the weapon, held in his huge hands, as though he had never seen it before. His gaze went to his weary pony, and suddenly a furious expression suffused his face. "Well, now, Alan Lacy," he said to the drooping horse, "you brought me all this far, didn't you? It's as far as you're going to bring me, goddamn you. I told you I didn't like it much. But you had to take folks off someplace where other folks got to kill them. It's time you paid for it, Alan. And here's the bill to pay." He put the muzzle of the carbine between the eyes of his pony and pulled the trigger.

The horse dropped dead where it was.

Somebody yelled over in the bunkhouse, but the cry might as well have come from the moon. Jock walked around the dead horse and leaned over the corral rail, cocking the carbine a second time. The six horses, alarmed by the first shot, had begun to mill around, snorting nervously, and showing the whites of their eyes. "All here, hey?" Jock said calmly. "*There* you are, Mark. Morning, Drury. Good to see you, Nelse. Howdy, Ollie, howdy. Sykes, I was wishing you'd be here, too." He raised the carbine to his shoulder and looked down the sights at a bay gelding. "Just killed your brother, Mark," he said. "Reckon I'll kill *you*, now. Sorry, Mark, sorry." He fired again.

The shot failed to kill the gelding. It started to rear and

scream. Jock continued to fire steadily at the now-crazed horses, who stupidly huddled and heaved in a frantic group across the corral from the man who was trying to slaughter them. "Good-by, Mark," he said in a level voice. He was speaking between each shot. "So long, old Drury Wynward. Good-by, Nelse, good-by, beard. Hate to kill you, Ollie. Pleased to kill you, damn you, Sykes." Here he dropped a horse with a single bullet, there he made only a wound. But he kept up the steady, calm fire and the calm, steady conversation.

Men were coming out of the bunkhouse, running toward him, shouting. They might as well have been running on the moon, too. Jock emptied the magazine of the carbine. Two horses were still on their feet, although one had a bullet in her, and her belly was running blood.

Jock brought out his pistol. His first shot killed the wounded mare. It took three more to kill the palomino that remained.

All six horses were down and dead. Two of Jock's cowhands, their faces strained by uncomprehending fear, had nearly reached him now, running as hard as they could. Jock looked down at the pistol in his hand, looked down at it with no curiosity at all, as though it were held by a stranger. Then he solemnly nodded his head.

A single unfired cartridge was left in the cylinder. "Howdy, Jock Menzies," Jock said aloud. "Good-by, now, poor old ox Jock Menzies. You told them you'd quit, and you did." He sent the final bullet mushrooming through his right temple.

The force of it drove him against the rails of the corral, and his brains stained the weathered wood. The pistol's kick sent it flying nearly two dozen feet through the air.

One of the men who was running toward Jock had to jump to avoid the damned thing.

CHAPTER 22

A<small>IN'T</small> that your Maw standing there?" Soap was asking.

Hallock's drowsy head jerked up. "Where, Soap? Where's my mother?"

"Yep, by God, it's her, all right." Soap kept the reins in his one good hand as he pointed ahead. "Under the tree by the house there."

The men who had made the long ride from the fight at Juncture Valley, traveling by starlight most of the way, had reached, an hour after the sun had risen, the long rectangle of meadow that marked the heart of the Randal holdings, and were within a quarter-mile of the ranch house. They had kept close together during the dark hours, but with the coming of the sun the group had gradually lost cohesion, so that now the fifteen living and three dead riders stretched in a long ragged line across a couple of hundred yards of meadow grass. The horses moved at a walk and their gunmetal lips were lathered; the shoulders of the men who rode them sagged.

Hallock looked toward the ranch house. There was still a steady, drumming pain in his head. His eyes were watering and he had to rub them before he could focus satisfactorily. After his vision had cleared, however, he too could see Harriet Randal, leaning alone against a tree by the ranch-house door, watching them all come home.

"There she is, sure enough," Hallock said. "Wonder what made her get up."

"Probably feels better," Soap said. "Wish I did, goddamn it."

"Maybe she does, maybe she don't," Hallock said, only half aware of Soap's words. Then he glanced at the grizzled trail boss. "Shoulder troubling you?" he wanted to know.

"Getting stiffer than an old maid's corset," Soap said. "All this jouncing up and down ain't doing it no damned good, neither."

"You'd best take to your bed for a spell," Hallock told him.

"Reckon I had," said Soap. "After a time, anyways."

"Look," Hallock said suddenly, "I'm going ahead to the house. You take the boys to Number Two corral, Soap. I'll be down in a little while." He jabbed his spurs into the sides of Arch Eastmere's horse. The beast needed no encouragement; seemingly as fresh as ever, it carried him off at a gallop.

By the time Hallock had reached the house, his mother was no longer alone; everyone else had come out to meet him—his father, Ann, Pax, even Ellen Lacy. Cora Randal, too, was there, her hair hanging loosely over her back and shoulders. She stood close to the door, away from the rest of them. All their faces were grave, but Hallock noticed, with considerable relief, that his mother seemed not only calm and controlled, but completely aware of what had been happening. He swung off the horse, went to his mother, and put his arms around her. Pax caught the horse by the bridle.

"No need for you to be on your feet," Hallock said in his mother's ear, holding her tightly in his arms.

"Never you mind, son," said Harriet Randal. "Never you mind. It's all right. You've hurt your head, dear."

"Bumped it, that's all," Hallock said. He broke away from her, kissed Ann, and nodded to his father. Pax and Cora he ignored. Ellen Lacy might as well not have been there.

"There's been more killing," Harriet Randal said flatly, looking at the distant riders, who had veered to the left toward the far corral. "On the horses back there—are those our boys?"

"Only one," Hallock said. "Sam Wadley. The other two're Randy Worth and Will Clough. You know, worked for Nelse."

"Poor boys," said his mother. "Poor, poor boys."

"You said *more* killing—" Hallock turned dark-ringed eyes on his mother.

"I know about Luke," she said. Her voice remained flat. "I even walked out to his grave."

"Who told you?" Hallock asked.

"Cora," said Percy Randal. "Last night." But when Hallock swung a half-angry, half-disbelieving gaze toward his sister, he found that Cora Randal had silently slipped back into the house.

"Don't talk about it now," said Harriet Randal. "It's done. And it may have been God's will. Now we should all of us thank God it's over."

"It's not over yet," Hallock said. "All we did was get out of the frying-pan. We drove 'em off, that's all."

"You must've hurt 'em pretty bad," Percy Randal said, "if you set 'em to running."

"I don't reckon they run too far," Hallock said. "They'll be back."

"Whose horse and saddle is this?" Pax asked suddenly.

Hallock didn't look at his brother. "Belonged to Arch Eastmere," he said.

Pax's face lit up. "You killed Arch, by God!" he exclaimed.

"Arch wasn't there," Hallock said. "It was Pace Gray on the critter."

"Pace, too," Harriet Randal said, and she closed her eyes with a sigh. "Poor Dorrie. Ah, poor Sallie."

"I figger he's alive," Hallock said. "Leastwise, they took him off with 'em."

"What about Mark?" Ellen Lacy wanted to know.

Hallock looked at her coldly, and for the first time. "I didn't see him," he said. "It was pretty hard to see anybody. But you could maybe go home, find out if he's there." He turned to his father. "Only other one of 'em we're sure of is Charley Samuels. He—" Hallock hesitated, watching his mother's face. "*He* got killed, too. That's all, four all together. And Pace Gray got hit someplace. And Soap got winged in the shoulder."

Percy Randal's eyebrows went up. "*Soap?*"

"He'll be all right," Hallock said. "Hell, Father, you could use a Parrott gun on old Soap and he'd still walk away from it."

Hallock's voice was beginning to rasp with fatigue, and he felt as though someone had used a Parrott gun on *him*. The headache, however, had started to lessen, once he had dismounted. "I'm going to get a little rest," he said. "I don't want to eat, just lie down and rest. Pax," he went on, still averting his gaze from his brother, "I told Soap I'd talk to him down by the far corral. But *you* go, hear? and say I said for them all to stretch out for a while. But tell 'em don't unsaddle, hear? And that goes for this mean critter, too." He indicated Arch Eastmere's horse.

"Tell Soap I'll come and dress his shoulder," Ann told her brother-in-law. "Soon as I've seen to Hallock."

"And afterwards, Pax," Hallock said, "you know what you better do."

"All alone?" Pax said heavily.

Hallock filled his lungs with air, then exhaled slowly. "If you can get some help," he said, "then get it. I don't care." As he made for the door Ellen Lacy stepped out of his path, and his father and mother and wife all followed him inside.

Ellen Lacy remained with her lover. "I'll go down with you, Pax," she said.

"Not this time," Pax told her. "Not now, gold honey." He led Arch Eastmere's horse down the slope of the knoll.

In the main room of the house Hallock kissed Harriet on the forehead. "Luke didn't suffer," he said. "Believe me, Mother, he didn't."

"I believe you, darling," said Harriet Randal. "But can't it be stopped before more boys're hurt? I'd like to believe that it could."

"So would I, but I don't know how," Hallock said.

"Nobody does, Hattie, nobody does," Percy Randal said glumly. "Nobody even knows how these things get out of hand."

"Couldn't the military be sent for?"

"Soldiers won't help it," Hallock said. "Just make it worse, like as not."

"*Why* will they, Hallock?" Harriet Randal asked. "They'll at least keep more boys from being killed—"

Hallock tried to answer and couldn't. He lowered his eyes and shook his head. "Maybe later," he muttered. "Maybe we can talk about it later. We'll go over a lot of things then."

He left the room, his dear wife beside him. Ann's arm was around his waist as, together, they mounted the stairs.

Percy and Harriet Randal stood silently for a few moments, each unbearably aware of the other's presence, but neither of them capable of speech. Then Randal walked over to one of the windows from which he could see the men dismounting in the far corral. "Reckon I ought to talk to Soap," he said.

"Yes, Perce," said his wife. "Talk to them all. They didn't have to do what they did. We're not paying them to get hurt or get killed for us. And I don't want for any of them to have to go out that way again. There's no need."

"Thing's turning into a feud, Hattie," Percy Randal said, continuing to stare out the window. "That's what it's turning into, sure enough. A damnfool feud. And I just don't know why."

"You *could* stop it, Perce. You could go to Mark Lacy or Alan or whoever it is, and you could *make* him stop it."

"No," said Percy Randal.

"Perce." She was facing him now, even though his back was to her. "Folks've always looked up to you around here. And if you talked to them, they'd listen. They would've before, too, if you hadn't gone and gotten mad."

"I can't even get *mad* now," Percy Randal said. "Now that I've got good reason to. That makes it worse. But maybe after Hallock's laid down for a spell and can make more sense, he'll—" The old man's voice trailed off.

"It shouldn't be up to Hallock, Perce. It's up to you. It always has been. And you've never failed us before, Perce."

He came away from the window. "I'm not failing anybody now, Hattie," he said, blinking his eyes. "It's just that I—" He frowned. "You know," he went on vaguely, "I don't even know where Sam Wadley hails from. He rode up here one day, and that's all there was to it. He never once said where was home." Percy Randal was walking toward the door. "Maybe Soap or some of 'em'll know."

"Ah, *Percy*—"

His hand was on the knob. "You better rest, too, Hattie," he said. "You had a worse night than anybody."

"Never mind me, Perce," she said, and her voice rose. "But

please, *please* mind what's to come. I don't want any more Sam Wadleys. And I don't want any more Lukes, Perce. It's got to stop, and stop quick. Because if it runs on, Pax might go, don't you see that, Perce, or even, my God! even Hallock. I want to *keep* the boys I have left, hear? If I have to go to the Lacys on my hands and knees, I want to keep my last two boys—"

Percy Randal seemed on the point of going to comfort his wife, but he must have decided against it, because his hand never left the doorknob. "Now, don't you fret any more, Hattie," he said. "We've had all the grief we're going to get." Then, offering her the unsatisfactory solace of half a smile, he went out and left her there, in the middle of the sun-patched floor.

Harriet remained standing where she was, dead center in a house full of silence, until the silence itself became a kind of sound, muffling what might have been heard beyond the morning-yellow windows. She stood motionless until the silence became even more oppressive than her thoughts, and then, with a sigh, she crossed to the window through which her husband had gazed.

Her own eyes ignored the men gathered there at the far corral. Instead, she fixed them on a certain distant place, where the first line of spruces fringed the broad meadow, and where her sweet youngest son, now never to be seen again, lay in the earth he had loved so much, close by the guardian trees.

"Did I know?" his mother murmured. "Did I somehow know?"

Ellen Lacy came into the house. She had nearly reached the door to the hall before she saw Harriet at the window. "It's terrible, Mrs. Randal," she said, "just the most awful thing ever. I never thought Mark'd carry on so and bring folks so much misery, I declare I never did. It's a good thing for me I left his house when I—" Ellen's white brow remained serene, but she pressed her red lips together in annoyance: she might just as well, she decided, be talking to an old dead tree. She allowed her left shoulder an exasperated twitch, then went on into the hall and up the stairs.

The landscape beyond the window blurred for Harriet Randal: she inadvertently had focused on the glass pane, yellowed and warming in the sun. "Or was I somehow guilty?" she whispered to herself, wanting to grieve, but as yet incapable of grief, which must be an entire thing. We cannot, she thought, grieve piecemeal, not in the face of future grief, still awaited. Only when we know there are no more sorrows to come can the present be given over to grieving for losses past and loves forever gone.

But as to her *knowing*—

Was it because of some unexpressed premonition of dread events that she had taken to her bed late Wednesday afternoon, not to leave it again until midnight struck on Friday? She had been overwhelmed by a new and peculiar exhaustion that would let her neither sleep nor wake—as though some power beyond herself had wanted to bear her beyond all these truths of rage and death. And so she had lain in an odd, troubled trance while two days and nearly three nights had swept past on their crazy, cruel course; and never once had she felt their wings. Perhaps— but, ah! such a thing *must* not be true—she had somehow foreseen what was coming and had, like a coward, turned from it, to take the temporary solace of her bed.

Well, then, as to her *guilt*—

If she had shaken off this weakness, this refusal, if she had risen from her protective bed and faced them all, might events not have armed themselves before they caught the shock of violence? But ah! if she had sensed this shock's descending arc, and yet had done nothing about it, would she not be someday billed for these lives already lost? And would *Luke* be the one who presented the bill? Might he not be alive there at his mother's side now, if his mother had only been strong?

Luke. Luke. Dear dear Luke. Never again. No more.

But when Cora had told her of Luke, Harriet had been very calm; it was, dear God! as though she knew.

What had it been, then? Was it as she remembered, that dead-of-night hour? Ah, yes. Yes, it *was*.

Perce had been asleep at her side, then, but she was awake, wide awake, for the first time in she didn't know how long. And hungry. She had risen from bed, put on her slippers, and drawn the long robe over her nightdress. The moon was still nearly an hour from setting, and the house was dusted by its silver rays. She could hear no movement upstairs, and as she came down to the ground floor the stillness shrank back into corners, avoiding her.

Harriet had started along the hall by the staircase, when her attention had been caught by a figure in the window of the main room, the same window at which she herself now stood. It was Cora Randal, fully dressed; and as the mother paused, the daughter swung around and saw her. "I was waiting for you," she said. Her voice seemed to have come from far away, she spoke so very softly.

"Waiting for me, Cora?" Harriet had said. She had entered the main room and walked toward her daughter, peering anxiously at her in the deceptive moonlight. She was worried about Cora, she realized; the girl had acted so upset after Drury Wynward had left, on that frightening Tuesday night past. "What made you think I'd be down?"

"Because," Cora had said in the same soft voice.

Her daughter looked quite well, Harriet had found herself thinking. "What's out there?" she had asked, coming up beside Cora and peering out across the moonlit landscape. She no longer felt hungry, but strangely relaxed and placid.

"More than you'd guess," Cora had said. "Do you want to see Luke?"

"Luke? What about Luke? Where is he?"

"Out there. They should've told you."

"Told me what?" But Harriet Randal must have had this instinctive knowledge in her, because even then she knew what Cora was going to tell her, and she waited peacefully until she heard the fatal words.

"That Luke's dead. Arch Eastmere shot him."

The hollow drum of her heart had sounded at least twenty times. Then Harriet Randal had put her arm around her daughter. "Yes," she said, "they should've told me."

"He's buried out there. Want to see?"

"Yes, Cora, I want to see."

They might have been going to shop at George Throstle's, so unhurriedly had they strolled across the meadow to the new grave, ignoring the dew-wet grass, mother and daughter calmly moving to where the trees and the meadow met. Nothing was said, little thought; for all the passion these women had shown then, the boy might have been a dozen years dead. And when they had reached the fresh grave, with its mound of clods scarring the meadow's green table, they had each retained this mute control. Harriet Randal, right then, saw only a low long pile of earth, which seemed to have nothing to do with her Luke; yet for all that she filled her eyes with the shape of that narrow mound until the moon was nearly gone. "Pax was the one that buried him," Cora had broken their silence to say. "And Hallock wants this for the family plot. It will be, too. Best go back now."

"To the house, anyway," Harriet Randal had said. Now what had she meant by that?

They had returned to the house, and Cora had gone meekly to her room, without another word to her mother. And Harriet Randal had sat alone by the fireplace, alone in the still hell her house had become, with the moon finally down and the night at last dark, while her own dreams were darkened and sank. She had wept awhile then, but without any fall of tears, suitable to the emptiness of a sobbing woman who had yet to be filled with her loss. And after a time she had ceased to weep. She had closed her dry eyes and waited for dawn.

They had found her, sitting there, as one after another they had come down the stairs. And gravely she had told them she knew Luke was dead and that all this, whatever it was, must have an end, *today* must be the end of it. And then she had gone upstairs and dressed, to wait for her eldest son's return.

And now—

Now the waiting would have to continue, until poor Hallock could have his rest, until there was another chance for them to talk, until this already bitter Saturday could be made an end of their troubles and put a seal to grief.

She went over and sat once more by the fireplace, in the chair her husband so favored. "Luke," she said to the soot-blackened stones. "Luke Randal. Pax Randal. Hallock." She sighed. "These are my boys. My three tall boys. My life."

Her mind was empty of Cora.

A thunderhead was swelling above the Marias's round peaks, whiter than carded wool or cotton, more beautiful than any green of mountains. Cora Randal knelt on the floor by her window, rested her arms on the sill, and watched the cloud's near-motionless progression above the far ridges. "It's ten o'clock now," she told herself. "It ought to be on us by noon." If the storm was already rumbling off there in the west, its note was still too distant for any human ears to catch, even those of sensitive Cora Randal. She gauged a stillness around her, however, as though the bottom were dropping out of the air. It was becoming humid, too, and the sounds that reached her from beyond her window had an odd, unnatural quality about them. They were not themselves, but rather echoes of themselves.

Cora was impatient for the storm. She wished that she might rise into the air, carry herself beyond the Marias, sweep behind the white wonderful face of the thunderhead, and drive it helter-skelter in crashing flight before her, over this damnable house and the damnable two who lived under its roof.

Not her mother, though—Cora didn't mean *her*—nor her father: these had already tasted their grief and would live to devour it all. Not Ann Dover Randal, the fullness of whose grief was yet to come. Not Hallock, either, not horse-breaking Hallock, whose own breaking would be but little longer delayed. For all these Cora was bowed beneath her own private sorrow, which none of them, alas, could ever believe or know or share. Yet Ann and Cora and Harriet and Percy Randal would dwell together in the thunder to come. Just these. As one.

She closed her eyes and clasped her hands together and the image of her father rose in her mind. "Oh, how will you like your world, Percy Randal?" she crooned in her misery. "How will you like that water world, when there's nothing but water and a memory of earth, and when the doves you sent out one by one— one at a time, the doves—they never come back at all? Will you accept the world you've been given, once you have only a daughter? Not three *sons*, Percy Randal. No sons at *all*, Percy Randal, dear *father, dear* Percy Randal. Just one lonely daughter, one *daughter*, no more. What will your world tell you *then*, Percy Randal? And what will you wait for in those days?"

She closed off her misery and opened her eyes. The image of her father went away, and over the Marias the thunderhead mounted in its power. "If they'd've believed me," she said to the palms of her hands, "it all might have turned out different. But I don't think so, no, not after—"

Pax and that Lacy woman, *they* were the damnable two.
There would be no peace while Pax—

Pax had cursed them all, back there when he'd—

And *now*, with Ellen Lacy—

Let *her* know, then. Let Ellen Lacy know. Let her get her fill
of Pax Randal, bloody Pax Randal, damnable Pax. And then
maybe maybe *maybe* it might—

We'll see. Right this minute, we'll see. With the thunder two
hours away. Maybe.

Cora Randal rose to her feet, unlocked her door, and went
out into the empty corridor. Cat-quiet, she padded past where
Hallock rested and stopped in front of the room they had given
to Ellen Lacy. The door was open wide. Cora saw this contented
flesh, who'd become such a bone of contention, sprawled across
the canopied bed that had once belonged to Harriet Randal's
mother. Ellen's wide placid eyes were beguiled by nothing, and
the ghost of a tune thrummed in her throat. Cora almost jumped
into the room and shut the door quickly behind her.

Ellen Lacy was startled, but she showed no surprise, save
that she ceased to hum. She turned the perfection of her face full
on her visitor, saw who it was, and sat up, fingering her golden
hair. "Why, Cora," she said, "how nice of you to come see me.
Do sit down, dear. I've been feeling so sad."

Cora, however, remained by the door, her arms drawn tight
behind her, clutching the knob in both hands. She shook her
head back and forth very slowly. "I only came in for a minute,"
she said. Her voice had deepened, and she was staring at Ellen
with a predatory, about-to-leap intentness. "I wanted to ask you
something."

"Well, now, just sit down and ask me. A chat'll be very nice."

The slow shaking of Cora's head continued. "What I wanted
to know," she said, "is—do you love my brother Pax?"

Ellen Lacy managed to blush and gasp at the same time.
"Why, Cora," she said, nor did her voice increase its pitch, "you
shouldn't *say* such a terrible thing. You know very well why I'm
visiting here, and why Pax was kind enough to bring me. That's
not a nice thing to say, at all." Ellen Lacy rose, made a half-circle
around the foot of the bed, pattered to the commode, picked up
the pitcher, and began to pour water into the basin. "It's getting

terribly close, isn't it?" she asked, hoping that Cora would drop the subject. "Almost like the dog days, and here it is only June."

"There's a thunderstorm coming," Cora said calmly. Her eyes never left Ellen Lacy.

"*That's* what it is, then," Ellen said. She put the pitcher down.

"Or does my brother Pax love *you?*" Cora went on.

Again Ellen Lacy gasped. With great dignity, she tilted her chin at Cora. "I mean it," she said. "I don't want to *hear* such terrible things. You've no call to talk that way about your brother. Or me, either."

"Then you *don't* love him, and he don't love *you,* is that it, Mrs. Lacy?"

"Please, Cora, don't carry on that way. There's no question of love, not at all. Pax merely—"

"That's what I thought when I heard you," Cora broke in.

Once more the rosy blush swept across Ellen's velvet face. "*Heard* us?" she whispered.

"Twice," Cora said. "Right here in this very same room. And you sounded like a bull and a heifer. Not a question of human love at all. Two *animals,* that's what I heard."

"Cora!" Ellen flounced to the other side of the bed and stared wide-eyed at Cora from across the counterpane. "I'm going to tell Pax what you said."

"Promise? *Promise* to tell him?"

"I will if you *don't* leave this minute, and stop saying all those terrible things."

"That's not a terrible thing," Cora said. Her neck was jutting toward Ellen now, and her eyes had grown big and bright. "I know you both more than I want to, especially Pax, that damned Pax. And I know *love* hasn't got anything to do with it. Because you're not woman enough to love anybody, and Pax never knew what love was, and, damn him, he'll never live to find out. He'll—"

"Cora!" Ellen Lacy was growing frightened.

"I'll tell you about brother Pax," Cora said fiercely, the words tumbling over each other. "Do you want to hear about down by the river one day, there by the Forkhandle bridge, when filthy Pax was only fourteen years old, and I was eighteen, full grown?

Do you want to hear how he threw me down on my back, *forced* me down, his own sister, and put one filthy hand over my mouth, and with the other—"

"No, stop!" Ellen Lacy cried, raising her hands as though to ward Cora off. "Oh, stop it, *please*—"

"*I* couldn't even say 'stop,'" Cora told her, "or fight to save my shame. He was strong as he was filthy, and he did what he wanted to, to *me*, his own *sister*, and him only fourteen years old. He made me different, and different himself. He ruined my life and went away laughing, and I've never let another man near me since, and I won't, and I'll see that damned, filthy Pax dead yet, and as bloody as I was—"

"I don't believe you," Ellen said. "It's a *lie*, you're lying to hurt him with me." She was beginning to weep.

"That's what *he* told me, Pax, my big strong dirty brother Pax," Cora went on, "looking down at me there, lying on the ground and most dead with the hurt and the shame. 'Go tell them,' is what he said, 'there's not a one of them'll believe you.' And I didn't tell them, because I knew he'd laugh and swear I lied and they wouldn't, not one, believe me at all. And I was right, because they've never yet believed a single true thing I ever told them since."

"I *will* tell Pax, I will, I will," Ellen said, and covered her wet face. "These awful accusations you're making, I'll tell him every one."

Cora's breast was heaving. A white ring encircled her mouth. "Go ahead," she whispered. "He won't believe *you*, either. Not if *I* said it, he won't." Then she was out of the door before Ellen knew she was gone.

When she realized that Cora had left, Ellen brought her sobs under control. Cora simply wasn't right in the head, she decided. Why, she might become violent any time. A woman wasn't safe in this terrible house. Mark had been mean enough to her, and that was the truth, but—goodness, he'd never made her shiver, the way Cora Randal did. And *saying* such things about a dear man like Pax. She'd ask Pax right out, Ellen Lacy would, just as soon as the two of them could be alone again, and right after they'd—

Shame on you, Ellen, she said to herself, don't think about *that* right now. But what if Pax really had forced his own sister to—

No, it had to be a lie, it *had* to be. And, anyway, it was too much for Ellen Lacy to think about all at once. She needed time. She had to be alone. But not in this house, not here under the same roof with Cora Randal. She'd find a place, and after she'd thought about that terrible lie for a while it would begin to make sense, the way everything else in her life had made sense once she'd thought about it for a little while.

She washed her face in the cool water, smoothed her bright golden hair, and went downstairs. In the main room she saw Harriet Randal sitting by the fireplace. Under a tree outside the door Ann was playing with the baby, Simon. Percy Randal was coming up the knoll. She passed every one of them by without as much as a nod, so anxious was she to find some undisturbed nook in one of the various buildings where she could be alone. She even failed to notice the thunderhead that heaved its white bulk above the Marias, the coming storm that, unknown to Ellen Lacy, had stirred up the nearer storm in the heart of Cora Randal, and had thus driven the fair Ellen forth, in search of an answer for which she had no question.

Pace's body was stretched along two bales of hay, in the center of Maude Fletcher's blue-shaded shed. The eyes were closed, the mouth was closed, the hands were relaxed along the sides, the feet were set together. Arch Eastmere had laid him out that way, after the shed door was closed and they were alone together. The flesh had the color and coldness of snow.

For three hours Arch sat on the feed bin and looked at the dead face. Bloodless and bland, the delicate lines were those of a boy asleep, but a boy asleep in marble. Beyond the cool gloom, beyond the dusty ghosts of sunbeams, beyond the two small dirty windows, birds sang and the rustling earth made quiet noises beneath the replenishing sun. Yet none of these sounds were heard by Arch Eastmere as, while the tawny morning shimmered outside, he let the ashes of his spirit be blown into a holocaust of wrath.

Wonder had overcome him at first, after the initial shock and numbness—wonder that Pace Gray could have crossed the border between life and death so suddenly, so unexpectedly, with never a word, never an apology, never a regret, and never an explanation. And to be so peaceful, so calm and unmarked, with that resigned, patient expression: was this *all* the achievement of his nineteen years, the end and the reward? Or the penalty and the beginning?

Disbelief, by degree, took the place of this wonder. Why, what Pace was doing was all a trick to plague Arch Eastmere, like borrowing his horse and saddle that way, when Arch hadn't really lent it. Pace was a cute one, lying there, pretending to be a gone goose, real cute. The kid even had this new trick of making his flesh feel cold when you touched it.

Desperately, and for but one moment Arch Eastmere believed in this disbelief. "Hoss?" he said. "*Hey,* old hoss. Pace?" But these hopeful and questioning words merely intensified the silence in which what had been young Pace Gray was now forever enfolded. And then Arch Eastmere shuddered and knew the truth of his loss.

Tears ran from his hard eyes and down his unshaven cheeks, to drop one by one on the dusty floor. But this was his sole outward show of sorrow, and Arch seemed not to know he was weeping. And at last the tears ceased of themselves, and gradually they dried of themselves as well, leaving faint salt trails below the hard eyes.

And as an accidental spark, mothered by dry wood and fathered by gales in some mountain valley, lurches into red and predatory life and then, its strength increasing, leaps up the flank of the mountain, augmenting always its voice and swift ascent, gulping down the fleet deer and the bounding lion, distending with each death the mass of its belly, to reach at last a high triumph as it engulfs the whole bulk of the mountain, closing its flame-fanged maw across the last anguished peak, so did a crimson wrath arise within tall Arch Eastmere.

And in the end, when this wrath, fostered by hatred and revenge, nourished by regret and hunger for blood, had filled to repletion his body, Arch Eastmere was no longer a man: he had become a walking destruction. Yet he made no show of rage. The molten steel of his anger seethed round his heart and vitals, but outwardly he was deliberate ice.

It was with a great calm and steadiness that he saddled Pace Gray's horse, led it across from the shed to Maude Fletcher's sagging porch, and tethered it to a post. Then, full of purpose and murder, he strode through the house to the bedroom, where Maude Fletcher lay on her side in her unhooked dress, flushed and perspiring, a corner of the sheet twisted between her hands. She watched Arch take his gunbelt from the back of the room's only chair and strap it around his waist. His flat-crowned black hat had fallen to the floor. He picked it up and put it on his head, careless of the dust on the brim. Then he faced Maude Fletcher for the first time since he had entered the room. His eyes held the savagery of a hawk or eagle, the coldness of a snake: there was no mercy in them.

"Time I went," said Arch Eastmere. "I'll be back."

"Arch—" she began, "oh, *Archie*—" Something was making her afraid. Not his hard eyes, but *something*.

"What is it, little Maudie?"

"I'm sorry, Archie honey, *ah!*" Tears were forming. "I'm so *sorry* about poor Pace, I'm all broke up by it, Archie, sad about Pace and you."

"A man tries," Arch Eastmere said slowly. "A man tries all the time. But it's no good, Maudie, never. No good, your whole life long. I'm killing Hallock Randal, Maudie, killing him dead as Pace. You stay where you are till I'm through, hear?"

"I love you, Archie honey, love you so, I don't ever care what you do, or how, but come back to me soon, please, Archie honey, safe and loving and soon." She stretched an arm toward him as though she hoped to drag him down for a kiss, but he paid no attention, and she let the arm fall.

"Wait for me, Maudie," he said, "and listen. Listen, and maybe you'll hear me come back. I'm going to burn your shed down now, Maudie. I'm burning your shed down before I go."

"You do that, Archie honey, and anything else you want, burn the damned shed, I hate it, Archie."

"I wish it was a city," Arch Eastmere said, and he left her.

As he came away from the porch, he saw the broken-backed body of Terry Sykes curving around the corner of the shed. Without breaking his stride, he went over to it, slipped one hand under Sykes's belt, and dragged the jackknifed corpse into the shed, where he dropped the limp thing by the hay bales, under the feet of Pace Gray. Then, without bothering to glance around to see if the shed held anything worth saving, he stood over the dead body and laid his hand gently on the white brow. "So long, hoss, old hoss," he said. "The next time it'll be different. And better for both of us, maybe. But now you'll always be nineteen years old, never a single day older, lucky old hoss Pace Gray. So long, hoss, so long for now."

He brought his weathered hand away from the forehead, felt in his shirt pocket, and pulled out a match. He lit it with his thumbnail. Then he bent down and laid the burning end against the bottom of one of the hay bales, which caught the tiny flame, swelled it, and sent it crackling up the bale's side.

Arch tossed the still-flickering match in a corner and went out of the shed. He pulled the door tightly closed behind him. Again he walked over to the porch, freed the reins from the post, mounted into Pace's old saddle, and veered the horse around to watch the shed. Within five minutes the whole interior was afire, and he could hear the continual muffled roar of flames unwillingly contained. Already small eager yellow tongues were beginning to dart through cracks and knotholes, tasting the outside air.

But Arch, with his own wrath hardly contained, could not wait for the fire to conquer, for the rickety building to crumble inward upon itself. He spurred the horse into a gallop, out across the road and then north, where the Randal ranch house was waiting.

A great cloud hung above the Marias. Within an hour it would come crashing across the Forkhandle country, bringing a sudden dark and a time thunder-shaken, shattered by lightning, rain-raked. And then, with the swiftness of its arrival, the storm would depart, leaving air that was new and clean above a wet, freshened earth. But before that racking cloud arrived, Arch Eastmere said to himself, Maudie Fletcher's old shed, which was serving right now as Pace Gray's funeral pyre, would be nothing but whitening ashes. And Hallock Randal, Arch Eastmere swore to himself, would have become another sacrifice, like Sykes, a somewhat better cut of funeral meat.

After Hallock had stretched himself on the bed, but before he closed his eyes, he had realized that he was concerned with Arch. "If anybody sees him coming this way," he said, "you wake me up in a hurry."

Ann looked at him with no comprehension. She had but then taken Simon from his cradle and was holding him in her arms. She was going to carry him out under the trees, for she was afraid that if Simon were left in his cradle he would manage, one way or another, to disturb his father's rest. As soon as the child was amusing himself somehow, she would go along and dress Soap Damson's shoulder. "Sees *who* coming?" she asked.

"Arch Eastmere. He just might be coming along here."

"Why should he?"

"Well, maybe because Pace there got himself shot."

"You didn't shoot him."

"Arch might get the idea I did. Anyway, if he chances to head this way—well, wake me up right quick, won't you?"

"You're *so* tired, dear heart, you simply don't know what you're saying. Go to sleep now, get your rest."

Hallock had tried to get his rest, but it had taken a long time. He had lain with his eyes shut and tried to formulate some plan of action by which everything would be neatly and instantly concluded. But he found that he was incapable of concentric thoughts that spread from a sensible central idea; so, in the end, since his mind was not at the moment serviceable, he used it to will himself to sleep.

The slumber which he managed to force on himself started out sodden and black, but then, for the second time in a week, he found himself caught up in the old frightening dream. Again he stood with his waxen men in line of battle at the clearing's edge, the little clearing whose sides, mottled with jagged pine stumps, sloped down to a soggy marsh. Again the Rebels swarmed out of the trees across the little clearing. Again they moved steadily down to the marsh, through it, and on up the nearer slope toward him. And again he was filled with the old horror, and covered with the same sweat of fear—but this time the fear was greater and the horror was almost unbearable. For the Rebels reached, and—*my God!*—went beyond the point where, always before this, choked with his terror, Hallock had jerked awake. Dear Christ, they were converging on him now, they were bringing their rifles to bear on his body, and his feet had become immovable, and the scream that bubbled out of his throat went unheard in the volley they—

Hallock Randal sat bolt upright in bed, his head dribbling sweat, his eyes washed with fear. The room had become very dark, and the echoes of the volley that had torn him apart could still be heard in the hills. And then there was the sound of a fainter volley from another part of the field.

Hallock gave a sudden, sharp sigh of relief, and then grinned like a fool. It was thunder that had aroused him, thunder that had brought on the dream. And getting mighty near, too; Ann ought to fetch in Simon, if she hadn't done it already. Hallock got off the bed, padded to the window, and peered out. Yep, the storm had nearly arrived. The landscape was darkened, and a wind was beginning to sough through the trees. And off to the southwest—Hallock leaned further out—there, off to the southwest, a tall man was riding toward the ranch house at a steady, deliberate gallop. He looked familiar.

He was.

CHAPTER 23

Tall Arch Eastmere rode with the thunder. He rode erect across the long meadow. His hard eyes bore on the spruces that flanked him. The wind beat his back, he felt the rain follow. He sensed before him the death of Hallock. He felt many deaths, save the last he would know. He recalled many dead men, but not himself.

He remembered Pace Gray, who was riding with him. The ghost of Pace Gray was beside him then. The clouds had gathered above Pace Gray. There was death in the air, and a dozen ghosts riding. But tall Arch Eastmere had yet to ride with them. Nor did he know it was death at his shoulder. It seemed like the wind, it seemed like Dolores.

Arch Eastmere rode toward the Randal ranch house. His thighs were spread on a dead man's saddle. Under him galloped a dead man's horse. A dead man's horse galloped on a high meadow, on its way toward a man who was soon to die, with a man astride who was not yet dead, for whom life was reserving one last cruel cheat.

Arch Eastmere had nearly arrived at the ranch house. The years of his life would be forty-two. The gun on his hip would be worn by others. The clothes on his back would never leave him. His heart marked time, marked time, marked time. The bolt in his heart he had yet to hurl.

Hallock Randal's years would be forty-one. The gun on his hip would be worn by no one. The clothes on his back would blend with his flesh. His dear wife would long for his body at midnight. His dear son would never remember his face. Neither slayer nor slain would leave any likeness.

The wind increased. The clouds were darker. A curtain of rain swept from the Marias. The horse was nervous. The knoll was reached. A roll of thunder was on the meadow. Lightning glared from behind a near hill. Arch Eastmere halted below the ranch house. Thunder and wrath were approaching their apex. The time had come for the dead to meet.

Arch Eastmere opened his angry mouth, which once, ah! hardly three days before, had been like someone's remembered childhood—

"HALLOCK!—HALLOCK RANDAL!"

The cry held a greater threat than any thunder, and everyone in the house heard it. Before his name rang out across the obscure air, Hallock had briefly left the window. Ann had run into the room, Simon clutched to her breast, pallor upon her grave face. "Somebody's coming," she said. "I think it's Arch Eastmere. He's riding—"

"I saw him," Hallock said calmly.

Ann put Simon in his cradle and embraced her husband, pressing her cheek against his coarse shirt, still damp with the sweat of his dream. "What'll you do?" she asked. The wet cloth muffled her words.

"Do what he wants," he said. "Settle things."

"Dearest heart," she started to say, "why don't you—?" Then Arch's great shout cut her short. Startled, she took a step backward and stared at her husband. But Hallock's whole mind was already centered on his adversary outside. "By God, now, but he's a cool one," he said with admiration, more to himself than Ann.

"I could gun him down from here." He went back to the window. "What you want, Arch?" he called down.

Arch Eastmere lifted his merciless eyes. "Man who killed my friend," he said. "Feller that murdered Pace Gray."

Hallock was silent.

"You," Arch Eastmere said. "*You.*"

Hallock hesitated a little longer. "All right," he said at last. "I'll be out."

"I'll be waiting," Arch said.

"Away from the house," Hallock told him.

"I'll be waiting," Arch said again.

"There'll be no gunplay around this house," Hallock said. "You get yourself back to the end of the meadow there, and I'll ride out to meet you."

Arch glared at him so fiercely that Hallock half expected him to draw and fire right then. But the tall man jerked his head once in curt agreement. "I'll be waiting," Arch Eastmere said for the third and final time. Then he went galloping off, toward the mountain end of the long meadow. As he passed near the bunkhouse, two cowboys, who had come to the door when they'd heard him bellow out Hallock's name, quickly scuttled inside. The only way that most men could have brought themselves to stand up to Arch Eastmere was in dead of night, and from behind damned good cover, at that.

Hallock watched Arch ride away, then, frowning, moved from the window. The frown was born of the new turmoil inside him, and the intensity of his concentration on how he might best handle matters during the next half-hour. Yet Ann's intentness was no less than his own, and so, in spite of himself, he found his eyes drawn to hers. Husband and wife were so full of emotion that they seemed to possess no emotion at all. Thus it was that Hallock, plunging into the cool depths of Ann Randal's eyes, sank past the question that lurked there. "You could have told him the truth," she said. "It wasn't you that killed Pace."

"First I even knew of the kid being dead."

"You could have said *you* didn't do it."

"I could've, yep. But I wouldn't. A man can't shame himself that way."

"You wouldn't shame yourself. Not with *me*."

Simon was on his knees at one end of the cradle, grinning and gurgling and stretching a tiny hand toward his father's arm. Hallock glanced obliquely at his son, then extended his index finger toward him. Simon grabbed it, made a happy, idiotic noise, and laughed. "Maybe not now," Hallock said, his gaze again on his wife. "But later—"

"No," she said. "Never. I'd *always* be proud." She went over to him and leaned against him, and he put his free arm around her warm shoulders. A crash of thunder shook the house. Simon, who loved loud noises, gave a shriek of joy.

"Anyway, that's not the point of it," Hallock said. "For one thing, I can tell that Arch Eastmere's crazy mad, worse than I ever yet seen him. And when he gets like that—well, there's not one damned thing you can do about it. He's made up his mind I'm the feller killed Pace, and the only way to get that notion out of his head is to blow it out with a bullet. And if I don't go out there and face him down, he'll, by God, come back here and burn the house down to get at me."

"He wouldn't dare," Ann said. "Not with all the men around. He wouldn't last a minute."

"He'd dare," Hallock said firmly. "And he'd last, too. But I'm goddamned if I want that, I don't want any more killing, for my own mother's sake, if nothing else." He pulled his finger away from Simon, and now, with both arms free, gently brought Ann around so that he could peer with great earnestness into her own earnest eyes. "Except the one man," he said, speaking slowly and spacing his words. "The man that owes me for Luke. I intend to take care of Arch Eastmere, and I reckon that once I do, things'll pretty much level out all over. It'll take the starch out of the Lacys, by God."

"You *can* take care of him?" Ann asked. Her expression was calm, but Hallock could sense her uncertainty. "If he's as wrought up as you said—"

Hallock squeezed her arms gently. A little confident smile ran along his mouth. "Hell," he said, "he's gone and made a mistake already. When we come together we're going to be on horseback, and I reckon to see we stay that way. I could out-fork Arch

Eastmere on the best day he ever saw, and I'll make damned sure he keeps off the ground till I put him there for good. If he has any advantage to start with, he's sure lost it now, by God."

"If you think so, Hallock," Ann said. She let her head press against his chest.

The smile left Hallock's face. "When I said before that I was going to kill him," he told her, "you said that's what I ought to do. Remember you said that?"

She nodded quickly, but kept her head down. "It was far away then, like something you think about when you're lying in bed."

"But now that it's real close, you want me to back down?"

"It's going to rain," she whispered.

"I reckon it will," he said. "And I'll probably get good and wet. But—"

"Hallock." Her arms were around him.

"My Ann."

Her eyes were lifted now. "I love you, dear heart Hallock." The words were spoken very quietly, and the tone that she used was low, and the simple phrase contained every moment of the more than ten years they had spent together. In it was all her faith in him and in what he now had to do, no matter what the result might be. Her arms tightened around his torso, and she held him as though she wanted her embrace to blend them into one body forevermore. "Don't be long, *please* don't be long," she murmured. Then, abruptly, she let her arms fall.

She brought his gunbelt to him, and watched while he strapped it on. She brought him his hat. She offered him gloves, but he refused them. She was collected, controlled and almost brusque—and her heart was ready to break. For, at some point in the past few minutes, she had felt black fear pass over her head, its shadow more grim than even the tempest sky. Ann Randal sensed that she had already become her husband's living urn; but never would she let him know it. She would go about the little time they had left together as though this day, ah! even *this* black afternoon of storm, were no different from the myriad bright others they had shared, as though the sun on high still warmed their world, and as though her dearest Hallock were on his way to no place more crucial than the far corral, and not to this dread accounting.

Yet even now he was standing over the cradle, over the consumation that was their son. Now he was lifting Simon high in the air, and the child was laughing, and Hallock was laughing, too. But suddenly, the man was no longer laughing. He was kissing the tiny face and the hands and one ear and the cloth that covered the little shoulder. And "If I don't get back by dark," he was telling the small wide eyes, "you put your mother to bed, hear?" And then he was coming toward his dear wife, and then he and Ann were clutching each other as though now *both* of them wished to be but a single body—and *Oh, God,* she thought, *he has the same fear.* Then his face was very close to hers. "And I love *you,* dear Ann," he was saying, and the kiss they both came to was agony and very long and sweet. And then he was saying: "Don't come down," and she was answering gravely: "No, Hallock," and then he was through the door and *Gone,* said her icy awful heart, *forever.*

Still she did not weep, but instead went calmly to Simon and tired to soothe his excitement. It was an impossible task, with all that thunder shaking the house.

In the main room downstairs, as Hallock had known and dreaded, Harriet Randal was waiting for him, with old Percy right at her side. "Hallock, you can't, you mustn't," were the first words she said when she saw him. "Please, Percy, tell him he can't." But all his father could say was: "She's right, boy."

"I don't have a choice," Hallock said. "There's no two ways about it."

"I heard what you and Arch Eastmere said, both of you," Harriet went on, talking much faster than was her custom. "But that doesn't mean you have to do what he wants or what you told him you would. Let him wait down there in the rain and the storm until he knows you're not coming. He'll go away then, he'll *have* to go off, and then when he's not so upset and all, he'll see how right you were. Won't he see that, Percy, won't Arch Eastmere see he was right?"

"Mother," Hallock said, "I swore I'd get Arch, for Luke. And that's just what I figger to do. It's as simple as that."

"I *can't* lose you, too, darling," Harriet Randal said, trying to keep herself steady. "Luke was all I could bear to have taken away. I want to keep you and Pax with me, you and Cora and Pax. We must never be any less, never—"

"You won't be *losing* me," Hallock said. He was growing restless and uncomfortable, even more so than he had, toward the end, upstairs.

"I'm scared," said Harriet Randal. Her lower lip started to tremble. "Very scared, and lonely. I don't want to be lonely, Hallock."

"You won't be, Mother," Hallock said. "But if this keeps up I'll be getting pretty scared myself, and that'll be bad. I reckon you've got an idea what *that* might mean, Father—so tell her *that*, for God's sake, and quiet her down."

"She'll be all right, boy," Percy Randal said. "You go on, now."

"Why do my boys have to run out and be killed?" Harriet said, "What have they done to deserve it?"

"Listen, Mother," Hallock said tensely, "you wanted today to be the finish of all this damned trouble, and that's what it's going to *be*, the minute I square things with Arch out there. Tomorrow, by God, they'll *all* call it quits, and Luke'll be resting easy."

"Son, son, I don't want Luke to be *paid* for. Dear God, it might cost me *you*—" Tears burst in a flood from her eyes, and as they flowed over her face they swept before them the last of her control; she tumbled back into a chair and huddled there, shaken and moaning, with her weary head hidden in her arms.

Hallock's mouth was distorted by the pain of the raw wound of his regret, he who, however agonized by sympathy and love, could not now accede to his mother's wish. He took a step toward her, full of pity, shocked to realize how shrunken she seemed to have become. But Percy Randal, with a shake of the head and a raised hand, stopped him. "Go along, boy," he said in a quiet voice. "I'll carry her up to her bed in a minute."

"She'll be fine when she sees me back," Hallock said. "I'll be quick, now, Father, don't you fret." He strode across to the door and went out of the house.

Four or five men, who had witnessed or heard the exchange with Arch, were waiting for Hallock by the far corral. One of them was Soap Damson, stripped to the waist and sporting a new bandage on his shoulder, still a tough, grizzled old rooster, for all the pain that he must've been in. "Now, you *get* that son of a bitch, Hallock," he said, "right where it'll hurt him the most, and then give him one for me, goddamn him."

"Sure, Soap." Hallock smiled thinly, his eyes on the horses in the corral. "I'll do that little thing." He glanced over at the group of hands and gestured toward the gate. "I'd be obliged if one of you boys'd bring me out that big gelding of Arch's," he said.

Soap Damson grunted with pleasure. "By God, now," he exclaimed, "that takes all the whisky in the barrel, for sure. I wish to Christ I could get a look at the face on the son of a bitch when he sees you setting on his own silver goddamned saddle. By God, now, by *God!*"

Nothing else was said between them. Arch Eastmere's horse was brought from the corral, nervous and inclined to toss its head, considerably spooked by the storm. But Hallock stroked the beast's head a bit and spoke calm quiet things in one flickering ear, and when he vaulted into the saddle the horse appeared to be soothed. Yet, just before he was about to touch spurs to its flanks, thunder shattered the air directly overhead, and the gelding exploded into a wild gallop.

Hallock had been carried for more than two hundred yards before he again gained control, and from then on he made sure he held the horse in tightly. Looking ahead toward the western end of the meadow, he was mildly surprised not to see Arch Eastmere waiting. What he did see, though, was an opaque curtain of rain sweeping over the grass, and in less than a minute it hit him.

It quickly soaked him to the skin, but meanwhile it seemed to deaden the thunder. He brought the horse down to a walk, and let it plod on, head low in the cascade of water, toward the end of the meadow. Behind Hallock, when he looked back, the bulk of the house was nearly obliterated by the gray wall the rain had put up between the man and the sunlit place he had known.

Again the horse spooked at a thunderclap, one fainter than before, but still alarming. Then it spooked at a bolt of lightning. And finally it spooked at nothing at all. Each time Hallock found himself hard put to steady the beast which, had a man less competent sat in the saddle, would have long since become a runaway. As it was, however, these continuing struggles for mastery were beginning to tell on Hallock, adding to the nervousness that his mother had first engendered. He was feeling singularly unsure of himself, and the fact that Arch was nowhere to be seen undermined his confidence still further.

He knew, of course, what Arch was up to. He was hiding in the trees at the edge of the meadow, perhaps for the temporary dryness they offered, but more certainly to upset and confuse Hallock, who would have no idea where to look for him. And then, when the right time arrived, there would be Arch, perhaps coming at him at full gallop and from an angle that would preclude Hallock's getting off a good first shot. "Bastard," Hallock muttered, blowing rain from the line of his lips and peering ahead toward the almost invisible trees. Somehow, with every fast beat of his heart, the façade of his courage was splitting down the middle; and the terrible thing about this was that Hallock was unaware that any crack had appeared, nor would he until all had collapsed and he lay among the ruins of himself.

Suddenly the downpour slackened, for the time it took the horse to advance a dozen yards. Hallock's alert eyes swept along the end of the meadow, now less than a quarter-mile away. A movement in the northwest corner caught his attention, and he saw it was Arch, riding out of the cover of the trees. Hallock veered his horse toward him, still holding to a cautious walk, then made an angry, meaningless sound as Arch entered the woods again, a moment before the curtaining rain resumed its vicious fall.

There was nothing that Hallock could do except proceed to the spot where Arch had shown himself and wait for him to make another appearance. But then, if Arch wouldn't come out in the open, Hallock would have to enter the woods to find him, with a prayer that he wouldn't be ambushed, and with his heart in his mouth, so far forward that its pressure would make his teeth ache.

"God *damn* him!" Hallock exclaimed. He had no mirror to reflect his face, to show the fear that was changing the lines there; but he himself was a mirror in which Arch Eastmere's behavior appeared in a very bad light. The least Arch could do, whether crazy mad to kill or not, would be to give Hallock Randal the courtesy of what, with both men on horseback, would be almost a fair fight. It wasn't proper for the two of them to have each a different campaign planned—especially when the one Arch was undertaking had put Hallock, even on horseback, at a certain disadvantage.

He pulled up at last in the open, twenty yards or so from the corner of the field where he had seen Arch, and waited, every muscle he'd need ready for instant action. He held the reins in his left hand and kept his right close to the butt of his .44, which he'd loosened in its soggy holster. But minute after sodden minute went by and nothing happened, nothing moved. Finally, when his fixed stare was degenerating and he had begun to blink, Hallock could stand it no longer. He urged his horse into the spruce.

He could see fairly well for perhaps a hundred feet through the trees, although there was nothing to look at except boles and branches. Nowhere was sufficient concealment for a man, much less a horse. Hallock continued on, weaving among the trunks, occasionally ducking wet limbs. Then he discovered hoof marks in the soaked forest floor, which allowed some slack to the taut fibers of his mind. From then on he guided one horse along the trail of the other, his attention divided between the tracks to be followed and any secrets that might be held by the dripping trees beyond.

In about ten minutes he came out of this patch of spruce and into another meadow, nearly square, and a mile across. The tracks of the horse Arch was riding led straight across this broad field. Hallock followed them at a gallop; he wanted to get the whole thing over with, to get back home and breathe easy. Had it not been for the rain and the way Arch was drawing him on, he might have been heading in the other direction right then, instead of riding over a field he hadn't been through in at least six or seven years. It was fairly close to the ranch house, but in all that time neither his work nor any chores had brought him there. As a matter of fact, he'd pretty much forgotten the damned place.

It was not long before the fact was brought home to Hallock that his forgetfulness also encompassed a narrow rutted road on the far side of the meadow. It led into another thicket of spruce, and tracks in the mud showed that Arch Eastmere had taken it.

Wet, cold, bitter, sensing the fingers of despair at his throat, Hallock started along this road. It bent now to the left, now to the right, not too much, but enough to cut off a view of anything beyond these minor turns. Hallock's problem had now become threefold; he had to watch the trail, survey the rain-beaten woods on either flank, and keep one eye alert for any sudden appearance of Arch around some bend up ahead. And meanwhile the rain continued, and the wind and the fading thunder.

After Hallock had gone half a mile down this road, it made a long curve. Hallock, as he had been doing from time to time, threw a quick, reconnoitering glance behind him. He saw nothing but spruces and the narrow road he was on, which suddenly vanished in its own curving, quite as though the trees had devoured it. He turned his gaze forward again and discovered that it was growing light up ahead, where the road came out on an open place. Hallock now had an uncomfortable feeling that he knew the road well, but he couldn't for the life of him recall when he had last ridden over it, or why. This bewilderment did nothing but depress him and load his spirit with an even greater weight than it already bore. The fingers of despair tightened around his windpipe.

As Hallock came from the road out into the little clearing the rain raged more fiercely than ever, for the storm had nearly passed and was shouting its last frenzied words. The downpour briefly blotted out the whole landscape. Hallock and the horse could do nothing but put their heads down and wait for the furious rain to exhaust itself.

Finally, and almost instantaneously, it did. At one moment the great descent of water was beating the earth with the sound of a thousand kettledrums; and a moment later nothing could be heard but a patient dripping from a thousand trees. Even the gray clouds scudding eastward held less of darkness, and the thunder had become a grumbling giant on a far horizon.

Hallock raised his head and shook his rain-heavy hat, scattering water all about him from the brim, then surveyed the immediate terrain. The clearing was roughly square and about three hundred yards across, and nearly every yard of it held the jagged stump of a spruce. He recalled the place at last, and remembered that over the past three years Art Cospatrick had cut all their winter wood here. From where Hallock sat on his horse the ground sloped gently down, leveled, and then rose again for approximately an equal distance before the trees began on the other side. A low place was thus formed in the center of the clearing, and the passing storm had made a small pond there, six or eight inches deep, above whose surface a number of stumps could be seen. But in all the area there was no sign of Arch Eastmere; even the tracks of his horse ended at the end of the road, along with the mud and the softer ground. Hallock craned his neck to take one more look at the road behind him. He saw nothing, but the idea came over him that the trees were closing in and that he was in some great danger. Skewered on his anxiety, he faced the open area again. Then, "Oh, Christ," he said, amazed and despairing, "it's—"

It was the clearing of his dream. It was smaller, perhaps, and instead of pine trees these were spruce, but for all that he recognized the fatal clearing. He had been here in awful sleep too often not to know the place when he saw it.

And then he watched in terror as Arch Eastmere rode out of the trees across the little hollow, the way the gray regiment had come in the dream, and began to walk his horse down the far slope, straight toward Hallock Randal. And seeing this final approximation of his dream, Hallock lost all his hope and courage. He became like the waxen, glassy-eyed dolls.

Steadily Arch came on, his eyes never leaving Hallock, holding the reins in his left hand, his right dangling loose near his old, worn Colt. Frozen in horrid fascination, Hallock gaped at the other's lethal approach, while his own fibers turned to jelly and his bones became India rubber. Somewhere inside his brain every impulse was being strangled and lulled. He had become a spectator at his own death, and he knew it; nor could he bring himself to struggle against this fate he had so long foreseen.

Arch Eastmere came on among the stumps of the trees. He

reached the small pond in the clearing's center. His horse splashed through it. His horse left the water. Rider and horse now moved up the near slope. They were less than a hundred yards from Hallock. Eighty yards. Sixty. Forty-five. Thirty-some.

Hallock continued to be entranced. He had become so indifferent to his fate, so disinterested an observer, that the only thought remaining in his mind was that he had never before had a real good look at the eyes of Arch Eastmere. They'd always been hard, but not merciless like this; the red that glowed in them could only be a trick of the rain-infiltrated light. Less than thirty yards. Twenty. Nineteen—

Whether the horse on which Hallock sat had picked up the odor of its old master, or whether it had taken the gelding all this time to decide that the storm had ended—whatever the reason, the great head was unexpectedly tossed high and it snorted and whinnied and shook its mane to and fro. The movement and noise jerked Hallock out of his ruinous lassitude, back to a reality hardly less deadly. His left hand dragged the reins to the left, forcing the animal's head clear of the line of fire, and his right hand encircled the butt of his pistol. He got the gun out— too late.

Arch Eastmere began to haul iron as soon as the gelding's head started its motion. The big old Colt had left its holster while Hallock's was still in leather, and before Hallock could swing his freed pistol to point it, Arch had already aimed and was firing.

The bullet hit Hallock on the left of his neck, just under the jaw. It missed the jugular vein, smashed curving through muscles, and came out near his spinal column. The impact bent him backward in the saddle, tilted his head with a hammer blow, and exploded white whirlpools inside his eyes. But it neither killed him nor even made him loose his senses. Blinded for the moment, yet still clutching pistol and reins, he fought to keep his balance and succeeded, even while he awaited the impact of another lead ball. But Arch Eastmere did not fire again.

He didn't have to.

The horse reared up under Hallock, at the very instant when its wounded rider's vision was returning and his shocked body had recovered from the bullet's crushing blow. As the animal's forequarters rose in the air Hallock was able to hold his seat, but blood was beginning to run out of the two holes in his neck, and he was seized by the faintness which was his body's secondary reaction to the slug that had so savaged it. The horse twisted in the air and came down with its forefeet far to the left of where they had been before the rearing. Hallock realized that he was half out of the saddle. His left foot, too, had slipped completely free. For the first and last time in his life he panicked because of a pony's actions. He let his pistol fall while he tried to get the reins in both hands. His left foot sought desperately for the stirrup, but encountered nothing but air. Then the damned horse reared again.

He cried out and clutched at the pommel as he felt himself leaving the saddle for the second time. But the gelding repeated its own convulsive twisting, and this time when it brought its forequarters down it brought Hallock off the saddle as well, slipping helplessly to the right, his fingers unable to cling to either pommel or mane, and making it impossible for him to free his right foot from the stirrup where it had caught.

As Hallock's body slid over its flank the horse shied in wild alarm and then vaulted away to the left, along the spruces that hemmed the clearing. Hallock screamed like a stuck pig as he was torn bodily from the saddle. His foot was now inextricably hooked in the stirrup, and he hung head down, his arms waving wildly, a defenseless, blood-dripping tangle in the air.

He screamed once more, and louder, when one of the iron-shod hooves laid open the side of his head. But that was the last living sound he made, for a moment later his skull was slung against a spruce stump and broke like an overripe melon. Pace Gray, whatever his destination, no longer traveled alone.

Arch Eastmere, sitting on Pace's pony, watched his own horse bear Hallock's limp body, battered by earth and hooves and stumps, along the edge of the clearing, more than halfway around. Then the beast spun at a gallop and hurtled into the woods. Arch could hear a faint snapping of branches, then a heavy silence came down on the place.

The wrath left Arch, dissolving like smoke, and with it went whatever Hallock had seen in the hard eyes while he himself had less than a minute of vision remaining. If Arch Eastmere's eyes held anything now, those things were shame and pity and regret.

He sat on his horse, as he had immediately after Luke had been shot, and waited for his own thunderous heart to crack and let his tortured life run out. But now, as then, nothing happened. Beat followed beat, his heart grew more quiet, and the tightness went from his chest.

The clouds in their thickness had nearly gone by, and over the Marias the freed sun was pouring its warmth across the inundated earth. Arch Eastmere sighed and stuck his pistol back in the worn old waterlogged holster and set out to find his own horse and silver saddle, and maybe what was left of Hallock Randal.

Before he found anything, though, he had to cover four miles of country and almost three hours of time. As it turned out, he saw his horse first, the silver saddle gleaming in the light of the descending sun. The horse was browsing by an aspen grove, and Arch had no trouble in switching mounts, after he'd taken some grass and wiped away Hallock's blood from the animal's moist flank. Then, with Pace's horse in tow, he began a search for the body.

In less than ten minutes he found it, not far from where his horse had been browsing. It lay at the edge of an old wallow, usually dry, which the storm had turned into water and mud. At first sight, what had been Hallock resembled a pile of reddened rags, but when Arch came closer he recognized it for what it was. It was far from pleasant to look at: a slimy jumble of dirt and smashed bones and raw flesh and tattered clothing, all overlaid with blood. Arch Eastmere could hardly bear to keep his eyes on it long enough to make sure it was the man whom he and his horse had slain together. Then, as soon as he knew, he rode south. He had business with Alan Lacy.

And behind him there, in the drying mud, Hallock Randal lay—forgetful of his horsemanship.

They were a glum crew, the men still gathered at Alan Lacy's ranch house, and therefore the only thing they'd seen all day, when they weren't dozing, was the ground at their feet, or maybe the toes of their boots. So it was by pure luck that Drury Wyn-

ward happened to look up, just before sundown, as Arch Eastmere rode in from the northeast. Drury, whose cigar had gone
out, and who had raised his head, along with his eyes, to relight
it, completely forgot to finish the operation, so surprised was he
at the sight of Arch approaching. He got over his surprise in short
order, however, when the neglected match burned his flesh in
two places. "Sweet Christ Aw-*mighty!*" he yelled, and he hopped
to his feet in a hurry, shaking his arm up and down to cool his
fingers, his hand flopping every which way.

"Always did say smoking was bad for a feller." Oliver Swindon,
who was sitting on the porch near Drury, spoke languidly. He
was about the only man there who didn't feel down in the mouth
and low; and the reason he was bearing up so well was that by
this time tomorrow he expected to be a good many miles from
Penelope Swindon and the Forkhandle country and everything
else he was sick of, maybe heading for the Pacific, maybe for the
Atlantic, it didn't matter much, just so long as a man could
smell sea water every day of his life and perhaps find a young
and pretty girl who'd be good to nuzzle at night. "Yep," Ollie
Swindon went on. "Smoking and drinking and marriage, they're
every last one of 'em wicked. And a man who'd do all *three* of
'em—well, by George, next thing you know that man'll be stealing
or killing his Maw and Paw or even playing cards for money.
Yep, I—"

"Shut up," said Drury, "and look who's here."

Oliver Swindon looked and Oliver Swindon, too, stood up.
"Got that greaser saddle back, didn't he?" he murmured.

All Drury could do was nod.

By the time Arch drew up near the porch, nearly thirty pairs
of eyes were fixed on him. A number of men called out greetings, but he answered none.

Arch had come here to Alan's ranch with a single purpose in
mind; he wanted to achieve it, quickly, and then leave—not only
Alan Lacy's ranch but indeed that part of the country. Ever since
he had seen what remained of Hallock Randal, he had been sunk
in a hideous sadness. He had made up his mind to say good-by
to the Forkhandle and never come back again. The place was
unlucky for him, and he was unlucky for the place. Trouble

might be asleep a thousand miles away, but the minute it heard that Arch Eastmere was back in his birthplace—well, then up jumped trouble and flew off to Arch. Now he had done the worst thing in his life, and, although he might have to carry the memory of that afternoon's wet hell with him wherever he traveled, he could at least leave the scene itself behind. And that included everything *in* the scene, even poor little hopeful Maudie Fletcher. She and Arch were unlucky for each other, too, and they both knew it, without having to put the truth into words. He'd write to her, maybe, someday. But first there was what he had to do at Alan Lacy's, then the sorrowful visit he must pay to Miss Dorrie and Miss Sallie Pace, and then—if the world would let him—one more stand-up to fate. First, though—

"Where's Alan?" he asked Drury Wynward.

"Inside," said Drury. "Where'd you find your horse and saddle?"

"Where I looked," Arch said bleakly. "Tell Alan to come out."

Drury didn't have to tell him, however, for the door opened and both Lacy brothers stepped out on the porch. "Howdy, Arch," Alan said cautiously. "Didn't expect to see you back here."

"Didn't say I wouldn't *be* back, though," Arch said.

"Something on your mind, maybe?" Nelse Macleod asked.

"Yep," said Arch. "Money and women." He was not joking, and the pitch of his voice precluded any laughter.

The way Arch was looking at everybody was making Mark Lacy nervous. "Too bad about Pace, Arch," he said.

"He's paid for," Arch said. "I collected."

"Who from?" Alan wanted to know.

"Old friend of mine."

"Hallock Randal?"

Arch nodded curtly. "Old Perce'll have to squeeze by with just Pax from now on," he said.

The group was stunned by this statement. While it was sinking into their minds, Lydia Lacy clattered up in the buggy, boldly returning at last from her long tryst with George Throstle. No one paid the slightest attention to her, and Lydia, curious about the cause of the silence and their abstracted faces, brought the buggy to a halt, just as Nelse Macleod managed to ask: "Where'd it all happen, Arch?"

"It don't matter where," Arch said. "All that matters is that I done it. But I can't say as I feel very prideful, and I didn't come here to talk big. Alan, there's a couple of things I'd like from you. One of them's my little Dolores, and this time I won't have to beg for a horse, because she can ride this pony of Pace's. And the other is, I'd be obliged for the loan of another hundred dollars."

"That's all?" Alan Lacy asked stolidly. "Nothing else?"

"Just Dolores and a hundred dollars, if you please, Alan."

"Can't say as I've got that much cash."

"Reckon you and these fellers can cough it up between you," Arch said. "And I reckon you can cough up Dolores all by yourself."

"Maybe," Alan said cautiously. "I can't rightly say where she is."

"Well, if you and all these other fellers was to look for her, I reckon you'd turn her up someplace."

"Seems likely, now, don't it?" Alan said in a mild tone. "But just let me look inside for a minute." His gaze went briefly to Lydia. "Once in a while a man can't find a female when he wants her." Then Alan, having acknowledged his wife's presence for the first and only time that day, went back into the house.

"Arch Eastmere, what're you going to *do* with that little girl?" Lydia Lacy called.

Arch, by no means apologetic, turned his head in her direction. "Her and me, we get along fine, ma'am," he said. Out of the corner of his eye he saw Alan Lacy coming out through the door. He swung his body around to face him, only to learn that he was now facing a little more than the man who had gone in search of Dolores. For Alan now held a double-barreled shotgun, with both hammers cocked, pointed at Arch Eastmere's belly. Arch's gun hand jerked inadvertently a few inches toward his holster. "Don't," Alan told him quietly.

"Reckon I won't," said Arch. He raised his hands until they were shoulder high.

Shock had been piled on shock, and every man there was astonished. "What the hell're you up to, Alan?" old Nelse Macleod exclaimed.

"You gone plumb crazy?" asked Drury.

"Get his gun, Mark," Alan said. "This bastard's given me all the trouble he's going to." He had eyes only for Arch Eastmere.

Mark went over to Arch and gingerly extracted the big old Colt from its holster. "What I gave you, mister," Arch said easily, "was a lot more help than you paid for." Mark went back on the porch with the pistol, and Arch, without waiting for Alan to permit it, dropped his arms.

"All we got from you was grief, goddamn you," Alan said. "It wasn't any cost to you when you murdered Luke Randal. But us —we're the ones who took the pounding for it. And now you've gone and gunned Hallock down, too, and Christ only knows what we'll all of us have to pay for that. But you come along here, bold as brass, saying you want this and you want that, and expecting we'll leap right out of our skins to fetch it for you. Well, Eastmere, the only thing you're going to get from me is a look at the barrels of this gun, and if you don't get yourself the hell away from here fast, I swear to God that what's in these two barrels'll tear your guts clean out."

"Ah, *look*, now, Alan—" Oliver Swindon began.

"You shut up," Alan told him. He raised the shotgun's muzzle as a gesture to Arch: "And *you*, git!"

"You better kill me now," Arch told him, "because if you don't, I'm going to come back here and kill *you*, mister!"

"Try it," Alan Lacy said. "You'll have to fight your way through a passel of men before you tangle with me. Won't he, boys?"

If he had expected a chorus of assent, he had good reason to be disappointed. Not a man of the group spoke up.

Arch Eastmere did, however. "Maybe," he said, "and maybe not. Tell you what I *will* do, though. I swear I'll kill every feller I find here when I *do* come back, kill him dead as a side of beef, same as if he was you." And with that he clucked his tongue at his horse and rode from them, with Pace's tired pony trotting along behind.

The men watched him disappear around a hillock to the southwest. Their eyes were uneasy, and their throats felt dry. Without a word Lydia Lacy slapped the reins on her mare's back and the buggy rolled smoothly toward the stable. Mark Lacy peered at the chamber of Arch's Colt, glumly noting that one bullet had been fired. Alan carefully let down the hammers of the shotgun. "Don't none of you fret any," he said, breaking the silence. "The son of a bitch won't be back here. He couldn't be that big a goddamned fool."

"Well, Alan," Nelse Macleod said slowly, "I've seen me a lot of goddamned fools in my time, but I never rightly could say just how *big* the critters ran. Me, now, I'm only a small-size fool. And seeing as how I am, I reckon I'll take what's left of my boys and head home."

Alan Lacy stared at the old man in furious disbelief. "Head for *home?*" he cried.

"Yep, that's the place, by God," Nelse said. "This whole thing started out bad, and it's worsening all the damned time. I'm turning my chips in now, and I only wish to Jesus I'd never went and bought 'em in the first place."

"You know, Nelse," said Drury, "I reckon I'll join you."

"By George," said Oliver Swindon, "that's the best idea I heard yet."

"My God!—here, listen—*all* of you," Alan exclaimed. "You can't go breaking off now. We're all in it together. We *got* to finish what we started."

"That's what I just *done*, for God's sake," said Nelse Macleod. He made a beeline for the corral, and, one by one, the others went, too.

And that was the end of that part of the trouble. Mark Lacy stuck with his brother, and the two of them stood and watched twenty-odd men mount their horses and ride away. By the time it had grown completely dark only sixteen men and two women remained in and about the Lacy ranch house. And an hour later only one of these women remained, for Lydia Lacy, who had left her horse standing in the buggy's traces, and was very glad that she had, was able to provide this transportation for little Dolores, when she sent her into town with a very private message for George Throstle.

He was going to do what she wanted, and much sooner than he'd thought.

When the storm had been over for more than two hours and there still was no sign of Hallock, Percy Randal, heavy in heart, called together every available man, with the single exception of Pax, and led them out to look for his lost eldest son. Even Soap Damson, bad shoulder and all, got himself on a horse and went along—and Ann Randal, too, insisted on going. Harriet Randal had cried herself to sleep in bed, and Cora was left in the main room, sitting in her father's chair and staring at a dying fire. Percy Randal had lit it while the storm was at its height.

Pax, who had sat out the rain in the barn, had returned alone to his grave-digging as soon as the downpour had ceased. Then, having finished all he had strength for, he had returned to the main buildings, only to realize that everyone seemed to have disappeared. Somewhat bewildered, he went up to the ranch house. There he found Cora in old Randal's chair, her face reflecting the flames that she watched. "Where's everybody gone to?" he asked. He was unaware that Arch had come seeking Hallock, and of everything else that had taken place on that black afternoon.

Cora did not look at him. "Hunting for Hallock," she told him. "He's dead."

Pax flushed in anger. "What the hell do you mean, *dead?*" he demanded. "Crazy bitch, you."

"You'll find out," she said calmly.

"Not from the likes of you, by God. Nobody ever has yet." He strode into the hall and up the stairs.

In a very short time he was back, his handsome face more petulant than ever. "Mother's in bed again sleeping," he said. "What's the matter with her now?"

"The same thing," Cora said. "*You.*"

"Oh, *Jee*-sus!" Pax rolled his eyes to the ceiling. Puffing out his cheeks in exasperation, he walked over to Cora. "Look, Miss Cora," he said, "simply answer me one thing, just *one*, do you reckon you're able to do that?"

"Not the whole of it," Cora said. "She went out, but I don't know where."

"How the hell did you know I was going to ask about Mrs.

Lacy?" Pax demanded. He was disturbed by his sister's unusual calm.

"Because you're a fool," Cora said. "And fools always want the same thing."

"All right, all *right*, goddamn it," Pax said. "When'd she go out?"

"This morning."

"And she hasn't come back inside *yet*, with the rain and all?"

For the first time since he had entered the house, Cora saw fit to look at her hated brother. "It was after we had our talk," she said quietly. "After I told her about you and me, and how you—"

"You told her all those *lies?*" Pax shouted. "What the hell's gotten into you, going around telling those goddamned old lies that you've told yourself so long that you believe 'em? By God, you damned thing you, they ought to bury you away somewhere—"

"Not till *you're* buried, *dear* brother Pax. Go find your Lacy woman and let me be." Suddenly her voice rose to a shriek. *"Please*—for the love of Heaven—let me *alone*—let me *be*—!"

Pax drew back, startled, from her contorted face. Then he whirled and ran out of the house.

He kept running, all the way down the slope of the knoll, and then he began to search for Ellen Lacy: in the barn, the loft, the stable, a shed, another shed, even the deserted bunkhouse. Nowhere could he find any trace of her. He was on the point of giving up the search when he remembered that Art Cospatrick's little shack was empty. He headed toward it at a dead run.

As soon as he opened the door he saw her lying, all golden, asleep on a straw mattress, on what had lately been Drew Cospatrick's bed. Her eyes opened slowly at the noise of his entrance. He bolted the door behind him and came over to the bed. "What're you doing alone out *here*, honey?" he asked her, sitting on the edge of the bed. "I been going plumb crazy looking for you. I was fearing you'd gone off home."

"I wanted to think," she said, still not completely awake.

"What about, gold hair? *Me*, same as I think about you all the time?"

Ellen slowly collected her thoughts. She had tried to do some thinking when she had first slipped into the little house, but then she had grown very drowsy. Finally, exhausted by the effort of thinking about thinking, she had fallen asleep. She had slept until the thunder had wakened her, but the pouring rain had made it impossible for her to get back to the ranch house. In the end, the sound of rain on the roof and fading thunder had lulled her to sleep again. And now here was Pax, and she still hadn't really done any thinking at all. "It was all about you and Cora," she whispered, averting her eyes, "and what she says you did to her—"

"Ah, *no!*" Pax groaned. "What did that crazy fool say *now?* My God, she's always making up something about me."

"You know—about down by the bridge, when you were only fourteen and— Oh, Pax, she told me a lie, *didn't* she? *Say* that she told me a lie. It was a terrible thing, she said, the most awful thing I ever heard."

His arms were around her and he was drawing his legs up beside her on the bed. "Ah, she *did* lie," he whispered. "She's crazy, the girl's *crazy*, all her life she's been telling lies like that. She's jealous because I love you, that's it, don't you see it, darling—?"

Now her arms were embracing him. "You *do* love me, Pax? You honestly *do?*"

"Ah, God, you gold honey, *how* I love you—oh, Jesus, Ellen, let me—here—no, *I'll* do it— *Ah*, now, that's better—just a minute, you gold-all-over honey—this—*there*—y-e-s-*sssss*—"

"God—Pax—oh, *God*—! Kiss me, Pax! Now—kiss— Ah-h-h—h—"

Thus made they funeral for Hallock, breaker of horses.

Dawn came as a flood of roses, and then the risen sun was coursing across a delphinium sky. A week had passed since so many had gathered in the meadow, to welcome Luke Randal to manhood. That Sunday, seven days since, had begun in what all had thought perfect weather, but now nature had outdone herself, unveiling new lucid marvels of the air that blandly laid bare the imperfection of what she had offered before. Cleansed and rewoven by Saturday's deluge, earth and sky together gleamed in a shimmering rainbow excitement. Even the drone of passing insects held a fresh, high-pitched delight. Everywhere the throats of birds were throbbing, and every tree, it seemed, was a green explosion of song.

Mark Lacy felt and was moved by the gentle aura around him as he slowly paced back and forth before his brother's ranch house. All night long they had spelled each other, at two-hour intervals, one lying down, one alert, while they awaited, with shotgun, pistol, and carbine, the dire return of Arch Eastmere. In the bunkhouse, too, a guard was kept; but there two men out of fourteen stayed on watch for the two-hour stretches. Arch, of course, had not come, which was what Lydia Lacy had told them, not without a ring of contempt in her voice, as she was going to bed. Her opinion had been that if Arch came at all, he would come in daylight. Whether she was right or not, he certainly hadn't arrived in the dark. Anyway, if he came on that gorgeous morning, they would be more than ready for him. The carbine hung in the crook of Mark Lacy's arm as he continued to pace by the ranch house. Everyone else was up and about, too, with the exception of Alan, who had stood guard during the two pre-dawn hours, and was now stretched out on the sofa inside, concluding his respite of sleep. From where he was, Mark could see one of his ranch hands and five of Alan's busying themselves with various chores, all of them wearing their gunbelts and each within easy range of his voice.

Since these six cowboys were occupied with their tasks, it was Mark, therefore, who first saw the small cortege coming down from the north. He could count five riders, but they were too far away for him to recognize individuals. "Hey!" he called to the nearest hand. "People coming. Get everybody along here." He ran into the main room of the ranch house and shook Alan awake. "Five fellers riding up," he told his brother, "and from Perce Randal's land, looks like."

"Five?" Alan Lacy said, instantly awake. "Only *five*? That's a mighty queer thing, now." He got to his feet, picked up the shotgun from the floor by the sofa, and went out on the porch with Mark. Half of the brothers' cowboys were already gathered between the house and the corral, and the rest were hurrying toward the group from various directions.

Alan peered across the near fields at the approaching horsemen, at the same time cocking both hammers of the shotgun. "Make out who they are yet, Mark?" he asked.

Mark Lacy shook his head, even as one of the ranch hands yelled: "That's old Perce Randal *his*self, by God."

"Yep," another cowboy said, "and Soap Damson with his arm all done up, and—why, *say*, one of 'em's a, by God, *fe*male."

"Straddled over that saddle like a man," said a third. "*Look* at 'er.*"

Alan Lacy knew them all now—Perce, Soap, Jim Good, the young Bannerman kid, and—"That's Ellen they got with them, Mark," he said in a quiet voice.

There was no answer from Mark, who stood there with his lips slightly parted, feeling as though some great claw had ripped his innards clean away. The sun, reflecting from Ellen Lacy's gold hair, seemed to dim its own bright luster. She sat astride Princess, her own horse, in the same way as when she had gone off with Pax, and the same dress covered her marvelous body. She looked beautiful, bland, and benign, and the mere sight of her made Mark Lacy break out in a nervous sweat. "They—you think they're bringing her back?" he finally managed to stammer.

Alan Lacy shrugged. "Can't say," he murmured. "Don't look to be a weapon amongst the lot of 'em. Can't rightly say what they're up to."

Whatever it was, he could see that all four men, and especially Perce Randal and Damson, had their faces set in the kind of tight-lipped resignation that Alan had always associated with hellfire-and-damnation preachers. But when the riders reined up by the porch and Perce Randal began to speak, his voice was as pleasant and gentle as ever a man's could be; and Alan Lacy uncocked the hammers of his shotgun without being aware he was doing it.

"Howdy, Alan," Percy Randal said softly. "Mark."

The two brothers nodded as one man. "Howdy," Alan said, addressing the group in general. Mark, who had been given a faint smile by his wife, became speechless; the words he might have spoken were trapped in his throat.

"Figgered I'd see more people around here," Randal went on. "Looks like all you've got're your own boys."

"Nobody's very far off," Alan said cautiously. "They're around."

"Sure, now, that's what I thought," Randal said. "Matter of fact, what we come here for, I'm hunting one of *my* own boys. Hallock."

"Reckon I can't help you there, Perce. None of us here've laid eyes on Hallock since—oh, Thursday, I'd say."

"*None* of you?" Percy Randal's voice remained mild. "How about Arch Eastmere?"

Alan hesitated. "Well, I don't know about Arch," he said. "He goes off and then comes back, and he don't talk much about where he went or who he went with."

"I'll tell you where and who with," Soap said angrily, "if *he* won't. And *what*, too, by God, in case you—"

"Now, you be quiet, Soap," Percy Randal said. He kept his tone on the same muted level. "It's all mine to handle now."

"Yes, sir," Soap grumbled. From then on, although he gritted his teeth from time to time, he kept silent.

"Like to talk to Arch, if I might," Randal told Alan Lacy.

"He's not here right now, Perce. I'll tell him when he comes back, though."

"Any idea where I might find him?"

"Nope. Can't say as I have."

Percy Randal was doing his best to sit erect and confident in his saddle, but it wasn't quite enough; he looked exactly like what he was, a tired old man with a broken heart. "It's been a bad week, Alan," he said. "I don't want any more of it. I want it to finish right now."

"No reason why it can't, Perce. You feel that way, Mark boy?"

Half drowned, but sinking content, in the blue pool of Ellen's eyes, Mark started when his name was tacked to the end of an unheard question. "Sure, Alan," he said awkwardly. "Sure, anything you say."

"All my boys're back from Juncture," Randal said. "There's none of 'em left up in the mountains. So if you want to take your people and go up there and see for yourselves that I never tried to dam up those streams, you ought to do it right now, today. And if you got some idea of being bushwhacked or anything, you're welcome to take Soap or Jim or Tim here, or all three of 'em, if you want, so you'll know it's in good faith. What do you say, Mark? You and me, we're the ones who started the wind to blow, so I reckon it's about time we come to a kind of understanding."

Mark's attention was finally drawn from his wife. And, with Percy Randal gazing down at him with weary dignity, he felt clumsy and uncomfortable and ashamed. He still possessed some vindictiveness, but it was half formed and, beneath the warm sun of Ellen's presence, it was melting like ice in July. "Seems to me, Perce," he said, but without much conviction, "it was *you* said you was building those dams. Right to my face, you told me."

"I was pretty mad," Percy Randal said. "And I was worse when I found out you were telling folks we were fixing to—

What?—*Steal?* Tote *off?*—I don't know.—Anyway, whatever it was we were supposed to be doing to Mrs. Lacy."

"Pax brought her home with him, didn't he?" Mark asked, trying to sound bitter, and failing completely.

"I reckon you know why, too, don't you, Mark?" Percy Randal said.

"Well, now—" Mark rubbed his hand roughly up and down his cheek. "Hell, she *might*'ve maybe had reasons for *some*thing, but not leaving house and home that way. We could've talked it over. Couldn't we, Ellen?"

He turned to her for support, but it didn't come to him in the form of words. Yet the ghost of a smile that she gave him was enough to answer his question.

"The way we're talking it over now, Mark?" Percy Randal was speaking to him again.

"Why, sure, Perce, the way we are now."

"Can I take it the thing's past and done with, then?" Percy Randal asked, looking from one Lacy to another. "Or what else do we have to do?"

Alan and Mark Lacy briefly faced each other with interrogatory glances, which were broken off when Mark let his eyes fall to the ground. Then Alan gazed silently up at Percy Randal for a space before he answered the old man. "Nothing, Perce," he said. "I reckon it's all been done."

"Yep," Percy Randal sighed, "all of it." He took a deep draught of the rain-washed air. "We brought your wife to you, Mark," he said.

"I'm obliged to you, Perce, much obliged," was all that Mark Lacy could say.

Behind him, Alan sensed a movement in the doorway. He twisted his head around and saw that Lydia had come out on the porch. "Calling it quits," he told her, and handed her the shotgun.

She nodded curtly, unsmiling. "Good," she said.

"How about coming inside for a drink?" Alan asked Percy Randal.

The old man shook his head. "Alan," he said, "I don't feel much like likker. My wife's lying home and letting herself pine away, and I can't seem to stop her at all. My Luke's lying dead in his grave, and my Hallock's lying off someplace where Arch Eastmere left him. We looked for him yesterday till it got dark and for half the night after that, and Hattie can't rest, and God knows I can't, till we find him and bring him home. But if you folks can't say where it was Arch killed him, I reckon we'd best wait here for Arch, and trust him to tell us himself."

Alan Lacy frowned in thought. Twice he struck a post of the porch with his open palm. "Might as well tell you, Perce," he said. "I didn't speak the whole truth awhile back. These boys you see here is all that's left. My own hands, and Mark's. What happened is, Arch come along here yesterday late and begun acting too big for his britches, so I laid this shotgun on him and Mark took his six-gun and we drove him right off the place. So Arch said he was going to come back here and kill me, and he said he'd kill any man else that was here when he came. And then that god-damned Nelse and the whole bunch of 'em up and run for home, like whipped dogs. Yep, he'll be showing up here sometime, Perce, but it won't be to talk."

"Oh." Percy Randal was silent for a moment. "What'll you do when he comes?"

"I can handle him. He'll be outside, I'll be in."

"Got any idea where he might be now?"

"Just the one, Maudie Fletcher's. He's been bunking with her since he got here. But that don't mean he's at Maudie's right now. He might be twenty miles away, he might be two minutes from where I'm standing."

"Well, we'll take us a ride down to Maude's place," Perce Randal said heavily. "And you keep your wife, Mark." The old man's attempt at a smile was unsuccessful. "She's good as new, and maybe better. We took mighty good care of her, hear?"

Mark Lacy nodded dumbly, then watched the four horsemen ride away. But not for long, for the sight of his wife's exquisite ivory calf, revealed by the drawing up of her dress across the saddle, irresistibly summoned his vision. The smile she was offering to him now was warm and sad and yielding. "Do you want to help me down, Mister Lacy?" she asked wistfully.

He blushed and shook his head. "No need," he said, and his voice had grown hoarse. "We're going right home."

"Yes, Mark," she said, and lowered her eyes, and he thought he'd go crazy with joy. "You, Tom, come here," he said to his foreman, Tom Quarles, who was taller by a head than the rest of the cowhands who stood there. Tom came over to the porch, and Mark pulled some crumpled greenbacks from his pocket. "It's Sunday," he told Tom, "and if you want to put this in the collection plate at Smiley Brann's church, you'd best get going. Just remember to be back by sunup."

"By God, now, we will, Mister Lacy," Tom said with a huge grin dividing his face, "even if we get brung home piled like cordwood in a wagon." He started back to the others. Alan's cowboys promptly took on, to a man, the expression of a pack of abused bloodhounds.

"Aw, hell," said Alan Lacy, "now I know why you've had all these money troubles, Mark. You give it away in church." But he was reaching in his pocket with one hand and summoning his own foreman with the other.

Ten minutes later, every last cowboy had gone pounding off toward town, and Alan and Lydia Lacy were standing on the porch, watching Ellen and Mark ride away.

Neither of these two riders waved, or even looked back at the ranch house. They moved for a time in silence, as they had on that previous Sunday, on their way from the blowout for Luke—but then the silence had been glum, and now it was pregnant with excitement and hope.

Ellen was the one to break it. "I was awful sorry about the terrible thing that happened to your mare. I really was."

"Me, too," he said. "That's why I said what I—well, you know."

"People ought to think before they say something or do something. Next time I'll remember to think before I—" Ellen flushed prettily, having managed to tie her present thinking in a knot she was unable to unravel.

However, it gave Mark Lacy the chance to wipe his mind clean of a dark idea that still clung there. "What about Pax Randal?" was how he phrased it.

"What about Mister Randal?" Her voice was like cool water.

"Did he ever—I mean, did he *try* to—?"

"What makes you think I'd let him?"

"I don't. But didn't he even once—?"

"He kept his proper distance. And if he hadn't, I'd've seen that he did."

"Ah, for Christ's sake, sure, *sure* you would, Ellen. My God, *trash* like Pax Randal. You must think I'm a goddamned fool."

"When we get home," she said softly, "I'll show you in bed what I think." For Ellen Lacy, the lodestone, the lodestar, the paragon of women, intended to abide by her own rule: from now on she wouldn't do *anything* until she'd thought about it for a while. Especially something so titillating.

Alan and Lydia kept their eyes on the dwindling figures of Ellen and Mark until a low ridge hid them from view. "You'll be wanting this shotgun, won't you?" she asked him. "If and when Arch Eastmere shows up?"

"The carbine'll handle it," he told her. "Never you mind, Liddie, hear?"

"I don't suppose I will," she said. "Not with the arsenal you're getting together."

"What arsenal?"

"You left Arch's six-gun on the chest in the bedroom."

"Oh, *that*. Well, hell, Liddie, *you* use that, in case I need help."

"What about if *I* need help?"

"You're one I'd never worry about, Liddie. Reckon you can whip your weight in wildcats, with maybe a bear, to boot. Me, I'm going to have a drink."

"I wouldn't go boozing, Alan, not with Arch Eastmere like to show up here any minute. You'll need sharp eyes."

"Now, look here, Liddie, a little drop of whisky never hurt a man's aim. And you can keep a lookout, too."

"All right," said Lydia Lacy. "There's nobody else here to do it."

She re-entered the house, lugging the big shotgun. Alan Lacy followed her in, got a half-empty bottle of whisky and a tumbler from the kitchen, and brought them back into the main room.

An hour later the tumbler was forgotten, the bottle was nearly empty, and Alan Lacy, nursing the residue, had gone out to sit on the edge of the porch. His senses were dulled, but he was by no means drunk; some of his sharpness had been blunted, that was all. He was able to recognize Lydia Lacy's footsteps as she came through the main room and out on the porch, and he saw no reason to turn to inspect her while she stood there on the boards behind him. He knew what she'd looked like an hour ago, and he reckoned that she hadn't aged much since. The hell with red-headed women, he decided: forthwith he gave himself another jolt from the lightning in the bottle.

"Alan," his wife said.

"If you want to do something," he said, without looking at her, "get yourself around to the other side of the house, watch for Eastmere."

"There's something more important to do here," she said. There was a flat, almost deadly quality in her voice that caught his ear and filled him with a vague annoyance. It also caused him to glance at her over his shoulder.

What he saw made him get to his feet in a hurry and spin full around to face his wife. Lydia Lacy was holding the shotgun on him, and both hammers were cocked, and the ugly twin muzzles were pointed at his chest. "What the hell're you doing, you goddamned fool?" he yelled.

"Put your hand on your gun, and you'll find out," she told him. Her lips were drawn thin, her eyes were slitted.

"You gone plumb crazy, Liddie?"

She didn't answer him, but her narrow gaze remained fixed on his face. "George!" she called.

Alan Lacy saw movement to his left, as someone came around the corner of the ranch house outside the kitchen. He looked, and knew George Throstle. Unpomaded, he was dressed for riding, he looked very frightened, and in his right hand he held Arch Eastmere's big old Colt. He came within a few feet of Alan and stopped. The hand that held the six-gun may have trembled a little, but it kept fairly steady on Alan Lacy's left side.

"My God, George," Alan exclaimed. "What's going on here, what is it, what're you two trying to—?"

"Go ahead, darling," Lydia said to George Throstle. "Shoot."

Alan Lacy's skin prickled as he realized his wife wasn't funning. "Liddie—" he said, "what is it?—You don't mean to *kill* me, do you, Liddie?—George, you can't be—?"

"Arch *East*mere's killing you," Lydia said. "Go on, George, shoot. This thing's heavy."

George Throstle gnawed at his upper lip. He seemed as scared as Alan. The hand that held Arch's big old Colt was trembling more and more.

"God *damn* you, George!" Lydia screeched. "Will you please, for God's sake, *shoot* him!"

Alan Lacy saw that he had one chance in a million, and he took it. He went for his gun. But even before his hand clutched the butt, his movement set off a chain reaction in George Throstle. The big old Colt roared. The impact spun Alan around and knocked him against one of the posts of the porch. He dragged his own short gun out of its holster, but he did this through instinct, not will. He was a gasp from dying as his pistol left his nerveless fingers for the ground, and he was completely dead after George Throstle's second bullet ripped through him and into the post; and George Throstle's third bullet, fired into Alan Lacy as he lay crumpled on the ground, was nothing but a waste of ammunition.

But George Throstle, an amateur at killing, didn't know that. "Oh, Lydia, dear God, Lydia, dear, oh," he whispered, staring wide-eyed at the corpse.

"You were very brave," said Lydia Lacy. "*Arch.*"

Unlucky Arch Eastmere, without his gun, the dupe and prey of trouble still, had seethed like a vat of acid as he rode from Alan Lacy's at sundown the day before. The shame of the insult he'd suffered had set his heart pounding in rage. It was not the wrath that had filled him as he sat by the dead Pace, which had been a red fire. This new and unexpected anger was cold and deliberate, nor was it so massive that it overwhelmed Arch Eastmere's power of thought.

In the first few minutes, however, his rage had nearly wrecked his reason; then he had been on the point of galloping into town, borrowing a short gun from Smiley Brann or somebody, and coming right back to kill Alan. But the glowing image of this idea began to lose its luster almost at once, when he realized that Nelse and Drury and the rest would have called what he'd said a big brag, nothing else. They'd all of them stick with Alan. If Arch got himself a pistol and returned there tonight, he'd end up a bloody sieve, and without, like as not, ever even seeing Alan Lacy. He'd have to come up with another way of doing things.

When a man holds within himself wrath and reason, at one and the same time, it very often happens that, unless he has a monstrous soul, he eventually reasons his wrath away. And so it was with Arch Eastmere, as he rode through the gathering night. As he wondered where he might be most apt to obtain a pistol, he found his thoughts drifting to Maude Fletcher's place. But he knew that Maudie never kept a weapon around, and Sykes's would have been ruined in the fire. Pace's short gun was gone, he remembered; the kid must've dropped it up at Juncture Valley, because Arch was certain it hadn't fallen out in the wagon. There had been nothing in the wagon except Pace Gray.

Gradually, and without Arch being aware of it, he began to forget about finding a pistol and instead concentrated on Maudie, until he saw her as a warmer harbor, a safer haven than ever before, a beacon in every storm, and perhaps, after all, not un-lucky. But the light she was flashing now, and that drew him inexorably to her, was not a single beam, but a reflection from the many facets of Arch Eastmere, as he was, as he rode through the night there.

One of these facets, indeed, was his emotional exhaustion. He was being beaten to his knees at last by the hammer blows of the harrowing, horrible day. Another was his physical condition. He had been drenched by the rain, and his clothes had dried on his back. Now they were stiff, and chafed him, and his boots were still wet inside. Too, he was beginning to feel a tightness around his throat and chest; undoubtedly, he'd caught a cold—which might develop into something ten times worse if he stayed out in the night air. And he was very hungry; he couldn't remember when he'd last eaten. There were a number of other facets, as well, but they all added up to pretty much the same thing: he needed sympathy, he needed love. He had gained little on this grim Saturday—gained little, and lost much. The fires within him that had been started by Pace, lolling dead in the wagon, were now all dead themselves.

And perhaps what had happened at Alan Lacy's had been just

what Arch Eastmere needed, in a way he hadn't needed either money or little Dolores. Come to think of it, he couldn't figure what had gotten into him between the time he left Hallock's mangled body and the time he turned his back on the muzzles of that shotgun. Dolores was a good-looking girl, that was the truth, but she wasn't so necessary to Arch's well-being that he had to court trouble to get her. And money wasn't necessary, either, not to such an extent that he'd be willing to chance a blown-off head for a measly hundred dollars. And then there was that crazy idea he'd had about him and Maudie being unlucky for each other—

A man made his own luck, the same way luck made his own life; and a woman had to do the same thing. Arch couldn't say that a woman was unlucky for him, not when she loved him and took care of him and kept him warm and acted like she worshipped the ground he walked on. Anybody who told himself *that* kind of woman was unlucky had a mighty peculiar idea of luck, either good or bad. And if Arch was making Maudie happier than any other man or thing in this world, he had no call to say that he was unlucky for her. The two of them fitted together real good, any way you looked at it, and he'd best face up to that fact, and then shut his fool mouth about luck.

Besides, Maudie had one very important idea that was the same as his own: she wanted to get out of the Forkhandle country. Women were supposed to have all this intuition, so maybe she could understand that staying in Eastmere, or keeping it as a kind of base to come back to, was unlucky for both of them. Well, there was only one way to test the truth about that: they'd *get* out of the Forkhandle country, the two of them, and head east or west or someplace. Day after tomorrow, they'd go—provided he shook off this cold he felt coming.

He didn't feel at ease about leaving, though, before he'd taken care of Alan Lacy for shaming him like that—but he'd always said, and he'd told young Pace Gray a million times, that he never went starting trouble. And to settle matters with Alan— well, that was starting more trouble than he ever wanted to get near again. So let Alan call himself cock of the walk, if he wanted to, telling the whole world how he chased Arch Eastmere. Let him: Arch had his own revenge. For no matter how many times

Alan told how he'd sent Arch packing, it would still be in his head
that Arch had said he'd come back and kill him, and for the rest of
his life Alan would have to keep looking behind him, to see if
Arch perhaps hadn't finally come back.

In spite of his exhaustion, Arch suddenly felt relaxed and at
peace with things. In spite of the dangers of riding at night, he
let out a whoop, kicked up the two horses, and booted it head-
down for Maudie's.

When he got there she was waiting for him on the porch, and
she stood in patient silence while he hobbled the tired animals.
Then he came up to her and threw his arms around her and
kissed her as he hadn't kissed her since he'd come back from over
the Border. They didn't have to say a single word to one another.
He picked her up and carried her into the bedroom and tossed
her bouncing on the bed. Before he turned out the oil lamp he saw
that she was wearing the same dress, still unhooked, that she'd
had on when he last left her. In thirty seconds, between them,
they made sure that she wore it no longer. Much later, she fed
him a huge supper. And, toward midnight, they went to sleep.

In the morning the band around Arch's chest was tighter. He
woke up coughing, some time after sunrise, and his hollow hack-
ing woke Maudie, too. She was instantly solicitous, but he said it
was nothing, dust in his throat, or maybe mud. And to prove to
her how well he felt, he made love to her again, and it turned
out to be simply the best there was, ever. Afterward, they lay in
each other's arms and admired the beauty of the morning. Then
Maudie got up and went into the kitchen, stark naked. In a little
while she started bringing their breakfast in, plate by plate and
cup by cup, bacon and new bread and steaming hot coffee that
eased the restriction in Arch's chest. They devoured each other
along with the food, and when they'd eaten they put the dishes
and cups by the side of the bed and proceeded once more to
make love.

"This is the way it ought to be, Arch honey," she said, very
dreamily, after a while, "this is *real* love, hear, goddamn you, old
catamountain, same as I've always felt it, the kind only old longhaunch can give me."

"That's the truth, little Maudie," he said. Then he coughed

twice. "Now don't you go fretting," he told her quickly. "We've sweated my dusty throat pretty nigh clear."

"Don't you go catching a cold, goddamn you, Archie, neither," she said, "not right after the other thing, old sick man, not after you've been so sick."

"I'm not sick any more, Maudie."

"Ah, sweet Archie, I could tell you weren't, oh, goddamn you, honey, oh, *couldn't* I, and whatever you were sick from, I'm sure glad it's gone."

"So am I, little Maudie, because we're going, too, someplace far off, you and me."

"Oh, *Jesus*, old long cat, do you mean it, you're not having fun with your Maudie, we're going off someplace together?"

"That's what I mean, little Maudie honey, we'll go off for good and all, tomorrow we'll go, if you're ready."

"Christ! but I *love* you, where to, Archie, where?"

"Maybe west, maybe east, Maudie, north or south, what does it matter where we go?"

"It don't, long as every day ends in a bed, or even a blanket laid down on the ground, goddamn it, Archie, we'll be warm together."

"And mighty poor, too, little Maudie, it looks like, here I don't have a cent to my name now, even my old six-gun's gone."

"We got us a hundred dollars and a loaf of bread and full canteens and clothes to put on when we see folks coming and two fine horses and blankets enough, we're goddamned rich, old hard-face you."

"We got us my fine silver saddle, too, Maudie, but I'd hate to sell that, it's my pride."

"Ah, I won't let you sell that bright shiny saddle, I won't *ever* let my Archie get rid of his pride."

"The way I feel, Maudie, I'd sell my old Colt, but I reckon it's gone forever."

"Where's your big six-gun now, Archie, damn you, what happened to your big old Colt?"

"That old Colt got took from me, Maudie honey, just like everything else this past week."

"Nobody took your Maudie, goddamn you, she's lying all

happy beside you here, what things did they take, warm old
Archie, what else did they take from a sick man?"

"I wasn't sick, now, you hear, and they took what I didn't take
myself."

"What was that, I want to know, please, Archie, you never
say what you do, what did you go and take?"

"Lives and bitter draughts, Maudie, pretty near more than a
man could stand. I'll tell you now, Mrs. Maude Fletcher, I'll
tell you the whole of what I did, I reckon you got a right to
know—"

And he held her tight against his body while he told her what
he'd done through that dire week, since he'd called her name in
the darkness outside her window, a thousand years ago, on another day called Sunday. He told her all there was to tell, of what
he did and what his feelings were, and his words dealt with
sadness and waste and lost things, and tears ran down her cheek
and fell on the flesh of his arm. There were only two truths that
he didn't tell her: what Phil Hyssop had said about his heart,
and what had been done together by Arch Eastmere and little
Dolores. The first of these didn't matter any more; the second
might matter too much. But letting Maude Fletcher know about
the other things made him feel clean and fresh and good, somehow.

Some of Arch's loneliness and loss rubbed off on her and made
her weep for a while, her small body drawn up and nestled in
his arms. Then the tears tapered off and she was smiling again,
more gay than she'd been in over two years, and, "Oh, *how* I
love you, long old catamountain, how I *love* you, body and heart
and soul!" she was saying, and he rolled over and kissed her hard
and deep, and was ready for love again—when she broke free and
hopped off the bed and went over to the window and stood
there, stark naked, looking at the sky and breathing the air and
stretching her arms out wide.

"Ah, it's the best, the most pretty day ever," she said, "and if
we're going away tomorrow, Archie, it's the last day we'll ever
spend here. Ah, let's get out in the air, old lazy Archie, let's walk
down to the river."

"Sure," he said, "you and me, together." The words hurt him

a little. It was a phrase Pace Gray always was using, old hoss Pace Gray, you and me, together. Now Pace was ashes, out under the— "Give me time to tend to the horses," he told her. He rose and put on his shirt and pants and pulled on his boots, still not thoroughly dry. While Maude Fletcher rummaged through the few things she had, trying to find a dress that was half as bright as the day, Arch watered the horses and made sure that plenty of grass was around. Then she came out of the house in a dress that was wrinkled and soiled a little, but which was nearly as blue as the sky. Her arm was around his waist and they had already passed the embers of the shed, without either one of them looking at it, when down the road and toward the house came Percy Randal and Soap Damson and Jim Good and the Bannerman kid.

Arch Eastmere's heart began to pound away, and he was tempted to pound away with it, but he knew he couldn't make cover and without a gun he didn't stand a chance, so he faced the four riders and waited for them to kill him dead, while Maudie gave a scared little scream and hung to his waist for dear life. Then Arch saw that the horsemen were unarmed, too, and it made him relax a bit, but his fool heart pounded right on, and maybe all the harder—at least, that was the way it seemed, with all the rest of him growing so calm.

Percy Randal and the others drew up in a line, and Arch saw that, with the exception of Soap, they all seemed pretty calm, too. Soap, who'd likely as not taken a slug in the shoulder up there at Juncture Valley, had his arm in a sling, and he was glaring at Arch as though he wanted to ride him down and make the horse trample him dead. "Morning, Perce," said Arch Eastmere, not even blinking an eye. "Sure didn't reckon to see you here."

"You killed my Hallock," Percy Randal said quietly.

Arch freed himself from Maudie's arms and moved a step away from her. "It was a fair fight," he said.

"I'm not saying it weren't," Randal told him. "But I want his body. Where'd you leave him, Arch?"

"That's all you want? The body?"

"That's all, just the body. The trouble's over, Arch. I don't hold you a grudge, but I—"

"*I* do, by God, you son of a bitch," Soap exclaimed. "And to your dying day, goddamn you."

"Shut up, Soap!" Randal said, with a flicker of anger.

"Maybe *now*, but not later," Soap muttered. "Not later, he'll see, damn him to hell."

Arch kept his eyes on Randal, ignoring the furious Soap. "Well, Perce, you'll find Hallock—" he began, then broke off, scratching his head in confusion. "It's—Perce, I *know* where he is, but I can't rightly tell you how to get there. Maybe I better come along and show you."

"Aw, Archie honey, *no!*" Maude gasped.

"I'd be grateful if you would, Arch," Percy Randal said.

"No reason you should be," Arch said, "not after I—"

"Goddamn it, *I* don't want to ride with the bastard," Soap said. "Don't he have enough *brains* to tell us where to go, without us having to ride along with him?"

"There won't be no trouble, Perce?" Arch asked.

"No trouble, I swear," said Percy Randal.

"Your word's good enough for me," Arch said. "But—uh—look, Perce, while I got the chance, I want to tell you that—well, you had a mighty fine and happy life, not seven days ago, and then I had to show up and ruin it. I— Ah, I recollect how folks always used to say you were *truly* blessed, if ever a man—"

"Let's go, Arch," said Percy Randal.

Ever since his father had ridden off that morning, still hoping to find Hallock's body, Pax Randal had been acting like a wild man, stomping around out there in the barn, busting things against the wall, even yelling his handsome fool head off. He hadn't dared to lift a finger when, on Percy Randal's orders, Ellen had left with the four men. If Pax had put up an argument, or refused to let them take her, it would have stood out clear for all to see that his main purpose in bringing her home with him hadn't been quite as Christian as it looked—and then there would be ten or a dozen hells to pay. God alone could guess what old Perce might do then—with Luke dead, and now Hallock, and his mother acting looney upstairs, and that goddamned Cora carrying on more crazy than ever. Why, his father might even shoot him down, shoot his own son down like a dog.

Pax was angry and Pax was bitter and Pax was resentful. After all, when you came right down to it, they'd treated him pretty much like a dog all week long, keeping him out there at the edge of the meadow with a shovel in his hands, when he ought to have been in the mountains with the rest of them. It was his fight, too—and yet, goddamn them, they hadn't given him one single chance to show what he could do. Hell, there wasn't a man within fifty miles who could handle a rifle as well as Pax Randal. If they'd only have let him, he'd have taken care of Mark and Alan Lacy and everybody else, too, one at a time, from a distance. And Arch Eastmere, in the bargain—particularly Arch Eastmere. God! there was a feller he'd love in his sights; at two hundred yards, or even three, he'd bet any amount of money he could nail Arch Eastmere solid, smack between his mean goddamned eyes.

But for all the good he'd been able to do for his family, he might as well have been a little boy with a slingshot—and now they'd taken away his warm-bodied gold-head honey, and *that* fixed it so that he'd had all he could stand, and then some. "God *damn!*" he screamed at the top of his voice. Then he picked up a pail he had slammed against one side of the barn and heaved it across to the other. He listened to it bang against the wood and clatter down, and then he ran out of the barn, intending to make for the house.

Soap Damson, mad as a bull in fly time, and coming along at a gallop, nearly knocked Pax sprawling. "What the hell're you trying to *do*, you damned old fool?" Pax yelled at him.

Soap reined up and came trotting back, trying as well as he could to keep his anger in check. "All right, for Christ's sake," he said, "nobody got killed."

"Not today," Pax said, growing calmer. "Not *yet* today, anyways. What the hell're *you* back here for? I reckoned you'd gone to find Hallock."

"That's where the rest of 'em went," Soap said. "Me, I took it as long as I could, then I come back. Be damned if I'll ride with that Eastmere bastard."

"Ride with Arch *East*mere?"

Soap spat a stream of brown juice that nearly carried inside the barn doors. "*Hell,* yes. He took 'em off up there someplace to find Hallock for 'em. I didn't want to ride with the son of a bitch even before we left that Maude Fletcher's, and finally I just had too much of the sight of him, goddamn the murdering bastard, so I up and cut for home. They can get Hallock out of there without no help from me, I reckon. Besides, my goddamned shoulder hurts." He swung himself from the saddle, wincing as he hit the ground. "Jesus, it *does* hurt, too. I hope to Christ Ann cleaned it good. Maybe she'd best take a look again, if she feels up to it, that is."

"Soap?" Pax Randal's head was suddenly spawning a clutch of ideas. "What'll Arch Eastmere do, once he's showed 'em where Hallock is?"

"How the hell do I know?" Get hisself back on Mrs. Maudie, I reckon, before some young buck beats him to it."

"Can I have the loan of your pony, Soap?"

"Your Paw said for you to stay here, didn't he?"

"With luck, I'll get back before he does. Can I borrow the pony?"

"Hell, Pax, I don't give a damn. She's kind of wore out, though."

"I don't reckon to run her into the ground." Pax patted the leather scabbard that held Soap's saddle gun. "This thing loaded?"

"Yep, and they's more in the saddlebag. But what the hell're you figgering on do—?"

But Pax had vaulted into the saddle and was galloping away. "Going to make up for something," he called back, and waved a cheerful good-by.

Cora Randal, standing at the window of the main room of the ranch house, heard what he said as he rode off. "Oh, you are, Pax, you *are*," she whispered to herself. "You're going to make up for a *lot*."

There was a lone gigantic boulder near the road a mile north of Maude Fletcher's. Jagged, cracked, quite flat on top, it seemed more a miniature mesa than a single rock. It rose abruptly from a point a hundred or so yards from the road, leveled off at a height of fifty feet, stayed level for a few yards, then sloped gently down into the meadow. South of this boulder was a growth of spruce, not too wide, but running east a half-mile or more from where its western end flanked, and nearly reached, the road. This narrow spruce grove cut off most of the view to the south for anyone who stood upon the great boulder, but otherwise from the height a fine panorama could be had along the rest of the horizon. And it was to this boulder that Pax Randal came.

He tethered Soap's horse to a bush, concealed from the road by the huge rock. He took a handful of cartridges from the saddle-bag, pulled the carbine out of its scabbard, and scrambled up along the boulder's easy eastern slope to the top. He went forward to a little hollow in the stone that gave him both protection and an excellent view of the road. He slid into this hollow, worked the carbine's lever to cock it, and settled down to wait. He felt like God—or even better.

Not more than twenty minutes had passed before he saw the figure of a man on horseback coming down the road from the north, and he was settled in a good shooting position and ready to fire by the time he could recognize the rider as Arch Eastmere. Pax was so excited that he could scarcely breathe, and the short time that it took Arch to come abreast of him was, every second, an agony. But there was Arch at last, trotting across his front, a perfect target, hardly a hundred yards away. Pax had never known a thrill like it; even Ellen had been nothing like this. He laid his sights at the place he figured the top of Arch's pelvis would be. Allowing for the angle at which he was shooting, Pax expected his bullet to harrow the man's heart. With a tense smile distorting his handsome mouth, he tightened his finger on the trigger.

A split second before the hammer fell, the sun, striking the silver rosettes on Arch Eastmere's saddle, reflected a glancing beam that caught Pax full in the eye, making him jump just enough to spoil his aim. The gun spoke, but even as it kicked against his shoulder he knew that he had shot low, although he couldn't say by how much, and he swore and worked the lever and, so anxious and excited was he, even rose to his feet to fire again.

This time, when he squeezed the trigger, all that he got when the hammer fell was a sharp click; there had been only one cartridge left in the carbine. He swore again, but it was too late to get Arch now, for the son of a bitch was shaking his fist up at Pax and yelling: "I'll be back, hear?" and then yellow-dogging it beyond the spruce and out of sight.

"And I'll be waiting, by God," said Pax.

This time he loaded the magazine full. He even shoved an extra cartridge directly into the chamber.

Then, once more, he sat down to wait for Arch Eastmere—in comfort.

The slug had slammed hard into Arch's left foot, a hairbreadth of time before his ears were assailed by the gun's sound. It had been thud of lead against leather and flesh, then the carbine's flat crack. The echoes rolled through the unaware target; he shuddered in brain and marrow and heart.

The ride to find Hallock's body had gone well enough, all in all, except for Soap Damson's angry defection just after they'd forded the river. The worst part of the whole thing had been when Arch brought the remaining three men up to the wallow, and the heap that had been Hallock Randal. Arch didn't much enjoy another look at the body, but he managed a quick glance. It was sufficient to show him that animals hadn't mauled it, although it wouldn't've made a great deal of difference, such was the present state of Hallock.

Percy Randal had the sense to see immediately that his son had been dragged by a horse, and Arch didn't have to explain that the horse had dragged a dead man; old Perce accepted that without saying. The entire affair had been carried out with a somber politeness, and with very little talk.

Arch had left the three men by the wallow, as soon as he figured it was decent to do so, and headed for home and Maudie. After he had forded the river again and left Randal land for good, he found that he felt even more warm and wonderful than he had while in bed with Maude as this best of all mornings began.

The cough still bothered him, though. He had done a lot of

it during the ride; his throat was more raspy and dry, his chest more constricted. But a chest cold was nothing; he'd had them before. They gave you a bad three or four days, and that was all there was to them. Nobody died of a cold in the chest, not in such weather as this. And, the way Arch was feeling now, he couldn't be killed by double pneumonia, with galloping consumption thrown in.

He was very happy, indeed, and with, he believed, good reason; for by taking this jaunt with Percy Randal, he had come through the last of the doors that had so long enclosed him. Now Arch Eastmere, and little Maude Fletcher with him, had broken out into the limitless and lucky plains of the future. He was deep in a dream of these succoring days, so near, when Pax Randal's bullet hit him.

The lead slug smashed its way through between the ankle bone and the tendon. His foot was driven back against his horse's belly, with force enough to make the surprised beast snort and pirouette left. Arch knew he'd been shot, because his leg went numb from knee to toenails. His chameleon emotions changed from gray shock to crimson anger as he struggled to steady his circling gelding, meanwhile trying to search out the man by whom he'd been bushwhacked. He had finally managed to get the horse faced southward again when he saw Pax Randal rear up from his hollow lair on top of the boulder and take another shot at him. It must've been a misfire, because the next thing Arch knew, Pax had brought the carbine down from his shoulder, and was jerking away at the lever. But whatever had gone wrong, Arch didn't wait around to see. He shook his fist at Pax, yelled: "I'll be back, hear?" and then high-tailed out of sight and range.

The numbness left his leg quickly. Before he had covered half the distance to Maudie's place, he was gritting his teeth with pain. He could see where the bullet had pierced his boot; blood was seeping out of the hole in the leather. There was plenty of blood inside the boot, too. His toes seemed to be awash in blood. Yet beyond the anger, beyond the pain, his mind was clear as crystal: he *had* to get his hands on a weapon—a rifle, a pistol, *any*thing, as long as what came from its muzzle would serve to kill Pax Randal. He'd stop the bleeding, first; and then, if he couldn't make it himself, he'd send Maudie to somebody, *any-body*, larruping all over the countryside until she could get a gun. A fit of coughing bent him over the horn of his saddle. He could get down off the horse, all right, but could he get *up* again? There'd be trouble, and that was the truth. The agonizing wound throbbed on, throbbed on.

He received the last cheat he would ever be given when he came thundering off the road to Maudie Fletcher's and saw her standing by the porch, wearing a different dress than the sky-colored one he'd left her in, and talking to a bandy-legged little man who was leaning on an old Henry rifle, a man with thick gray eyebrows, shiny shoebutton eyes with watery pouches beneath them, and a scraggly gray mustache that drooped below his jaws on either side of his sad mouth, a man who had barely turned fifty and who looked a good sixty-five: Phil Tate. And that old Henry repeating rifle was better than gold, pure gold. Arch Eastmere had never in his life been so glad to see a friend.

Phil Tate felt pretty happy, too, until he got a look at Arch's face. Maude Fletcher, before she realized that her long old cat was hurting somewhere, had also been flooded with happiness, now that Arch was back with her, safe. But when he reined up, grinning with pain, his teeth set and showing, they both hurried from the porch toward him, Phil coming on slower and limping a bit. "Archie honey," Maude was crying, "oh, Archie, what'd they *do* to you?"

"Whatever it was, it weren't fatal," Arch said. "Tether this critter to the post there, please, little Maudie." He let the reins fall into her hands. "Phil, would you kindly get my fool foot out of this stirrup?"

"Sure I will, Arch, bless your heart, now. Just leave me lay my old repeater down." Phil Tate set his rifle on the ground, then eased Arch's left boot away from the binding iron. Considerable blood got on his hands. "Looks like somebody took a shot at you," he said. "Looks like he hit you, too."

"Pax Randal," Arch said. "About a mile up the road." He threw his right leg over the pommel. "Careful, Phil, I'm coming down."

He slid off the saddle, keeping a firm grip on the pommel, and reached the ground easily, with his wounded foot held a few inches off the earth and all his weight on his uninjured leg.

Maude Fletcher was weeping as she tethered the horse. "I'll *kill* him," she said, "that goddamned Pax Randal, I'll kill him goddamned dead, the Randal bastard."

"I'll save you the trouble, Maudie honey," Arch said. "*Ah!*" He winced as he lowered his left foot to the ground and shifted some of his balance to that leg. "Reckon you two best help me inside," he said. "Sorry to bother you, Phil. Know you ain't rightly healed yourself."

"Hell, I got myself *up* here, didn't I? And in the nick of time, too, Lord love you." Phil moved in close to Arch, who draped his left arm around the smaller man's shoulders. Maudie came in on Arch's right. She wasn't much help, but she was better than nothing. Her tears had become half sympathetic, half angry. "I didn't *want* you to go, Archie, dear?" she said. "There was something told me it couldn't stay so perfect and good. I could tell those goddamned men were going to pay you—"

"Ah, stop your bellering, Maudie," Arch said through his clenched teeth, as he hopped toward the porch between his two human supports. "Perce Randal didn't put Pax up to it, I'm willing to swear Perce didn't."

"Who did, then?"

"His own cussedness, most-like," said Arch.

They got him up on the porch with some difficulty, and it wasn't easy to help him through the two doors and into the bedroom. They managed it as well as they could, though, and they didn't hurt him too much. He refused to lie on the bed, however, and hopped by himself to the chair. "It's mighty hard for a feller to get off *Maudie's* bed," he told Phil Tate, still able to make a small joke, "but it ain't hard to get off *anybody's* chair. And I figger to get off this one before very long. Maudie, go fetch me a piece of rope and the sharpest knife in the kitchen."

"A *knife*, Archie honey, what for, not for to cut off your goddamned leg?" Maude, who was tough when she had to be, had wiped the last of her tears away. Arch's poor joke about her bed made her feel better, too; she guessed it couldn't be as bad as

she'd feared at first, not if her old catamountain was beginning
to sound more cheerful.

"Bless your heart, Maudie Fletcher," Phil Tate said, "he wants
it to cut off his boot."

Maude darted out into the kitchen, and Phil Tate let himself
down on his knees, very slowly, by Arch's outstretched left leg.
He nodded his head toward the kitchen. "That pretty little
Maudie woman's been telling me what's been going on," he said.
"Lord, Lord, it sure don't make much sense."

"That's the truth, Phil," said Arch. He pointed at his blood-
soaked boot. "And *this* don't make even *that* much."

"Pax Randal, Pax Randal. He that blond boy of Perce's?"

"Yep."

"Don't reckon I've laid eyes on him these ten, twelve years.
And taking up bushwhacking, hey? About a mile north of here?
He wouldn't've been setting atop that big old rock there,
would he?"

"He would, and he was."

"Nice handy place. Good to be on, hard to get at."

"We'll see about the *hard* part," Arch Eastmere said, "when
I get back there and root him right off his perch."

"You won't be doing no rooting the rest of *this* day, bless you,"
Phil Tate said. "Not that the boy's fool enough to hang around
there, anyways."

"He's fool enough," Arch said. "And I'll get me back there if
I have to crawl on my hands and knees and tote your rifle between my teeth."

"Lord, Lord," Phil Tate said.

Maude Fletcher returned with a Bowie knife and a three-foot
length of frayed rope. "The knife's sharp," she said, "but I don't
know how strong the rope is, Archie honey."

Phil Tate took them both from her. Arch held out his hand
for the rope. "I can do that part," he said. He swiftly looped it
around his thigh, tying it tightly for a tourniquet.

Phil prepared to slit the side of Arch's boot. "Let's us have a
drink of whisky, hey?" he suggested.

"Fine and dandy, provided you got some," Arch told him.

"Some in my saddlebag. Would you please go and fetch it for

us, Maudie? And afterwards maybe some rags and water." As soon as Maude left the bedroom again Phil Tate deftly slit Arch's boot from the top, all the way down to where the upper part met the sole at the boot's very tip. Then he drew the knife half-way around the boot on both sides, sliding the blade along under the naked flesh of the foot. By the time Maude came in with the bottle of whisky, the ruined boot was off and had been tossed in the corner.

She bent over Phil to look at the wound with him. Arch's foot was red with blood, but now that he had the tourniquet on his leg the bleeding had stopped, and she couldn't even see where the wound was, it was all such a mess down there.

Phil Tate, however, had a clear idea of the situation. "Hell," he said, handing Arch the bottle, "it ain't such a bad one after all, bless your heart. Anyplace else, and a feller wouldn't think twice about it."

"It don't hurt as much as it did," Arch admitted. "Don't hurt much at all, any more."

"Ah, I'm glad, old longhaunch," said Maudie, "I hate to have you hurting, anyplace, anytime, it tears my heart out when you hurt."

"That's a nice little woman you got here, Arch," Phil Tate told him. "You're a plumb lucky feller, bless your heart."

"About time I got to be, too," said Arch. He took a long pull at the bottle. Then another. Then a third. "*Well*, now," he said. "That's better." He gave the bottle to Phil. "Rags and water, if you please, Mrs. Fletcher," he reminded Maude.

"I for*got*, goddamn it," she exclaimed. She scampered into the kitchen again.

Phil Tate let some whisky gurgle down his throat. "She tells me you folks're leaving," he said.

"Tomorrow."

"Not with that foot, Lord love you."

"I figger to be a *far* piece from the Forkhandle by tomorrow night, Phil. And that's *me* talking, not the likker."

Phil handed the bottle back to Arch. "*You* go ahead. I take any more, and I'll start to believe you."

Arch was having another long drink as Maude appeared with

a kettleful of water and some torn bits of cloth that were dusty and soiled, but the best she had. "They're not maybe clean enough, Archie," she said, "but I'll tear up a dress if you want, hear, maybe I'd better go tear up a dress, yes, I will, and my best one, too, he deserves the best, my old shot catamountain."

"Maudie honey," Arch Eastmere began, "I only want a bandage that'll hold for a while, and something that can be stuck on right now, because I been wasting too much time, and he's wai—wai—*waiting* for me—"

As Arch started to say the word "waiting" his face went completely white and his mouth dropped open and hung slack and loose; and when he finished the sentence he seemed to have expended the last breath in his body to do it. He stiffened in the narrow chair, his eyes became wide as marbles, and every cord in his neck stood out. Then he tumbled off the chair to the floor.

Maude Fletcher screamed and Phil Tate gaped. Phil recovered first and crawled across to Arch. "Lord, Lord," he muttered, and he reached out to roll Arch over. Maudie snapped out of it, then. "Don't touch him," she said, "please don't touch him, Phil."

Phil Tate looked up at her, uncomprehending. "Maybe that Randal boy shot him twice."

She shook her head. "It's an attack. He had one before."

"Attack of what? He tell you what?"

"I don't know, he didn't say, the doctor told him to live real easy, but I guess he never said what was the matter right out." Her eyes were fixed in fascination on Arch Eastmere's face. She knew he was fighting to get his breath back, and she also knew that there was nothing she could do to help him. All little Maudie Fletcher could do was wait. And pray, of course. And love.

Phil Tate slowly got to his feet. "The one before, how long did it last?"

She kept her gaze on Arch. "Maybe a half-hour, I don't know."

"And afterwards?"

"He rode into town to the doctor."

"Where's this doctor live at?"

"Anybody'll tell you, *any*body will, are you going to bring him back here?"

"He must be a goddamned poor doctor, not to tell a man when he's got heart trouble."

Now her eyes were on Phil Tate. "Is that what it is, his *heart,* how can you tell it's his heart?"

"I seen another feller that way once."

"Did he live, he *did, say* he did, Phil, he come out of it and lived, didn't he?"

"Couple of times," Phil Tate said gruffly. "I'll be back." He hurried out of the house as fast as his bandy legs and healing wound would let him. Little Maude Fletcher, meanwhile, dropped to her knees beside Arch, and gave his contorted body all her attention. She didn't even hear Phil Tate when he clattered off to the north.

Phil Tate, bless his heart, Lord love him, wasn't going into any town to look for any doctor. Whether Arch Eastmere lived or died depended on Arch himself, and all any goddamned doctor could do would be to waggle his beard and look thoughtful. But if Arch were going to die—and Phil Tate had an idea he might— old Phil was going to see he died happy. For old Phil, with some help from his old repeater, intended to do a little rooting of folks off their perches.

He might have been bad on names, but Phil knew terrain as well as he knew the roof of his mouth. He also hated to waste either time or ammunition. He was a very workmanlike man.

And on Pax Randal he did a very workmanlike job. He didn't bother to face him frontally; in fact, he didn't even trouble to pass the growth of spruce that cut off a southern view of the road from anyone on the rock. He left the road just south of the spruce, rode east for a hundred and twenty-five yards, maybe a little more, dismounted, tethered his horse to the nearest tree, and plunged straight through the narrow strip of woods, cocking his old Henry repeater as he went.

He came out midway along the huge rock, in a position from which he couldn't see Pax Randal, but from where he had a very good view of Pax's horse, browsing by the bush it had been tied to, and invisible from the road. Thereupon Phil Tate, who hated to waste time and ammunition, who was a thorough worker and no gentleman, promptly killed Pax Randal's horse dead.

The sound of the shot, with the animal's scream, did exactly what Phil Tate thought it would. It disturbed Pax sufficiently so that he had to find out what had happened. He rose out of the hollow in which he had been concealed and came crouching along the top of the rock to see what kind of a son of a bitch was low-down enough to shoot horses.

He didn't get this information, not for the moment, anyway, because Phil Tate spotted him first. Phil didn't see all of Pax— merely a hat and an inch or two of head—but it was all he needed to get on with the job. He used his second bullet to crease Pax Randal's skull, knocking the hat twenty feet away, and knocking the owner of the hat unconscious.

Phil Tate then came from the edge of the trees, circling the rock, and mounting its mass over the easier slope. He couldn't climb very fast, because every step he took sent a twinge of pain from the wound in his groin, and he couldn't bear the thought of re-opening it. So, as things turned out, not rushing, he reached the level top of the rock at the very moment that Pax Randal was heaving himself to his feet. Pax was still dizzy, and he was holding one hand to his head, his left side turned toward Phil. Finally, though, after Pax had let his bloody hand fall and given his head a good shake, he happened to look along the rock and saw Phil Tate coming toward him. Up went the carbine to Pax Randal's shoulder.

And there the carbine stayed, unfired, until it fell out of his hands. For Phil Tate, firing from the hip, put a hunk of lead from his old Henry repeater plumb through both lungs of Pax Randal, reading from left to right. Pax staggered back, tripped over his own feet, went down, and lay there sprawled on his back, his head hanging down in the hollow from which Phil's first horse-killing shot had enticed him. Blood was coming up Pax's windpipe, and some of it was running out of his nose and mouth; but he was drowning, quite literally, in the rest of it, exactly as Cora had said he would. He was dead in a matter of minutes.

And, although Pax would never be around to appreciate the wry illogic of fate, and the justice or injustice of the event, at almost the same time, high up in the Marias, the South Tine finally filled up the great hole that had opened in the earth beneath its bed. Again it started its old course down its ancient bed, first as a mere trickle of water, coming over the lip of the hole, then, after not very long, with the force it had always possessed. It would be eight or ten hours before the people in the Forkhandle country would realize that the river was rising again —but they would, indeed they would. And some folks might even be thankful.

Phil Tate, meanwhile, came down from the boulder. It had taken a bare half-hour to return this small favor to Arch, and he had carried out a very workmanlike job. The worst part of the whole thing, as far as Phil Tate was concerned, had been climbing that big goddamned rock.

He was back at Maude Fletcher's almost before Pax Randal got around to dying.

After Phil Tate had left, little Maude Fletcher waited. Arch's wide eyes were fixed on her, unseeing; in his head, she was sure, he watched terrible things—but he couldn't tell this was his Maudie kneeling beside him, too awed and fearful for any tears, waiting for him to live or die, and wanting—*dear* God!—wanting him to live, even if his return to life had to mean Maude Fletcher's dying.

The time that passed while she kept her vigil was a vacuum in the bright day. She didn't know how long it was before Arch gave a deep sigh and relaxed, but it seemed to take even longer than had her entire life. Yet at last he *did* sigh and relax, as he had when the other attack was over, and recognition came into his eyes as he looked at her, and he even managed a weak smile. "That was a fool thing I did, little Maudie," he whispered.

"Oh, dear sweet honey Arch old cat honey," was all she could say, choked by her joy and relief.

Then they both were silent for a while, as he let some of his strength come back and some of his pallor depart. Finally, and with great care, he raised himself on one arm, his wounded leg held straight out. "Help a feller up on the bed, will you please, Maudie?" he asked her in an uncertain voice.

She jumped to her feet, bent down, and encircled his chest from behind. He did what he could to help her, and between them they managed to get him on the bed, not exactly straight up and down, but in a good-enough position. Maude fluffed out both pillows and put them under his head, one on top of the other. "Thank you, Mrs. Fletcher," he said. "Reckon you got me on your bed after all, didn't you?"

"I don't like to see you on my bed, Archie, not this way, goddamn it, never *this* way, poor sick Archie honey."

"There's no feeling left in my leg, Maudie. Could you please untie that rope? Maybe the bleeding's stopped."

Clumsily, but with all the speed that her trembling hands could give, she untied the tourniquet. "Not bleeding, is it, now?" Arch Eastmere asked her. She shook her head, and he sighed again. "That's one thing out of the way," he said.

"I'll wash and bandage it," Maude said. "Want me to?"

"Don't trouble," said Arch. "It'll keep. Where'd Phil Tate go, little Maudie?"

"I don't know for sure, I think for the doctor." She sat down beside him on the bed.

"No, he didn't, not Phil, not for any doctor, he hates 'em."

"Then I can't say, poor sick Archie, all he told me was that he'd be back."

"Reckon I know where he went. After Pax Randal. I wish he hadn't gone and done it, though. I'll get that boy myself."

"I hope to God he kills that goddamned Pax Randal, and so do you, Archie, hear?"

"I hope Phil Tate don't come to no harm, that's what I hope, Maudie, not on account of me. Still—" he smiled and touched her hair, "a feller don't have many friends. We're both of us obliged to old Phil, Maudie honey."

She leaned forward intently, caressing his cheek with a gentle hand. "Why didn't you tell me, goddamn you, why didn't you tell me your heart was the trouble?"

"Well, little Maudie—" He brooded for a moment. "Reckon it was because I thought I'd been lied to, reckon I didn't want you to fret."

"Was it old Phil Hyssop you thought that lied?"

"That's who I thought, sure enough, Maudie honey, because

he said if I did this thing or that I'd most-like be mighty sorry. He told me to rest, remember, I didn't keep *that* from you, Maudie. But I plumb forgot to rest, myself, and I went and did the this thing and that he told me not to. But nothing come of it, the way he said it would, so I figgered old Phil was lying to me, or least-wise having some fun. But I figgered all wrong, little Maudie, or was it that I lied to myself?"

"Ah, Archie, you should've told *me*, I'd've kept you quiet and on your back even if I'd had to tie you down, old damned fool catamountain you."

"Looks like now you won't have to, Maudie."

"Oh, God, Archie, I wish I *had*."

"You changed your dress, little Maudie Fletcher, you took off that blue-sky dress."

"I couldn't abide this place any more, Archie, I changed to a dress to travel in, hear, I wanted to go soon as you came back, I couldn't wait till tomorrow."

"Poor little Maudie, wait just a bit longer, then we'll go off together."

"How long, Archie, ah, how *long*?"

"I'll tell you when it's time, Maudie, as soon as I know myself. You wait, little Maudie, and listen, and you'll hear me say it's time."

"I'll wait and I'll listen, old dear cat you, and I'll never be out of your sight."

"Not any more, no, never, Maudie, never the rest of our lives, wherever we go, whatever we do."

"Where will we go to, long sweet Archie, where'll be some of the places we'll go?"

"This way and that, around and about, up and down, every-where, Maudie, wherever the sun shines good, wherever the wind blows gentle." He closed his eyes on the present, letting them open inward on the future, but then a frown creased his pale brow and he raised his eyelids again. "That's after I go one place else," he said, "after I see those two poor old ladies and tell 'em what happened to Pace. That'll be hard, little Maudie."

"No worse than seeing you suffer like this."

"I'm not suffering, sweet little Maudie, I won't never suffer again. From now on old Arch'll rest and live easy, right by his Mrs. Maude Fletcher, keeping all warm by her soft, pretty side."

"Ah, Archie, goddamn you, honey, if you're going to rest you start *now,* hear, you're talking too much, you lie easy."

He gave her a happy soft smile, and his eyes didn't look hard at all. He smiled like a happy small boy. "Yes, ma'am, Mrs. Fletcher," he said.

"That wagon they brought Pace in—the horse wandered off with it someplace," she said. "Maybe Phil Tate can find 'em again, and if he does, old longhaunch, I'll take you off in that wagon, flat on your back till you're fit again, when you and me're far far away."

He took her wrist in his big brown hand and fixed her with a tender gaze, all the hardness gone forever from his eyes. "One thing more, little Maudie," he said. "I've had me a mighty fortunate life. There's been lots of luck in it, and lots of my Maudie Fletcher. Lots of my little Maudie, but still not *enough,* by no means. I'll make it all up to her, though, I swear, the rest of her days I'll be with her, making it up."

What she said to him then was very simple. "I love you, Arch Eastmere." Five words—and the last he ever heard. For suddenly, then, a wild look came into his eyes and a great glacial fear spread over his face. He sat up on the bed, reaching out for her in blind desperation, and as her arms went around him he embraced her like a metal vise, and his cheek against hers was like cold metal, too. "Maudie—little Maudie honey—*hold* me—!" he said in a loud voice. "I—love—*loved*—"

Abruptly he went limp in her arms, and even before she lowered his lolling head to the pillow she sensed that she handled a dead man. Still, she wouldn't let herself believe it. "Arch?" she said. "*Archie?*" But somehow she knew that he was gone from behind the face she was looking at, that the calm pale face on the pillow there was indeed the one he had left, ah! thirty-some years ago. She let her head sink down on his motionless breast. "Oh, God *damn* you, Arch Eastmere," she murmured, "God *damn* you, my old dead catamountain." And that was all the mourning she allowed herself then.

When Phil Tate returned he found her in the kitchen, stuffing odds and ends into a pair of saddlebags on the table. She had changed her clothes again, and now she wore an old cut-down shirt of Arch's, and a shapeless pair of men's trousers that made her seem more tiny than she was. Every movement she made, every word she said, was precise and controlled. When she spoke she sounded like another woman. "You kill that son of a bitch?" she asked Phil point-blank.

The question surprised Phil Tate somewhat, since he'd seemed to have gone for a doctor, not Pax. "Yep," he said.

"Good."

"How's Arch?"

"He's dead, too." She said it matter of factly, without any pause in her packing.

"Oh." Phil Tate watched her busy hands for a long time. Then he said: "Can I go in and see him, please?"

She nodded.

He went into the bedroom and stood over Arch Eastmere's body. The tall man's face was relaxed and placid; the lids now covered forever the hard and lonely eyes. Phil Tate hadn't realized until now that the lashes were so long, so black. "Bless your heart, son," he said softly. Then he felt uncomfortable; that hadn't been exactly the right thing to say, considering how poor Arch Eastmere had died. "Well, now, I mean—" Phil went on. "It's—well, *hell, you* know—you were a pretty good man, all things considered. I'm sure sorry to see you this way, Arch, and yet I'm kind of glad I had the chance. Yep, Lord love you, a pretty good man."

He returned to the kitchen. "You're what I said, a fine woman, Maudie," he told her. "Bearing up well."

"No, I ain't," said Maudie.

"What you figger on doing with him now?"

"What he'd want. You'll see. I'm going on down to Divide with you, Phil."

"There ain't nothing for you down there, Maudie."

"Nothing here, neither." A faint note of sadness now entered her voice. "And there never was, I guess. But I listened. And I waited. I must've liked to wait. *Hell!*" Her last word scattered what sadness had lurked in the others.

"Got any idea what you'll *do*, down to Divide?"

"The same thing. Listen. Wait."

She finished packing the saddlebags, and he took them out to the horses. She had two more things to do in the house. One was to kiss Arch Eastmere for the last time. The other was to set the place afire, which she did by dropping a match on oil she had poured from the bedroom lamp.

Not many minutes later she sat on Pace Gray's horse, with Phil Tate beside her on his own mount, to which Arch's big gelding was tethered, all of them up on a hillock near the road that led down to Divide, watching her old shack burn.

"That's what Arch would've wanted, hey?" Phil asked her.

"Wanted, and won," she answered. After a moment she went on: "Ah, I *hate* that goddamned house, I always have, and I'm glad to see it go. All the living I did in there, when Arch Eastmere wasn't around, wouldn't even fill up a thimble—and when he *was* around there was so much life in me that there wasn't room for it in the whole goddamned Heaven and earth. Let's get on, Phil, now—and quick."

They started southward on the road to Divide. "If you don't mind," Phil Tate said, "I'd just as soon ride cross-country, because of one thing or another."

"All right." She veered her horse clear of the road, with Phil right behind her. "Before it gets on to night, though, I've got to stop off and tell Pace Gray's aunts about him."

"Pace Gr—? Oh, sure, that nice young feller that come down to fetch me for Arch. That's right, he got hisself killed, didn't he? Why, I've knowed them aunts of his since I was a small child. Dorrie and Sallie Pace. Right pretty girls they was, too. But I heard tell they changed a lot, stayed hid at home for years. Reckon it'll cut 'em up considerable when they find out that fine boy's dead."

"Especially when *I* tell 'em," Maude Fletcher said heavily. "They heard of me, and they know what I'm like. They'll end up as much ashamed of Pace as ever they'll be sorry for him."

"Well, now," Phil Tate said, "suppose I go along and see those two pretty girls? Two pretty *old ladies* by this time, I reckon. And suppose I tell 'em Arch Eastmere and Pace went off on this little trip someplace? To seek their fortunes, I'll tell those ladies."

"*Will* you do that, Phil? It'd be fine, if you would."

"Why, *sure* I'll do it, bless your heart," said Phil Tate. "After all, it's the goddamned God's truth, ain't it?"

Behind them the house fell in on itself.

Around the middle of that beautiful afternoon, Nelse Macleod went looking for Drury, down by the river where he'd been told he could find him. Old Nelse had been restless and unhappy all day. He had gone first to Oliver Swindon's, only to learn from Nell Swindon that her husband had never come home. She had no idea where he'd gone, nor did she seem to care much. Nelse had been vaguely distressed by this news. Then, riding across to Drury Wynward's, he recalled an incident long past that had evidently been lurking in the back of his mind for several days— and this memory depressed him further. So, by the time he saw Drury, sitting on the bank of the Forkhandle and smoking a cigar, Nelse Macleod was a glum old man.

Drury noticed it as soon as Nelse got off his horse and creaked down beside him. "Hell, Nelse," he said, his white teeth clenched around the big cheroot, "it can't be *that* bad."

"I was over to Ollie's," Nelse said. "He's run off."

"Good," Drury said. "Got a hankering to do something like that myself."

"You fretting, too—about what we all went and got ourselves into?" Nelse asked.

"I'd be a fool if I didn't," Drury said.

"They better get it over with fast," Nelse said. "Before any more fellers get killed."

"Can't be many more hung than they'll settle for now. They sure can't hang fifty, sixty men."

"It ain't the hanging-bee I'm worried about," Nelse said.

"What is it worries you, then?"

"Damned if I know," Nelse sighed. He moodily pulled at his beard. "Sound foolish, don't I?"

"Not especially."

"Well, I am, by God, and in my second childhood. I woke up this morning and I said to myself: 'Nelse Macleod, you're going to up and die pretty soon,' and so I—"

"You'll live to see a hundred, Nelse."

"I ain't funning, Drury. Why, hell, I scared myself so, I goddamned near went to church. What for do you reckon I'm riding around today? I'm not *working*, by God. No, sir, but it's a mighty fine day, and I got this feeling they ain't many more fine days left to me—"

"Now, you shut up that talk, Nelse, or I swear I'll go off and leave you to sit here alone."

"I just wanted you to know, Drury."

"All *right*, then.—You see that fire south of here awhile back?"

"What fire?"

"I don't know what was burning, Nelse, but there was one hell of a lot of smoke coming from it."

"How far off?"

"Five, six miles."

"Ain't no houses down there, except that shack Maudie Fletcher lives in."

"Maybe Arch Eastmere got mad and burned it down."

"Reckon he wouldn't do that, Drury."

Drury spat out a piece of tobacco. "Hell, Nelse, we might as well blame old Arch for *every*thing, instead of spreading it around like we're going to have to."

"Just who do you reckon's to blame for starting the whole business, Drury?"

Drury pondered the matter. "Well, Nelse, if you come right down to it, I reckon it's a toss-up betwixt the Lacy boys. Mark was the feller that first talked things up, and Alan was the one that got the wagon to roll."

"Want to know something, Drury? *I* begun this trouble. A long, long time ago, too."

"*Now* what the hell're you jawing about, Nelse?"

"Something that started, oh, it's thirty years since, easy. I recollected it while I was on my way over here. Don't know *why* I did, it just come into my mind. There was this time Arch Eastmere and Hallock Randal took it into their heads to run off—I forget why—and, my God, they was a bunch of us out looking for 'em all day, these two little boys, neither one of 'em more than ten years old, if that. Well, me and old Perce—he was *young* Perce then, and me, I had the finest set of ebony whiskers you ever did see, somewhat like Black Jack Eastmere's, only better—Perce and me, we finally come into this meadow and, Jesus, it was jam-packed with this funny kind of grass, god-damned nigh tall as a man's head, with all these big red flowers on it. Perce didn't want to go through it, but I had this feeling, so finally I got him to fan out through it with me. And, by God, there were those two boys. Perce caught young Hallock, and I got me Arch. I reckon he thought I *was* old Black Jack, too, be-cause he fit like a goddamned wildcat at first. And the little buggers never *did* tell anybody why they was going to run off together that way. And that's the story, Drury."

Drury gave old Nelse a bewildered glance. "And a mighty nice story it is, too," he said. "Only thing is, *you* forgot to say what it's got to do with you being the cause of all the trouble."

"Goddamn it, you'd know if you *listened*," said Nelse. "If I hadn't gone into those big red flowers, they might've got clean away together, that's what Hallock and Arch might've done. And what do you reckon *we*'d be doing now, if I hadn't found those runaway boys, those two little boys in the flowers?"

HARRY BROWN was born in Portland, Maine, in 1917 and grew up there. He studied at Harvard and then, before World War II, worked briefly for both *Time* and *The New Yorker*. While in the army he was attached to *Yank* and later transferred to the Anglo-American Film Unit. After the war he concentrated on film writing for many years. One of his screenplays, *A Place in the Sun*, written in collaboration with Michael Wilson, won the Academy Award for the Best Screenplay of 1951. He has also won several poetry prizes. His play, *A Sound of Hunting*, was called the best of the 1945–6 season by the late George Jean Nathan.

Mr. Brown is the author of a number of books of poetry and fiction, among them *A Walk in the Sun* (1944) and *The Beast in His Hunger* (1948).

[*January 1960*]

A NOTE ON THE TYPE

THE TEXT of this book is set in Caledonia, a Linotype face designed by W. A. Dwiggins (1880–1956), who was responsible for so much that is good in contemporary book design. Caledonia belongs to the family of printing types called "modern face" by printers—a term used to mark the change in style of typeletters that occurred at the end of the eighteenth century. It is best evidenced in the letter shapes designed by Baskerville, Martin, Bodoni, and the Didots.

This book was composed, printed, and bound by KINGSPORT PRESS, INC., Kingsport, Tennessee. The paper was made by P. H. GLATFELTER CO., Spring Grove, Penn. Typography by VINCENT TORRE.